GROWING UP TWICE

Rowan Coleman is thirty and lives in London with her husband and baby daughter. In 2000 she won Company magazine Young Writer of the Year Competition. *Growing Up Twice* is her first novel.

Lydia

GROWING UP TWICE

Rowan Coleman

ARROW

Published by Arrow Books in 2002

3 5 7 9 10 8 6 4 2

Copyright © Rowan Coleman 2002

Rowan Coleman has asserted her right under the Copyright, Designs and Patents Act, 1988 to be identified as the author of this work

This novel is a work of fiction. Names and characters are the product of the author's imagination and any resemblance to actual persons, living or dead, is entirely coincidental

This book is sold subject to the condition that it shall not, by way of trade or otherwise, be lent, resold, hired out, or otherwise circulated without the publisher's prior consent in any form of binding or cover other than that in which it is published and without a similar condition being imposed on the subsequent purchaser

First published in the United Kingdom in 2002 by Century

Arrow Books
The Random House Group Limited
20 Vauxhall Bridge Road, London, SW1V 2SA

Random House Australia (Pty) Limited
20 Alfred Street, Milsons Point, Sydney,
New South Wales 2061, Australia

Random House New Zealand Limited
18 Poland Road, Glenfield
Auckland 10, New Zealand

Random House (Pty) Limited
Endulini, 5a Jubilee Road, Parktown 2193, South Africa

The Random House Group Limited Reg. No. 954009

www.randomhouse.co.uk

A CIP catalogue record for this book
is available from the British Library

Papers used by Random House
are natural, recyclable products made from wood grown in
sustainable forests. The manufacturing processes conform to
the environmental regulations of the country of origin

ISBN 0 09 942768 0

Typeset by Palimpsest Book Production Limited,
Polmont, Stirlingshire
Printed and bound in Great Britain by
Cox & Wyman Ltd, Reading, Berks

For Erol and Lily with all my love.

Acknowledgements

With thanks to Kate Elton and Lizzy Kremer for all their help, support, inspiration and spelling corrections.

Also to my dear friends Jenny Mathews and Rosie Woolley who graciously lent me their names when I couldn't think of any for two of the characters, and on whom neither namesake is based!

Especial love and thanks to Erol for his unwavering support and belief in me, and last but in no way least to my daughter Lily who grew at more or less the same rate as the book and was born just after its completion. She has made growing up wonderful.

Chapter One

'Listen. I need you to be honest now. Have I gone cross-eyed? I have the strangest sensation that my eyes are no longer operating in tandem.'

We are sitting in Soho Square and it is the last Saturday morning in August. We spent last night club hopping and then drinking coffee in a twenty-four-hour café just off Charing Cross Road.

I am with Rosie and Selin. We have all known each other since primary school and have been best friends since we swapped our 'first kiss' stories, real and imagined, drinking mugs of Cinzano Bianco. That was fourteen years ago at a sleepover at Rosie's house. About eight months ago another chapter opened in our friendship when we found ourselves simultaneously single for the first time in ten years. The last time we hung out so much we were drinking Lambrusco on the swings at our local park and singing Meat Loaf's 'Dead Ringer for Love' to any passing likely-looking lads.

'Look at me. No, look *at* me,' I say to Rosie, wondering if maybe she really has lost the ability to focus. 'They're fine really; a bit red round the edges but definitely working in unison.' A look of total horror passes over Rosie's face and she dives for her bag to fish out her make-up. I smile to myself, I knew she wouldn't be able to live with red-rimmed eyes.

1

'I swear to God, it's that Red Bull that does it, it's evil. We should write to *Watchdog*,' she says, as she sets a complete pocket-sized cleansing, toning and moisturising regime out on the grass in neat little Chanel packages.

'I think it was the coffees, *let's never have coffee again*, it's poison,' Selin says, lifting her hand in front of her face to cast a shadow over her eyes. 'Look! Look at me, I've got the DTs!'

I take her hand in mine and examine it. 'It's fine,' I say. 'God, you two are *so* paranoid.' And I flop back on to the grass, arms outstretched, waiting for the warmth of the sun to find me. Selin lies on her front, propped up on her elbows and Rosie, looking for all the world like Doris Day on a picnic, packs away her used cotton-wool balls in the plastic freezer bag she carries for just such an occasion. She begins to apply her foundation with one of those funny little triangle-shaped sponges. The square starts to fill as the sun climbs and draws last night's casualties out of the shadows.

We are secretly waiting for pub opening time and hair of the dog, pretending we are going to look at a photographic exhibition at the National Portrait Gallery. We all agreed last night that we would definitely go today, as we have been meaning to go for the last four weeks and it closes this weekend. We all know we are lying.

One other fine morning just like this one Rosie decided that Soho Square is the last place left in London where fresh clean air is stacked in cubic feet right up to heaven. We often spend this part of Saturday right here, breathing and gossiping. Recuperating from the high jinks of the previous night.

This fine morning the air has only just become warm, the dew is beginning to disappear and we turn our faces to the sun like the cottage-garden flowers that border the square.

'This is not good. We have to face it. We are old. We can't

do this any more.' Selin sits up, pulling her fingers through her long and curly midnight hair and shades her eyes from the sun. 'Look at those nu-metal kids over there. They probably think we're on an OAP outing. I should have a mortgage by now and a car. In fact, I should *definitely* have a car by now and *definitely not* be sitting in a park surrounded by teenagers recovering from a hangover. I should be having a *café latte*, in a bed bought from Habitat, reading the *Independent on Sunday* and, and I should have a husband – who looks like the bloke from the Gillette ad – squeezing me fresh orange juice in my fitted kitchen.' She laughs while she makes her demands to the heavens.

'What do you want a car for in London?' I ask, ignoring all the other stuff of distant dreams.

'I don't *want* a car.' She slams both palms down on the grass making Rosie jump a little bit so that her eyeliner goes wonky. She scowls at Selin, Selin ignores her. 'I just *should* have one. The option to have a car should be open to me.'

'You can't even drive!' I think I know where she is coming from but I'm having trouble with her analogy.

'I'm just saying that I'm thirty in nine months' time and I haven't got a car. And I had planned to have a car by now, a red one.'

'Look, I'm thirty *way* before either of you two and anyway,' I say, 'when we were fifteen we all thought we'd be married by now and have a house, a proper career and two children and do that every day until we died. But we're not at that stage yet. Life is still beginning, and it's fantastic. So let's enjoy the good times while they last.'

'Yes,' Rosie contributes, 'and I've already been married, so I know it's not all it's cracked up to be. Apart from the dressing up, the dressing up was fantastic. And the presents, of course. Oh, and do you remember the hen night? Now *that* was good.' Rosie blots her lipstick. Her marriage lasted six months and it was a pretty dreadful six months. Still, she did look great in that wedding dress.

Selin sighs in that way she does when she feels Rosie and I don't take life seriously enough.

'Mmm, well it's the "still" bit that worries me,' she says. 'What if life is "still" beginning for us when we're eighty and getting our kicks on a Stannah stairlift? Or worse, the three of us have had to sell our houses – assuming we ever earn enough cash to buy our own houses, that is – to keep us in an old people's home and we look at each other and say, "What have we done with our lives?"'

'Selin, I think you are deliberately choosing to be negative,' I say. 'Remember your positive affirmations – "I smile, the world smiles with me."'

'I smile, I get some more wrinkles,' she says but she is smiling all the same.

'And let's face it, you can't afford any more of those!' Rosie throws in, ducking to avoid the balled-up crisp packet that Selin aims at her head. 'Anyway, we had a good time last night, didn't we? There's life in the old dogs yet.' And she checks her eyeliner again before lying back on the grass, shading her eyes with the back of her hand. If the last few months have been anything to go by Rosie will keep looking on the bright side until the hangover fully sets in, an eventuality she will doggedly postpone until the early hours of Monday morning.

'*You* can call yourself "old" and "dog" in the same sentence, lady, but leave me out of it,' I say and suddenly we're laughing in the still-sparkling grass; the weak delicious unpreventable sort of laughter left over from too much vodka and a very old friendship.

'Whoa there.' Rosie clambers to her feet a little unsteadily. 'I can't handle this witty banter any more. Let's go and have a

Bloody Mary, I feel a bit queasy and I need something to settle my stomach.'

'Yeah, come on, kill or cure.' Selin stands to join her, catches my eye and a 'someone had better look after her' look of understanding passes between us. Their shadows fall across me and make me cold.

'You know, girls, I'm gonna stay here for a little bit and chill. I'll catch you up,' I say, feeling the goose bumps rise on my forearms. I just can't face the smoke and smell of a pub right now.

'Hang on, not at the pub for the first BM? You're not breaking ranks, are you?' Rosie challenges me.

'No, I just like it here. I'm going to stay for a while and get it together and I'll be along in a little while, OK?'

'OK, lightweight,' they chorus and walk away arm in arm and, as always, laughing.

Chapter Two

I lie back on the grass and look at the sky through the lenses of
my shades. I have always been in love with summer, not in the
sun-worshipping sense as my pasty freckle-prone complexion
will attest, but in the sense that I love sunlight. As a child
I wrote rigorously rhymed poetry about golden streams of
summer chasing through the leaves and making the shadows
dance. Looking into the cloudless sky as it bends over my head,
full of city echoes, I get a non-specific kind of nostalgia. A vague
wistful feeling I can't put my finger on.

The rest of the congregation on the benches and the grass
is made up of a curiously harmonic mix of winos; *Guardian*
readers; retro-grunge teens drinking from cans, smoking roll-ups
and laughing ostentatiously; and about six near-identical couples
with croissants and fully interactive sets of tongues. A gay couple
lie side by side not far from me, silent and hand in hand. Looking
at them I remember the touch of warm skin.

'Are you OK?' I ask myself. I've got that star-crossed feeling
again, an intuition that fate is about to make a delivery. My
skin is tingling, and my temples are beginning to throb. It
seems that very soon the hangover will arrive in earnest. I stay
absolutely still, feeling drowsiness seeping through my veins
and enjoying it; it is a badge of honour; combat colours to
prove I'm still kicking and breathing. The star-crossed feeling

is probably just a toxin overload; I *must* stop thinking I'm so mystic.

'Hey erm, hello, Jenny? Remember me?' I have a visitor. I inspect him from behind my shades; it's a ginger teenager from the retro-grunge gang in the corner. It's a bit early for beery breath in my face.

'You're a ginger teenager,' I tell him, as if he needs no further reason to leave. But he only laughs.

'Yes, that's it, you do remember me, I was at the party you and your mate had in Ladbroke Grove. We were well hard core, the last to go in the morning, remember?' His smile stretches from ear to ear.

Suddenly I recognise his air of false bravado and I do remember. That had been *the* party. The one good party you throw in your whole life when everyone you invited comes and everyone you didn't comes too. We had a DJ and a mirror ball and every inch of the carpet caught it.

I met a Spanish truck driver in the kitchen, some Dutch tourists on the stairs and this couple of kids, probably just about sixteen, on their first ever E. One of them had danced like a puppy all night and the other one had passed out after twenty minutes only to wake up in the morning with just his mate, Rosie and me left. This was the kid right here. We had never called him by his name, only 'ginger teenager boy'. They had had cups of tea and we pleased them by laughing at their jokes until one of them remembered that he would be late for Sunday lunch at home. They'd gone as quickly as they had appeared, a charming juvenile mystery.

We discovered that they had left us their two telephone numbers, one of our names bracketed beside each, expressing a preference. We had laughed even more and binned them. The ginger kid had written my name next to his number and here he was again. A little bit older but no nearer any real facial hair, apparently.

'How are you? Still living in that flat? That party was well cool, man.' He smiles and flops on to the ground next to me. 'New trainers? We went to see Slipknot last night, they are *sick* puppies! Do you like them? I've got an imported CD with two previously unheard tracks.' He produces the aforementioned item like a child at Show and Tell and hands it to me for approval. All of their tracks are previously unheard by me.

'Very nice,' I say, without looking at it, and drop it on the grass. 'What can I do for you?' I sit up now and feel the blood drumming in my head. I feel older even than I am, my eyes are aching.

'We're going for some breakfast. I thought, you know, as your mates have gone you might like to come with us.' I look at him and try to remember his name; he's a pretty boy really. His hair is short and spiky and he has a sweet smile and brown eyes, the true best friend of the much-beleaguered ginger person. I wonder what his agenda is.

'Look, I've forgotten your name.' I'm being downright rude and still he sits there with a soppy grin on his face, looking pleased as punch.

'That's cool. It's Michael, Mike. So, do you fancy breakfast with us?' He gestures at his mates across the grass. Two other boys, one with the sides of his head shaved and some attempt at dreads; one with a scrawny pony-tail, both messing about with a box of matches; and a girl, slim and fair, sitting with her knees drawn up beneath her tassel-trimmed skirt, looking right at us. I make the deduction.

'Is that your girlfriend?' I ask sweetly with my best and first smile for him.

'Yeah, she won't mind, I told her we're mates.' He sends a little wave to her over the grass, she sends him a little scowl back.

I ignore the world's most ill-advised assumption and say, 'OK, I'll come for a coffee.' He doesn't hide the look of surprise on his face as I hold out my hand for him to help me to my feet. And neither can he stop himself from flinching in surprise when I swing my arm over his shoulder as we stroll over to the café. The second sign of thunder rolls over the nameless girl's face.

There is just something about the opportunity to minx a much younger, thinner woman that overrides all of my tenuous, subjective and flexible notions of loyalty to the greater good of the sisterhood. I'm not proud of it, but to be honest I'm thinking about the story I can tell the others when I get to the pub; I am writing them a joke. I always used to say I wouldn't become a jealous-old-harridan type, the type that used to snub, bitch and bully me during *my* thin and pert period. But . . . oh well. I expect it's evolution.

Chapter Three

In the café, one of those shabby genteel affairs, a mixture of Formica tabletops and gold baroque-style mirrors, the kids look quiet and nervous. They probably think I am from the same generation as their mother and the realisation give me pins and needles. Thank God it's not possible. I wonder if I can work that fact into the conversation, just to make it absolutely clear.

Michael introduces the boys first – Jake and Andy.

'And this is my girlfriend.'

'*Sarah*,' she says and gives him a 'I-do-have-a-name-you-know' look. I like her, she's feisty.

The coffee comes and just the smell of it makes my stomach lurch. Michael is looking at me a lot and I like it. Sarah is looking at me a lot and I like it. Jake and Andy are trying to catch the coasters they are flipping from the table edge – well, it keeps them occupied.

'So what are you up to these days?' I ask Michael. I talk just to him, and lean a little bit closer; he smells of grass. He gives me a wide and disarming smile. I bet he gave that smile to Sarah across the playground before they got together. His eyelashes are dark at the root and curve up to golden tips. I begin to see why Sarah is so possessive.

'Well, we've just done AS levels. I was bloody crap – reckon I failed them *all*.' He gives a kind of Gallic shrug, confident and carefree. 'It's the end of the summer holidays now. Ages off, it was fantastic, man. But I'm eighteen in a few weeks so I'm having a right big party, with a DJ and that, like you did. You should come.'

Sarah has taken the end of the ribbon of her draw-string top in her mouth and is chewing it. Now she is looking at him. He is definitely not looking at her.

'I'd love to.' I put my hand on his wrist. It turns out he has light golden skin and fair little hairs on his forearm. He has long fingers stained with biro. They remind me of a guitarist I once knew.

'Yeah, your mum said you should have *adults* present,' Sarah says. Michael blushes, until the pink flush clashes with his hair. I think he is more embarrassed for me than himself, but her words sink in and I suddenly catch my reflection in a mirror and see a dishevelled twenty-nine-and-nearly-two-halves-year-old woman flirting with a kid who is not even eighteen yet. Trounced by a newcomer, I feel panicky. I need to see the others. I need to get back to my world. My excursion is suddenly over.

'Look, I should go, I've got to meet my friends. It was nice to see you, though.' It is the lie I tell most next to 'I'll call you next week.'

I walk down the street about to call Rosie on my mobile to find out where they are, when suddenly he is walking next to me. I stop. If I had run that far that fast, I think, I would have been out of breath. He isn't.

'Can I borrow your phone?' he says and takes it out of my hand. He dials and a few moments later I hear a ringing from the pocket of his combats. He hands it back to me.

'Now I've got your number and you have mine,' he says quietly. He is looking at me again and I am suddenly aware that he is taller and broader than I am and that the sunshine makes me want to touch his hair.

He places the palms of his hands either side of my face and kisses me. A breeze is shaking the petals from the tree we stand under and they float down like snow. I feel a sense of déjà vu; he is reminding me of something that I miss, I lean towards a memory. We part and he stands back and looks at me, he bites his bottom lip. I have nothing to say.

'I'm going to call you,' he says with resolution and turns, walking away quickly without looking back. I stand there for a moment to collect myself; there is a gradual subsidence of physical sensation. I find I am regretting its regression.

My phone rings and makes me jump. I half want and expect it to be him but Rosie's name flashes. I press 'OK' and everything clicks back into place.

'You are *never* going to believe this,' I say.

Chapter Four

I press 'End' on my phone two seconds before I push the door of the pub open, and I don't have to look around for them because a two-double-Bloody-Marys-at-least cheer greets me as I walk in.

'Here she is!' Rosie shouts. 'A Mrs Robinson for the twenty-first century!'

Selin is wiping the tears of laughter from her eyes as I sit down at their table. It's almost twelve o'clock; there aren't many people in the pub, but the few that are there are the faithful, the Coach and Horses characters.

Long coated, long haired or shaven headed, designer glasses, notepads and pens in pockets, portfolios and Filofaxes tucked under arms. Poets, painters, media boys and girls all Guinnessed up or whisky chased rather more than is recommended and thoroughly disapproving of us, flippant, drunk and laughing as we are.

That is one of the reasons why we come in here. It wasn't long ago that I was in a relationship with one of these types, for three years, in fact. I have a vague female notion that I'm annoying him by proxy with my flippancy. Owen was a serious man. He always carried a volume of Proust, he thought a lot about death. It would have been no surprise if I had been presented with the opportunity to annoy him in person in this pub where we had our very first date. But in the last few months since our relationship finally ended for good I haven't seen him once. I've gone to the same places and hung out with the same people but our paths never crossed. Selin says it's God's way of protecting me from myself, but then she never did approve of us very much. Actually, none of my friends approved of him very much and all of his friends disapproved of me.

'Tell us again, *pleeease*,' Selin pleads, 'I only got Rosie's half of the conversation.' Her black eyes sparkle and she flashes her famous three-cornered grin at me.

'Get the drinks in then!' I say and sit back in my chair smiling. I'm happy; not ten minutes ago I was kissed and now here I am with my two best friends, the greatest story to tell and a large Bloody Mary. Daylight fights its way through the frosted glass, bouncing off glasses and bottles, illuminating the slowly turning unfolding swirls of smoke. The smell of ash and old beer seems suddenly appealing. There is nothing like the slow and somehow illicit pleasure of daytime drinking.

'He's sixteen,' Rosie says, leaning back on her chair so that it balances on two legs (just like she used to in the back of the class), fanning her flushed face with a beer-mat.

'Nearly eighteen, actually,' I say, slightly annoyed that she is hijacking my moment.

'He's a ginger,' she continues, putting her hand on my wrist as if to restrain me, but really to stop herself from tipping over.

'No. *No*,' I protest. 'More sort of blondey auburn.' Selin looks at me over the top of her glass and raises one of her dark, beautifully arched eyebrows. She is the only one of us who can do this. Many a teenage evening was spent practising in front of mirrors and only she managed it. She's been flaunting it ever since.

'He is skinny and has spots.' Rosie drains the last of her drink and rattles the remaining ice-cubes under my nose. 'Your round.'

'He's filled out a lot since you saw him last, and his skin has cleared up. God, I'm twenty-nine and I still get spots,' I say, aware that I'm losing all comedy value by defending him too much. The bar is only two feet away and we carry on talking as I go to get the drinks in. A man with a long grey pony-tail turns his back on me and tuts.

'I don't remember seeing him at that party. Did I see him? Why didn't I see him?' Selin says.

'Because he passed out after about five minutes on Jen's bed and you were too busy snogging that Spanish truck driver,' Rosie reminds her.

'Oh yeah, Raoul,' she giggles quietly to herself. 'It turned out he was from Bromley.' I return to the table carrying three glasses simultaneously, a trick I learnt back in my barmaid days.

'No, you're joking! He was so convincing,' I cry. 'He gave me a recipe for paella! Hang on, why didn't you tell us this at the time?'

'Wasn't even of Spanish extraction. I can't remember why. It wasn't *that* good a story.' Typical Selin. Rosie and I will tell anything to anyone, but Selin is just a little bit more remote. Always up for a carefree snog and a dance when we're out but she hardly ever gets involved past that, never swaps phone numbers, never arranges dates and *never* takes anyone home. I don't mean she hasn't had her wild moments, and she's certainly no virgin, but some time over the last couple of years she just decided to become much more reserved and cautious. I wouldn't be surprised if Rosie and I hadn't put her off men for ever. She's had one long-term relationship (with a boy from her street) and they only split up because she felt she was too young to get married; they're still really good friends. She never gossips about her personal life, never spills her guts the way Rosie and I do. It's like getting blood out of a stone. Sure, she complains sometimes about her job, or money, or the lack of a good man, but in general she is very serene and sort of complete. She doesn't seem to carry the angst that Rosie and I have been investing in so heavily for so long. Well, not her own angst. She's carried a lot of ours over the years.

'This country. Can't trust anyone,' Rosie sighs, and I'm not sure who she is referring to.

'Back to the boy!' Good, Selin is curious.

'Well, he just ran up to me, grabbed me and kissed me. Right there in the street! It was kind of sweet really. You know, romantic.' I can't help the coy little smile that curls up the edges of my mouth.

'*Romantic!*' they cry and grab each other in a mock melodramatic clinch.

'Wasn't it sloppy and dribbly?' Selin asks.

'No!'

'Tongue like a Rotavator?' Rosie enquires in her usual forthright fashion.

'Certainly not.'

'Teeth and nose bumping?' Selin.

'No. None of that, it was nice, he was good. I mean, look, we all had our first snog at around fifteen, right?'

'I was eleven,' Selin said.

'I was nine,' Rosie chimed in. 'Edward Stone, back of the art class.'

'OK, I had *my* first snog at fifteen.'

'And eleven months and two weeks. I remember because it was at Cathy Barker's sixteenth and yours was two weeks later. You snogged that bloke who went mental a couple of years ago. It could have contributed.' Rosie grinned.

'His name was Sam Everson and he didn't go mental, he had a breakdown and it was years later when I didn't even know him. And my point is, even I, late flowerer that I was, had had three years' intensive snogging practice by his age. I was pretty good at it by then. So our kiss was accomplished, romantic and even a bit sexy and anyway, god-damnit, I haven't had a snog in ages and I enjoyed it!' I'm slightly flushed and the tingle of the Tabasco is melting the back of my throat.

Rosie and Selin look at me. They look at each other. They look at me. Selin purses her lips, getting ready to be maternal.

'You fancy him,' she says.

'I don't! I'm just saying it was nice!' I roll my eyes up to the nicotine-coloured ceiling.

'You fancy him. You fancy him, you do. Please God don't tell me you're going to phone him, because I *know* you're not. You're not, are you?' Selin is anxious and I know why. She has seen me merrily trot off, usually in cahoots with Rosie, into one outlandish and disastrous encounter after another. She has been at our respective doors with two bottles of wine and a large bar of chocolate on more occasions than we can remember. When Rosie moved in with me after she split up with her ex, Chris, just after Owen dumped me for the last time, Selin even remarked on the fact that our flat sharing would save her a bus fare at least (and God help the neighbourhood).

'Of course I'm not!' I say and I mean it. I'm not. Really.

'You should,' Rosie says. 'You might be his first. You could teach him how to *pleasure a woman*.' And she says it with a fake French accent.

'I doubt it very much, if his slutty-looking girlfriend was anything to go by,' I say, somewhat unfairly, driven by an unhealthy and arbitrary competitive streak. 'But it doesn't matter because of course, *of course*, I'm not going to phone him. And if he phones me, I shall be very sweet so as not to drive him to breakdown in later life.' I look pointedly at Rosie. 'And I shall say I can't see him again, thank you very much.'

'Unless he has two good-looking friends.'

Oh, Rosie.

Chapter Five

This morning when I open my eyes, for the first time since spring the electric light from the hallway is casting a yellow glow under my bedroom door. Rosie is up already and autumn is on the way. I can see a chink of blue sky through my curtain, but the cast of the light bulb somehow reminds me of being cold and I turn my back on the window and curl up. Now I can see my phone.

The third requisite day between swapping your phone number and getting the call isn't, strictly speaking, until tomorrow. I had thought that, being young and presumably impetuous, he might have called me sooner, but I guess they learn the mind tricks even earlier in man development these days. I think he will phone me tomorrow. I don't mind if he doesn't phone me. It will be easier in a way. It's just the waiting. It's annoying, and even more annoying when you're waiting for a call from someone you don't want to call you.

But I'll leave my mobile switched on, just to get it over with. I mean, I don't want to have to call him back, do I?

It's Monday. I imagine Rosie is up before me because she has got today off and a day-long date planned with this man she met through work. They are going boating. It's an original idea for a date and Rosie likes to be original. Her last first date took place in a yoga class. 'Well, at least you'd know if he was up to it,' she had said mysteriously. But apparently he wasn't, because she had only seen Yoga Date Man the once.

She has this strange superstition that to refer to a man by his actual name, until they have seen each other at least four times, means that the relationship will end prematurely. Consequently I have never learnt the names of very many of her acquaintances. Her ex, Chris, was Total Fox Man the first few times I met him, which I thought was a debatable tag. Self-important Slimy Git Man was how Selin and I referred to him in private, until the shock news of their whirlwind engagement. After that we thought it best to be more polite about him.

I'm not good at mornings, they get me down. I always stay in bed a bit too long, spend a bit too much time over breakfast and a bit too long in the shower. I never *can* find anything clean or nice to wear and it takes me two and a half cups of instant before I can really take in the day. Although I don't mind my job, because for the first time ever I'm earning a real wage, and the people are nice and I get listened to sometimes, I just sort of stumbled into it rather than found my vocation and usually, just before I open the door to leave in the morning, I take a deep breath and say, 'Oh well, here we go again.'

Rosie comes out of the bathroom. She looks dreadful: her blonde hair is in tangles, she has dark smudges under her bloodshot eyes, and her face is still creased with the marks of a restless night.

'I feel awful.' She slumps against the bathroom door. 'I've been throwing up since dawn.'

'Oh, poor love, did you get a take-away last night?' I ask her.

'No, toast.' She must feel poorly, she can't string a sentence together.

'Booze?' I ask cautiously, it was my first guess. Over the last week or so I have noticed the effects of her hangovers keep her in the bathroom longer than usual, but she gets sensitive if you mention her drinking and it's too early to face a fight.

'No, not a drop.' She rubs her eyes and tucks her usually silky hair behind an ear. 'I feel strange.' I follow her into her room and she sits on the bed.

'Do you want me to phone thingy and cancel him?' I offer. It wouldn't be the first time. Once I told someone she had had to emigrate overnight for legal reasons.

'Mmm, yes please.' She gets back into bed and pulls the duvet up under her chin.

'Jen?'

'Yes, love?'

'Mumphalaeneltnt,' she mumbles.

'Pardon?' Three or four deep breaths pass and she repeats herself a little more clearly.

'I think I might be pregnant.' A brief moment of horror passes through me and I take a deep breath and calm down. This is probably typical Rosie overdramatics. She couldn't possibly be sick just because she ate or drank too much.

'Don't be silly, you haven't done it with anyone since the husband, right? And that was months ago.' I can say this with confidence because we really do know everything about each other's lives. And if ever there has been something we haven't told each other for one reason or another we always break the ice by buying each other a Mars Bar. Over the years it has become a symbol for big news. Selin blames our gradual weight gain throughout our twenties on Rosie's erratic and tumultuous life, which seems fair, as most of the Mars-Bar-related news *has* come from Rosie, with quite a bit from me, and there has been none from Selin for years. And of course Rosie eats what she likes and never puts on a pound.

'I've missed two periods, I'm about to miss a third.' This comes from under the duvet. Two periods, that's OK. This girl from work didn't have a period for a whole year, sometimes it just happens.

'I think you're overreacting, Rose. I mean when? Who?' Personally I think it's probably stress and a lifestyle that doesn't exactly bode well for the natural rhythms of the female cycle.

'Chris!' The name comes out in a high-pitched little screech. Chris her erstwhile husband, Chris?

'But, mate, you've been living here for eight months. The last time you saw Chris was at that dreadful work party and he was there with his new bird and you said she was fat . . . although she probably wasn't, you think anyone over a size eight is fat.'

Another muffled strangulated sound comes from under the covers.

'Rosie? Come on, tell me.' A hand appears and fumbles around on the bedside cabinet, around two glasses of stagnant water, a pewter hip flask, an aromatherapy candle, some neatly folded lottery tickets and an empty packet of Hula Hoops, until it finds the edge and then the knob of the drawer. Opening it, the hand disappears briefly and returns clutching a Mars Bar. King size.

'Oh, Christ,' I say and immediately unwrap it and take a bite. It's 7.45 a.m. The ritual now complete, she pushes back the covers and looks at me.

'I'd check the sell-by date, if I were you, I've been meaning to give it to you for weeks.'

'What happened?' I say, not sure that I really want to know.

Rosie's alarm-clock radio clicks on suddenly and the room is filled with the intrusive blare of some dreadful carping 'breakfast crew posse'. She reaches over, turns it down and leans back against the wall holding her spare pillow to her chest like a child with a toy. I can see she has hardly slept. She must have been thinking about this for weeks, poor love. She rubs her fingers across her tired eyes and begins.

'Well, it's mostly like I told you. Remember I had to take some clients to that ridiculous awards ceremony a few weeks ago? I knew that Chris would be there because his team was nominated for Best Child-orientated Campaign which is why I got that new dress and shoes. And bag. And my hair done, purely for the "ha–you–sucker" factor. And of course he *was* there and he brought "her" with him. And she *was* fat, honestly. Or if she wasn't fat she shouldn't have worn a skirt that short. Well, he clocked me, of course, and we sent each other a few glares and I was very happily having a few glasses of champagne, because you know it was free, and talking to Yoga Date Man, that's where I met him, remember? Well, then I went off to "powder my nose" so to speak and . . .' She stopped and clapped her hand over her mouth.

We were supposed to have given up cocaine, it was our New Year's resolution.

'. . . But it was free, so it doesn't count really and anyway it seems that he followed me down the stairs and well when I came out there he was, waiting. Before I knew it he had me back in the ladies' in a cubicle and we sort of . . . well . . . we accidentally had sex.' She stops talking and looks at me. I can't think what to say. Part of me is thinking that the months and *months* of us helping each other get over our exes have been for absolutely nothing and I feel angry with her. The other part of me just wants to give her a hug and help her get through it. I go with the hug option for now and decide to save the good-talking-to option for later. I climb into bed with her and put my arms around her.

'You think I'm a dreadful old slapper, don't you?' she sniffs and rests her head on my shoulder. Her hair covers her face but I can tell by her trembling shoulders that she is trying not to cry.

'Well, yes, but let's not discuss that now. Come on, darling,

22

it's OK. You're on the pill, anyway, so you can't be pregnant, can you?' I say softly to the top of her head.

'That's what I thought. But the morning before it happened I was sick just after breakfast. A few too many vodkas the night before. I didn't even think about it affecting my pill working. Not until I was late.' Well, it was a minor setback but not conclusive proof.

'Ah, but you always use a condom, because we promised each other, didn't we?' That was our New Year's resolution *circa* 1992 and as far as I knew we had always stuck to it. Maybe if taking the pill hadn't made me blow up like one of those poisonous fishes and turn into a tearful Attila the Hun it would have been harder to stick to but, as successfully integrating into society for at least three weeks out of every four is somewhat essential in the customer-care environment in which I work, I had decided to give the pill a miss and stick to traditional methods instead. Owen used to complain about it a lot, about the interruption, the loss of sensitivity and all that. He used to give me a really hard time in fact. But I just think it's unfair that when you're a girl you have to either take chemicals, stick a wire contraption up your bits, fiddle about with a sponge and spermicide or wear an internal version of a sou'wester. I mean, it's incredible what lengths men have gone to to avoid having to deal with contraception at the business end. If you're a boy all you have to do is pop a bit of ultra-thin latex on your willy. Just do it and shut up. The three of us have agreed on this countless times, in countless conversations, in countless bars over the years. So you make them use a condom, don't you?

Don't you?

'Not with your ex husband in the bog when you're off your face, you don't.' Oh well, that blew that theory.

I don't think Rosie is pregnant. A girl who drinks as much as her and eats as little food, who lives on coffee and is no stranger to illegal narcotics, can't be that fertile. My sister-in-law gave up everything from alcohol to crisps for two years before she conceived. And besides, Rosie and Chris only did it the once. By the time you get to our age you know it's actually damn hard to get pregnant, whatever way you look at it. You just don't tell the teenagers. It's probably the worry that has stopped her coming on.

'OK, look, I'll take the day off sick,' I say. 'We'll go to the pharmacy and get a kit. It'll be fine, we'll go to the pub. It's really hard to get knocked up, you read about it all the time. Girls our age are always missing periods; it's probably stress, or too much booze or something.'

'OK. I love you.' She raises her head and looks at me.

'You've been worrying about this for ages, haven't you?' I say gently. 'Why didn't you tell me sooner?'

'Because I thought you'd kill me. Especially after everything we said about "never going back come hell or high water". And because I needed to decide what I would do about it, if I were, you know . . . *thing*. I sort of needed to get it straight in my head first, before it all became real. I thought you and Selin might not understand this time.' I climb out of bed, sit on the edge again and hold her hand.

'Look, if anyone can understand it's me. Look how many times I went back to Owen over those last three years, despite all the promises I made to myself and to you two. It's a painful lesson to learn, but well, sometimes I think you have to keep going back until you learn it. It'll be fine, you'll see. I'm sure you're not pregnant.'

I stand up and stretch as Rosie disappears under her duvet again.

'Where's your phone? I'll phone thingy and cancel him.'

She hands it to me and I scroll down through her address book.

'What's he listed under?'

'Boating Date Man, of course,' the disembodied reply comes.

Chapter Six

By the time we leave the flat, dirty grey clouds have descended over our end of the grove and are leaning menacingly on the rooftops of the Georgian houses that line either side of the street.

Our flat is on the top floor of a flaky purpose-built block right at the wrong end of Ladbroke Grove, just a few hundred yards away from the Harrow Road and quite literally only just on the right side of the railway tracks that run directly behind the building. The trains thunder past every twenty minutes during the day and once an hour throughout the night, which many of my guests over the years have found unbearable, but I like the comforting rumble that can sometimes make the night seem more friendly. And it used to really piss Owen off, so that was a plus.

I have lived there for seven years, on my own for most of it, only able to afford it because it is squalid, damp, mostly broken and prone to little outbursts of small-unidentified-black-beetle activity. I like it because it is only fifteen minutes' walk from Portobello Road and I have two bedrooms, a big broken kitchen and a living-room with a ramshackle collection of damaged goods from Ikea.

The landlord has never bothered to put the rent up in all these years and I have never asked him to fumigate the house, fix the leaky roof or mend the cooker so that more than one ring on the electric hob works. I am a domestic slut and so is Rosie. Our life together is a cheerful amble through the boundaries of reasonable hygiene until we reach a kind of critical mass and rush around picking things up, washing them and hoovering up the beetles (which, I'm sure, when they reach the rarely emptied-out fluffy crumb-filled haven of the hoover bag, yell, 'Yippee – beetle heaven!') until we are ready to begin again. The only exceptions to this rule are clothes, the bathroom, cosmetics and us. These are the only items and areas we pay attention to every single day.

As much as I love it, I have had my toughest times here too, the worst times with Owen as well as the best. I had been thinking about upping sticks and getting a house share in the *Time Out* tradition of making new friends, but I felt so low I didn't think I was brave enough to go through the endless rounds of flatmate interviews. Trying to look trendy enough to be fun but not annoying, and clean enough to be liveable with but not an obsessive compulsive. Pretty enough to hang out in bars with, but not so pretty that your boyfriend would want to sleep with me, that kind of thing.

When Rosie came to live with me she saved me from having to make that kind of lifestyle-changing decision and frankly I was relieved.

She was in a bad way back then. Chris had just upped and told her he didn't love her and he didn't think he ever really had. He had told her it was a huge mistake, that he had asked her to marry him just to get him out of a fight they had been having and that he hadn't really thought of the consequences. That he had met someone not long after they got back from honeymoon who he thought might be 'the one'.

Looking back, I think we saved each other. The very night that she turned up on my doorstep with two suitcases, no money to pay her cab and her face streaked with mascara-tinted tears was the night that Owen had left a Post-it note for me to find when I went round for dinner that evening. It was stuck to his front door.

'Gone out. Can't face tears. It's over,' it had read, fluttering cheerily in the breeze. I stood there for a long moment in the rain before turning and walking away, back to the bus-stop and home. I suppose that, during the three years of on-and-off passion, infidelity and violent drunken eruptions, I had got used to his mood swings, the sudden sea changes in his regard for me. Earlier that afternoon we'd been talking on the phone about the poached salmon *en croute* he was preparing and the nice bottle of wine he had chilling in the fridge. If I'm honest, as I trudged back to the tube station, all I really felt was a kind of weary resignation, a 'here we go again'.

At that point I fully expected two or three weeks apart, news of another girl picked up in the park or a museum, shortly followed by long earnest conversations, declarations of our imperfect but irresistible love and before you knew it we'd be back to the beginning of our cycle. Perfect blissful passion.

In retrospect it's hard for me to explain how life was with Owen. When I met him I was out in full spin, living the city life to the city limits. It was a time when Selin was studying, Rosie was seeing some guy and I was drifting between second- and third-generation friends and a series of half-hearted boyfriends. I often had the dizzy feeling that gravity only just had a hold on me and that any moment I could slip away into a cloud of stars, lost from the real world for ever.

I was looking for love, I suppose, but more than that I was looking for something solid and strong to hold me down to earth, the kind of firm dependability I felt I'd lacked since my dad had walked out of my life over fifteen years before. Although I had a romantic idea about self-destruction by vodka and kisses, a notion that stopped me going mad from boredom between five in the evening and nine in the morning almost every day of the week, I was really waiting to be rescued.

Owen is eight years older than me. He lives in a rooftop flat in Clerkenwell, which he moved to before it became so trendy, when it was still an eclectic mix of fishmongers and second-hand bookshops, before the five-star restaurants and the hottest clubs sprang up on every street along with another branch of Starbucks. His walls are lined with shelves heavy with all kinds of books. He doesn't own a TV, only a battered old radio that is always tuned to Radio Four. He has the look of a dissolute Leonardo Di Caprio, twenty years older and after several crates of Irish whiskey, with dirty-blond hair and slanted green eyes.

When we met he was strong and paternal, I thought he'd give me some kind of guidance. He was besotted with me and passionate. He made me feel as if there was no other woman in the world. He persuaded me that I was beautiful and clever, that I had depths that only he could reach. He wanted to possess every last fibre of my being, he said and, happily, I let him.

It was after about three months that I came bounding into his flat one evening to find him in a quiet and unresponsive mood. Hurt and confused, I badgered him for an explanation for his coldness until he eventually exploded in anger, hurling the book he was reading at my head. He told me I bored him, that he needed more excitement from life, that there was someone else, a French girl who had asked him for directions just outside the British Museum. She was vivacious and interesting, he said. Not stuck in some dead-end job going nowhere, without a meaningful thought in her head, like I was. He told me to get out of his flat. When I refused, when I cried and begged and pleaded with him to change his mind, he threw me out, leaving bruises on my wrists that took a long time to fade.

If he hadn't come back to me it would have been fine really, in the long term. I would have been down for a while, back on my night-time odyssey of bars and clubs, but in time I would have lurched on to the next thing, maybe *the* thing.

Only he did come back. It was less than two months later when he called me at work and asked to meet me. I was holding my breath when I saw him; I used to think that he was so beautiful. We sat over coffee and talked for hours about our relationship, how he missed me, his hang-ups and problems. How he needed me and needed me to understand him. He said, 'I think that I love you too much to even admit it to myself. I think that's why I behave the way I do. But God, I *do* love you. There has *never* been anyone like you, you *have* to come back to me.' He took me home and when we made love that night I felt as if I *was* drifting out of control in that cloud of stars.

It was six months after that that the next girl came along and our cycle began again. For three years I really believed that the pain and the abuse was all worth it, just for those first few weeks when we were back together again and life was as wonderful as I had ever known it could be.

When Rosie showed up at my front door the night I found the Post-it note, I got that star-crossed feeling again. Somehow her being there with news of Chris brought the situation with Owen home to me. This time it was really finished. Something was different; something in the cycle had broken.

I believed that it might be me.

I got in maybe ten minutes before Rosie rang the bell. We didn't tell each other the details that night, we just opened the bottle of vodka I had bought on the way home and then the bottle of gin that Rosie had brought with her and swore and wept and laughed. But in the following weeks we talked about nothing else. We followed each other from room to room, cups of coffee or tea or glasses of wine in hand, trying to explain our lives to each other.

I'd sit on Rosie's bed trying to understand how it had taken me three years and all those broken promises to finally see what he had done to me. I was angry with myself, and angry with Owen, three wasted years. She'd wake me up in the middle of the night to tell me that she couldn't sleep. All she could think about was her wedding day, the speech he had made and the message he had written in a card on some flowers he had sent her on the eve of the wedding: 'Yours always,' In our own ways, both of us felt like fools but at least we were fools together.

Selin would come over most evenings and sit quietly with a glass of wine in her hand as we talked it all out, nodding and agreeing, offering to get the Turkish mafia on the case for a small fee, making us laugh and letting us cry, just listening.

Gradually the three of us created a kind of equilibrium. Mornings became less painful, Friday and Saturday nights became more fun and our years-old friendship, which had always been true, re-formed once again into the kind of closeness that we hadn't really had since we'd left home for different colleges over ten years earlier.

Soon after she moved in Rosie began to drink even more than we were used to, but we were all drinking a lot and it didn't seem right to preach. Anyway, mentioning it was a sure-fire way to start a stream of denial that devolved into a fight. Selin was working too hard, still trying to prove to her dad that she was as good a partner in the family accountancy firm as her brother would have been if he hadn't decided to become a starving artist instead. Still trying to prove it even though her dad had realised it years ago and was as proud of her as any father could be.

I got used to not seeing Owen. I got over expecting to meet him around every corner or to hear his voice every time I picked up the phone. An intonation in someone's voice, an advert or a carton of milk stopped making me cry and gradually I began to feel free. Things moved on and got better, and right now things are pretty good.

Rosie couldn't really be pregnant, could she?

Chapter Seven

As I wait for Rosie outside the flat it occurs to me that in all the years the three of us have known each other we have never bought a pregnancy testing kit. I'm sure I must be infertile.

'Christ almighty, I feel like I've been beaten up by a big fuck-off bastard,' Rosie says articulately as she stumbles out of the doorway in a fake-fur coat and aviator shades that she really doesn't need, considering the overcast sky. She makes me smile, for despite her situation she has managed to pull her hair up into a chic little topknot and apply some lip gloss. Whatever the morning will bring she is determined to look presentable.

'Well, you can stay here if you like and I'll go,' I say kindly, taking my phone out of my coat pocket to check that the keypad is locked and that the battery is charged.

'No, no, come on, fresh air and all that. Who are you waiting to call you?' she says, nodding at my phone.

'Are you going to ask for the kit or shall I?' I digress nonchalantly.

'Oh, you, you please. I can't ask, he knows me.' She lights up a cigarette.

'Well, he knows me too, we both go in there all the time, remember?' We are often in the small corner-shop chemist on a boring Saturday afternoon, rifling through the bucket of bargain

33

nail varnish, or buying silly hairgrips shaped like butterflies, or five bangles for 99p.

'Yes, but he knows me because I go in there to get my prescription for the pill cashed. What's he going to think if I get a pregnancy-testing kit?' Rosie turns up the collar on her coat and nuzzles her chin into the fur.

'But he knows me too, I go in there to get my inhalers. He's going to think I'm asthmatic and that I have irresponsible sex!' I say, though I'm not absolutely sure why that should worry me. We stop at the shop front and look in. I notice a little basket full of nail transfers at half price.

'Oh come on, I'll ask,' I say, as I knew I would, and we push the door open and go to the counter.

'Hello, ladies, what can we do for you today?' Mr Chemist is always the nicest and politest of men, he loves us because we spend a fortune on his lovely but useless bits of shiny frippery.

'We need a pregnancy-testing kit for our friend Selin, who you may have seen with us before,' I say, shamelessly. 'She's married, has been for years.'

'Well, good for her, babies bring much joy.' He turns and places three kits on the counter in front of us. 'Did she request any brand?' I look at Rosie, who is closely examining a false-nail kit.

'The cheapest?' I say, wondering how much cash I've got on me.

Rosie springs into life. 'No, no. It was definitely the most expensive. Which one is the most expensive?' Rosie's philosophy of life is that you get what you pay for. We get the most expensive test, which is flipping expensive, and has two stick things in so that Rosie can make sure for definite twice that she is not up the duff. I buy the nail transfers and Rosie buys a pair of silver-effect false eyelashes and some stick-on glitter nails. We both get some diamanté-effect heart-shaped tattoos.

When we get back in there is a message on the answerphone. It's my boss, Georgina.

'Hello, Jennifer. I was just calling to see how you are. I expect you're in bed and can't hear the phone. Call me when you have managed to drag yourself up for a Lemsip and let me know if you will be in tomorrow.' Kind of her to give me a ready-made excuse, I think, and I go to the kitchen to put the kettle on.

'Well, go on then!' I call through to Rosie, who I can see is slumped on our black velveteen foam-filled sofa. She seems to be unpicking the sleeve of her sweater.

'It says to wait until the morning,' she calls back in a gloomy tone.

'It *is* the morning.' I am looking around the kitchen for the box of tea bags. I can't remember where I had it last.

'Yes, but for your first *pee* of the morning. I did mine ages ago. Hours ago. Shall we watch *This Morning* instead?' she says hopefully.

'You know very well that it's not on for another hour. Does it *really* say that?' I sound like her mother, not her best friend.

'Yes! I'm not making it up! You can read the leaflet if you like.' She's bordering on petulant now.

I'm not going to let her get away with a Rosie-tantrum this time. I find the tea bags in the fridge.

'Well, do you need to go now?' I ask sternly.

'A bit, I suppose.' I can hear her pouting.

'Well, go on then! You can do the other one in the morning if you have to.' I'm not sure if this is how it's supposed to work but I'm working on the theory that if you're knocked up, you're knocked up and it doesn't matter what time of day you pee on the stick. I hear Rosie mumble something derogatory about me as she pads along the hallway to the bathroom and shuts the door. I lift pots, pans and plates out of the sink until I can find two mugs to rinse out and I lean against the counter waiting for the kettle to come to the boil. What are we going to do if she is pregnant?

I can't picture Rosie as a mother. I can't picture Rosie in anything other than four-inch heels, with a cigarette in her mouth and a cocktail in her hand. If she has a maternal streak I haven't seen it yet. That doesn't mean she wouldn't be a good mum one day, though. I mean, she's loyal and kind. She's funny and good at listening; she's emotionally generous and always thinks the best of people. I suppose all of us have it in us to make good mothers one day, it's just that I have never thought of that day as being anywhere but around some far distant corner, and after some very radical changes of direction and circumstance. And the thought of someone as vain and superficial as Chris becoming a father? Well, it doesn't bear thinking about. No wonder she's been a bit madder than usual recently, with this on her mind.

I'm trying to think of the best way to be for her. Non-judgemental, supportive and practical, I decide, at least until I can get Selin on the phone to be in charge. We've got £820 in the emergency holiday fund if we need cash to get anything over with, and if she isn't pregnant, well, then straight over the road to the Duke of York and have two pints of bitter for old times' sake. The kettle clicks off and I pour the water on two tea bags, milk and the two sugars which neither of us takes except for regular daily emergencies.

I hear the bathroom door click open and Rosie running down the hallway.

I turn to look at her in the doorway. She is grinning from ear to ear and there are tears in her eyes.

'It's all OK then?' I ask, clasping both mugs of tea for dear life.

'Yes, it's brilliant!' She rushes to engulf me in a hug. I hold the two mugs out either side of her, trying not to spill anything else on to the sticky floor.

'Oh thank God, what *would* we have done!' I say, laughing with relief.

Rosie takes a step back and puts her hands on my shoulders. Her smile is radiant. 'Everything is going to change from now on. It has to.' I can see that the result has overwhelmed her.

'Well, you know, Rosie, you may have got away with it this time but—'

'I mean,' she interrupts me in a rush of emotion, 'I'm going to be a mum!' She is hugging me again and hot tea splashes on to my thumb. 'I'm having a baby!'

From the other room I can hear my mobile phone ringing.

Chapter Eight

We are both sitting on our black velveteen sofa, tea in hand, staring at the opposite wall.

'You're definitely pregnant? You haven't read it wrong?' I ask her. I'm still reeling from the news.

'Definitely. Blue stripe, the works.' She is already resting the palm of her hand on her abdomen. I can't quite believe this.

'But Rose, mate, are you sure? A baby? Single mother? You don't want to keep it because you think Chris will come back, do you?' I turn to look at her. That would be a typically Rosie move.

'No! God no, I don't want that bastard near my baby. Jesus!' she spits. I'm starting to wonder how long Rosie has been thinking this through. Maybe she knew even before she took the test. She seems to have everything planned out.

'I earn good money, I get good maternity leave and a childcare allowance from work and then there's the settlement from the divorce. It'll be fine, you'll see.'

But just at this moment I can't see that it will be fine, I can't see that at all. I lean my head on the sofa's back and look at the watermarked stains on the ceiling.

'But, Rose, a new baby. Your life will change for ever. Nothing will be the same, you'll have to grow up – and for real, this time, not just in terms of the clothes you can afford.

And what about Chris? Will you tell him? What about future boyfriends? What about Saturday nights?'

Rosie puts her tea on the floor, squashing a small beetle as she does so, and picks up one of my hands. 'I know I've been . . . a bit . . . well, a bit out of control in the last few months.'

'Years,' I interrupt.

'Years then, but *especially* in the last few months. On the sauce a bit too much, taking more drugs than I've let on about and all that. I know I've been a bit tricky sometimes and I've been worried about myself too. It's almost seemed as if it wasn't really happening to me: living here, it's been like having a holiday from my life. But maybe this baby . . . maybe this baby is my chance to get out of all that. Maybe this baby is it, the thing that is going to get me on the right track again.' She pats my hand. 'Holiday over.'

'You decided all that while you were in the loo waiting for the stick to go blue?' I'm worried. Typical Rosie; life-changing decisions made in two minutes. I generally think that life-changing decisions should take, well, a lifetime; makes it much less likely that you'll have to live with the consequences if you don't *actually* change anything. 'Because this is about more than saving yourself. This is about a real person, another person, who will rely on you always and for ever,' I say, feeling an odd sense of vertigo at the pace at which her life is changing.

'I know that, of course I do. Jen, I promise I'm not going into this lightly. I promise this *will* change my life and I *will* be a good mother. I know I will.' She grabs my hand again. 'I know it won't be easy, I'm not that naive but I really feel I can do it, I can make this baby's life a happy one. And that's a really important thing to do with your life, isn't it? The *most* important thing really.'

I look at her and think: non-judgemental, supportive and practical.

'Honestly now. How can you have decided all this so quickly? You knew already that you were going to keep it, didn't you?' I ask her.

Rosie shifts in her seat and takes a deep breath. 'Yes, I suppose I did. I can't explain it really, I mean the vomiting thing has only been recently, but for weeks I've felt . . . well, I've felt different, it happened almost immediately.' She laughs. 'I mean, it's pretty fucking weird, really. I don't know how anyone is ever surprised to be pregnant! I tried not to think about it for a while, but you can't ignore it in the end. *Everything* changes.' She hugs her legs up to her chin and looks at me over the tops of her knees. I decide to keep quiet and just let her talk.

'For the last few weeks I've been awake every night thinking about what I would do if I was pregnant. At first I was scared, I thought this couldn't be happening. Not now, not with Chris, of all people. I mean, how could I be ready for something like this? I was all sick and panicky. To be honest, I thought if I just drank and partied enough the problem would go away on its own. God, that sounds awful, doesn't it?' I shake my head and pull my own feet up on to the sofa in a mirror image of her. She looks like a little girl.

'That's not awful,' I say softly. 'Not at all. I expect loads of people react that way. It's just the shock.' She smiles a little smile and continues.

'One night I found myself worrying that I *wasn't* pregnant, that that time with Chris was just another pathetic, demeaning encounter which meant nothing. I found myself thinking, no, *hoping*, that maybe this baby is the reason I met him in the first place. If I'm honest this baby became a reality to me a lot longer ago than with that positive test result. This is my baby, *mine*. This is my chance to do things right for a change and I'm going to take it.' She lifts her chin a little with a determined air. 'And yes, I did make up my mind long before I took the test.

The thing I've been stressing out about most recently is how I was going to tell you two!' She laughs sheepishly.

'God, you shouldn't have been scared about telling us! Well, not me anyway.' I hesitate, and then continue. 'Look, I'm not sure I would have made the same choice and I'm not sure how we're going to iron out the details, but if this is what you want then of course I'm with you one hundred per cent. I'll help in whatever way I can. And so will Selin, I know she will. Once she comes down from hitting the roof.'

We reach out and hug each other and settle back on to the sofa in each other's arms.

'No more booze, you know. You drink a lot,' I tell her.

'I know. No more booze. None.' She shakes her head and crosses her heart.

'No more pharmaceuticals.' I think about the last few week-ends out we've had with regard to foetal health and decide not to mention it right now.

'Nope,' she concedes.

'The fags will have to go. Right now.'

'Right now.' She pulls a pack out of her jeans pocket and gives it to me.

'Tea, coffee, Red Bull. You'll have to cut all that out.'

'Well, I've been waiting for an excuse to detox.' She shrugs and pulls the ends of her sleeves over her fingers.

'And you'll have to kiss goodbye to your hipster Versace jeans before long.'

'Oh, bollocks. I've changed my mind.' And we fall into a fit of the giggles.

I have the strangest feeling of unreality as I watch the indestructible little beetle struggle out from under Rosie's mug. Things will have to change so much, things that neither of us have any idea about right now. I wonder if evolution really meant it to be this easy to bring another life into the world.

'Imagine, a baby in the house!' I say, feeling light-headed in a tipsy kind of way. 'We can paint a nursery! What fun!'

'Oh yes, but not baby pink or blue, something a bit more hip. I *have* to have a hip baby!' Rosie says and I nod in agreement.

As we sit with stupid grins on our faces, we watch the little beetle crawl over a discarded toast plate and amble under the sofa. Then suddenly Rosie sits up and inexplicably dives for the Yellow Pages.

'Bloody hell, we have to move! We have to move like *now*. This week — we can't live in this flea-pit with a baby on the way!' She's turning the pages but there doesn't seem to be a section called 'Reasonably priced three-bedroom flats just over the road available now'.

'God, yes, we have to move,' Rosie continues in her new hygiene rant. 'We'll definitely need more than one ring with a baby. Hot water and stuff, I expect.' And then, 'We'll never afford anywhere round here,' she says, matter of factly.

I sit back, a little stunned, and think about it. I had just started to come to terms with the fact that her baby would change all our lives but I hadn't expected it to change my life *quite* so much.

'We do?' I stand up and look out of the window and down the Grove, and think about the hundreds of nights when brim-full of wine I've strolled up it with Owen. This flea-pit has been my home.

'What about south of the river? Brixton or Streatham?' Rosie used to live there with Chris.

'Well, you know, *south* and all that. It's just not my cup of tea,' I say, rather than point out that we'd practically be moving in next door to the evil absent father of her love child. 'And I see your point, what with the "wildlife" and everything, but maybe we could buy some kind of spray?'

Rosie picks up on the uncertainty in my voice.

'Jen, darling. I have to move out of here, you know why.' She points at the dark recess beneath the sofa where who knows how many beetles are eavesdropping on our life-changing morning. 'I, well, I'd love it if you came with me. It could be a new start for us both, but well, look, if you don't want to come I'll understand . . .' Her voice trails off and she looks at me, her expression a mixture of concern and panic.

I look around the room and see memories of Owen in every corner, smirking at me. Leaving this flat is exactly the kind of life-changing decison I don't like to make in a hurry. This place has been my refuge for so many years. On the other hand, Rosie has suddenly altered her life beyond recognition, always and for ever in the space of a few minutes and well, maybe moving flat wouldn't be so bad, in fact maybe it would be another way to distance myself from Owen, to show solidarity with Rosie's determination to get over Chris, even while she's carrying his baby. Owen always said I was never impulsive enough. I hesitate a moment more, that sense of vertigo creeping over me once again, and then I decide. I'll show him.

'OK, yes. Come on, let's bloody move!' I catch on to Rosie's excitement. 'But I'm not moving south, you can't make me move south, OK?'

'Ha!' Rosie jumps to her feet. 'I've got it. We'll move back north, we'll go home to Stoke Newington and live near Selin! They've got cafés there now, an organic supermarket and everything.'

Stoke Newington. No tube, but the number 73 would take me straight to Tottenham Court Road, which is only two minutes' walk from the office. And we'd be going home really, so it would be much less of a change than it might have been. Rosie is a genius.

'Of course!' I agree. 'Then the three of us will be close and Mrs Selin loves babies, I bet she'd babysit any time you liked.' I'm talking about Selin's mum. We have always referred to parents as Mrs Rosie, Mrs Jen, Mr and Mrs Selin. 'I'll go and get a copy of *Loot* right now.' And I already have my coat on when a sudden sinking feeling stops me in the doorway; I turn and look back at Rosie. I can tell she has just had the same thought I have.

'How *are* we going to tell Selin? She'll kill us,' I say, forgetting for a moment that none of this is my fault. 'And what about your mum?'

'I'm not worried about telling *her* . . .' Rosie says. We look at each other a moment longer and I shut the front door behind me. In times of difficulty, denial is always the safest place.

In the newsagent I buy a token copy of *Loot* – though I know in my heart that it is probably already useless by 11.45 on a Monday morning – and a large bar of Cadbury's. Before I go back into the building I take out my phone and check the received-calls register. I check the last number to call my phone and compare it to the number he left. They aren't the same. I dial to pick up my messages and find that it was the bookshop calling to tell me my ordered items are now available.

I stand in the doorway for a moment longer and look at the dark sky. It's funny to think that only a couple of days ago it was bright blue and warm enough for a vest top. I remember the touch of the sun on my face as he tipped my chin back to kiss me. A small knot forms in my stomach. I close my eyes just for a second and think of his kiss. My lips tingle.

This is insane. I'm twenty-nine, he's far too young for me, one of my best friends is pregnant and anyway he hasn't even called yet. I think about switching my phone off. In the end I just put it back in the pocket of my coat and go inside.

'Rosie, get some biros and get ready,' I call as I walk through the door.

'OK. There was phone call for you, while you were out.'

'Michael?' I ask before I can stop myself, even though I know he doesn't have the land-line number.

'No.' She sighs and crosses her arms. 'Owen.'

Chapter Nine

Rosie has gone into the kitchen to put the kettle on again. Rain has just started to hit the windows and I reach under the three-legged dining table that leans against the wall, bring out the buckets and situate them around the room. Usually the ceilings don't leak unless the rain gets really heavy, but it's better to be safe than sorry.

Owen used to laugh at my *faux*-destitute lifestyle. He used to say it was bohemian and I used to think, 'Yeah, right. I'm a very bohemian Customer Service Administration Manager (UK) for a hardware-component manufacturer.' And then, when he was back into writing his literally fictional novel, with so far not one word actually committed to paper, as far as I knew, I'd be Miss Mundane Bureaucracy. I'd be Miss Lower Middle Class Mediocrity. And I'd know that I was shortly to be dumped again for a poet called Alicia or an editorial assistant called Hermione.

Of course, I'd never meant to find my way into customer services. I'd meant, upon leaving university, to be Kate Adie, an intrepid and courageous journalist, but with more make-up and hopefully less chance of getting hit by bullets. If I ever stop to wonder why it has never happened I comfort myself with the thought that only about two or three people get to be like Kate, and only a few hundred, maybe fewer get to work on the really interesting papers or news programmes. Knowing my luck I'd probably have ended up reporting on a mischievous parrot called Reggie who turned out to be the mysterious cause of the neighbourhood knickers disappearing, and so my life wouldn't have had *that* much more meaning than it does now.

And then, of course, coupled with the enormous odds against me ever making it, is my relationship with personal commitment. My mum had always encouraged me, all through my childhood and early adult years. 'You can do it, but it's very competitive; it's competitive and it requires commitment and even after all that hard work, you might not make it. But if you believe you can, you *just* might,' she'd say when I told her I wanted to be an actor, ballet dancer, singer, fighter pilot, writer, and then finally journalist after one night when Kate's new report left me emotionally aghast for the first time ever about the state of the world. I went to bed that night fired up with determination, but woke up the next day thinking, 'Mmm, hard work, commitment, might very well fail . . .' I managed to carry the flickering ambition as far as two weeks post graduation, but when faced with the nitty-gritty of making it really happen I'd got a temping job as receptionist on a science park instead.

'Are you going to call him?' Rosie says, bringing more tea in from the kitchen. She is probably the only person in the world who would understand if I did.

'No,' I say. 'It's weird. This time last year, or this time six months ago, I would have done like a shot. But I'm not calling him. No. I just don't want to.'

'You know he'll call you again. And again. You know what it's going to be like. It'll be flowers and tears and letters and poems and books again, just like it always is when he wants you back.' This is unusual for Rosie. Over the years when I've asked her what to do about Owen she has always said, 'If you want to go through it again you have to go through it again.

I can't stop you.' So I always used to ask her and not Selin, because Selin used to say what I didn't want to hear.

'Yeah. I know,' I say. 'But we're moving soon, so sod him.'

Rosie sits down and shuffles in her seat. 'You're going to kill me,' she says, chewing her bottom lip.

'What, even more?' I ask her, thinking she is changing the subject.

'There's . . . there is something that we haven't told you. Selin and I.'

'What? A Mars Bar kind of thing?' I say in a small voice. I've got that quiet feeling of dread in my chest.

'Well, yes, strictly speaking, but I haven't had a chance to get another one in. I'll put it on the slate.' She smiles nervously. 'It's about Owen. Selin heard something about him through Josh.' Josh, Coşgun, Selin's older artist brother, whose name sounds like Joshgun and whom we all call Josh.

'What about him?' I am beginning to feel panicky and cross.

'The last time he split with you, it was for this girl Josh has met a couple of times through his collective, a sculptor or something. Well, after a while she wised up to him and didn't want to see him any more. I guess that was a bit of a shock for Owen, he didn't like it. I mean, he usually does all the hiring and firing, doesn't he.'

Instinctively I walk away and turn my back on her to try and collect my thoughts. A small part of me still hurts when I hear about the other women. A small part of me feels afraid of what Rosie might say next.

'Why are you telling me this now?' I ask her. I feel hurt. I feel hurt, frightened and fucking angry.

'He refused to leave her alone, mate. He started following her around. Calling her all hours. Sending her nasty e-mails. Josh says he heard that he broke into her house and trashed it.

She wasn't in, luckily. She got an injunction against him and he's on bail for breaking and entering.' She looks at her feet. 'We didn't tell you because it was over between you two. We didn't want you to worry about him any more. We didn't think you needed to know.'

'Well, why are you telling me now? I *don't* want to know.' Strangely I am not surprised by this information, but the uneasy sense of dread has spread to my stomach. Owen was always going to do something like that to someone one day. I'd always known it really.

'Because he's called you, called again. Maybe he wants you again. It sounds mean but I hoped he would stay fixated with this girl. Jen, he's a nasty piece of work. He treated you like shit for years and he thinks he owns you. I'm just afraid of how he might react when he realises he doesn't.'

I turn and march up to Rosie, furious. I stop inches from her face. 'He's an arsehole, but he's not a stalker, for fuck's sake,' I shout, well aware how much the evidence suggests otherwise. I rationalise: 'He was probably drunk. He was always doing fucking stupid things when he was drunk. Like that time he punched out the ticket bloke at Tottenham Court Road tube station because he didn't have the right ticket!' My words ring hollow, bouncing off the bare walls.

'I'm not saying he is a stalker,' Rosie lies for my sake. 'I just thought you'd like to know that stuff before you call him back, if you decided that you wanted to call him back, I mean.'

'I'm not fucking calling him back!' I shout and I've slammed the door shut on my bedroom before I realise I've left the room.

Lying on my bed I can feel the heat in my face and the sting of tears in my eyes. I blink hard. I am determined not to cry.

'Are you all right?' I ask myself. I try to work out why I'm feeling so sick and angry. It isn't because Selin and Rosie have kept something from me; any two of the three of us would have made the same choice. And it isn't because of this other girl, not really. I knew when he left me the Post-it note that there would be someone else along the way.

It's because I know – and I think I always have known – that there is something else to Owen, something a bit darker and more threatening than his self-obsessed narcissism. Because somewhere just behind his sweet romantic moments, the passion-filled afternoons and repetitive tearful reunions, I've always been a little bit afraid of what he might do next. Up until now I've always complied with what he wanted. Always gone back to him when he wanted me and always left him when he didn't; in a sense he has owned me. Now things are different. I don't need to go back any more. I don't even want to speak to him. I don't want to hear the sound of his voice, let alone see his face. Whatever he did to this girl is no surprise. Something like this was always coming, I am just glad I got out soon enough before it came my way.

There is a quiet knock on my door.

'I'm sorry.' Rosie comes in and sits on my bed. 'We should have told you. Josh was getting ready to tell you himself, but we stopped him. He was a bit pissed off with us, I can tell you.' Sweet Josh has always been big brother to all three of us and looked out for us since we were kids. My head hurts and my stomach is in knots but I know I shouldn't take it out on Rosie.

'No. It's not you. It's him. I'm just fucked off that he's still fucking me off nearly a year after we've finished, and just when I thought I'd got him out of my head.'

Rosie pulls the hair back from my face and tucks it behind my ear. 'Yeah, I know. But we're going to move and then he won't know where you are or anything about you any more.' She flops down on the bed next to me, clutching *Loot*. 'Look,

I've phoned this place here, not far from Selin's. It costs quite a bit more than here but at least it's got a roof and central heating and they're viewing this afternoon. Apparently there will be two couples and two other girls there at the same time. Do you want to go?'

I take the pink paper from her hand and look at the ad as if it will give me a clear picture of the flat she has in mind. Two double b/room, fitted kitchen, f/freezer, balcony, gas c/h, close to b/stop and shops. 'Yeah. Let's get there early, and take your cheque-book.'

She smiles and nods, leaves again and closes my door behind her.

I should be out there talking about her baby, not in here moping about a long-gone ex. A train rumbles past. It's all finally gone, I think. Every moment that I spent with Owen in this room. Every book he gave me, with a message scrawled in the front. Every shell he picked up for me and every poster he bought me. None of it means anything any more. Not even the seven years I have spent in this flat. I just want to be as far away from every association I have with him as possible. I want to go. I want to go now. Before he calls again.

Chapter Ten

I got up this morning with Rosie just after six and held her forehead until the queasiness subsided. Between bouts she told me this had been going on for days before she'd plucked up the courage to tell me. Looking back, I can see that it all fits in with the way she's been acting recently, early-morning bathroom bouts and all. Feeling guilty that I hadn't picked up on the clues earlier, I didn't leave for work until the doctor's surgery opened and I could call and make her an appointment. I had to say it was an emergency, even though Rosie doesn't seem to think there is one, as the only other appointment they had on offer meant she would have been taking the baby to primary school by the time her pregnancy was confirmed.

Unsurprisingly, we had had no luck with the flat we went to see. The two bedrooms turned out to be one bedroom and a large cupboard, the central heating a dodgy gas fire and the balcony a decidedly unstable-looking railing that was apparently designed to prevent you from falling out of an entirely arbitrary third-floor french window. Anyway, both of us had forgotten that the advent of a child would require a third bedroom, one day at least, so the next thing I did after booking Rosie in at the doctor's was to pick up another copy of *Loot* on the way to work.

I had phoned Selin last night but we got her answerphone,

and her mobile was switched off. Needing to talk to her and knowing she wasn't one for going out mid-week, I phoned her parents who live two streets away from her in a flat over the family business on Green Lanes. Even though she officially left home over three years ago, she spends at least four evenings out of seven with her family.

'Hi, Mrs Selin, it's Jenny Greenway,' I say, even though she's known me for nearly fifteen years and no one but Rosie or I calls her Mrs Selin.

'Hello, Jennifer, how are you, darling?' Selin's mum and dad moved to London from Turkey in the sixties, and I never grow bored of listening to the remnants of her accent combined with years of north London life.

'Pretty good. Is Selin there by any chance, please?'

'No, sweetheart, she's out with her dad. Don't you know? On Monday they play pool down the road, they've been going for weeks. Selin has beaten him the last two Mondays. Now it's a grudge match.' I didn't know, and I was surprised that Selin hadn't mentioned this unlikely bonding exercise with her father. She adored her dad; her conversation was usually littered with anecdotes and stories about him. I adored her dad too and he'd gamely stepped up to the plate to fill the absence of my own dad at various points over the years, stopping by to put up shelves when I'd first moved in, once giving me a lift to a job interview when it was pouring with rain and there was a tube strike. I laugh when I think about Selin and her dad playing pool and I suppress a little burst of jealousy. Maybe she was getting ready to hustle us on one of those afternoons when it seemed like a good idea to put as many pound coins as we could find between us on the pool table in our local and wind the men up by taking all day about it.

'Oh, we're thinking of coming over to see her tomorrow if she's around, that's all.' Rosie and I had discussed a plan of action and decided we'd tell her face to face. Selin would know immediately that something was up – we hadn't been north in six months – but we decided it was the best way.

'Tomorrow? Well, if you're coming over this way I'll make you girls dinner. It will give me an excuse to feed up that girl of mine. You children with your mothers so far away, you need a good meal too.' A sensible person would never pass up the opportunity to eat at Mrs Selin's table. At the risk of offending my own mother, she is the best cook in the whole world. However, I sort of thought under the circumstances that it might not be the best place to discuss the baby, the move, Owen's reappearance.

'Oh, we don't want to put you out . . .' I said feebly, knowing that nothing bar nothing in the fifteen or so years I've known Mrs Selin has ever put her out.

'Don't be silly, the children will love to see you and I'll get Coşgun over too. That boy never eats. Up all hours, up to goodness knows what, but he never eats. Drinks, too much in my opinion, but never eats. Runs around with all those girls but—'

'Let me guess . . . never eats?' I finished, and wondered about the universal preoccupation of mothers with force-feeding their offspring. My own mother thinks I'm anorexic if I don't have two slices of cake for dessert and then has the cheek to comment on my weight. I wondered if Rosie would turn into a feeding maniac. Considering how sparingly I've seen her smear her disgusting low-fat spread on her crispbread I'd be surprised but, well, the mystery of motherhood is uncharted territory for us. The thought of seeing Josh again was nice, but in a way I didn't want to hear any more news that might bring Owen nearer.

'Well, I'd better check with Rosie – hang on.' I put my hand over the receiver and called, 'Rosie?'

'Yes?' Her disembodied voice came from her bedroom.

'Mrs Selin has invited us to dinner tomorrow?'

'Yippee, yes please!' Rosie obviously didn't have the same reservations that I did; in fact maybe she was pleased to have a reason not to come straight out with things. And one thing was true – we could both do with a good meal.

'Rosie says yes please, if you're sure that's OK?'

'Of course it's OK, of course.'

'Should you check with Selin?'

'Don't you worry, darling, Selin will be here waiting for you tomorrow and then you girls can go and have a drink after dinner and talk about boys or whatever it is you don't want to talk about in front of us old fogies. So I'll see you tomorrow about eight?'

'OK, thanks again.'

'No problem. How's your mum these days, out in the country?' My mum moved out of town a couple of years ago with my brother and his family to just beyond Watford; the countryside, I suppose, in comparison to N16.

'Oh, she's good, she loves being a grandmother,' I said politely, wondering why it is that women of a certain age feel the need to talk longer on the phone than is strictly necessary.

'I should be a grandmother by now. At your age I was married eight years.' I briefly wondered how Rosie's 'young' mum with her trendy hairdo and Calvin Klein wardrobe would feel about being a grandmother. It's almost as hard to imagine as Rosie changing a nappy.

'I know, but there is only one Mr Selin and you don't want to share him, do you?' I said, making her giggle before she blew me a couple of kisses down the phone and said goodbye.

Now, after dropping Rosie safely off at the doctor's and turning my fingers black thumbing through *Loot* on the tube, I'm back at work in the Customer Care and Sales call centre, phone headset on, picking up calls from clients on average every two minutes. I periodically yell from my little goldfish cubicle that it would be nice if someone else on the sales floor could manage to interrupt their dissection of last night's TV to pick up some calls. We all wear Madonna-esque headsets so the phones don't ring here, they beep; all I can hear around me is a cacophony of monotonous beeps and they all seem to be coming my way.

The one good thing about all this is that I haven't really thought about Michael and the fact that he hasn't called me yet. OK, last night as I was drifting off to sleep I did think about the kiss and wondered what else it might have led to, but I know that's dangerous territory. I mean, we all know that the more of a dream personality you attribute to someone you hardly know, the more you will be let down. But it's OK with Michael because I'm not going to get to know him at all, so if I use him to take my mind off real things that's OK. It will be OK until he actually phones me, and then I'll put a stop to the whole thing. So for now it's OK to dream about his sweetness, the soft warmth of his mouth and his long guitarist's fingers.

Day three and he hasn't called yet. My phone has been turned on and charged up since Saturday, although I will never know why I bothered to buy it – the only people who ever phone me on it are Rosie and Selin and the occasional shop. When I chose the tiny model with its glittery casing and 'Disco Inferno' ring I had the vague notion that I'd need it for emergencies. Really, I wanted it because Rosie had got a pink one that plays the theme tune to *Top Cat* and Selin has a holographic cover for hers that makes it look like it's covered in 3-D love hearts. Deep down we are still the three little teenagers who used to swap coloured shoelaces to go in our trainers and badger our mums for stiletto-heeled patent-leather shoes from Freeman, Hardy and Willis, just like our friends had, still not proper grown-ups.

Today my phone is sitting like a tiny glittery little toad next to my work phone, sparkling provocatively under the daylight-effect strip lighting. I look at my calendar, 28 August. When do kids go back to school these days?

My work phone beeps a long single beep which means it's an internal call and the display tells me it is my boss, Georgie.

'Hello, Georgie.' I try to remember to sound a bit croaky.

'All right, darling? How are you today?' When I read Georgie da Silva's name on my interview letter three years ago I pictured some horsy long-faced Sloane, fished out my fake pearls and turned up the collar of my shirt especially for the occasion. When I met her and found out that she was an East End princess with a thing about new-age alternative Eastern therapy I couldn't have been more surprised. But it's partly her faddy experiments with crystals, *feng shui* and the like that make life here fun. She is a brick really, I feel bad lying to her. But not enough so I can't live with it.

'Yeah, much better thanks. I think it was one of those forty-eight-hour things, you know.' I cough, pretty realistically I think.

'Those girls giving you trouble?' She is referring to the call-centre team I am in charge of (in theory), two of whom are actually boys. In practice, I think I just preside over the natural rhythms of their work pattern: gossip until ten, work like bastards until one, dawdle around until three and then pretend to file until it's time to go home. I don't mind really, my pattern is the same. As long as the calls get picked up and I don't get any customer complaints and we meet our targets, I don't mind. It's not exactly the world's most dynamic career but at least I can afford good shoes, which goes a long way towards making up for a lack of personal fulfilment any day of the week.

'No, they're a good bunch, really,' I say.

'The floor looks a mess, doesn't it?' she says.

Oh no, here we go again. The paper will be blocking the flow of our *chi* and causing a build-up of negative forces or something.

'Do you think? I'll get them to do a tidy-up,' I say, thinking there isn't a cat in hell's chance.

'No. I've got an idea I want to go over with you. Pop over and see me, will you?' And in a typically Georgie style she hangs up without saying goodbye.

Emerging from my little office, I pick my way through old photocopying paper boxes full of, well, old photocopying, navigate my way around the green bags of rubbish that accumulate by the recycling bin and stop short at the fax where the orders seem to have piled up beyond the collecting tray and are now fluttering on to the floor.

'Carla,' I turn to the youngest member of the team, who is clearly going to have to work for at least five years before she's any good at anything, much like myself at her age, 'can you pick up these faxes and distribute them amongst the team, please?' I turn to the floor as a whole.

'Ladies, and Kevin and Brian, can you please *try* and remember that we are here to process sales, therefore when orders come through on the fax we need to deal with them quickly? Thank you!' There is a general murmur and a couple of them get up from their desks and come to help Carla sort out the pile of orders. Well, Brian and Kevin actually, Carla being exceptionally pretty, with her waxed blonde curls piled up on her head and her *very* short skirt making the most of her *very* long legs. Sometimes I wish my powers extended to enforcing a dress code.

A couple of years ago I was the one slacking behind my VDU and ignoring the hum of the faxes. I never thought I'd get to the stage where I was confident enough, efficient enough and grown up enough to run a team of people every day, it just sort of crept up on me. It's a bit scary when I think about it.

Georgie has her feet up on her desk and the crystal that hangs above her chair glints in the sunlight that I can't see from my office. She is an attractive woman, and looks exactly the way I want to look when I'm her age: pretty in a mature way, with clear blue eyes that are surrounded by pleasant laughter lines when she smiles. Of course I have the laughter lines; I just don't find them very pleasant just yet.

'Ah, hello love . . . ooh, you do look a bit peaky.' I nod pathetically and cough a bit. I'm not offended. I am the sort of person who does look peaky at the drop of a hat; it's the pale complexion and dark hair that does it.

'You want to get some Echinacea down your neck, that'll sort you out sharpish.' And she shoves a couple of brown-looking capsules at me, which I pocket with a grateful smile and a plan to dispose of them later.

'Now. Hypnosis, what do you think of it?'

'Well, in what context do you mean?' I can't figure out where she's going with this one. The Christmas party maybe?

'You know, like, helping you give up fags, stop being afraid of spiders, lose weight, that sort of thing.'

'Yes, well, it certainly seems to work for some people,' I nod. It's best to be noncommittal on these occasions or before you know it she'll have you enrolled in a retreat for Buddhist nuns for six weeks.

'Well, anyway, hypnotherapy. I'm thinking of having you all done.' And she waves her hand expansively towards the now seemingly orderly office floor. 'What do you think?'

'Done?' I am almost afraid to ask.

'Yes, a group hypnotherapy session to make you all tidier. You know, something along the lines of seeing your in-tray full of paper making you feel compelled to process and file it. What do you think?' she repeats.

I'm silent for a moment. The air-conditioning makes the

wind chime by the door tinkle and I can see a tiny spider busily weaving a web between the leaves of her money plant.

'You see, Georgie,' I say slowly, 'the thing is, hypnotism used in that way might, you know, contravene the basic human right of free will – don't you agree?'

She looks disappointed. 'I thought it might be a bit iffy, but I thought, well, as it helps everyone to improve themselves it might not be a bad thing? And we've got this American due to visit any day now, so I thought it couldn't hurt to make a good impression.'

'Yes, but there is something faintly megalomaniac-fascist-despot about that way of thinking, isn't there?'

'Well . . . if you say so. What about an early-morning yoga class?'

'Super,' I say, wanting to cheer her up even though the likelihood of the young ones getting in early enough or the more mature ones being arsed is slim.

'Really?' She smiles.

'Great idea. Count me in.'

She smiles again and starts flicking through her Rolodex. 'I'll sort someone out now. Oh and Jen, love, there are some special deals I want you to take the team through today. We're launching them tomorrow; the targets are on the sheets.' She hands me our new project.

As I walk back to my desk Carla is sitting on Kevin's desk and conspicuously holding a piece of paper as if it were her passport to flirting. When she sees me coming she gives him a little smile and goes back to her desk.

'We've caught up on those faxes, Jenny,' she says as I go past.

'Super,' I say, in a boss-like fashion. 'Well done.' And I walk back to my desk, still in awe that anyone pays attention to anything I say.

Chapter Eleven

One thing after another happens at work and I get in about fifteen minutes before the taxi is supposed to pick us up to go to Selin's mum's. Rosie is waiting for me, reclining on the black velveteen sofa in a nice pair of khaki linen trousers from Hobbs, her yellow hair in a neat French pleat and her face perfectly made up, all peaches-and-cream natural. By her feet there are three old cups of tea, two small plates with toast crumbs on and an empty foil carton that contained Chinese food some time last week. I get a little heavy feeling in my heart and I am glad the time is coming when we must finally be tidy.

'Hello,' she says, absent-mindedly staring at the TV.

'Hi, how was the doctor's?' Aware that I won't have time for my planned shower I sit at the three-legged table and reapply the make-up that I keep there over the make up that I put on this morning. Rosie, who would no sooner consider doing such a thing than she would eat leftover take-away out of a rubbish bin, looks at me with distaste.

'You'll clog your pores and your skin won't be able to breathe and then you'll go all grey and get spots, and then when you've got spots *and* wrinkles don't come running to me for a miracle cure. The doctor was very nice. She gave me official confirmation and a leaflet. I have to make appointments for scans and things after that. You'll come with me, won't you?' She waves a bit of pink paper at me and I nod mutely, contorted, as I try to drag the mascara brush through my already-mascaraed lashes.

'Oh, God, I look like a drag queen,' I say when I examine my handiwork. Talk of the baby seems like a distant reality. Almost like our childhood discussions of what we wanted to be when we grew up.

'There are three messages for you, all from Owen. One polite, one whiny, one pissed off.' I look at the blinking red number three on the answerphone and without any hesitation I press Delete. We both watch it as it makes its little whirring and clicking noises and resets itself to nought. I had hoped he wouldn't call again, a vain wish, I suppose, given his track record. He's not a man who likes to be ignored. It crossed my mind in the early hours of this morning that maybe seeing him would be the best way to get him to leave me alone, but as soon as the weary sun had pushed its way through my bedroom curtains I knew it would be madness. The best thing to do is to put him out of my mind and move on. Funny really, not so long ago I would have been pacing the floor, desperate for him to call me again.

I pick up my comb and I'm pulling it though my hair when the buzzer goes, making us both jump, as it always has every time it has rung as long as I've lived here.

'Here he is, right on time.' Rosie waves down to Kaled, a driver from the taxi office over the road. She has an account with the firm for work purposes and during the course of several trips took a particular shine to Kaled, whom she now asks for by name. He has even given her his private mobile number, which she does not hesitate to use much to the annoyance of his girlfriend and the pleasure of Kaled. In fact, over the last few months they have become firm and, by all accounts, platonic friends. I check my bag, keys, purse, inhaler, cheque-book (you never know) and phone, still switched on and three bars of battery showing. Still no call from Michael and the end of day four approaches.

In the taxi Rosie sits in the front seat and chats away to Kaled nine to the dozen about the baby, the house move, Owen and anything else she can think of. It's really nice to see her so relaxed and laughing; those two really get on well. I think they will miss each other a bit, or at least they would if it wasn't for the fact that Rosie has already invited him to our moving-in party for the flat we have yet to acquire. It's a shame Rosie can't have such an easy and open friendship with all the men in her life, but then again none of us lives up to that ideal very often.

Chapter Twelve

The bottom of Green Lanes where the Mehmet family business and home is located is always busy and the traffic is always heavy. The many Turkish restaurants and cafés are always full, mostly of men drinking coffee and whisky and just talking.

The accountancy firm Mehmet & Mehmet has a shop front covered by venetian blinds and a brown-and-cream sign with back lighting that Selin's dad is extremely proud of. He had it installed the day that Selin passed her first set of accountancy exams. Selin grew up in this house and the rest of her family still live in the two-storey turn-of-the-century apartment above the building, part of a dark and ornate red-brick block complete with turrets, tower and ornate balconies that now sits uneasily over rows of newsagents, mini-marts and pizza places. As we press the buzzer Rosie and I exchange glances, feeling nervous.

'Have you brought some wine?' I ask.

'Yes, red so that I won't be tempted,' she says – she hates red wine.

'And have you got the stuff?' She winks at me and opens the blue carrier bag to show me. We are prepared.

Ayla, Selin's ridiculously pretty and slender sixteen-year-old little sister, opens the door to us. She has her hair smoothed back into a neat bun and two long gelled ringlets hang just below her jawbone. With the family olive skin and molten brown eyes she is a beautiful young woman.

'All right?' she says with a bright smile and kisses each of us on both cheeks.

'Looking forward to the new term?' I ask lamely, hating the fact that I sound like my Auntie Marge. As we follow her up the stairs I notice that she has literally no bottom. I guess she would think I was a mad old fogey if I asked her where she got her hipster jeans shot through with a silver shimmer. Jeans like that are a long-distant memory for my hips.

'Yeah, thanks,' she replies cheerily. 'I've made some new mates already. Quite a few of the girls who'll be in my class have summer jobs at Sainsbury's too. They're really cool.' I'm pleased about that. Ayla was very shy as a child and watching her gradually come out of her shell as she grows up has been a pleasure to see. Last year she had to move school as for no apparent reason she had become the target of some bullies. Despite her best efforts to face it out and numerous trips with her parents to see the head the problem continued. Ayla had had a terrible time. She lost weight, broke out in a rash and cried all the time, until her GP tried to prescribe her Prozac. The only solution it seemed was to move her to a new school. Shy and sensitive as she was with strangers, it took her a little bit of time to settle in to the new school so I was really pleased when she made new friends and managed to take her exams despite all the upset, ready to start back at the lower sixth.

'How were your GCSEs? Sclin said you did well.' That's it. I have been possessed by the ghost of my Auntie Marge, and she's not even dead.

'I got nine: four As and four Bs and a C for maths. Dad wants me to retake it.' She looks over her shoulder and rolls her eyes at us.

'Nine?' Rosie chimes in. 'How can you have nine? You must

be a genius. That's bloody millions. I only got four.' She taps me on the shoulder. 'How many did you get?'

'I got five, but we did O-levels back then, it was different.'

'Yeah, much harder for starters,' Rosie says, and it's my turn to look over my shoulder and roll my eyes at her, secretly thinking she is right. 'Rosie, GCSEs are equally difficult and hard,' I say out loud.

'Yeah, and don't forget Selin got nine O-levels and an A in maths, as my dad is always telling me,' Ayla says lightly and without malice. Damn it, she's right. Rosie and I were just lazy and preoccupied with clothes and boys. Selin wasn't lazy, and she was preoccupied with clothes and boys *and* algebra. It's a winning combination.

We are led into the warm and bright sitting-room, which is covered in original seventies wallpaper that has just come back into fashion. Selin comes out of the kitchen to kiss us both. She has twisted her copious black hair into an unruly up-do and is wearing her favourite red silk shirt, and she looks gorgeous. Mrs Selin, elegant and curvaceous, follows, kisses us both on each cheek and offers us some Hula Hoops in a little glass dish. Then the baby of the family – the child that was a surprise after the surprise of Ayla – Hakam, who is just eleven, is pushed our way. After vigorous and physical prompting from his mother he comes and kisses us both and then looks as if he wants to vomit.

'You wait,' his mother says, ruffling his hair. 'In a few years you won't be able to wait to kiss beautiful women like these two and you'll wish you got the chance more often.' Everyone laughs; Selin digs Ayla in the ribs and they wink at each other. Hakam, who will one day be very handsome, goes a lovely deep rosy colour and sticks out his bottom lip. I think about Michael, briefly, who seven years ago might have been going that special kind of red-haired-person pink at being forced to kiss family friends. Seven years ago I had my second-ever job as the world's worst PA to a very tolerant boss who used to do all his own typing because I couldn't. I was seeing a philosophy student with a beard at the time; he was a lot of laughs.

'You girls sit in here and have a glass of wine. Ayla, come and help me in the kitchen.' Ayla sighs, rolls her eyes again and follows her mum to the kitchen. Hakam, seeing a temporary escape route, legs it up the stairs to his PlayStation. Poor kid. Being the youngest in a house regularly full of dominating women can't be easy.

'Dad's gone out to fetch some wine,' Selin smiles, as she throws herself in an armchair, swinging her legs over the arm. 'So? To what do I owe this pleasure?' She knows that something unusual has happened as we hardly ever come to visit her. It's not that we don't see her all the time. It's just that for some reason, coming back to the place where we grew up has always seemed like a pointless exercise when there is so much to see and do out there. My mum moved out of town with my older brother a few years back when my niece was born. Rosie's mum went to live in Florida with an American she met whilst working as a tour guide at Tower Bridge. Both our sets of parents divorced in the eighties and neither of us really knows our dad any more although Rosie has tea with hers about twice a year and he gives her money. I know mine lives in Battersea with his clichéd ex-secretary second wife, who is about six years older than me. He wears a leather bomber jacket, drives a sports car and has a firm belief that his comb-over makes him look less bald. Despite my efforts to make sure he has always had a number to contact me on, he never calls me and on the few disastrous occasions when I've seen him since he left he patently wishes he could be elsewhere, back in the life where he can forget he ever had a former family. For a long time, I thought there must be something I could do to build bridges, but gradually I realised that he just didn't want to know. It made me feel like an over-persistent, clingy ex-girlfriend.

But on the way here tonight, seeing the school we all used to go to and the café we used to drink Coke in after school, hoping to get a look at the sixth-form hunks, made me smile. These places and others, like the bus shelter where I avidly kissed my first boyfriends in full view of the poor commuters, and the park in which we cracked open those first illicit bottles of Lambrusco, formed such a seminal part of my early life that they suddenly seem inviting and reassuring once again. There must be something about getting older that makes reminiscing pleasant and the country of your childhood a safe haven. Just at this moment, though, that country seems very far away. Of all the news we've broken to each other over the years, this must be the biggest.

'We brought some wine.' Rosie hands Selin the bag and she looks into it.

'Oh, red, that makes a nice change from your usual . . .' She stops dead in her tracks. She pulls out a large party pack of fun-size Mars Bars from our off-licence carrier bag. She looks from me to Rosie and says, 'Who?'

Rosie and I, still standing like the accused in the dock, point at each other.

'Hang on,' I say uncharitably and unfairly. 'Yours is much worse than mine.' I can see that Rosie has changed her mind about wanting to tell Selin the news. I can see she is considering moving countries, changing her name by deed poll and undergoing plastic surgery in order to avoid telling Selin the news. And when you consider that earlier today she phoned her mum in Palm Beach and had no trouble telling her at all, you'll understand exactly how much we care about each other's opinions. Especially Selin's, who in all of our years of friendship has never ever been wrong, not once. That's not an exaggeration.

'Owen is back in touch,' Rosie says, shrugging her shoulders

for my benefit and waggling her eyebrows. I think she is trying
to tell me she wants to abort the mission. But this is going to
have to happen at some point between now and next May and
I'm not letting her off the hook.

'Oh no, tell me you aren't going to see him again.' She looks
at Rosie. 'Did you tell her about, you know, the thing that we
discussed?'

Rosie nods.

'Yes, she did tell me, thank you, oh, and thank you for deciding what I am and am not grown up enough to deal with myself.'
I am still indignant about that even though I know they were
just trying to protect me and that Rosie's tactic of prolonging
the moment before she makes her revelation is working.

'I'm *not* going to see him again. I wasn't even before Rosie
told me her bombshell, I'm not interested. No, Rosie go on,
tell Selin the real news.'

Rosie gazes longingly at the glass of wine in Selin's hand and
then, looking as though she has had the best idea in the world,
says brightly, 'We're moving back to Stokey to get away from
Owen.'

Selin breaks into a huge smile, leaps up from the chair and
hugs us both at once, dripping a bit of wine on to my foot. I
wish people would stop hugging me when there are beverages
involved.

'That's fantastic news! It will be so great having you around
the corner, *hooray*! And a good idea too, Rosie, well done.'
Rosie smiles and nods in the style of a sensible person, enjoying
her last few seconds of Selin's approval.

'Rosie,' I say sternly.

'What else?' asks Selin with a tone of cautious resignation.
The three of us are now standing in an uneasy triptych, like
guests at an unsuccessful cocktail party.

'Oh well, I'm pregnant too, so that, I suppose.' Rosie turns and picks up from the mantelpiece a school photo of the three of us aged around sixteen, when were all into U2 and wore tight black jeans, fake biker jackets and lace fingerless gloves. 'God, we were thin, weren't we? I'm going to join an aqua–aerobics class for mums–to–be at the sports centre, by the way.' There is a nano–second of silence.

'*You're pregnant!*' Selin roars at the top of her voice and just at that moment her older brother Josh walks in through the living–room door.

'Pregnant? Which?' He looks astounded.

'Rosie,' I say quickly, and he breaks into a huge smile and engulfs Rosie in a massive bear–hug. It's so typical of him to be instantly sweet and non–judgemental.

'Are you OK with it?' He steps back and looks down at her with concern.

'Yes.' She smiles up at him. 'I am pleased and I'm keeping it, aren't I?' She looks at me for back–up and I just nod in agreement, knowing that whatever Selin might be about to say now, she will certainly have a whole lot more to say to me about this very soon.

As Selin stands open–mouthed and for once pretty much speechless, clutching the party pack, her mother comes in and snatches it out of her hand.

'You girls, your teeth will fall out,' she says. 'Don't you ruin your appetite with these things.' She sees Coşgun standing with his arm around Rosie. 'Ah, my oldest son, come here, darling.' She kisses him on both cheeks several times, taking off his coat and pinching his flesh as she does so. 'It's not a prerequisite to be starving when you are an artist, you know. Why do you never eat?'

'I eat the entire time, Mum, I'm just lean and I can't help it. High metabolism – don't worry about me.' He kisses the top of her head.

'He lives in a squat,' she tells us. 'He works as a gardener all weathers when he's not inhaling paint fumes, he has had more girlfriends than the Leaning Tower of Pisa.' None of us understands what she means but we keep quiet. 'And he tells me "Don't worry". Don't worry? You get a proper job and a nice girl and then I won't worry. Now, Jennifer, you'll have wine?' She goes over to Rosie and kisses her again, breaking into a huge smile. 'Rosalind, I'd better get you some juice as you're expecting.' And then, 'worse things happen at sea, you know,' she says to Selin, patting her on the arm as she returns to the kitchen, chuckling quietly and leaving us standing about in an embarrassed silence. So much for keeping it between the three of us for now.

'I don't have *that* many girlfriends,' Josh mumbles. 'None for ages, actually.' He has had his black hair shaved close to his head. It suits him, funnily enough. His quest to find the inner artist has seen him go through more silly hairstyles and clothing items than your average workaday clown. In fact, half of the fun of having him as my surrogate older brother is teasing him about his latest tortured-artist look. I remember with a smile the time when he used to wear his black hair long and use Selin's hair irons to straighten it out. That was back in the days when one idle eye-linered glance would have my teenage heart in paroxysms of desire, my God, I loved him so! I'll have to give teasing him a miss today though, as he looks quite presentable for a change, even bordering on sexy. He takes a seat at the table and watches us.

Selin sits down again and drains her glass. She leans forward, resting her chin in the palm of her hand for a second, and looks at the bottom of her empty glass.

'When did you find out?' she asks me. Rosie has gone to sit on the sofa in the corner and is looking very interested in her new false nails.

'Yesterday,' I say. 'We tried to call you, but you were out.'

'Who's the dad?' She is still talking to me, and I can't work out if she is cross or not. I know that I feel like a naughty schoolgirl, standing here alone in the middle of the room.

'Chris,' I say quietly. Selin says nothing for a moment and then goes to sit beside Rosie.

'Rosie,' she says gently. 'Are you sure about keeping this baby? Have you thought it through?'

'Yes,' Rosie says, and now that she lifts her face I can see her cheeks are streaked with tears. 'I think I really can do it. I really want to. It's a person in here.' She pats her stomach. 'I want to give my baby a good happy life and I know I can. It's not ideal that the father has the maturity of an undeveloped Teletubby or is about as likely to want to be involved with his own baby as he would to live in a monastery, I know. But I'm lucky I have the means and the support to make this work. A lot of people don't have that. And I've got the best thing in the world. I've got you two, and if you'll help me I know I can be a good mother. And even if you won't I'm going to give it a damn good go.'

All at once we are together in a big hug, each one of us in tears. Josh watches from the other side of the room and as I catch his eye he smiles at me and nods. The front door bangs shut and a moment later Mr Selin walks into the room.

'My God, my house is full of crying women! Don't tell me, don't tell me, it's hormones, right? I am a man who knows about hormones.' He shakes his head indulgently and comes and hugs us and kisses the tops of our heads. His show of kindness makes us cry even more.

Chapter Thirteen

Mrs Selin has made us some *dolma* because she knows we will complain if she doesn't, but the main part of the meal is a lemon-roast chicken with roasted vegetables and it's beautiful.

'We can help you find a place round here,' Mr Selin says. 'Seli, what about Mr Carlton? He rents some properties, I believe?' He smiles so that his many chins dimple and crease.

'Yes, he does, I'll call him tomorrow. Might be able to get you a good deal.'

'And Adem of course, why not ask him?' he says. I knew that they would be able to help us out.

'Mmm, OK, I will. Good idea,' Selin says, studying her plate before exchanging a glance with her mother, who then proceeds to tap Mr Selin on the back of the hand with her fork. Mr Selin shrugs and shakes his head and the whole bizarre pantomime ends, inconclusively in my opinion. This is one strange family. Selin smiles at Rosie and me in turn. I want to ask her about her pool nights, but I can't find the right moment to bring it up, and anyway, judging by that performance, maybe we are not supposed to know about them, although goodness knows why not.

'I think it's well cool that you're pregnant,' Ayla says, sending her father's eyebrows and blood pressure sky high. 'God, don't worry, Dad, I'm not going to get pregnant, I'm going to university, remember? But, you know, when you're a bit older, Rosie's age, it's cool. It's the twenty-first century, man. You don't need men for anything these days.' Josh leans back in his chair and laughs, tipping back his chin and closing his eyes.

'You need us for at least one part of that scenario, don't you?' he says.

'No. We'll all be able to get sperm donors soon, just like going to a supermarket. In the chiller cabinet,' she says with a sweet little smile, and poor old Hakam gags into his glass of Coke.

'Oh, really.' Josh's eyes are sparkling with mischief. 'And have you told this to Jamie Bolton yet? I'd expect he'd like to know your view on these things before he gets around to asking you out.'

'No!' She giggles and covers her eyes with a beautifully manicured hand. 'Leave it, Josh! You're gonna be in big trouble!'

'Oooh, who's Jamie Bolton?' Rosie joins in. I think she is glad to have the conversation steered away from her, which must be a lifetime first. Selin joins in now with the same wicked sibling-teasing smile her brother is brandishing.

'Jamie works behind the record counter at Woolworths,' she says. 'Ayla *loves* him, don't you?' Ayla laughs good-naturedly and her eyes sparkle with the first-crush flush of excitement and anticipation.

'No! I don't love him!' She turns to me in a touching kind of conspiratorial way and says, 'He's well cute though, seriously, and he's a nice bloke too, well safe.'

'Good,' I say, feeling the spirit of Auntie Marge entering my body, 'I'd hate to think of him being in peril.'

Later, after coffee so strong it could launch a rocket, ice-cream and some *baklava* from the bakery on the corner, Rosie and Selin get out boxes of old photos, Mr Selin nods off in a chair and Ayla becomes engrossed in a phone-text conversation with someone who makes her giggle a lot. Hakam, free at last, has gone back to his bedroom. Mrs Selin refuses any help with clearing away and I flick through her collection of easy-listening LPs, looking for a Dean Martin track that I really love. Josh sits opposite me rolling a fag and now he goes to the balcony doors at the back of the room and steps outside saying, 'This is my last, giving up today!'.

'It's still pretty mild out here,' he calls back though the nets and I go out and join him to look at the outside world.

We have a wonderful view of the back gardens and rooftops of North London. The brown and grey houses and scatter of aerials and satellite dishes have the gentle rosy glow of one of the year's last summer evenings. The sound of the traffic has abated a bit, somewhere nearby kids are playing football and we can smell a barbecue a couple of houses down.

'So, how are you doing in all this?' Josh says. He smiles at me in that way that makes the stubble on his chin crinkle into dimples and I think how nice it is to have had a big-brother figure around all these years. When I first met him I used to have the maddest crush on him. It's funny really; we laugh about it now. I used to clam up and go red whenever I saw him. Funny because he's just not my type any more, and we have become firm friends.

'Rosie is very lucky to have a pair of friends like you,' he says. 'Are you sure you're OK?' He always takes the trouble to ask.

'Yeah, I'm pretty good, really,' I say. 'We're lucky to have Rosie.'

'They told you what I heard about Owen, didn't they?' I nod and sigh, biting my lip as I look out over the neighbours' back gardens.

'Well, I'm glad you're over that, it sounds like he's gone a bit mental from what I hear. If you ever wanted me to, you know, sort him out for you I would, you know.' I smile at him and pat the top of his hand which is resting on the railing. I think to myself that I can't imagine Josh getting heavy with a cuddly toy, never mind someone like Owen.

'You're sweet. But I think this will all go away on its own and I don't want anyone getting into trouble over him. I just feel so stupid.'

'Stupid? Why?'

'Because looking back I can't believe I ever had anything to do with him, let alone loved him. I would have done anything for him. I often did.'

'You weren't stupid. I saw you together, he was a plausible bastard. He even had me convinced the first couple of times. All that charm and bohemian bollocks did wear a bit thin after a while, though.' He smiles at me. 'Maybe you were a *bit* stupid.' I laugh and thump him lightly on the chest.

'Bastard. What about you? Your mum thinks you're the Casanova of Church Street. Is *anyone* safe from your charms?' I flutter my eyelashes at him in a mock flirt.

'Oh, you'd be surprised.' He rolls his eyes and grins.

'What happened to Wanda?' I ask. She was a many-plaited art-school beauty queen – they had been the Stoke Newington art collective's celebrity couple for most of last year.

'Some bloke from Scotland happened to her. In my bed.'

'Oh. I always thought she was a no-good slut,' I joke, but I'm not just saying that for Josh's benefit. I found her and Owen talking very intimately at the back of the garden at a party once. 'But you're such a nice bloke, you should have girls queuing up after you.'

He chuckles a bit and says, 'No, girls never like us "nice" blokes, do they? What about you? Met anyone who lights your fire lately?' I think about Michael and the kiss and the touch of the sun and the falling leaves and the resounding silence of my phone.

'Well, put it this way, someone kindled the ashes a bit.'

'Really? Do you think that some*one* might turn into some*thing*?' he says, nudging me in the ribs with his elbow.

'Mmm, no. No, it won't, it can't really,' I say, sounding a bit guilty despite myself.

'God, he's not married, is he?' Oh dear, Josh really does think I'm a lost cause.

'Oh no. It's way more complicated than that.'

He's quiet for a moment and turns to look at me, rubbing the back of his newly shaven head self-consciously. 'Just take care of yourself, OK? No more Owen-type experiences – promise me? I mean, you're like family to me, all of you. I mean, well, Seli is obviously, but you and Rosie too. I don't want to see you hurt any more. Promise me.'

'Promise,' I say, thinking that you can't get much more different from Owen than Michael.

Josh nods in approval and changes the subject. 'I've got an exhibition coming up in a few weeks in Hoxton, with the collective. You lot should come down. It's sponsored by Smirnoff, some bloke from *Time Out* is coming to give it a review.'

I laugh at his attempt to bribe me with a free Moscow Mule.

'I'd love to. And you know I'm going to rope you into helping us move, don't you?'

'No problem,' he says. We go back into the living-room where Rosie and Selin have just found photos of us on our first-ever lone holiday to Bournemouth, sporting sunburn and a bottle of Thunderbird. Mrs Selin has set the record player to play Dean Martin's 'Sway' and she and Selin's dad are dancing a makeshift rumba. Things are good.

As we leave Selin walks us down the stairs and says, 'We have a lot more to talk about, you know, there's a shit load of stuff to work out.'

'Yeah, I agree,' I say, nodding vigorously.

'I know,' Rosie says, 'let's go out on Saturday night!'

Selin and I look at each other.

'Oh, for God's sake, I'm not ill, I'm just knocked up. And if I'm not drinking or anything the baby will be fine, and if I feel a bit dodgy I'll go home.' She looks at me. 'We could go to Starsky and Hutch?' She knows that a bit of seventies disco will almost always tempt me.

'Well, if we just go for a bit?' I say, looking at Selin, who shakes her head in resignation.

'If we just go for a bit and I can stay at your place and we go out for Sunday lunch and talk things through *properly*. OK?' Selin says like a mum working out a compromise with a couple of unruly kids.

'*OK*,' we say in unison like a couple of unruly kids.

As I get in the back of Kaled's cab I fish my phone out of my bag. There is a little envelope sitting in the top left-hand corner of the screen. I have a text message. This is only the second text message I have ever had. It must be from Ayla, I think, who sent me the first one as soon as she got her phone for her birthday. I open it up and it reads, 'sry hve not bn in tch. things hve been difclt hre. will call sn, hve bn thinking of u. mike xx.'

It takes me a couple of seconds to work out what he's saying and a couple more to feel a rush of delight; *yes*, he's called me, messaged me, whatever, not that I care. All I mean is that I've still got the old charm. I should probably just ignore him but I'm a bit tipsy and I have a fluttery feeling in my stomach. I press reply. 'speak 2 u sn. j xx.'

I think about it for a moment, my thumb hovering over the Send option, and then I press Erase. What on earth am I thinking? The wine and emotion must have gone to my head.

But at some point before we get home I'm dreaming of kisses again, kisses and sunshine, holding hands and the smell of grass.

Chapter Fourteen

It's Saturday afternoon and I'm in the bra department at Selfridges when I hear from him again.

I want a strapless bra, to go under the Barbie-pink glittery halter-neck top I have bravely bought just minutes ago from TopShop, having successfully picked my way through the plethora of child women that shop in hordes sporting exactly the same hairstyle and exactly the same fake-leather jacket.

Between TopShop and Selfridges I have had two big thoughts. The first is that little girls today dress and wear their hair the same regardless of race or religion. This, I decide, is a leap forward in the quest for world harmony until I remember that Selin and I had exactly the same taffeta skirts with gold embroidery when we were teenagers. Mine was red and hers was dark blue and that was in 1987. 'Maybe we led the way,' I think. 'Power to the child women, right on.' I also think if I could be blessed with any prescient wisdom between the ages of fifteen and twenty, it would be, 'Enjoy. You will never be this thin again.' But that isn't a big thought so I'm not counting it.

The *second* big thought I have had is that my shopping habits now precisely reflect my age and financial status. My one hundredth purchase of a glittery jersey top followed up by maybe my fourth visit to Selfridges to buy underwear illustrates this. My glittery life has begun to require more and more expensive and serious support to keep it afloat, literally. And by the looks of this item of lingerie engineering I'll be going to Rigby & Peller next.

The fitting assistant is staring at my breasts. 'You see,' she says, referring to the bra I am sporting round my midriff, 'these bras are only designed to hold you where you already are.'

'Oh, really?' I stutter, working out how I can say, 'Fuck off you stupid bitch, you've got no tits at all so what would you know about big breasts? Nothing! You probably think it's all a bed of roses well let me tell you my girl . . .' in a polite and rational way. But I can't, so I hold my stomach in more instead.

None of my friends has ever been able to understand my rant about breast size, so I have long since given up trying to make them understand. Just to clarify, having big breasts handed to you by nature is fun, sure it is. But when you get the sneaking suspicion that all the men who have ever fancied you did so only because of them, or that modern culture has deemed that the female IQ diminishes in exact proportion to the increase in bra size, you start to wonder. Or when your boss talks to them and she's a woman, or when you pay the best part of a grand a year in supporting them and *even then* they don't have the good grace to behave like plastic ones. The fact that you can't walk down any street, anywhere, at any time of year without some idiot noticing them through two jumpers and a winter coat and saying, 'Nice tits on that.' And that you can't wear the strappy little numbers your friends do. Then you do think, 'Well, what *is* the upside?' Oh yes, the hundreds of men who fancy you simply because you have big tits.

But any time I have ever mentioned it my friends say, 'Oh, shut up, you love it, you sex bomb.' And I have to agree with them so I do shut up.

'Oh, really? What's the point of wearing it then?' I smile at the girl.

'You can buy it, take it home and bring it back, if you don't like it?' she suggests helpfully. At this point my phone rings. I pick it up and I don't recognise the number.

'Sorry, I've been waiting for this call – emergency, sick . . . cat.' And I pull the curtain in front of her.

'Hello?'

'Oh hi, Jenny, it's me?' It's Michael. I know that it's Michael straight away.

'Sorry, who?'

'Oh, it's Michael, Mike, who you met in the park last week.' I think about the time I have spent framing a kind and mature reply as to why I couldn't see him again and how he would get over it eventually and laugh about it one day. All week I've been waiting to deliver it and he hasn't phoned. And now, after one barely legible text message, here he is all blasé. Some things in the male behavioural pattern *must* be genetic; failure to call within a reasonable time frame and the compulsive urge to kick any kind of object (including soft-drink cans) around any kind of open space (including the office) are two.

'Oh, you. Hi.' My tone is offhand, but I have to admit that inside I'm feeling a bit flustered.

'Yeah, I'm sorry I haven't called earlier,' he says apologetically.

'I wasn't expecting you to call me.'

'Ummm, yeah, you know, after we kissed and everything.' Candid youth. 'Look, I'm up in town with my . . . I'm up in town, I thought you might like to come and meet me for a drink this evening?'

'I can't, Mike, I've got plans,' I say haughtily. 'I usually have plans for Saturday night by about four o'clock on a Saturday afternoon.'

Why aren't I just saying that I can't possibly see him again, as he is a child? I am letting him down gently, of course. It just sounds as if I'm disappointed and upset so he doesn't feel so embarrassed.

'Oh, OK, where are you now?' He isn't returning the favour.

'The underwear changing room in Selfridges,' I say, hoping to get a fluster.

'Cool!' And he laughs. 'I'm just at Bond Street tube, so I'll come down and meet you and we can go for a quick one. Drink, I mean.' He laughs again. He definitely is just about eighteen then.

'Well, OK, but give me twenty minutes, all right?' It would be kinder to tell him face to face and I have grown far more compassionate as I get older.

'OK, I'll meet you in Hosiery in twenty.' And he hangs up the phone.

Hosiery?

Chapter Fifteen

I look at myself in the mirror. I can't possibly let him down gently looking like this. I have no make-up on, or even with me. I was waiting until I got home before washing my hair and I am wearing my comfortable, but faintly whiffy – even from five feet six inches away – trainers. I'm sure when he looks back on this in a few years' time and laughs he'd rather be picturing a sophisticated, stylish woman than a has-been in last year's Nikes.

The lingerie girl has won. I pull the tag off the bra, take my new top out of its bag and put it on. I study my profile, I study my back for blemishes, I decide to keep my jacket on but I feel a bit better.

Mercifully the queue at the counter isn't too bad. I hand the girl my ticket.

'I'm going to wear it now.'

'Yeah, I heard. Better is he, your cat? That's 24.99 please.' She smiles. I glare at her and depart, pausing briefly to pull up my bra.

Next stop, shoes and boots.

I am not good at designer labels, which is why I would never normally buy clothes or shoes in Selfridges. Because I'm not really sure who's in or out, who's hip and who isn't, and if I do buy something by someone I've heard of it never has the desired effect because they are usually *passé* by the time I have heard of them. Anyway, I'm sure you have to be under a size twelve at least to wear anything that has 'S' or 'M' listed as the size, or 'One' or 'Two' for that matter, and I haven't been under a twelve since 1996 so I just buy clothes in places with proper size labels and roomy trousers. But at least I'm on safe ground with a pair of boots − as long as they aren't knee length, we all know knee-length boots are designed for women who don't have calves. But I'm not going to get started on that with only fifteen minutes to spare.

I see a shiny ruby stiletto ankle boot with a crocodile-skin look and a zip. I pick it up and march over to the assistant.

'How much is this?'

'£139.99, madam.' She is arranging the evening party-wear mules.

'Mmm . . . got anything around the eighty quid mark?'

I finally get her attention and she briefly looks me up and down. Without speaking she picks up a pair of patent-leather granny boots with a pointy toe and laces and a clumpy heel. Like I say, I don't know, but I'm pretty sure they aren't cool and anyway I don't like them.

It's time to rationalise. I have ten minutes until I meet the eighteen-year-old I want to look nice for, so that after I chuck him he can look back and yearn for a glamorous elusive older woman and what might have been. In order to achieve this I am considering spending £80 on a pair of boots I don't like and will not be able to walk in after ten minutes. So, really, what is another fifty quid for a pair of boots I could love sincerely and won't be able to walk in after ten minutes? In fact, it's an economy to get a pair I at least like. I hand her the crocodile-skin-looking ones hoping they aren't real but deciding not to check just in case.

'I'll take these in a size seven. I'll wear them now, I don't need a box, here is my card,' I blurt out before I can change my mind. Five minutes later I'm approaching the escalator with some wobbly trepidation.

Cosmetics next, Clarins counter. Genius plan on the verge of implementation.

'Hello, I'm not sure if I'm using the right foundation and I'd like a makeover please?' I smile brightly at a lady called Denise.

'I'm sorry, Madam, but our makeover technician has gone home now. She will be available tomorrow though, if you would like to book?' she informs me as she busily refills the lipstick dispenser.

'Gone home? Well, can't you do it?' I plead.

'I'm sorry, madam, I'm not qualified yet. I've only done blusher and lips. I've not even started on eyes.'

'Oh well, can you just give me some stuff and I'll do it?' I find myself saying with more than an edge of desperation.

She leans back and looks at me. 'You've got an unexpected date, haven't you,' she says, crossing her arms and pursing her perfectly drawn lips into a thin line.

'Well. OK. Yes. In less than ten minutes . . . does this happen a lot?' I am shocked, but only because I thought it was the best idea I'd had in ages and I was planning to boast about it later.

'All the time. You'd be surprised, they come queuing up in here on a Saturday, don't know which foundation to use, can't do blusher, ya de ya de ya. Any excuse. We usually get at least two purchases, though.' And she eyes me meaningfully. Oh well, what's another fifty quid?

'OK, I'll buy the mascara and the lipstick but please please please lend me some foundation!' I beg her, clasping my hands together in quite a pathetic display of neediness. It seems to work though, as she smiles at me with a pitiful look and relents.

'OK, it's a deal. Do you want me to do your blusher?' Seven minutes later I'm done.

'Thanks, Denise, you're a brick.' I am about to make my way to Hosiery when she calls me back. She is offering me a can of Batiste dry shampoo and a brush from her own bag.

'Look, don't take it personally, but . . . after you've gone to all that trouble?' It is one of those moments of one sister reaching across boundaries to connect with another.

We acknowledge one another with a silent salute and two minutes later, with my hair brushed through and a quick squirt from a tester at the Chanel counter, I am ready. It has taken over two hundred pounds and exactly twenty minutes. Ten pounds a minute. Not bad.

I am ready. So I am definitely going to meet him. In Hosiery. Now.

Hosiery?

Chapter Sixteen

As the only tall ginger-haired boy in the tights department he is easy to spot and I think I have finally found my feet in these boots by the time I reach him.

'Hiya!' I say and smile at him. He is holding two packs of black tights, one in each hand.

'Hi! Wow!' He bends and kisses me on the cheek. 'You look really nice.' And he goes pink. Success! He looks briefly down my top and then back at the tights. He smells of the crisp early-autumn evening and London rain.

'What's a denier? And what is the difference between forty and seventy?' He has a kind of charming insouciance about the absurdity of the question he is asking.

'Are you a teenage cross-dresser?' I ask him. I mean, if he was it would give me another very good reason to let him down gently. It wouldn't be the first time I've used it.

'No! No, man! Fuck, I'm not *gay* or anything. God!' And he laughs a nice deep throaty uninhibited laugh. 'No, I was up here with my mum, buying stuff for the new term and . . . oh fuck, that is so not cool, oh well, anyway, she forgot to get tights so I said I'd pick her some up. Opaque she said, but she never mentioned no denier shit to me.' And he laughs again, a little dimple appearing either side of his curly grin. Well, he's not a cross-dresser *or* gay, but he *was* just getting back-to-school gear with his mum. Keep that in mind, Jen.

'Get her seventy denier and you can't go wrong. Let's get out of here, I've had enough of this shop for one day.' I catch Denise's eye as I'm leaving and see her eyebrows shoot so far up her forehead that they almost meet her improbably high gelled-back hair-line.

The first thing he does is to freak me out by taking hold of my hand. I am not sure how to react so I calculate the odds of anyone I know seeing us together, realise that they are pretty low, imagine for a second the utter mortification of running into Owen with a Titian-haired teenager in tow and pull him off Oxford street and on to a side road taking deep, panic-abating breaths as I go.

'Have you got somewhere in mind then? I thought you might fancy walking down to Soho and going to the Coach and Horses?' He releases my hand and drops his arm around my shoulder. I get the impression I might be letting him down a bit too gently. But it's a bit chilly in this halter-neck and it's nice to have the warmth of another person nearby, especially another tall person. A tall male person with nice hands.

'No, not there, there's this really nice place down here,' I say on the off chance that there might be. 'It's called the . . . ummm . . . the . . .' We turn the corner into a street I have never been down in my life. 'Ye Olde Parson's Nose.'

'Oh right,' he says as he takes in the mock Tudor frontage. 'You've got a thing about scuzzy old pubs, haven't you? Irony, nice one.' The irony is that he's not actually wrong. During my life of sporadic financial security I have worked behind many a bar, and most of them scuzzy just like this one. Scuzzy pubs are nicer and also no one I know goes into them, and that is definitely a plus when one is on a letting-down-gently mission. As we approach the bar I have a brief moment of panic in case he's asked for ID. He looks older than eighteen to me. I wonder if I look older than twenty-nine?

'I'll have a Stella, please, mate.' He seems at ease with bar staff at least. He turns to me. 'What are you having?'

'Large gin and tonic please, ice and lime if you've got it, lemon if you haven't.' The barman nods and I see Mike surreptitiously checking the note and some change he's got in his hand. Well, good, he should know it's expensive going out with an older woman. Especially an older woman who has got butterflies and isn't exactly sure what it is she is meant to be doing, who keeps thinking about the last time he kissed her and who needs a large G and T even to be here.

'Shall we sit down?' he says. I follow him to a little niche in the corner and he steps aside, gesturing that I should sit down first. Instead of sitting opposite, he slides in next to me. This is bad for two reasons. Firstly, it seems as if he has far more sophisticated first-date experience than I gave him credit for, and secondly, after I've finished this drink I'll probably need the loo in about three minutes and I'll have to ask him to move. You can't see the bar from where we are sitting and I can't see any other customers. I think I saw this set in a German porn film once.

He looks down at his hands so that his fringe flops forward over his eyes, and then smiles at me sideways. 'I didn't think you would meet me tonight. I mean, you didn't reply to my message or anything,' he says and turns a little to face me. This would all be much easier if he wasn't so my type. I really didn't think that ginger hair *was* my type, but the summer seems to have lightened his with little gold flecks and I am finding the slightly almond shape of his brown eyes disconcerting, more so even than the way that he is biting his soft lower lip that kissed me so nicely only the other day.

'Well, I thought it was best,' I say. This is it. I have to do it.

I have been around the block enough times to know exactly what misery and mayhem will come my way right now if I say and do the wrong thing. I open my mouth to speak but he gets there before me.

'It's just, well, the first time I met you, you were so cool and everything and you were really nice to us and you looked really beautiful even though you were mashed from the night before and I was really pissed off because you got off with that bloke who was obviously a twat.' I couldn't fault him so far. 'That bloke' was my most recent rebound fling after Owen (break-up number six), a friend of Josh's called Danny, very pretty but a complete jerk and the cause of an embarrassed silence between Josh and me for a couple of weeks.

'And then when I saw you again in the park, even though it was a year later, I thought, you know, this means something like fate or something and you're so sexy, I've never met a woman as sexy as you and you looked great, even though you were a bit hungover. And after that kiss I couldn't stop thinking about you, I thought about it all the time and I chucked Sarah last week because she kept going on about you and now her mum's not speaking to my mum. It took me ages to get up the guts to phone you, after you never replied to my message, and then I thought you were pissed off with me when we spoke, but when you turned up looking like *that*, like really beautiful, I thought well maybe she does want to know me? I know you're a bit older than me, twenty-two or something, and you think I'm a geek probably, but I think that kiss was *so* good that you must have felt it too and so well I want to ask you if you will go out with me?'

As he makes his speech he flushes pink from the hollow in the base of his throat up to his temples and if I could see into a mirror right now I'd see two red spots on my cheeks too. I can't remember the last time anyone said something like that to me and I don't think there was ever a time when I heard that kind of speech and believed that it was sincere. The romance of it all is going to my head and I need to get my feet on the ground. He said he thought I was twenty-two.

'Mike. Mike, I really like you, you are very attractive to me and we haven't spent much time together but I have really enjoyed the time we have. But we can't see each other. I'm not twenty-two. I'm twenty-nine. I'm too old for you.'

There. I've said it. I have done the responsible thing, I have learnt from all those impulsive encounters that left me messed up for weeks, months, years, depending on the encounter in question. I cannot go out with someone this much younger than me. He's very attractive, impossibly sincere and forbidden-fruits sexy, but despite all that I just can't do this.

'You aren't twenty-nine. You're not.' He looks at me and shakes his head.

'I am and in a few months I'll be thirty. So now you know that you feel different, don't you?' I am really hoping he doesn't.

He sits back and looks at the ceiling. 'No, I mean all that stuff I just said, it doesn't depend on your age. I still mean it. And it's not that you're too old for me, is it. It's that I'm too young for you, right?' He's got an angry, slightly hurt tone to his voice and his long fingers clench the edge of the seat so that his knuckles show white.

'I can't stop thinking about you,' he says, as if that is reason enough for me to throw every reservation out of the window.

The really scary thing is that I think it might be. At least some of them. When was the last time anyone felt that way about me? The large gin on an empty stomach – along with the sensation of his knees pressing against mine and the pull of being near someone who wants me – has made me feel light-headed. I should get up and leave now. I've done what I meant to do, I have behaved in a responsible way and walked away from a situation doomed to failure. I can't go out with him, of course I can't, but I suddenly realise I am about to say something I know I am likely to regret at some point in the near future.

'Look, you and I aren't going to have any kind of relationship. It's not going to happen. But I do fancy you like mad and so I have decided to have sex with you tonight, for one night only. OK?' I say quickly.

The flush on his face deepens another shade and he crosses his legs in a none-too-subtle way.

'Fucking hell,' he says. 'OK then.'

Chapter Seventeen

We have been sitting in the back of this black cab for about the last fifteen minutes and we've made it about halfway down Oxford Street.

We haven't said a word. I look out of my window and he looks out of his. Across the wide expanse of the black leather seat our arms are outstretched and our fingers stop just short of touching each other. I look at him and smile. He looks at me and smiles.

'Sorry, I don't mean to clam up or anything,' he says. I smile at him even more and reach out to pat his hand; it feels freezing cold. Freezing cold probably *isn't* the temperature most desirable prior to carefree, fantasy-fulfilling sexual abandon, but as my nan always said, cold hand, warm heart, or something.

This is not the first time I've jumped into the back of a black cab with the intent to liaise. But this is the first time that my love interest and I haven't been making free in one corner, embarrassing or entertaining the driver depending on what type of driver he is.

Michael shifts a bit in his seat to face me. I smile at him so much that I am afraid I have probably started to look a bit scary and mad. My face hurts. I should have slipped another gin in to relax me more while I was waiting for him to come back from the loo. He seemed to spend quite a long time in there, composing himself I expect, but anyway by the time he came back, still looking pink and a bit flustered, I could easily have had two more doubles, neat over ice, one after the other just like I used to when I was too poor to afford mixers.

I was only young back in my part-time waitressing days and although no one can actually prove any correlation between the number of undiluted doubles I sank and the number of total toss-pots I pulled, they seem to tally up pretty much percentage wise. Michael isn't like any of those mishaps. Michael is the kind of boy I would have died to have a date with back then. Come to think of it, he isn't the first eighteen-year-old that I have kissed, it's just that at the time I was eighteen too.

'What about, you know . . . condoms?' he asks. I can't help the childish giggle that escapes my mouth before I catch the eye of the driver in the rear-view mirror and look guiltily away. He's the type that won't be entertained.

'Well, I'm pretty sure I've got some. If the sell-by date hasn't run out, that is!' I laugh with cartoon-calibre hundred-watt voltage but Michael nods solemnly. I wish he'd stop being so mature and not take it all quite so seriously. I wonder if, in a few years from now, when he's sitting in the back of another cab with another woman he doesn't intend to see again, he'll think about tonight. The night that he first had sex.

It's not that it has suddenly occurred to me that he might be a virgin – it's crossed my mind around the same number of times as he has over the last few days – but it *has* suddenly dawned on me that it might be a problem. For me, if not for him. I never intended for things to get to the cab stage. I hadn't planned to act out my last sleepy thoughts before I drifted off every night and besides, in those fantasies I have a flat stomach. I reach over and slide the glass across to close off the passenger compartment from the driver's ears.

'Michael, don't be embarrassed or anything,' I say as I am

about to ask the most embarrassing question I have ever asked next to, 'is that erect?' 'But, well, are you a virgin?' I say it quickly, avoiding his eyes and trying to act as if someone else must have asked him such a personal question. I really hope that glass is soundproof.

'A virgin?' He splutters. 'No! Well, not *completely*. I mean Sarah and I got pretty damn close, I can tell you. We didn't actually do it, but it's not like I haven't had plenty of dry runs. OK, yes I am.'

He looks at me closely and completely straight-faced, trying to gauge my reaction. I look back at him, trying to gauge my reaction. I think how much the girls would laugh if they ever heard this story, but they are never going to hear this story. Even now in the midst of the most surreal taxi ride of my life – and I have had a few – I know which secrets to keep and this is one of them. So I just smile at him, transfixed, with a manic grin that feels as if it has bisected my ear lobes.

'I made her come,' he informs me anxiously.

I turn and look out of the window and take a deep breath. Tears sting my eyes and my face is hot enough to fry an egg on. As soon as this is over I have to go out and make some new friends to tell this to. Just about composed, I turn back to him.

'Perhaps now isn't the right time for you,' I say softly. The gentle tilt of the not-enough gin has subsided and the virgin thing has somehow taken the edge off the whole idea.

I'm not the virgin-busting type. I have never knowingly had intimate dealings with a virgin before. I'm not sure I'm up to it, it's a big deal. There would be things I would feel obliged to do, I know; I spent much of my early teens reading about it in fat books featuring busty virgin mayor's daughters/novice nuns and naughty swarthy pirates/highwaymen. There should be candles, four-poster beds or a full moon and a windswept empty beach.

First overcome protest. Remove clothes (forcibly if pre-ferred). Place hands. Whisper encouragement. Make them float, float on a burning sea of desire. Just not sure I have what it takes.

My virginity was lost on a single bed in a squat in St Albans. I hadn't quite picked Mr Right, more a Mr All Right, but it was just about as romantic as cider-and-chip-fuelled passion could be and it was perfectly nice. I had just wanted to get it over and done with. Selin, Rosie and I had all told each other we'd done it when we were sixteen. I told them I did it with an Italian twenty-year-old in the local graveyard, but in reality I was eighteen when I finally went through with it. We only found out a couple of years ago that we had all lied to each other because the others said they'd already done it. Good old peer pressure, where would we be without it? Non-smoking, teetotal thirty-year-old virgins probably.

Actually this sort of thing *has* happened to me *once* before, about five years ago. I went to this rooftop party in Old Street with an old friend I had known since sixth-form college who I was secretly in love with. It was entirely futile as he was not secretly in love with me, and I suspect that he thought I was a bit too flighty for him anyway. The fact that I followed him to parties, got drunk because he wasn't in love with me, and then pulled an assorted variety of his friends probably didn't help much, but you know how it is. Logic flies out of the window when you are in a futile crush situation.

Anyway, I was at this party on a roof in Old Street. It was a summer evening and the sun had sunk to the level of the building, making it very bright and hot, I remember having to squint at everyone and shade my eyes to see who I was talking to. My friend who did not love me was nowhere to be seen and the combination of sun and neat double vodkas over ice had made me feel dizzy and nauseous.

Without warning a cool hand took mine and led me out of the sunlight and into what looked like a cool dark bicycle shed. On a roof. Pretty strange, but I was drunk so I wasn't too bothered. My rescuer seemed a handsome chap with a confident smile. He handed me a glass of water and before I could work out that it was another vodka and tonic we were kissing. The oldest trick in the book, but my friend didn't love me so I didn't care and anyway this would show him how popular I was, and then he'd ask me out and one day we'd get married.

The rescuer was quite funny and not a bad dancer so I ended up going back to his place. I remember he lodged with this incredibly gorgeous male model who was lounging half-naked on his sofa looking like an Athena poster when we got in. He took one look at me and nearly fell off the sofa. At the time I thought he must have been stunned by my sunburnt, mascara-blurred beauty, but later on I realised that it probably had something to do with his tenant, bringing home an actual girl. For the night.

It was going quite well. I'd told him I didn't have sex on the first night, which is something I have always said until I get to know the lie of the land, so to speak, and most of the time I stick to it. He acquiesced like they always do and you secretly know that the next eight hours or so will be spent trying to change your mind.

If you're wondering, *yes*, this kind of thing has got me into trouble in the past, and *yes*, I have been lucky with the blokes I've pulled. None of them have turned out to be raving psychopaths – well, not murderous ones anyway – but if, for example, Ayla was about to embark on a voyage of discovery similar to the one that occupied most of my twenties I'd stop her right in her tracks and say, 'Don't be stupid, you'll only end up hurting yourself.' But no one can tell you that, can they? You have to find out for yourself.

Alarm bells rang when I saw that he had a poster of Celine Dion above his bed and a model aeroplane hanging from a bit of cotton over the computer desk, but boys are strange. We got on well, made out, giggled, made out, slept, and talked until around five in the morning when I realised he hadn't tried to talk me into sex once. Feeling mildly offended and anxious and deciding that I liked him after all, I rolled on top of him and said in my best husky seductress voice (which luckily coincided with my dehydrated and sleep-deprived voice), 'I want you to make love to me.' The poor lad nearly choked to death. Then he told me he was a virgin and that was it.

I think when a man finds out you're a virgin it's a turn-on. Rosie and I have kind of reinstated our virginity a couple of times (purely in the interests of research) and I know this to be true. However, when you are a girl and you find out that the man in your bed is the less experienced one it's a turn-*off*. At least for me it is. I can't explain it. It's the sudden fear that you won't be up to it. You'll fail in some way, it'll be dreadful and he's the man and he's supposed to do all the hard stuff anyway. Sorry to all those who have struggled for the last hundred or so years for equality, but this is about more than equal pay and the vote. It's sex. In your heart of hearts, what do you really want from sex with a new partner? To lie on your back, suck your tummy in and look pretty? Or to engage in potentially humiliating acrobatics that turn gravity into a Very Bad Thing. I know what I'd rather do.

'You know what?' I had said at about 5.05 a.m. 'I'm late for church. I'd better go.' And in fifteen minutes I was out of the building, realised I was somewhere in Forest Hill and spent most of the journey home wondering how I could persuade my friend who I was secretly in love with that I wasn't such a slut after all. I never did manage it. He's married now to a primary-school teacher from Stow-on-the-Wold.

And so right now here I am, five years later, halfway along the Edgware Road with another virgin, one years younger than me. One that has all the hopes and expectations that I usually have myself. One who has romantic ideas about *me*. A fragile, young, fairly innocent virgin boy entirely in my hands. I can't do it. I might have to go on top.

As I turn to Michael to tell him that this just can't happen, that I'm not the right one to remember in years to come, he slides across the seat and with purposeful resolution takes me in his arms and kisses me in a way so different from the kiss in the square that it makes my head spin, my heart pound and I literally swoon.

'God, I want you,' he says in a deep voice. Without hesitation, I draw him down to kiss me again.

The way I look at it, we have another ten minutes at least in this cab before we get back to the flat and I really have to decide what to do.

Chapter Eighteen

While I pay the cab driver Michael is kissing the back of my neck. As I turn the key in the lock he slides his hands under my top and runs his fingers down my spine. We get into the hallway and he pushes me up against the wall and pulls back my hair to bare my neck to his kisses. Blimey.

We pause briefly and hear the sound of breathing echoing against the walls. He chews his bottom lip and looks at me intently. Poised on the brink of something, I feel the need to take a moment. I gently push him away and slide from under him.

'Hang on,' I say, fanning my face with my hand. 'I'll pour us some wine and I've got to phone the girls and tell them I won't be coming out. Take a seat.' I point him towards the living-room and take a deep breath. As I go into the kitchen I feel the taut beginnings of a new adventure about to uncoil. This could be a really bad decision. I don't care.

I call Selin's mobile but she doesn't pick up, so I leave a message telling her I have a headache, I've gone to bed and not to worry about me; I'll see them in the morning. I look in the fridge for the half bottle of wine I had left over from yesterday. It isn't there. I find it in the cupboard next to where the tea bags would be if they weren't in the fridge. It's warm, the tea bags are nicely chilled and it all seems to fit in rather well with this topsy-turvy evening.

Rosie and I are such dedicated spirit drinkers that we are bound to have at least one tray of ice-cubes on the go in the freezer, which has frosted up so much that there's now only room for two ice-trays. Sure enough I find a little dolphin-shaped rubber ice-cube maker that is still half full.

I tip its contents into two plastic half-pint beakers left over from a party and slosh the wine over it. I taste it. It's revolting. I down half of mine before I go into the next room and top it up again. I feel brim-full of nerves and anticipation.

Michael sits on the sofa with his long legs stretched out, his head flopping back and his eyes closed. He is smoking a spliff. I suppress the shock, resist the urge to tell him off and slide into the space created by the curve of his arm. This is going to be fine. Eighteen-year-olds today are much older than they used to be in my day.

I hand him the wine. He smiles in that lovely slow way he has and offers me the spliff. I feel the geeky embarrassment that I have always felt in refusing it, knowing that I'd probably just have an asthma attack, which really would ruin this most precarious of moments.

He puts it out on a saucer that's been by the sofa for a couple of days and takes the wine from me. If he thinks it's revolting he doesn't say and he takes a couple of healthy sips. We hold each other's gaze for a moment, and he runs the blunt tip of a long finger down the side of my cheek. Both of us put the wine on the floor.

'You're so beautiful,' he whispers as he winds his fingers in my hair. 'You're so incredibly beautiful.' Usually when I hear those words I don't quite believe them, but with Michael I do believe, and that is more than enough.

We're kissing again and I find myself pushing his T-shirt over his head and running my fingers down his toned and hairless torso. His skin is soft and lightly golden, like all the colours of a summer morning. He sits back from me for a breath and his hands are trembling as he lifts my top over my raised arms. He stares at me and his scrutiny makes me close my eyes.

I feel his fingertips run down my neck and over the curves of the top of my breasts, then he is kissing me again. Arching my back, I reach behind and unhook my bra, keeping my eyes closed as I let it slide to the floor.

His hands are on my breasts and then his lips and I open my eyes to watch him and I feel like I haven't felt in ages; adored, desirable and ready for this moment. I want to devour him whole.

Suddenly he shudders and makes a little noise in the base of his throat. With his head still buried in my neck he becomes completely still. I lie quietly for a moment, unsure of what to do, and wait, stroking my fingers through his hair.

'Michael?' I whisper. Oh God, I hope he hasn't passed out. 'Michael?'

He raises his head to look at me, and his face is a picture of horror and shame. He clambers up, flings himself to the other side of the sofa and buries his head in his hands.

'Fuck , fuck, fuck. I just . . .' He looks as if he might be sick. 'I just . . . *came*,' he mumbles. 'Fuck, how embarrassing.'

He fancies me *too* much, Christ what relief.

Half naked and feeling suddenly bereft, I try to take in the implications of what has happened. He came in his pants. I try not to laugh, but as he is too embarrassed to look at me I allow myself an indulgent smile. It's hard not to feel smug about how much I turned him on. Poor bloke, remember he hasn't quite had his eighteenth birthday yet. Actually, let's forget that. I try not to be pissed off that I didn't come. I try to think of something to say to make him feel better.

Reaching for the floor, I pick up the first bit of clothing I come across and tug his T-shirt on over my head. Sensibly covered I lean over to him, stroke the hair back from his face and kiss his forehead. He backs away from my touch.

'Michael, please don't worry. Things like this happen sometimes. It's all right,' I say, even though I can't think of a time when it actually has happened to me or a time that I have even heard of it happening. I mean, it's happened too fast during sex for sure, but not *before* it.

'But it's not all right, is it. I only had this one chance to prove to you how good we could be together and I blew it. Christ, like some stupid fucking kid.'

Well, I think, in a lot of ways, you are a stupid fucking kid, but a lovely one who I really like.

'You haven't blown it!' I whisper on impulse, pulling down all the sex-only barriers I constructed in one fell swoop. 'I bet if we have a bit more wine and go to my room, listen to some music, Barry White maybe, we can relax and pick up where we left off.' I love Barry White so much, but I will never forgive myself for using his name in the context of a conversation about sex. *Never*.

'Really?' I am touched to see tears in those lovely brown eyes and I suddenly feel an unexpected rush of tenderness towards him. That kind of display of emotion would normally send me running for the hills but everything about Michael is so new and untouched. The last thing I want to do is break him.

'Really,' I say, and I am holding him in my arms when I hear the street door downstairs bang shut.

'Oh no,' I whisper, and I grip his arm perhaps a little more tightly than can be comfortable. He winces and disengages himself.

'What's the problem?' I can see he's worried that I've changed my mind, but I don't have time to reassure him now.

'It's Rosie and Selin. They're back!' Panic escalates my voice until it is a high-pitched squeal. I leap off the sofa and drag

Michael into the hallway. 'Bloody hell! Right, right, go into my room. It's the second on the left, go in there and be quiet and don't make a sound.' I'm piling all his stuff into his arms and shoving him in the right direction.

'But why?'

Oh yeah, I forgot to fill him in on the no-one-must-ever-know part of our relationship.

'Because I told them I had a headache!' I lie, not wanting to compound his misery.

'But . . . ?' He backs down the hallway with the hint of a petulant pout forming on his mouth.

'Just go *now*,' I whisper as forcibly as I am able. As I hear him shut the bedroom door I leap back on to the sofa, the flat door opens, I chuck my glittery halter-neck top and bra behind the sofa, and shove the spliff end under it. I pick up his glass of wine, drain it, roll it under the table and flop back on the sofa. My head spins and my stomach protests, but the upside is that I actually do feel ill and can keep the acting to a minimum.

'Hiya!' they call as they come in. Rosie flops next to me on the sofa and Selin kicks her legs over the arm of our only easy chair.

'You're back early,' I say, looking at the video clock. It's not even nine.

'Yeah well, we were in this bar and the smell of smoke started to make me feel *sick*,' Rosie says incredulously. 'Imagine that! I didn't even *want* a fag. Mother Nature is a miraculous thing. Only thing is, I would still kill for a lovely chilled glass of Sancerre.'

She eyes the last two inches of wine in my plastic glass and I say, 'Try that and you'd definitely be put off.'

Selin hangs her coat neatly over the back of a chair and sits next to me on the sofa, taking her shoes off before tucking her feet under her legs. She picks up the story of their evening.

'Yeah, and you were late so I checked my messages and you said you didn't feel well. How are you now?'

I smile weakly and shrug in an 'oh, OK' kind of way.

'Then "Last in Music" didn't seem like an inviting prospect, not quite the classic of twentieth-century music you always purport it to be,' Rosie adds. 'And besides I seem to be knackered all the time at the moment. I think I overestimated myself.' She nods to herself and pats her belly reflectively.

Selin conitunes, 'And so we decided to come back and keep you company. Thought we could get a take-away.' She pats me gently on my arm and smiles at me in that old-friend way so that I feel just about as guilty as a girl can feel without wanting to spontaneously confess. I'm going to make it up to them, I promise.

'I want healthy take-away though,' Rosie says optimistically. 'But you can choose, Jen, as you're poorly.'

'First of all,' I say, wanting to stop them being so nice to me, 'Sister Sledge were geniuses, every last one of them, and second of all, can we have Chinese?' How the hell am I going to get Michael out of the flat without them noticing?

Rosie looks at me and frowns. 'How long have you been into surfing?'

I look down and realise I'm still wearing Michael's O' Neill T-shirt. 'Oh, it belongs to some bloke I pulled once,' I say so shiftily that they must surely rumble me. 'I found it in my drawer today. Thought it would be good for slobbing out in, you know. Poorly like.'

Rosie, who never slobs out in anything but Nike sportswear, wrinkles her nose at me and Selin, taking control as usual, gets off the sofa, turns on the TV and rifles through the various take-away menus we keep on top of the video. Now's my chance.

'I'm just going to the loo,' I say blithely.

'Mmmmm,' they reply in unison, mesmerised by the last five minutes of *Casualty*. I leave the room, on my way into the hall casually kicking the old bit of brick that stops the door from swinging shut. I go straight into my bedroom. It's in darkness. He isn't there. He isn't in the bed. He isn't under it. He isn't in the wardrobe. He must have gone already. He must have sneaked out. I sit on the bed and breathe a sigh of relief, then pull his T-shirt over my knees.

Hang on. If he's gone, he's gone topless. Fuck. He's in Rosie's room.

I run next door and hiss at him, 'What are you doing in here, moron!' He looks offended.

'You said second on the left!' He's definitely pouting now.

'I did not!'

'Did too.'

Oh God, I haven't got time for this.

'Did not!' I stop myself. 'Anyway. You've got to go *now*.' I pull his T-shirt over my head and hand it to him before I remember that I am naked underneath.

'Flipping heck,' he says, unable to look me in the eye. I grab Rosie's dressing-gown and hurriedly put it on.

'There's no time for that now,' I whisper. 'Come on, get dressed. I'm getting you out.' He puts his top on and steps closer, forcing me to look up at him, making me feel like the girl again, instead of the mother.

'Have I blown it for good with you?' he says, pulling me close by the lapels of the dressing-gown. I don't have a chance to respond before he has slipped his hands inside the towelling and is rubbing his thumbs across my nipples. I still his hands so that I can think. I do want to be here again. Not here in Rosie's room likely to be found out at any second, but here in his arms. Yes, I do want to be here again. I push his arms back by his sides.

'You haven't blown it. We made a good start tonight. Maybe we should just try again, another night when we can really be alone. Maybe go on a date. It doesn't have to be about sex,' I say, not sure what else it is we might have in common.

'Like as if you're my girlfriend?' he says with such a hopeful expression it almost makes me want to slap him. Instead, the palm of my hand just rests on the side of his face.

'Yes, but let's keep it quiet for now, OK? Let's keep it our little secret.' As I say this I am filled with a vague feeling of discomfort and I have to remind myself that he is almost old enough to die for his country as I push him towards the front door.

'I'm just taking this rubbish down, it stinks!' I call through to the living-room. I imagine the raised eyebrows and quizzical looks between the girls as I push him out of the door and walk him down the stairs. He is muttering something about being called rubbish.

In the shadows of the porch he whispers, 'So I can call you?'

'Yes, or I'll call you,' I say quickly. We will call each other but now let's go home.

'And what about tonight?' He pulls his long T-shirt uncomfortably over his hips and looks at the toes of his trainers.

'Don't worry about it, tonight was lovely. It really was. Are you OK to get home?' I say and I pat my jeans pockets looking for some cash.

'Oh yeah, I'll be fine. Mum bought me a return ticket this morning.' He bends to kiss me goodbye and I watch him lope down the grove.

As I walk back up the stairs I realise the extent of my inebriation. How much of what I feel at the moment is the cheap warm white wine churning in my stomach, and how much the tingly pleasure of unconditional adoration, and how much is actually about Michael himself? Will Rosie and Selin notice that I haven't taken the rubbish out and that it still stinks and still overflows from the kitchen bin?

I shut the flat door, change into my pyjamas, exchange my own dressing-gown for Rosie's and wander back into the living-room.

As Rosie hands me the menu for the local Chinese and Selin puts *Dirty Dancing* in the video again I lean back into the sofa, drunk and almost content.

Right now I don't care what my motives are, I just want to live with the pleasure of the moment. Yes I know that at some point it will all end in tears, but tonight I just want to enjoy it. Tomorrow I'll work it all out and do the right thing. Honest I will.

Chapter Nineteen

This morning, I've woken up wishing that I were a singer. I don't mean a midriff-baring teen sensation that looks like a souped-up spaniel puppy. I mean me in some smoky old-style nightclub, some jazz café, in a full-length red-velvet hip-hugging number and elbow-length gloves. Me belting out 'Cry Me a River,' or 'Smoke Gets in Your Eyes' or some classic sixties soul number. Head tipped back, throat exposed, eyes shut tight, feeling each word to the tip of every finger, the whole room in my thrall.

The only drawback of no longer living alone that I can think of is that my imaginary singing career has been somewhat curtailed. I still find myself doing a number in the shower, singing along to the kettle, or pulling the curtains and shutting the windows in the living-room to do a whole dance routine along with Ginger, Doris or Julie depending on which Saturday afternoon musical is on BBC2. But if Rosie catches me she'll tease me mercilessly for hours on end and come out with an ever more bizarre list of people she thinks I should impersonate on 'Stars in Their Eyes'.

I used to be able crank up 'Lady Marmalade' while washing up, loud enough to make sure I couldn't hear my own voice, never actually finishing the washing-up as I was too busy shaking my stuff round the kitchen, singing to the scouring pad, wearing soapsuds in my hair like diamonds and Marigolds on my hands like silk.

We all have our little showbiz fantasies, don't we? In another life, with another voice (and an American passport) I would have been a torch singer, a jazz siren, a Motown mystery or disco diva. Somewhere around 1979 the history of music lost its charm for me and I stopped caring about chart stuff any more.

My devotion to all things post-1900 and pre-1980 would be sad if I had been eighteen back then when punk came to town, because that would mean I was stuck in my youth unprepared to move on with the times, unable to embrace my own generation. But I was only eight at the time when my brother and I stopped watching *Top of the Pops* to enact out our own version of *Rockin' Robin*, and started to watch it to diss' the hairstyles and shout 'Crap!' after each track in the top-twenty countdown. My brother got a parka and took up smoking on his first step to becoming a Smiths fan, and I refused to give up my lime-green nylon flares with the elasticated waist even when they flapped a good two inches above my purple sneakers. So I'm not sad, I'm retro funky classic, just like my favourite nightclub in town. A singer in a jazz club, one of the things I promised myself I'd do if only once before I got to thirty, along with journalism and learning to drive. Oh well, you can't do everything, can you? Or sometimes anything.

There was one time when Rosie joined in with my 'secret' love of singing.

There was one time when the pair of us decided to hire a car and go to the country for a week for an epiphany. We didn't find ourselves but we did find an old country-and-western compilation tape stuck in the tape deck. Left with no alternative but to play it (have you heard local radio?), by the end of the weekend we were whizzing down those country roads belting out Leanne Rimes like troupers. But country lost its appeal as we got closer to London.

We never spoke of it again.

And once Selin and I did 'Stand by Your Man' at some karaoke night, except Selin rediscovered her dignity before the end of verse one and left me standing there all alone finding it hard to be a woman, and toughing it out solo. But everyone cheered at the end and no one laughed, so that was fun.

Lying in my bed I can see the chrysanthemum-shaped patch of damp that has been slowly blossoming over my head for the last two years and the brown-and-orange floral curtains my mum gave me as a stopgap when I moved in, and which I never got round to replacing. I look at my £12.99 Ikea bookshelf, now dusty and bare since I packed all my books into five boxes from Sainsbury's, and the four black dustbin liners full of clothes piled up in the corner.

It is one week since Michael and I had our near miss on the sofa, one week since Selin announced that she had found us a flat we might fancy, and one week since Rosie and I began the probably futile task of straightening the place up sufficiently enough to merit the return of my deposit.

We are moving today.

Selin told us about the flat last Sunday, in a café on the Portobello Road. The three of us must have been the only people in an establishment awash with *lattes* who were actually eating. No wonder the waitress loved us so much, although she looked as if she could benefit from a good fry-up and a couple of cakes herself.

'Mmm, by the way I think I've found you a flat,' Selin had said through a mouthful of waffles, whipped cream and maple syrup. The offhand way she dropped the news into the conversation had made me smile. In reality she had probably been waiting all of that night and most of the following morning to tell us that she had rescued us again. As we always expected her to. We weren't in the least bit surprised and not nearly grateful enough.

'Really, how?' Rosie asked, ostentatiously waving smoke from a neighbouring table of thin second-hand-leather-coated types out of her face. They say the reformed ones are the worse.

Selin's excitement at having found us a flat caused her cheeks to flush and her eyes to glitter, making her look exceptionally pretty. Like a teenager in the first flush of love, almost. She is the only person I know who can get this worked up about organising stuff.

'This bloke my dad knows, I know him too, a bit. He's cool, straight as a die. It's a nice flat too, just off Burma Road, ten minutes from mine, rent's not too much, two double bedrooms and one little box room. What d'ya think?'

'Sounds perfect. Can you give us his number so we can go and see it?' I asked.

Triumph spread over Selin's face like a sunrise. 'No need,' she said, reached into her bag and pulled out a bunch of keys. 'We can go right after lunch.'

Kaled turned up about twenty minutes later even though it was his day off, and as we travelled across town he told Rosie he had sacked his bird for doing his head in. Rosie agreed that she did sound a bit unreasonable. Kaled asked Rosie if she fancied going to this underground garage anthem night he was DJing at and Rosie said she'd love to but what with the baby and all that she should take it easy. Kaled said how about this chilled night at an after-hours bar he knew in Brixton, and promised to look after her if she came along. The back of Rosie's head looked very tempted but yet another flash of the new Rosie that's developing along with her baby made her say, 'Thing is, Kaled, all I feel like doing at the moment is eating burgers and throwing up.'

'Just like Elvis,' Kaled said dryly, making her giggle. 'No probs man, it's cool, some other time, yeah?'

'Yeah.' Rosie said as we turned into Burma Road.

We loved the flat. It was clean, it was roomy, it had one of those mirrors in the hallway that make you look thinner than you are, and best of all it had an original sixties L-shaped kitchen with bright orange-fronted units and Formica worktops covered with a stylised flower-power design. We wrote out our deposit cheques immediately. For some reason the mystery landlord had instructed Selin to deal with the contracts, which I did think mildly weird, but I guess if he was a client it might be an accountanty type thing to do. Anyway, at least we knew Selin wouldn't rip us off so we signed them and we had a new home.

I called my old landlord, Mr Bilton, that very night. It took him a few minutes to remember who I was, but when I gave him a week's notice he wasn't too bothered. Turned out he had just been about to chuck us out and sell the flat to a housing association anyway.

So here we are a week later, and I'm about to say goodbye to seven years of variable luck, a few dozen beetles and the brown floral curtains.

My new room already has curtains, and they look as though they might be from Habitat. They're not, but they look as though they might be.

Josh is bringing over a mate with a van to help us shift the heavy stuff. Selin is already here, having stayed the night and, judging by the sound of movement, is probably already labelling boxes with the marker pen that she brought from the office especially.

I suppose I should feel sentimental, sad even. I have had some good times here. But every single happy memory I have is eclipsed by some low-down thing that Owen did to me. All the laughter I have had here is hidden by the shadows of the tears; I think I'd have to live here another hundred years to wipe out all the bad memories – and just imagine what the beetles might have evolved into by then. As it turns out I'm really glad that Rosie's pregnancy forced my hand. Sometimes I think that if the whole of my life were left just up to me nothing would ever change.

Rosie walks in without knocking, wearing only jeans and a bra, and points at her breasts.

'Look at these! Look!' She climbs up on the bed and kneels in front of me, shoulders back, hair tossed back, chest thrust out as if she is about to do a photo shoot for Page Three. I check I'm not dreaming. I'm pretty sure this is not the same kind of drunken, drug-fuelled situation as the very short, extremely embarrassing let's-have-a-go-at-lesbian-sex-episode that happened back in 1993. That and the country-and-western episode are the two things we never talk about.

'They're very nice, Rose, always thought so,' I say, pushing myself up on to my elbows and attempting to run my fingers through a tangle of hair. 'But why are you showing them to me?'

She rolls her eyes, as if I've missed her second head or something. 'Because they've got bigger! Look! They're massive.' She jumps off the bed and goes over to my mirror, stands in profile, admires her cleavage and turns to smile at me.

'Ha! Baby, there's a new cleavage in town.' I laugh along with her but I've got to tell you they look exactly the same to me. Rosie bounds over and grabs my wrist to pull me out of bed.

'Let's go and buy some new tops, quick, before I get to the tits-*and*-belly stage!' I sit up in bed and pull back the brown curtains for the last time; the 8.22 from Paddington rumbles past.

'Well, we could, but I really think we should move house first, don't you? Doesn't really seem fair to leave it all to Seli.' I tip over the edge of the bed, root about underneath and bring out four mugs, one replete with beetle corpses. When I surface Rosie is looking mildly sulky. I think she really did forget we were moving. I continue in my best cheery girl-guide voice, that I learnt during my two weeks before I was chucked out for setting fire to the church hall curtains. 'For starters, we've still got washing-up to do.'

Rosie pouts. I think it's charming that Rosie pouts and flutters at anyone regardless of sex, sexual inclination or longstanding friendship, so strong is her faith in her flirtatious ability, but it doesn't wash with me. Not today.

'But they *are* cool, aren't they?' she reasserts in a childlike voice.

'Pammy would be proud,' I say and I kiss her on the cheek as I walk past. Leaving her with my mirror for a few more minutes of self-admiration. What on earth will happen to my breasts if I ever get pregnant? It doesn't bear thinking about.

'Proud of what?' Selin asks as she turns up in the doorway.

'My new breasts, silly!' Rosie says, pulling her shoulders back.

Selin glances at her chest with mild amusement. 'Of course, how could I be so blind? Now come on, you two. I'm not doing the whole thing on my own, you could at least make a token effort.'

'OK,' we sigh in unison.

The door buzzer makes me jump just as it always has done for the last seven years. As I skip down the stairs to answer the door I think about our lovely new doorbell at our lovely new flat that goes 'ding-dong' in a lovely Big Ben kind of way, not remotely like the final death charge of an electric chair in Missouri, or some other state where they fry people, anyhow.

My good mood evaporates almost entirely as I open the door.

It's Danny.

Danny, Josh's-friend-who-I-slept-with-at-that-party Danny. Danny, who Michael so accurately referred to as 'obviously-a-twat' Danny.

In the space of a nano-second I squint at Josh over his shoulder with murder in my eyes, and Josh shrugs and mouths, 'He's got a van.' Or at least I hope that's what he mouths. I swallow my pride and break into a smile that says, 'So we've done it, so what? We're all adults here.'

'Hey, babe.' Danny's slow, designed-to-be-sexy smile breaks out over his pretty face and he looks me up and down. Danny is the kind of guy who has definitely got it going in the looks department. He is the sort of bloke who you'd never imagine would go for *you* in a million years, that kind of male-model Levi-ad look that heaven has surely reserved only for its natural counterpart, the slender elfin-waif woman. And that is his secret weapon.

So surprised are you by his attention, so flattered by his compliments and drawn in by his charm, that you start to believe. As he quotes poetry at you and talks about art you start to think that he's not just a vacuous lovely. You start to think maybe he could be into you, even maybe he could be the one to get you over your ex, and a damn fine-looking one too. You drink the booze, dance the dance, laugh the laugh and sleep with him. It's usually dreadful sex (in this case he had the *tiniest* willy I have ever seen and that's no word of a lie) and then he doesn't call you and even though after that experience you'd rather snog Hannibal Lecter when he's feeling a bit peckish, you feel pissed off and cheated.

Well, not this time.

No chance, sucker, I think. I'm sober, I'm busy and I've got an almost-eighteen-year-old secret lover who knocks the socks off you in the trouser department. At least I'm pretty sure he will do when we get past that over-excitement thing.

It's funny but it's true, indifference makes you the most attractive thing in the world. As I make it clear to Danny that he is nothing but a distant regret, I just know that for the rest of today Danny is going to go for me hell for leather.

I usher them both up the stairs and Josh whispers in my ear. 'I'm sorry, he was the last resort, honest. This other bloke I know has gone to a folk festival in Surrey.' He grins at me with what I would normally refer to as his winning smile. Oh well, you can't win them all. I purse my lips at him and follow Danny up the stairs.

When Rosie sees Danny the first thing she does is laugh, really hard, bent double at the waist, and she is barely able to resist pointing at his crotch. When she see *me* she laughs even more. Selin covers her mouth with her long fingers and looks studiously at the ceiling, her shaking shoulders contradicting her apparent composure. And I know why. It's because I told them about his assets (or lack of them), and how he likes to talk during sex and say stuff like, 'Hold on, baby, my love rocket's gonna take you out of orbit.' Which in retrospect is made all the more hilarious by his very *very* tiny little appendage. Put it this way: at one point I wasn't even sure we had taken off. I bite back a giggle, Danny looks at Josh and Josh – who I hope to God hasn't heard that story from Selin – shrugs and taps his forefinger on his head: 'Mental.'

'Don't mind me,' Rosie says, her eyes filling with tears, 'I'm knocked up. It's hormones. By the way, thanks for helping . . . Danny.' She's off again.

Selin shakes her head. 'I'm sorry. When she laughs, I laugh. I'm just a sheep in that respect. Herd animal. Shocking lack of independence,' Selin splutters.

I glare at them both.

'Still, Dan,' Rosie says, 'now you're here at least we know things will go with a rocket!'

Josh looks on in utter bemusement as the pair of them collapse to the kitchen sink, patting each other on the back and wiping tears from their eyes. I'll get them for this. Later.

'Weird,' Danny says, his blonde dreadlocks tied back into a muppet-style pony-tail, so self-assured that he would never guess they were taking the piss out of him. He saunters over to me and drapes an arm around my shoulders.

'So shall we start with your room?' He raises a probably plucked eyebrow and I raise both of mine back at him with contempt kept only in check by the fact of how very much we need his van.

'Can if you like, it's all packed away in boxes in the living-room.' I pick his hand off my person as if it were a flea and sashay Mae West style into the other room. Josh shakes his head at me and Danny follows like the dog I always knew he was.

It's going to be a long day.

Chapter Twenty

In her new capacity as pregnant girl Rosie neither carries nor lifts but only points and directs, a role she was born for. Selin labels things and then cleans things and then sponges things down. As we don't really have that much stuff and as the boys seem to be doing such a good job I tell everyone I'm going to phone Mr Bilton to see what's keeping him and I retreat into my old room with my mobile. Bare of the meagre things that made it my room, it looks seedy and naked. For a moment I reflect on the pivotal moments that I have spent here and my sigh fills out its corners.

I phone Michael. He answers after two rings.

'Jenny, hiya,' he says expectantly. We texted each other mid-week but this is our first live conversation since the sofa incident. It doesn't take any intuition to realise that he has been anticipating and dreading this call just as much as I have, if maybe for different reasons. The immediacy of a live conversation after a series of cute but short text exchanges is a whole new ball game. In this world of electronic communication the old-fashioned phone conversation has almost become a sign of affection and esteem. Who do you call any more who you don't really like or respect?

'Hiya,' I say. 'Where are you?' I ask with the habitual opening gambit of mobile-phone users the world over. I sit on the edge of the bare-mattressed bed and then lie back on it. At least I'm not leaving a memory of Michael behind here, never got this far.

'Hiya,' he says again. 'Um . . . I'm in the park with some mates, playing footy.' His voice rises at the end of the sentence as if he is asking me where he is. I listen to his breathing, which sounds even, and I listen for the background noise of boys shouting and I can hear none. For whatever reason he's lying to me. I consider pushing it, but instead I retreat. I don't want to discover any secrets Michael might have that would spoil my involvement with him, I want him to be my golden- (OK, ginger-) haired and impulsive dream. I want him to be playing in the park with his friends.

'Yeah? Are you winning?'

There is a beat of silence.

'Actually, I'm not playing football, I just took the dog down the river . . . I've been sitting here for the last hour wondering if I should phone *you*. I just didn't want to sound sad.'

Whenever I wonder what I'm up to with this boy, a boy I've met three times, kissed on two separate occasions and somehow managed to slip into some kind of relationship with, he opens up my heart to show me. The knot of tension in my stomach explodes into a sunburst of warmth and the mid-morning light that finds my face through the bedroom window seems to seep in through my skin. I love it that he had been moping down by the river, and I love it that he didn't lie about it. I love it that he had thought about this call just as much as I have.

'I'm moving flat today. It feels strange,' I say, wanting to talk to someone close about the oddly detached absence of mixed emotions I have about this day.

'Yeah? I've never moved,' he says and I try to imagine his house, the house where he took his first steps, rode his first bike and sneaked his first girlfriend up the stairs to fool around with. Which number am I, I wonder?

'Anyway, school's crap,' he continues, ignoring the conversational road of me moving house for the first time in years, missing his chance to discuss it with me in a boyfriendy way. Lying on my bed I shrug my shoulders and smile as I listen to him.

'It's my birthday party in a couple of weeks. You are coming, aren't you?'

It seems like such an improbable scenario that I say, 'Yeah, of course I will.' I'll think up an excuse as to why I can't between now and then.

'Cool . . . so when will I see you again?' His voice drops a little, I guess in case the dog or some ducks hear him being soppy. 'I miss you,' he whispers.

I run the palm of my hand under my T-shirt and over my belly. An intriguing little thought crosses my mind but I've got a feeling Michael wouldn't be much up for phone sex and anyway I am supposed to be moving.

A deep little sigh escapes from my throat and I say, 'I miss you too. It's difficult, though, isn't it? You know. To be alone.' Once again crackle-filled air takes over the silence for a moment. He breathes in sharply and I can almost see him leap to his feet.

'I know!' he says excitedly. 'You can come here!' I laugh out loud and think of his mother offering me tea and asking me about my A-levels.

'Michael, you live with you parents.' I state the obvious.

'Yes, and for the whole of next weekend they're away. Anniversary. You could come for the weekend.' I think about it. It would be crazy. It can't happen. But it *would* be great to be with him somewhere far away from everyone I know. In his big house where he assembled his first record collection, where he lay on his bed and wondered about what kind of person he was meant to be. Why not be there at the beginning of everything he is now? What harm could there be? No, it's just too stupid.

'OK, you're on.' I find myself laughing as I say it. Where did I develop this ability to kid myself right up until the last second? He whoops at the other end of the phone. I can hear his dog bark, and somewhere behind him kids are playing.

'I just want to say,' he says, 'about the other night . . .'

I stop him. 'Michael, it's fine, really. I had a *great* time.' I giggle as I remember. 'It was a little strange when the girls came back, but it was fun, really fun. You were . . .' I can't think of the right thing to say. 'Great' or 'wonderful' doesn't seem appropriate. 'Sexy' seems a little out of proportion and 'sweet', 'lovely' and 'fine' all seem too patronising.

'You were . . . fun,' I finish lamely, hoping that I don't sound as though I mean I found his enthusiasm hilarious.

'I just want you to know that um . . .' He coughs. 'I want you to know, um, well, when I get you on your own again, things are going to be different.' His stolid and determined tone curls my mouth into another indulgent smile. If this was any other man, by this time I would have been wholly overtaken by the Creeping Repulsions. That retrograde feeling of horror and disgust that, for reasons unknown, only seems to cruelly manifest itself after you have committed some intimate act with an individual who, in the cold light of day and the sharpened perception of hangover induced clarity, turns out to be the very person who you would not sleep with even if they were the last living example of your opposite number in the whole wide world. Even worse than that, they think you are now going out together. Which means all the awkwardness of having to come out with gems like you are (option one) 'still in love with someone else', or (option two) 'just not looking for anything serious right now' or in the very tough cases (option three) 'would never dream of going out with a psycho like you, unless under the influence of strong lager and a full moon'. Once I tried reverse psychology and told one CR candidate I wanted

122

commitment, commitment, commitment and children, lots of them, right after we got married. He must be the only man I have ever met who wanted all that too. It was a nightmare, and only option three worked in the end.

But this is Michael. Sun-filled, innocent, happy–go–lucky Michael. He is all the games of spin the bottle that I have ever played, he is all the tight-lipped moments of tension I have spent trying not to laugh while some poor lad has been grappling with my bra fastening. Michael is the last moment before the first kiss under the glow of an orange street lamp, in the days when I could still see the stars in the sky. He is everything I was before I met Owen, and what I love about him most is watching him find his way. The smile resounds in my voice.

'I look forward to it,' I say. There is a short silence of smiles coming back at me.

'Look, I'd better go,' I say. We both smile silently for a moment longer.

'OK, I'll call you in the week to sort it out?'

'Yeah, see you,' I say softly.

'Good luck with your move. See you,' he says and hangs up.

I stretch back on my naked bed and try to imagine his bedroom. There is something about Michael, something that doesn't exactly remind me of Owen but something they have in common. Owen is very charismatic, maybe that's it. One of the reasons I fell for him so totally at the beginning was his charm, which was genuine in the original meaning of the word, in that his manner could be beguiling and bewitching. In the early days after a reunion his displays of authoritarian love for me made me feel warm and secure. His romantic indulgences coupled with an innate sense that he was right about me prevented me from having to worry about deciding my own fate; for the first time since Dad left home I had someone else to make those decisions.

But it's not like that with Michael, it's almost the opposite. I close my eyes and picture him in the sunlight in the park, in the shadows in Rosie's room. It's the way he sees me. Owen used to look at me in that way, with that desire and emotion, but the difference is that with Owen I would be living on tenterhooks waiting for that expression to suddenly vanish or dry up. With Michael I know that every time I see him he will look at me that way. He reflects my glory.

'Jen!' Rosie shouts along the corridor in a mildly frustrated tone. 'What are you *doing* in there?'

'Phoning Mr Bilton!' I reply. 'What do you think?' Her voice is suddenly right outside the door and I sit up abruptly. She opens the door.

'Oh. Well, he's here now, so you can stop.'

'Is he? I must have the wrong number, I wondered why I kept getting an unobtainable tone,' I say, and I follow her out to meet Mr Bilton. Normally that would have been a close thing but I'm finding another side-effect of Rosie's pregnancy is a short-term memory to rival a goldfish. If any suspicion crossed her mind I'm pretty sure it will be lost in her baby-filled ether by now, drowned out by a cloud of anchovy-craving hormones and the much more interesting prospect of real life, the actual process of creation, right inside her, right now. It pretty much blows *my* mind when I think about it.

Mr Bilton is a very tall, very fat man, who wears a very old, very brown, browner than the original colour, very smelly jumper. Mr Bilton is probably London born and bred but for some reason (maybe he has watched too many episodes of *Coronation Street* and *Emmerdale*) he feels compelled to call us lasses, miss whole chunks out of sentences and add the letter 't' to the end of random words. Somewhere down the line he must have done a dreadful impression of a northern person and was never able to revert to normal, or he is a northerner who has lived in London so long he sounds half cockney. Either way, on the few occasions that we have spoken it freaks me out. That and his personal hygiene habits.

I follow him around the flat trying not to gag every time a whiff of stale smoke, sweat or fried food wafts in my direction.

'Of course, there were no subletting allowed.' He nods at Rosie who leans on the door frame of the living-room, her nose stuck in a permanent wrinkle.

'Rosie? She's just a mate who's come to help me move out.' I smile at him as sweetly as I can whilst holding my breath and he makes a grumbling noise deep in the recesses of his massive girth.

'Table's broken.' He points at the three-legged table.

'Yes, but it was when I moved in. You were going to come and fix it. Look, I have the inventory.' I wave a random piece of paper in his face, hoping he won't want to take a look. The windy intestine noise erupts and echoes around the empty room.

We finish our tour, and he points out the iron-shaped burn on the floor (guilty), the broken handles on the kitchen cupboards (guilty) and black bubbly mess of melted lino in the bathroom (not guilty, it was Rosie and I have no idea how she did it). Luckily he doesn't try the cooker and the beetles seem to be staying in hiding, maybe as a farewell gesture. He tucks his chin into, well, more chins and looks at me from two tiny red-rimmed eyes.

'I'll give you two hundred back, not a penny more, no point bartering, lass, you'll get nowt more out of me, y'hear?' I nod in disbelief and accept the slightly smelly-looking cash.

I give him the keys and carefully prop open the front door as the last few bits are carried out. He strides off over the road and heads straight into the pub.

'You can't let him get away with that!' Rosie says indignantly. 'This flat was a hell hole when you moved in!' I tuck the cash in the pocket of my jeans.

'Listen, Rosie, between you, me and the lino incident I'm grateful for whatever I get. I thought *he* was going to charge *me!*' Rosie rolls her eyes at my non-negotiation skills as I grab the last box and take it out.

Everything is in the van, Rosie and Josh are having one more look under beds, Selin is having a last-ditch attempt at making the hoover pick something up and Danny is in the driver's seat tuning the radio. He has already offered me the seat next to him. I have declined in deference to Rosie's condition.

I take one last look around me as a resident at the Grove, expecting sentiment to kick in at any moment.

That's why when I hear Owen's voice, I think for a moment it's a daydream.

'Jenny?' There it is again, fake upper class with a faint trace of Brummy. Owen, he's here. My stomach takes a tumble for my feet.

I take a deep breath and look back at the open door. Selin, Rosie and Josh will be down any minute. Finally I look at Owen.

'Owen, hello. What do you want?' I ask in measured tones. I can't help giving in a little to the pull that his blue eyes have always had on me.

Danny must have found the station he wants on the radio, as the volume soars and blots out the noise of the passing traffic, leaving Owen and me standing alone able to hear only each other and hard-core chart rap. Some skinny white guy is extolling the virtues of raping his kid sister and then murdering her.

'What's going on?' He gestures at the van. Even though he's smiling and his voice is reasonable I don't want him to know

I'm moving, it's just a gut thing. There is still something about him that makes my stomach lurch and my heart pick up pace. The rising volume of the base coming from Danny's van seems to drum inside my head. Owen takes a step closer to me. I take a step back.

'Owen, why are you here?' I cock my head to one side and smile at him, attempting to appear as relaxed as possible. Somehow the noise around us has become an inescapable wall.

'Why do you think?' His genial tone disconcerts me. 'You're not answering my calls. Why?' His smile is still present, a little more tight-lipped but still there.

Danny's changed his mind about the rap and for a moment the air is filled with deafening static before the baleful tones of some indie popster wash back in and then out again, complaining about the weather. As Danny searches, snatches of voices, tunes and empty noise buffet the air around me. My irritation with Danny and his god-damn radio and Owen and his god-damn smug smile finally begin to simmer and I start to lose my brittle composure. Any lingering remnants of nostalgic romanticism that I might have felt about him evaporate like mist and I am suddenly certain that I want Owen to go.

'Owen, we split up. You finished with me. Why should I answer your calls?' I am annoyed with the tight girlish tone in my voice.

He brushes his floppy blond hair back from his face and chuckles. Yes, *chuckles*.

'You're upset with me, of course you are,' he patronises. 'I do nothing but hurt you. But *you* know. It's always you that I come back to. Those other girls mean nothing to me. They just prove to me more each time how much I love you.' His voice softens and he steps a little closer to me. 'This time, Jenny, I think I really have learnt my lesson. This is the last time, I swear to you.'

As I listen to his litany of clichés I find the anger that rises in my chest almost impossible to quell, but my instinct tells me not to lose my temper. I speak in measured tones.

'Owen, the last time? The last time *was* the last time.'

He shakes his head in disbelief and laughs again, almost a giggle this time.

'OK, OK, so you don't want to be together any more,' he says, clearly not believing a word of it. 'But what about being friends? We've been too close for too long just to throw it all away.'

This time I can't help the angry laugh that escapes my throat.

'*Friends?* After everything you've put me through, you want me to be your *friend*?' His face hardens at my tone and I glance over my shoulder again, hoping to see Rosie or Josh, and say, 'Owen, just go.'

Another radio station phases in and for a moment the Grove is filled with 'Hit Me Baby, One More Time'. The volume decreases but Danny doesn't turn it off.

Rosie's voice precedes her down the stairs.

'Right, that's the last of it, we're good to go!' As she emerges on to the road she is saying, 'Christ, who is playing that awful . . .' she sees Owen, '. . . music.'

'Good to go where?' he asks, looking at me.

'Nowhere,' I say.

Rosie joins me and links her arm through mine. 'Owen,' she says flatly.

'Rosalind,' he replies, using the full name she can't stand. I can feel her bristle.

She sweetly steps in front of me. 'Look, you might as well just go. Jen's moving and there's nothing you can do about it.' The secret's out. It's at times like this that I wish the psychic connection we have often imagined between the three of us really existed.

'Moving?' Owen's voice rises sharply. 'How can you move without letting me know?'

Rosie speaks for me. 'Why should she tell you?' she hisses. Her eyes narrow and she almost bares her teeth.

'Because I need to know where you are, you fucking bitch!' As always his sudden verbal violence stuns me into silence. I stare at him, fighting back tears.

The flat door slams and suddenly Selin and Josh are at my side.

'What's going on here? Owen, why are you here?' Josh demands, instantly taking control. Despite his anger Owen takes a step back.

'This is none of your business,' Owen spits at him. Josh stands in front of both of us and takes another step forward until he's looking down at Owen.

'No, you're wrong. This is *my* business, this is *my* friend. Now, she doesn't want you here and neither do I. So why don't you just fuck off?' If I'd seen this on TV I'd have just laughed, Owen and Josh standing eyeball to eyeball getting ready to fight over me. I have never seen Josh look so angry. I've never seen Josh look angry at all. I wonder if I should try and calm the waters and ease the tension, but I find that I'm rooted to the spot. I've seen that look on Owen's face before. I'm afraid of him.

All at once the music spins off and the noise of the street rushes back in. Danny hops out of the van and takes in the scene. He saunters over and says, 'Need any help, man?' in a noncommittal way that could be addressed to either Josh or Owen in any context. In a second he becomes another best friend. Owen breaks the deadlock and turns on his heel.

'I'll be in touch,' he shouts, and his coat-tails flap in the breeze as he marches down the street. I want to thank Josh and Danny, to tell Rosie off for giving it all away and to love her for sticking up for me, but before I can speak I'm in tears and Rosie and Selin are both hugging me tightly.

Danny lights a roll-up and leans against the van.

'Uptight guy,' he says.

Chapter Twenty-one

The living-room of our new flat is an assault course of boxes and bin bags. We have plugged in the TV and the kettle and although there is a perfectly nice sofa we are sitting on the floor with fish and chips. Selin, Josh and Danny are still here.

Our encounter with Owen seems like years ago now, just a dream that has already faded and which I have half forgotten. Which I would have completely forgotten if everyone would only stop talking about it.

'So, then I told him to get lost or else,' Josh proudly tells us again as if we hadn't all been there.

Selin eats another chip with a furious expression. 'Thank God Josh was there, hey, Jen?' she repeats for the third time.

'Yes,' I say quietly. 'Thank God.' They assume that Owen has made me quiet and withdrawn but actually I am totally, unfairly angry with Josh.

I don't know why I'm angry, I was really glad he was there at the time, but this constant harping on about how Owen was clearly insane and probably dangerous, and who knows what might have happened if Josh hadn't been there to rescue me, is starting to grate. His new-found role as the local knight in shining armour is beginning to get on my nerves. I mean, it wasn't that big a deal. It seemed scary at the time but really it was just Owen getting on his high horse again. I'm pretty sure he would have left of his own accord if Rosie hadn't turned up when she did and let the cat out of the bag. Because of Josh's heroics the rest of the day had been about that little scrap outside the van. Today was meant to be about my new beginning. Now I just want to forget it.

I change the subject.

'I'm going away next weekend,' I say. Rosie takes her eyes from *Blind Date* and looks surprised.

'Oh? You didn't mention it. Where are you going?' I think she might be a little peeved that I'm abandoning her for only our second weekend in our new home.

'I'm going to stay with my mum for a couple of nights,' I lie. 'I just felt like getting out of London and being made a fuss of,' I say honestly.

'Yes, good, she needs to get out of town,' Selin says. 'Get that cunt Owen out of her head.'

'Selin!' Rosie exclaims and presses her hands over her ears and then her belly and then her ears again in quick succession. 'You can't say that!'

'What, "Owen"?' Selin asks, winking at me. Selin is so rarely foul-mouthed that whenever she is it just makes me giggle.

'No! You can't say the "c" word. It's detrimental to women,' Rosie says indignantly. Josh is also open-mouthed and Danny looks a bit embarrassed. This is just what I need, some obscenity reclamation to turn the evening round. Maybe Selin does understand how I'm feeling after all.

'I think girls *should* say it.' Selin climbs on to this evening's soapbox. 'It desensitises it. I mean, we all say "fuck" all the time and who cares about that?'

'It's not the same,' Rosie protests and I wink at Selin.

'OK, Rosie, calm down. I've got a joke,' I say, suppressing a giggle. Rosie smiles at me and abandons her new mum-to-be priggishness.

'Why does Rupert the Bear wear chequered trousers?'

Selin, who has heard this joke before, nearly chokes on a chip.

'I don't know,' Rosie sings in a nursery voice. 'Why does he?'

'Because he's a cunt!' I holler with fish-wife hilarity and the tension and stress of my day dissolve in a helpless fit of the giggles. Selin and I catch each other's eye and neither of us can stop laughing. Eventually even Rosie joins in. Danny and Josh exchange a look.

'I still say you can't say that about Rupert the Bear. Not Rupert!' Rosie says, wiping the tears from her eyes.

Selin, who seems particularly sparkly-eyed ever since she took a fifteen-minute call on her mobile in the kitchen, lies flat on the floor with her arms folded on her belly.

'Let's say some more swear words,' she says. 'It's like being back at school.'

But we can't think of any other rude word that makes us laugh so much.

Not even cunnilingus.

Chapter Twenty-two

I'm the kind of person who loves train stations, trains and train journeys much more than I have ever actually enjoyed arriving anywhere.

I especially like Waterloo station, with its bright vaults of light and high-topped creations of space. I like the smell of coffee and burgers, the rushing shoals of single-minded people moving as one, pushing past and around each other, and I like the odd collections of shops selling knickers and ties, the very things you need when you are about to travel. I feel almost like a ghost in stations like this, as I always arrive at least thirty minutes early and I am never in a rush. I float dreamlike and invisible through the crowds, free from stress or worry, watching those who can't even see me.

I feel blissfully at peace today on the very Saturday morning that I'm about to leave the comfortable confines of the centre of the city and go to see Michael in the country, well, Twickenham, which counts as the country in my book.

This morning should be filled with the kind of nagging foreboding that normally insinuates itself into the back of my mind whenever I think about what Michael and I are up to, but even that has subsided and instead I am filled with a sense of peaceful contentment that has got everything to do with this train station, I'm sure.

I wonder if there are other people like me out there who feel calmed by public transport terminals? Maybe I could start a therapy group, and lead hoards of fretful women trapped in inappropriate affairs, downtrodden by work and harried by failure into the roomy peaceful caverns of London's mainline stations. It works better for me than a jacuzzi, isolation tank or half-bottle of vodka ever has – maybe it's the promise of a new beginning. Even if that beginning does happen to be the beginning of a short trip to see my teenage soon-to-be lover.

Damn it, the nagging foreboding is back. It always comes back when I think of the 'teenager' bit.

At last the train I'm waiting for is ready for boarding and I walk down past the first-class compartments and find an empty carriage. It is a sunny September day and I pick a window spot where the velveteen seat is upholstered in warmth. I look out of the window and check the departure screen just to make sure I'm on the right train, something I have always done since I ended up on a non-stop train to Birmingham on my way to see my mum in Watford.

I should be in Twickenham in about thirty minutes. Michael will be waiting for me at the station, and although I have never been to Twickenham before I imagine a rural train station with late-flowering hanging baskets swinging from ornate Victorian wrought ironwork. I imagine a platform empty apart from his tall lean frame lounging gracefully against a red-brick wall, his tangerine hair washed out by the sunlight. Somehow, in my daydream, when I step from the train I am wearing a pair of red shoes and a matching hat. As the train pulls away it leaves a gentle mist of steam that keeps us apart for a few moments longer before we are in each other's arms, kissing without tongues and with a lot of cheek rubbing, in that old black-and-white film way. Well, this is the kind of thing that happens when you let your imagination run away with you.

The dirty junkyard no man's land that always seems to exist alongside city train lines slips by and my thoughts turn to the real issue at hand. This weekend – what with us having a lot of time to ourselves, just us two together for longer than a few hours for the first time ever (but never mind, that's another thing to worry about later) – we will probably have sex.

The thing is, the last time I saw him in the flesh, so to speak, I really wanted to do it, really I did. He had been so sweet in the pub, so romantic, and so sexy in the taxi. I'd had some gin and about half a pint of that wine and I was all fired up for base four. I haven't had sex since that dreadful encounter with Danny, which was a disappointing episode. The kind of sex that makes you think a full-length mirror and a box of Kleenex would have served your partner just as well, and that makes you a bit pissed off that you even bothered in the first place. Michael had been so impressed with me that I wanted to eat up his admiration. It's been a long time since I've felt that confident in myself. But, to be really honest, the moment I closed the door on him and walked out of the little bubble we had created for ourselves I felt relieved that nothing too concrete had actually happened, that I hadn't crossed any kind of boundary.

You know what? I can't imagine any thirty-year-old man racking his conscience over whether or not to have sex with a willing eighteen-year-old girl. I think I think too much.

Twickenham is the next stop and if I want to have sex with him I damn well will. Probably. Always supposing he doesn't blow it before we get to the crunch, that is.

Chapter Twenty-three

Twickenham station is nothing like I imagined, it's more of a concrete post-war concoction with some half-dead flowers in what used to be a rubbish bin, before rubbish bins were banned.

Michael is not on the platform and there seems to be more than one way out. I follow the signs and the people until I find myself outside by a taxi rank. I button my cherry-red leather denim-style jacket up to protect my probably too-bare cleavage from a sudden breeze that goes right through my jeans. I stand on one high-heeled booted foot and then the other. There is no sign of Michael.

This is very annoying. I had especially planned my journey so that my train would arrive fifteen minutes after we had arranged to meet, but I can't see his red hair anywhere in the crowd and now *he* is twenty minutes late. I think lateness is so rude.

I could phone him but I don't want to seem too keen. I'll wait for another ten minutes and then get the next train back to Waterloo; I'll take it as a sign that this was never meant to be and prepare myself for the comforting welcome of my favourite terminal and McDonald's. The prospect suddenly seems rather inviting.

Except that here he is now, running right at me, the pockets of his combats flapping in the wind. Does he have any other type of trouser option apart from combats, I wonder? Does he have more than one pair, for that matter?

'Hi!' he says, halting millimetres from my face, eyes wide with smiles. 'God, sorry I'm so late, I had to wait ages for a bus and the battery on my mobile is dead so I couldn't even call you. God, I'm sorry.' He grabs my forearm a little awkwardly and kisses my cheek with cold lips. Wanting to reassure him, I pat the small of his back and look up into his brown eyes.

'I've only been waiting a few minutes. My train was late.' It seems as though all the intimacies we established last time we saw each other need to be recreated. We touch each other clumsily, and as he leads me away he takes my hand the wrong way and we laugh, break hands and re-engage in a self-conscious way. It's been a long time since anyone wanted to hold my hand in public.

'The bus-stop is over here,' he says, and I follow him, silently considering and deciding not to offer to pay for a cab. As we reach the stand he sits down on one of the narrow benches and gestures for me to sit on his knee. I think of the weight of my behind and the slenderness of his thighs and I can't think of anything worse, so I decline. From a barely discernible gathering of his eyebrows I think he is slightly hurt, but not half as much as he would be if I sat on his unsupported knee.

'So, what fun have you got planned for me this weekend?' I say, waggling my eyebrows in a suggestive way, against my better judgement. His eyebrows smooth out and he laughs at me, shaking his head.

'I thought we could go to my local tonight and play some pool, my mates will be down there. Sarah might be there too, but she'll be cool. At least she should be by now, it *has* been nearly a month.'

I nod in agreement and think 'poor old Sarah', and then I think there is nothing I want less than to be in the pub with his beer-mat–flipping fraternity putting pound coins in the jukebox to listen to tuneless nonsense I've never heard of and then pooling the last of their change on the table to see if they've got enough for another round. Been there, done that. So vehement is my reaction that I almost turn around and head back to the station, but just at that moment Michael's long fingers reach out to hook around mine and he tugs me close to him and stands up to put his arms around my waist.

'I'm so glad you're here,' he says, kissing me softly and drawing me into the fold of his body, blotting out the cold.

I decide to stay.

Chapter Twenty-four

His house is not exactly the TV-land suburban semi that I imagined. The avenue he lives on is tree lined and quiet, with only a few cars – probably aged cars for the children to drive – parked along the road. The grown-up cars reside side by side in married pairs on wide and accommodating driveways.

As we walk down the road I half listen to Michael's faithful rendition of his favourite scene from *Star Wars*, but my more attentive half takes in huge basement kitchens with stainless-steel hoods presiding over gleaming white worktops, or glimpses of a living-room that has surely never been used for living, with curtains in the same material as the sofa.

I have no idea why I am so fascinated by this other-world lifestyle, so different from mine. Maybe it is because where I grew up houses this big had invariably been turned into flats by the 1960s. Maybe it's because no one in my family had a car at all after Dad left so there hadn't even been the possibility that at age seventeen I might be presented with a car myself to park on the street or anywhere else. But more than likely it's just because I'm nosy, because I'm awestruck that some people really do have lawnmowers you can drive, and others really do go to John Lewis to get soft furnishings that match their sofa.

Mainly, I'm impressed that some people who don't live in America have swimming-pools in their gardens, judging by the pool-filter van that's just pulling out of the house up ahead.

Michael takes two steps ahead of me, turns to face me and, walking backwards, says, 'And then, and *then* right, Darth Vader goes . . .' He cups his hands over his mouth to add the required sound effect. '"Your powers grow weak, old man. First I was the pupil but now *I* am the master. Ha ha ha ha ha!"' His hand drops to his side and he falls back in step next to me. 'And then Obe Wan Kenobe gets killed but he becomes more powerful than when he was alive, so it's cool.'

This is the sort of thing that might make me wonder how much intellectual stimulus I can expect dating an eighteen-year-old. Except that I've been on the receiving end of exactly the same monologue about either *Star Wars*, *Withnail and I*, *Monty Python*, *The Young Ones*, *Blackadder* and, more recently, *Buffy the Vampire Slayer* with so many men of so many different ages and backgrounds that I can't really pin it on immaturity. Well, not the kind you measure in years anyway. Michael continues.

'That is a classic, classic moment. I did sort of like episode one, but I do sort of think Lucas shouldn't have directed it himself, and what about . . . oh hang, the pool people have come early. I'd just better go and check what they've done. Hang on.'

He bounds off to catch the van as it's turning on to the road. I watch him sign something and confidently pat the van on the side as it drives past me. He stands at the gate of his house waiting for me to walk the last few steps to his side.

His house isn't a semi-mansion, it is an *actual* mansion, at least in my book. Set in actual ground with an *actual* swimming-pool (now safely netted against autumn leaves) and a summer-house gazebo-type thing in the back. I mean, I thought he was nicely spoken but, well you know, I hadn't imagined him to be actually *rich*.

Once inside, Michael takes my jacket and hangs it in a double-doored closet in the hallway and leads me into a kitchen so enormous that in the middle there is a central isle of working top for no apparent purpose at all other than to cover a built-in (fully stocked) wine rack. A dark blue glass vase holding those really expensive, almost real-looking, fake sunflowers sits demurely at its centre. Despite the unseemly amount of cupboard space, some of which probably hides a fridge, washing-machine and dishwasher, there is a wrought-iron pan-rack thingy hanging from the ceiling, replete with brass pans that I guess are probably just there for show. Also hanging up are bunches of dried herbs and a large bunch of my arch-rival nemesis, dried lavender, guaranteed to set off an asthma attack if I get too close. I pull my inhaler out of my bag and retreat to a breakfast bar that runs along the wall to french windows that overlook a patio running down to the pool, which precedes the gazebo which hides some sort of secret garden behind.

I must be some kind of snob; the whole thing makes me feel extremely uncomfortable and Eliza Dolittle-ish. The only thing saving me is the blindingly obvious fact that Michael is so shaken up by having a potentially willing sexual partner in his empty house that he is rattling on about bollocks like there is no tomorrow.

'And so I said, if Sigourney Weaver can be cloned in *Alien Resurrection* then of course they can make *Terminator Three*! Coffee?' He holds a brightly glazed mug up for my attention.

'Yes, I'd love some,' I say. 'Your house is amazing!' He looks around him as if he has suddenly been transported to another universe.

'Is it? I suppose growing up here, you just get used to it.' His offhand tone rankles.

'Mike, you've got a pool, for Christ's sake! No one has a pool!'

He smiles and carefully folds a filter for the kind of percolator Rosie would give her eye teeth for.

'You never call me Mike. I like it. I like it better than Michael.' He spoons in three scoops of rich-smelling coffee, pours some bottled water into the measuring jug and then into the filter tank. Viva instant.

'We are better off than some people, I suppose, but I still go to a comprehensive and Dad votes Labour. We aren't fascists or anything.'

'I didn't say you were, *Mike*.' I say, not remotely interested in talking sixth-form politics with him.

'I didn't say you did, *Jen*,' he replies with his deep chuckle. He seems to have relaxed a little. As the coffee begins to bubble and gurgle in the pot he walks over and joins me at the breakfast bar, pulling his stool close to mine.

'Come here often?' he says in the most appalling and entirely inappropriate small town nightclub lingo. 'Jen, Jennifer, Jenny, Jen?'

Without waiting for an answer he leans over and kisses my smile, pushing my mouth open with his tongue. He really is a great kisser for his age. His hands run up from my knees to my thighs and my hands remain primly folded in my lap. I sit still and let myself float in his kiss until the percolator has brewed three mugs' worth of coffee and sits quietly simmering. Then I pull away from him and say, 'Black no sugar, please.'

He opens his eyes and smiles at me, jumping off his stool with careless abandon.

One of the sad things about life post virginity is that you hardly ever kiss just for the sake of it any more. It's almost always a prelude to sex. Just like that kiss was too, I suppose.

'Come on, let's go upstairs,' he says, handing me my coffee. My stomach ties in little knots and flips over. I am the one feeling eighteen again. Well, I'm the one feeling an eighteen-year-old anyway, ho ho.

His room is not on the first floor, nor even the second. Instead, at the end of the second landing, he pulls on a rope and a sturdy-looking pine staircase emerges from the ceiling.

'Loft apartment,' he laughs, and standing aside takes my coffee. 'After you.'

I've not been keen on the steep-perilous-looking-stairs-and-high-heel combination ever since I fell down the escalator at King's Cross, sliding on my shins and leaving long deep parallel gouges that took ages to heal, and which at one point created a whole new pulling persona for me of recently attacked tiger trainer. But nevertheless I gingerly make my way up the stairs and emerge into the biggest teen room I have ever seen.

Covering the length and breadth of the house it has gable windows either side, and even more light flooding in through skylights. The floor is covered with real wooden boards and there is a sofa bed, a TV and a stereo covered with extensive and unruly piles of videos and CDs, then at the other end a door opens on to his own bathroom. There is also a kitchen unit and a mini fridge. Scatter rugs cover some of the floor and instead of heavy-metal posters on the terracotta walls, Picasso prints decorate the room, framed and hanging neatly side by side.

'Bloody hell, Mike,' I say, using his new pseudo-pet name. 'This is bigger than my entire flat!'

'Yeah,' he laughs, 'my parents decided I could use my own space soon after I got into nu-metal. Then when I leave home it'll be a good guest room.' Along with the other six or seven, I think to myself.

'Music?' he says and plunges on to the floor to start going though the CDs. 'What do you fancy?'

'*Not* Slipknot,' I say pointedly and he laughs.

'I don't have any disco.' We have never talked about music, I don't know how he's picked up on my tastes.

'What about David Gray?' he says. 'I got *White Ladder* last week, it reminds me of you, sort of.'

I smile at him, despite not having a single clue what David Gray sounds like, and say, 'Sure.'

Pleasant-sounding tunes fill the room and I am still standing looking around, diligently drinking my coffee, as he begins to pile his CDs into miniature tower blocks. I watch him until he abruptly stands up, walks over to his sofa bed and flips it open. I'm sort of shocked at his forthrightness and my stomach does that little flippy thing again.

He lies on the mattress and pushes off his trainers without undoing the laces in a way that would make his mother weep if she could see him. Actually, the whole almost-thirty-year-old-girl-in-his-room thing would probably make his mother weep, so let's skip over that.

He holds out his hand to me.

Self-consciously I set my coffee on the floor and unzip my boots and lie stiffly next to him.

He pulls himself up on to his elbow and looks at me.

'Are you ready?' he says bluntly. I almost choke and for a second I feel like I'm lost in the absurdity of the situation.

'Are *you* ready?' I say. He looks at his hands and then looks back up at me through his eyelashes with a heartbreakingly sweet smile. He nods.

'Ohhh Babylon,' David Gray sings.

Michael slowly unbuttons my top and pushes it back off my shoulders with the palms of his hands. 'You're pretty hot,' he says, laughing at himself as he says it and making me giggle too. The laughter seems to have released me from my nervous thrall and I sit up and pull my top right off, dropping it to the floor.

145

Watching me, Michael pulls his T-shirt over his head and starts his own pile on the floor.

'You next,' he says, and watches me as I stand and unbutton my jeans. There doesn't seem to be any especially graceful or sexy way of taking off jeans, but I manage OK, remembering to grab my socks at the last minute.

'Now you,' I say, and he stands opposite me, dropping his combats in one easy movement, stepping out of them, leaving his socks on. He nods at me, and raises an eyebrow.

Oddly enough, stripping for him seems to be the easiest thing in the world and I'm glad, really glad that we aren't fumbling around with each other's catches or zippers.

I reach behind and unhook my bra, trying not to envisage what my breasts will look like without its support. I slip each strap down from my shoulders and ease it away, letting it fall to the floor and finally uncovering myself, letting my hands fall uneasily to my sides.

We both bend simultaneously to remove the last of our underwear and for one second longer we look at each other across the expanse of his sofa bed.

Then, both kneeling on the bed, his hand reaches out for my hand and he brings my fingers to his lips, kissing each one in turn. I tip my head back and close my eyes, unable to stop myself smiling as he turns my fingers over, kisses my palm and then my wrist and gradually inches his way closer to me as he works his way along my arm. Afraid that we could be here for hours, I break away from his kisses and fling the same arm around his neck pulling him flush to my body. The shock of the impact of flesh makes him moan and I am overwhelmed by the full force of his long lean body as he embraces me, his hands in the small of my back, pushing me closer as we kiss.

He lowers me on to my back and hovers over me, his eyes roaming across my torso. Straddling me, he cups my breasts in both hands and as he looks at them whispers, 'You're so beautiful.'

I watch him as leans to kiss one nipple and then the next, gently sucking and licking each one in turn until I feel my stomach tighten with the promise of pleasure. I hadn't expected this.

I feel his hand begin to trail its way to between my thighs, but I shift a little to block its path. As much as I would love to just let this happen to me I take control and I shake my head, knowing that too much delay, too much worrying about what I'm feeling would spoil the moment for him. I'm already turned on all I need to be by the way that he wants me. I roll him on to his back and he grins with delight as I reach over him to pick up the condom he has at some point placed on the bed and, straddling him, I put it on as carefully as I ever have, not wanting to set anything off before time. His smile fades and his eyes are fixed on me with an intense gaze. The muscles in his throat contract and I can see longing, nerves and anticipation crowd into his face.

I lean over him and kiss him, lean forward a little more to let him kiss my breasts and then slowly I lower myself on to him, pleased with the way he seems to fill me. He sighs and closes his eyes, furrowing his brow with concentration, his hand reaching out to grip my forearms either side of him.

His eyes open halfway and we hold each other's gaze as I slowly begin to move. It is moments, only seconds I suppose, before he comes with a shudder and reaches up to clasp me to him. Although I haven't come during those short moments of fusion I feel like the sexiest woman on earth.

I've done it, I had a virgin and I think he thought it went pretty well.

I lie with my head resting in the curve of his neck for a while as his fingers run up and down my spine and then gently I roll off him and to his side. He looks at me.

'Fucking hell,' He says. I say nothing and, smiling like the sphinx, I roll on to my back and stretch.

'God, I mean, *fucking hell*. But fuck, I'm sorry, it was so quick, I'm sorry.'

I take his hand and pat it. Cringe and drop it like a hot brick. 'It was lovely,' I say dreamily.

'Yeah?'

'Yes,' I say.

He rolls on top of me and says, 'Do you mind if we do it again then?'

Chapter Twenty-five

When it comes right down to it we all do live our lives from one cliché to the next.

It's maybe about four in the afternoon and it has started to get gloomy in that winter's-coming way and Michael is fast asleep, his sweet face half buried in the pillow and his arms flung above his head. He does look very young right now, but then we all do when we're asleep.

I, on the other hand, have been wide awake since the last time, lying next to him and looking at the ceiling. I don't resent him being asleep at all, I'm glad. At least it'll give me a bit of a break.

I'd like to think that the reason boys fall asleep when they're carnally satiated and girls still lie there, minds buzzing, fingers drumming, harks back to a primeval time when, black-widow style, we used to off them when we were done and have them for tea. Not because I have psychotic tendencies, but because I think it mildly more cool and interesting than the usual reasons:

1. What does he think of me now that we've had sex?
2. Was I any good?
3. Did my thighs put him off?
4. I wonder if he'll chuck his girlfriend now?

And in this case:

5.   I haven't come yet, but if I start to do anything about it I'll probably wake him and that would be so embarrassing I'd die.

Neither do I resent the fact that he didn't get me floating, floating on a sea of fire and all that. I mean it *was* his first time, and his second and third. In fact, I really didn't want him to start in on trying to make me feel good, I would have found it more awkward than anything else. That he wanted me so much made me feel fantastic and I'm sure he will make me come at some point, it's just that, well, he might not be there when it happens.

Owen did not go to sleep after sex. He read a book. Actually, he would get out of bed and go and sit in his high-back winged chair and read a book. Sometimes he'd get up right after we had finished without saying a word.

If we had been apart for a while he wouldn't be able to get enough of me and the post-coital cherishing would go on for hours. Then, after a few weeks, I'd begin to feel that that whole side of our relationship would dwindle to nothing if I didn't make all the moves, wear all the right underwear and turn all the right somersaults. Even then I'd feel compelled to coax him to bed. He had me so wound up I'd feel that we had to be having sex at least once a day or he'd leave me. He really did have me completely where he wanted me. He had me up for anything to keep him interested, and then he'd leave me anyway.

I suppress the nasty tide of anger and bitterness that begins to well up and look at the sleeping Michael instead. He's smiling in his sleep. For a fleeting moment I wonder if he is dreaming about Sarah and her size-eight teenage thighs and then I laugh at myself and get out of bed and get dressed.

First of all I look in his wardrobe. There seem to be piles of T-shirts and sweatshirts hastily bundled into one corner and only two shirts hanging up. One is a crisp white dress shirt and the other a rather alarming black satin number with ruffles on the sleeves. This boy harbours Gothic tendencies. I delicately rummage through the pile and find another pair of combats. So he does have more than one.

I look in his bathroom, smile at his shaving gear; I have never seen or even felt the tiniest graze of stubble on him. He has an untouched bottle of CK One on his bathroom shelf, and I decide Sarah gave it to him last Christmas, but that it isn't really his style. Or maybe his mum, who hadn't sussed that no one wears CK One any more. I pick it up and give myself a spray. Typically, I only discovered that I liked it when Rosie gave me a half-full bottle. Which of course was long after it was cool.

Flicking through his CDs I can' t find anything that I've ever heard of or would ever want to hear until I find a copy of *Never Mind* by Nirvana.

'Kurt!' I whisper to myself, as if coming across an old lover. Lovely Kurt Cobain. The only period of my life when I have been utterly seduced by of-the-moment music was in my university days in the early 1990s. I was drinking 50p-a-shot dog-rough vodka in Spiders, Hull's cheapest and grungiest night-club, when suddenly 'Smells Like Teen Spirit' filled the dance floor with head-flinging, feet-stomping, hands-held-behind-backs naval-gazing abandon. I loved it and I loved everything Nirvana did after that. OK, so basically it was slow, slow, QUICK LOUD QUICK LOUD, slow slow on every single track but I loved the quality of Kurt's voice, the sound of real guitars and his eyeliner. Three reasons that I'm sure would make any Muso worth his sort weep in desperation.

I clearly remember the day Kurt topped himself.

Rosie and I, in possession of our fortnightly dole cheques, met up in The Sussex off Leicester Square at eleven in the morning and drank until eleven in the evening, every time raising a toast to Kurt and shouting, 'Never mind!'

It might have been that night that we ended up in Tottenham Hale without ever quite knowing why. It's a sobering thought that I'm nearly three years older now than Kurt was when he died.

So I was twenty-two back then and Michael would have been, let me see, maybe around about, dum de dum, ten. Ten. He was ten the day Rosie and I were toasting Kurt in The Sussex. That's *TEN*.

What am I doing here? What am I doing in the room of this boy who I have nothing in common with, who I hardly know, having sex with him, why? I like him, sure, I like him but it's wrong. I know it's wrong, it's wrong for *him*, it's wrong for *me*. He's not going to marry me is he? I don't even want to get married right now but it's the total and utter lack of the very possibility that scares me. And, and I'll be thirty soon and what about if I ever want to have kids? And just because he reminds me of life before Owen, I mean just because of that, it's not a reason at all really. If it were fine, if I was happy about it, I'd have told the girls, we wouldn't be having secret shag trysts in the attic of his parents' house. It's wrong, wrong, wrong.

I'm going.

I grab my bag and stuff in the knickers I did not put back on and run to the window to reccy the terrain. An azure-blue Land Rover pulls into the drive. Must be very useful for all the off-roading they do around here. But that's OK, they'll ring the bell, whoever they are, find out no one is in and then off they'll go again. I just hope you can't hear the bell up here.

A tall and vaguely familiar-looking man gets out of the car and then goes round to the boot. As he opens it a red setter leaps out and dances around his feet while he takes out some bags. If my brain has been lagging two beats behind, alarm bells finally peal the moment a flame-haired middle-aged woman draped in a sea-green Pashmina steps out of the car.

I slump on the edge of Michael's sofa bed and wonder: why are his parents back now?

Chapter Twenty-six

Feeling my weight on his side of the bed, Michael stirs and snakes his arm around my waist.

'Mmm baby, come back to bed,' he says with none of the ironic, jokey tone that is appropriate when using that phrase. I slap his hand away.

'Michael, how long are your parents away for?' I ask him in a brittle school-marmish whisper. He sits up, blinking and rubbing sleep out of his face.

'Relax, will you. Tomorrow night, I said.' He rolls his eyes.

'Oh, so why are they downstairs *now*?' I hear my voice rise in panic. Michael smiles at me as if I'm an idiot, registers the severity of the expression on my face, leaps naked out of bed and straight to the window.

'Oh, shit,' he says, seeing the car. 'It's OK, you can just stay up here until they've gone to bed and I'll sneak you out.' I am surprised to find myself offended. Half of me had thought, considering Michael's apparent devotion to me, that he would suggest we go downstairs, have a cup of tea and get to know the folks. Obviously I would say, 'Don't be so ridiculous, I'll sit up here until they've gone to sleep and then you'll have to sneak me out,' but it comes as something of a shock to realise that he wants to keep me a secret from them just as much I want to keep him a secret from the rest of my life.

'I'm not waiting here until then!' I hiss just to be contrary. 'It's only early, I'll be holed up here for hours! Get me out now!' He looks at me, taken aback by my temper. And then before we can come up with any ideas, we hear his mother calling up the stairs.

'Mikey? Darling, are you in?' I look at him and mouth '*Mikey*?', caught between horror and hilarity. He frowns at me and hastily begins to dress.

'Mikey? Darling? You'll never guess what your father did!' The voice, now a floor nearer, is light and humorous.

'I bet I can guess,' I whisper bitterly. Michael just manages to pull his T-shirt over his head when a ginger head appears in the floor as the sofa bed clicks back into place. I am reminded of a post-modern play written by somebody Irish.

'Oh, you *are* here?' She smiles brightly, her eyes adjusting to the autumn afternoon gloom. 'Why are you sitting in the dark? Hello,' she says, nodding at me.

'We were watching a film, Mum. Um, this is Holly, from drama club, you remember I've talked about her?'

First of all, who is Holly and why has he talked about her? Second of all, why call me Holly? Why can't I be Jenny from the drama club? And third of all, how old is this flipping Holly meant to be? Is she his tutor? A parent of a fellow student? And fourth of all – *drama club*?

Michael's mother, now fully in the room, switches on the overhead spots. I brush my fingers through my hair and pray to God and Clinique that the money I have invested in their anti-wrinkle cream pays off.

'Hello, Holly dear, I've heard an awful lot about you. Michael says your improvisation skills are something to behold.'

Oh, are they indeed?

'Hello, Mrs . . . um . . . Mrs . . .' I don't know Michael's second name.

'Oh, just call me Fran, dear. All of Michael's girlfriends do.'

All of them? Well, I wouldn't want to break the tradition, would I?

'So, why *are* you back? Tonight's the anniversary night,' says Michael, attempting to hand me my jacket at the same time. I ignore him.

'Your father! He would forget his head, really he would! He only booked the hotel for *next* weekend. Can you imagine it? There we were checking in and the girl's saying, "Sorry, Mr and Mrs Parrott, you're not in the register," and your father's getting quite blustery as he does in those sorts of situation and then she says – she was charming, very well mannered – "I'll just check next weekend's bookings," and there we were! I knew I should have done it myself. It's so difficult finding a good hotel that will take pets.' She and Michael roll their eyes at each other in a spooky carbon-copy sort of way.

This is an afternoon of revelation. First of all I discover that the man I have just slept with is called Mikey Parrott. Then I discover he has had girlfriends, in the plural, and that he talks about some teen slut called Holly. And then I witness a woman on her twenty-fifth wedding anniversary laughing about how it has been completely ruined. A split-second comparison with what I remember from my own parents' married life explains why I find it all so surprising.

Mrs Mikey pats my arm and says, 'Come downstairs, Holly dear, and meet my dreadful husband. We can all have a nice cup of tea.'

'Actually, Mrs Parrott, I mean Fran, I have to be going. Mum's expecting me.' Michael nods vigorously at my side and the minx in me thinks, 'But oh, what the hell,' and I conclude, 'But one cup of tea won't do any harm.'

As soon as I am installed on their wine-red sofa (that matches the pelmeted curtains) with Charlie the red setter's head ensconced snugly on my lap, I regret my impulse to wind Michael up.

So far they haven't got me under a bright light and shouted, 'Ha, impostor! Anyone can tell you're practically middle-aged!' No, it's worse than that.

First of all, Mrs Mikey brings me a silver-framed photo of her and Mr Parrott on their wedding day back in 1977. They look sweet and so disco and Mr Parrott looks so much like Michael that I smile with genuine affection. This encourages her. Next she brings the wedding photos of her daughter, Michael's older sister, something else I didn't know about him. I'm trying to think of the things I do know about him.

Candice, or Candy as the family call her, was married two years ago, when she was twenty-two (twenty-two!). She's as ginger as her mother and brother, but her wedding photos are quite different from her parents', awfully posed with that misty Vaseline-on-lens effect. But worst of all is seeing Michael at fifteen-ish, gangly, even more spotty, with his shoulders hunched and that kind of sheen on his skin that just says 'smelly boy who masturbates too much'. Only three years ago. I've been here before today, haven't I?

Throughout all of this Michael just hangs around sheepishly in the corner, occasionally getting up to fetch biscuits or put on a CD of a Welsh choir as and when requested by his parents; a dutiful son.

Finally I see the chance to go and say, 'Well, thanks for the tea, Fran, but I really must be going. Mum will go spare!' She smiles at me, clearly thinking what a nice girl I am, and I feel a moment of guilt thinking about my real mum, who I haven't visited for ages.

'Michael, go and get Holly's coat, will you?' He must have left it upstairs because without a word he leaves the room and bounds up the first set of stairs two at a time, his rhythmic thuds gradually fading into the rafters.

Mr Parrott, who until this point has been merely nodding or laughing at the anecdotes provided by Fran, takes it upon himself to engage me in conversation.

'So Holly, any ideas on which uni you'll be going to?' I like his voice, it's deep and fatherly. I like fatherly men, I can't help it, it's all down to not having one around myself I guess.

'Hull,' I say quickly. It was the university that I went to, after all. Well, actually it was Humberside Polytechnic, but they're all the same these days, aren't they?

'Hull? You seem very sure? When Candy was getting ready to go she couldn't decide right up until the last moment.' Oh well, I expect Candy had more than one choice.

'Oh yes,' I say, feeling vaguely like a time traveller with a sudden rare opportunity to look into my future and see every detail mapped out for me. 'I'm definitely going to Hull.'

'And after college? Something drama-y, I expect?'

I consider saying Customer Service Administration Manager (UK) for a hardware component manufacturer, but let's face it, it wasn't exactly my cherished dream when first I got on the train to Hull full of hope and looking forward to three years studying whatever 'humanities' might turn out to be. Somehow during those three years I was going to pick up the mythical abilities needed to be a journalist, I remember, without much of a clue of what it might entail. At some point immediately after graduation I expected to be discovered by someone and to start my career with a brief stint as a local reporter on *Humberside Today* or something before my star ascended to the *News at Ten*. I never imagined that hundreds of people with actual experience went for jobs reading the news on even *regional* radio stations even in the North, and I had a cat in hell's chance of ever getting one. It still comes as something of a shock.

'Journalism,' I say. 'That's what I'd like to be involved in.' I'm surprised to hear myself sound a little wistful as I remember.

'Oh yes, journalism, very good. Nice little job on a good local gazette. Good steady trade. Well, good luck.' He has a lovely smile, and Michael's eyes. From his wedding photo I can tell that when he had hair he was dark and very good-looking. The non-sexual way in which he talks appeals to me, and in a funny kind of way I find it rather sexy. You never know, maybe if I was ten years older . . . ? Just kidding, it's that father fetish again. You always want what you don't have.

Finally the jacket arrives and I say my goodbyes to Mr and Mrs Parrott.

Michael walks me outside and to the end of his driveway in silence. It's dark now and I'm cold.

'Which way is the bus-stop?' I ask him, looking up and down the tree-lined avenue.

He points to my right. 'Down the end of the avenue, turn right, across the road. It's the 246.'

'OK,' I say briefly and peck him on the cheek.

He grabs my wrist. 'You're annoyed with me, aren't you?'

'No, no, I'm not,' I say, obviously annoyed.

'Look—' He starts to explain but I cut him off.

'This was just a bad idea, that's all. I'll see you.' I stride off down the road to my left. Stop, turn around, and stride back past him in the direction of the bus-stop.

'I had a really fantastic time!' he calls after me, lamely.

I foolishly expect him to run after me but when I am two-thirds of the way towards the end of the road I conclude that he is not going to. Why do men never do that in real life?

This is the time that I should stop and really question what I thought I expected of this relationship. You know, why I got so jealous and pissed off with him. Especially considering that as far as I'm concerned I'm only meant to be taking a short excursion back to the good old days and it hardly seems fair of me to overreact. Maybe it's like those situations when you meet someone pretty and probably on the rebound from his beautiful girlfriend who has gone travelling for a year without him. Someone who is obviously going to mess you around from the word go. Someone with whom you agree to have a casual-sex, no-commitments liaison, no problem at all, fine by you. And then what do you do? You promptly fall in love with him. It's no wonder, then, that the poor sod gets a bit peeved when you ring him on the hour every hour, run out of restaurants after him or burst into tears at your own birthday party because he ended up snogging another girl, who happens to be your arch rival who you only invited so she could see how pretty your boyfriend was. Things like that can happen; I've heard of it.

What I'm saying is, you go into some things saying one thing out loud and thinking something entirely different deep inside. Serious denial, it's pathetic.

But I'm not going to think about this now, I'll think about it tomorrow.

Chapter Twenty-seven

Everything is changing. Since my return from Twickenham I've noticed it all around me. Not small imperceptible changes but big wheel-turning movements. For the first time in my life I have the impression that I am getting older, or no, maybe that's too drastic. I can feel time passing.

After ten years of living with the back scent of washing-up and wet laundry, Rosie and I have developed a taste for household objects, more specifically kitchenware. Rosie kicked us off with a matching orange Bodum kettle and cafetière set, the perfect shade to complement our kitchen. Later that same day I brought home six retro fifties-style coffee mugs that I picked up on a lunchtime shopping trip that was supposed to be dedicated to the purchase of underwear. Black underwear, as white always goes grey in the wash.

And then on the Wednesday after Twickenham I found myself getting out of bed half an hour earlier than normal and brewing some of the fresh coffee that magically appeared in the cupboard. As I spooned in the coffee, Rosie, fresh from her turn in the shower, followed me into the kitchen, produced some fresh crusty bread for toast and scrambled some eggs. We sat together at the tiny kitchen table and ate breakfast in a comfortable silence, finishing by clearing the plates and mugs to the empty draining-board. Every evening we have lived here one of us has washed up. And it doesn't even take very long if you do it every day.

Neither of us has said anything about it, we have just accepted it with relief, like two children who have been trapped in a funfair hall of mirrors and suddenly come across their true reflections.

And of course there is Rosie. Rosie changes every day. Twelve weeks gone, some of her changes only she can attest to, like needing to go and buy maternity tights even though her hips and tummy would still make the average woman reach for the Slim-Fast. Or her pilgrimage to Mothercare to buy some trousers that she insists fit her despite the fact that they bag around her middle like a kangaroo's pouch, and slip halfway down her bottom when she walks.

And then there's the crying. She stopped being sick just after we moved into the new flat. She still looks a little wan without the right amount of sleep or enough food but generally speaking we thought the worst was over. Instead she started crying. First off she cried at an RSPCA appeal on TV. Well, we've all done that without the aid of added hormones so we thought no more about it. But now she cries all the time. She cries at the news, *EastEnders*, trailers for films, the books she's reading (she's reading Harry Potter), the death of her first ever pot plant. Maybe that would merit some sentimental reaction but she had only bought it a few days earlier.

Underlying the arbitrary crying episodes, is something else. The Rosie I've always known has flitted from one day to the next, always restless and always searching. Somehow that Rosie seems to have settled down and now, beneath the tear stains and the baggy trousers, I can see she is fully centred on herself, happy to believe that she is enough to get her through.

Of course, some things never change. After reading about what can happen to your perineum during labour we both got so scared by the pregnancy book that Selin bought her that we have hidden it under a pile of hardbacks, a doorstop and the remains of Rosie's pot plant.

'I'd just rather not know that bit,' Rosie said.

'Neither would I,' I concurred and we both shuddered as though someone had walked over our graves.

As for Selin, now Selin has started to – well, the only word I can think of is bloom. Always beautiful Selin, tall, raven-haired Selin. Normally elegant and reserved, she has suddenly acquired a little glow, a different smile has appeared in her repertoire and a new tone in her voice.

'Selin, you're different,' I told her one day over two sneaky bottles of wine whilst Rosie was out at a function.

'No, I'm not,' she laughed, tossing her hair in a black glossy tidal wave, rejoicing in the very difference she denied.

'Yes, you are. You've sort of become . . . ostentatious. Which is nice, by the way.'

She looked at me for a long moment and then reached over and gave me a hug. 'I'm just happy. You and Rosie are nearby. The dreaded Owen has gone for good. I'm getting on really well with Dad. I've landed a couple of new clients. I feel as though I'm moving forward and, well, Jen there's . . .'

'Oh, God, everyone is moving forward but me!' I cried with dramatic self-pity. 'There's what?'

'Oh nothing, never mind. I'm just happy,' she said, and we left it at that, although I did wonder for a moment what secret knowledge about how to live life Selin had secretly acquired, and if her new expression of pleasure at her never-changing daily life somehow meant she was leaving Rosie and me behind, still stuck in the same jumbled, disorganised, it-will-sort-itself-out-one-day rut. Maybe she has achieved that mythic nirvana of being happy with her lot and her single status that all the books and magazines tell us we need to achieve. If she has, and if the prophecy is true, she'll be mobbed by hundreds of relationship-friendly men any day now.

Repeat after me, I am happy with my life, I am happy with my life, I am happy with my life. Honest I am.

Even Josh is different. For starters, he comes around all the time. I haven't seen him this much since he and Selin still lived at home, back in the days when we used to root through his drawers looking for his meagre collection of porn. We'd spend hours giggling through our fingers on Selin's bed before sending him a ransom note made out of letters clipped from the pages threatening to tell his mum. On three occasions that little enterprise had got us enough money to go down to McDonald's in Wood Green and flirt with the sixth formers. But then he fitted a lock to his door and we had to go back to flat Diet Cokes in the café.

It's not that I mind him being there when I get in, it's nice to see him, I even look forward to it. It's nice that he'll drop round with a video or a pizza and the three of us will veg out in front of the TV. But the thing is, I can't quite work out his motivation. I mean, OK so we're new neighbours, we're all between official partners, but he's got loads of mates in Stokey and it's not as if he has a ton of time on his hands. Even though we're used to seeing him pretty often, it's usually with Selin, some social occasion we all attend, not just because he fancies a visit with his little sister's mates. In fact, we're beginning to see him more than Selin, who seems to be constantly busy with something else these days.

I occasionally wonder if it might be that he fancies Rosie. Most people do. And Josh always talked about wanting kids one day. If he does fancy her I don't think Rosie has cottoned on yet, which is probably for the best. I love Rosie and I'm very fond of Josh, but although I can't quite put my finger on why, I just really can't see them together.

Now me. The usual routine of work trundles on. Nine days since Twickenham and not a word from Michael. I turned my phone off for three days because I didn't want to speak to him, but when I switched it back on there were no messages waiting. I'm not really sure why I got so cross, I'm not really sure why he hasn't phoned and I'm not sure if I should phone him. But a memory of his touch, the way he holds his head or his redundant aftershave lotion suddenly creeps up on me and I'm surprised by how much I miss him.

Chapter Twenty-eight

Something has happened to make my workplace more interesting – OK, to make it interesting at all. There's a new addition to the office. Jackson from New York City. I have to say New York City, because whenever any one of us says something like, 'Wow, New York, living there must be *so* cool,' he says things like, 'Well yes, New York State is very pleasant. New York *City* is way cool.'

I'm giving him the benefit of the doubt because he's new and I sometimes behave like a twat when I'm nervous.

Apparently he is Georgie's opposite number in NYC, which gets her back up, because he's probably about twenty-five and worse, he's a vice-president or vice-something. Georgie tells me they are all vice-presidents over there, post room up. I'm not sure she's giving him the benefit of the doubt.

He is far too strait-laced and serious to be her type of person, despite the fact that he is totally gorgeous in that kind of 1980s longish-hair and sleeves-rolled-up kind of way. In that kind of Rob Lowe, piercing-blue-eyes, with-a-Texan-drawl, St-Elmo's-Fire kind of way.

He's here on an ideas exchange. They are going to cross-fertilise creatively and are striving to push the envelope in order to concretise a more dynamic transatlantic symbiosis and become more successful rainmakers.

Your guess is as good as mine.

All I know is that he is here for a month and that Georgie's PA, the long-suffering Alice, has brought her more cups of herbal tea in one morning than she usually consumes in two days. Alice flashes me the packet as she walks past on her fourth trip of the morning. 'Tolerance Tea.' Figures.

Ten days and counting and I still haven't spoken to Michael, but I think he might be working up to talking to me. He's called me a few times at work, I'm pretty sure. I've picked up the phone but as soon as I speak he hangs up. Either that or I've been unlucky enough to have my direct line input on to the auto dial of a fax on Repeat to Sender mode. This happened to me a couple of years ago, so I wouldn't be that surprised. It was a girl from accounts called Lizette, who had taken exception to my Owen-related rebound fling with her boyfriend (break-up number two). Well, OK, he *was* her fiancé at the time but I was a crazy mixed-up kid back then, I have a much more responsible attitude to other people's relationships nowadays. Lizette is still here, but shortly after our 'episode' her fiancé went to Mexico to find himself and found a beach-bar job in Cancún instead and then married a local girl. Lizette has never forgiven me.

After the acute embarrassment of Twickenham has died down I just keep thinking of Michael, asleep beside me in his attic room. I never expected him to have reservations about what we were doing. I never expected that he would want to keep *me* a secret. He seemed so keen that I went to his party, meet his friends in the pub. Maybe I read it wrong, maybe he was just trying to protect me, respect my feelings. When it comes right down to it, if he hadn't mentioned this Holly person I'd probably have laughed all the way home.

I sigh and look blankly at the Excel spreadsheet in front of me, trying to muster up the energy to take it seriously. This is another legacy from Owen. So many names thrown in my face so many times. So many other women that every time another woman came up in conversation I had to brace myself for the worst. At some time in my life all the anger and bitterness I feel will fall away and I'll see this as another hour that turned the clock. It's just that I can't imagine when.

All at once my mobile springs into life with its tinny version of 'Disco Inferno' just at the exact moment that my work phone starts beeping for attention. Professional to the last, I dive for my bag and spend a frantic few seconds rooting my phone out. Pulling it out, I can see Michael's name on the display. The moment I press 'OK' to answer it both phones go silent. My mobile must have gone to messages and the work call must have gone off into the mysterious world of my 'hunt group', in other words it will be directed to someone else in the office to pick up.

My work phone chirrups into life again.

'Hello, UK Sales, may I help you?'

Silence, but I get the feeling that someone is there. If I press my headset against my ear I think I can hear the passing rush of traffic.

'Helloooo,' I call moronically. 'If this is your fax machine this is not a fax number!' I press the Release button, wondering if in the unlikely event that people should happen to congregate around the fax area they can actually hear me shouting down a fax machine.

I'm still trying to figure it out when Jackson slides, yes, slides in the manner of Michael Jackson, into my office singing the tune to my mobile phone ring.

He smiles at me with exceptionally white teeth and sits down.

'Hey!' he says brightly. I have watched enough TV to know this is American for hello.

'Hello,' I say in my best Lady Di voice. He leans back in the chair as far as it will go and with his arms folded across his chest focuses his blue eyes on me from under a floppy fringe. There is something about a floppy fringe on a bloke.

'Man, I love that number,' he says with a twinkle. I think his teeth really do do that advert thing and gleam; it could be the strip lighting but I'm pretty sure they are gleaming. Now I know not all Americans look like extras from *Ally McBeal*, because I've seen Jerry Springer, I've seen Mr and Mrs Tourist, 'fanny packs' slung high, matching anoraks zipped up tight, laughing on the tube at 8.15 in the morning. But this one really does.

I want to ask him what he does to his teeth and if he is wearing tinted contacts but instead I say, '"Disco Inferno"? Really? Do you love disco or just "Disco Inferno"?'

You have to be cautious in the early stages of finding a kindred disco spirit. These days many hopefuls turn out to be people who bought an afro wig for someone's stag do and when they talk about the Bee Gees' 'More Than a Woman' they mean Westlife's version. At least I think it was Westlife, it could have been A1.

'Disco? I *love* it. Where can a guy go to get down to some decent disco in this town?' He's probably gay but given that I'm the only person in the world who was surprised about George Michael I don't think I'm the best one to judge. A straight good-looking rich American man who loves disco? There hasn't been one of those since John Travolta, surely?

'Well, mmm, I know a few clubs, we could go one night if you like?' I say casually. I don't want him to think I fancy him, just in case. Well, I don't want him to think I fancy him at all, because I don't. Much.

'Really? Thanks, that would be really good. It looks like I might be here quite a while, it would be nice to meet some people.'

'My pleasure,' I say, my smile spreading faster than a charm tsunami.

'And listen.' He leans in a bit closer and beckons me to within inches of his chiselled nose. Here we go, he's going to ask me about gay clubs. 'I just wanted to say, sorry about acting like a prick when I first arrived. Nerves.'

'A prick!' I cry, just loudly enough for Kevin to look over and giggle. 'Nonsense. No one thought you acted like a prick!' I say with sincerity. No, we thought you acted like a *twat*.

'I'll see if I can arrange something for this Friday, shall I?' It's not that all thoughts of Michael have just gone instantly out of my head. It's just I want to show Rosie and Selin my pretty new friend.

'That's really kind of you.' He gets out of his chair and heads for the door.

'Not at all,' I say, 'it's nice to have a new disco friend.' I sit for a moment, caught up in a nostalgic fusion of seventies music and my 3D-effect Rob Lowe poster that I used to snog so inexpertly but intensely. Gradually the moment fades and I think of Michael. I pick up his message.

'It me. It's Michael. I just wanted to say hi. I haven't called because, well, I didn't think you wanted me to. But I just want to talk to you. OK? Please call me back.'

The sound of his voice brings back the sensation of the pressure of his hands in the small of my back. I call him; he picks up straight away.

'Um, hi!' he says. He sounds surprised.

'I'm sorry,' I say, straight out. I just want to see him.

'*You're* sorry? I'm sorry I acted like a pig.'

'I just got a bit jealous about this Holly person. It was stupid, I'm sorry.'

'No, but you don't have to be jealous. Holly is just a friend. I only said her name because Mum knows most of the people

I hang with. I didn't want her to ask you too many awkward questions. But it was a stupid plan. I had only just woken up, remember? And you might well have drained me of my mental powers as well as everything else that afternoon.' His chuckle is low and dirty and I feel a little tingle at the memory. He does think I'm the best thing in bed ever.

'I did have a good time,' I say slowly, 'before the parents incident.'

'God, so did I. Look, can I see you again?' His voice is so tense and sweet and I'm charmed by the fact that he hasn't taken it for granted that my calling him means I want to see him again.

'Yes, I want to see you. But I don't know when.' I'm guessing that whenever we do see each other someone's bed will be involved, and gaining access to a bed without any complications is tricky.

'Let's go to the movies,' he says out of the blue.

'The pictures?' I'm surprised.

'Yeah, like a proper date. I'll take you to see a film up the West End and then we can queue for an hour to have some Häagen-Dazs and then I'll walk you to the bus. What do you say? This means more to me than sex, you know.'

I pause. I mean more to him than sex. I'm just not quite sure how to take that. Maybe he doesn't think I'm a sex goddess after all. Maybe he's putting up with me in bed because he likes me as a person.

'I really like you,' he says into the silence. A date. I haven't been on a date since . . . I can't remember the last time I went on a date. Owen didn't do dates.

'I'd love to,' I say. 'How about tomorrow? We can meet outside the Hippodrome at 6.30. You can pick the film.' I have tomorrow off to go to the hospital with Rosie so I know I won't be kept late in the office.

My work phone starts to beep again.

'OK, cool. I'll see you then,' he says happily.

'OK, better go,' I say, bugged by the beeping of my head-set.

'Jenny?'

'Yes?' I say a little testily.

'I think I love you.' He hangs up. His words are still ringing in my ears when I pick up the call from the other phone.

'Hello, can I help you?' I say on autopilot.

Silence.

'Michael?' I say stupidly.

Sodding bloody bastard fax. The line goes dead.

Chapter Twenty-nine

Waking up in my new bedroom almost makes mornings a pleasure. The day is gloomy and the orange glow of the street light that burns reassuringly yards from my window still shines brightly through my white voile-type curtains. I stretch out my legs and press my toes against the carved pine base of my bed frame, and sitting up I can see my reflection in the panel of mirror-fronted wardrobes that run the length of one side of the room.

Yes, the wardrobes are MFI, the pine bed has deep crayoned scratches on it from some past encounter with a creative child, and an intriguing set of teeth marks on the headboard, but in the first moments of the day basking under the sunrise of the street lamp I feel happy that finally I have a lifestyle. Second-hand and lived in as it may be.

Today is Rosie's first scan. Selin, who can only stay the bare minimum of time away from work, is planning to go back to the office straight after, but Rosie and I intend to catch a cab to Oxford Street and buy some more maternity clothes that she doesn't need yet, and have lunch. I have stopped telling her that she doesn't really have a bump yet, as it makes her cry, and so for the first time in any female relationship I have ever had I find myself reassuring her that she is looking fat.

When I get up Rosie is already in the kitchen, wearing her

new white pyjamas with little pink rosebuds coming into bloom left right and centre. She is setting out plates, two knives and a pot of strawberry jam. Yesterday I bought a butter dish that caught my eye in the Marie Curie shop window as I left work, and now it sits in all its steely ex-B&B splendour on the centre of an orange-and-white gingham tablecloth that Rosie must have acquired at some point. The pair of us have become addicted to breakfast. And not just any breakfast, but breakfast in the style of Doris Day.

'Tea?' she says. She seems a bit quiet, even for her. Maybe she's a bit nervous.

'Lovely,' I say. 'I meant to do this for you, it being scan day and all.'

'Jen . . . ?' she begins in a tone I have heard a thousand times. She puts a round white teapot on the table and sits down. So overawed am I by the appearance of a teapot that it takes me a moment to notice the big fat tear that rolls silently down one cheek.

'What's up, sweet pea?' I say softly. I am fully expecting her to break down because she fancied raspberry jam this morning.

'I'm worried about the scan.' She wipes the tear away with the heel of her hand and looks about seven.

'It'll be fine, silly,' I say in what I hope is a brusque and positive manner, using the very phrase that winds me up so much when others say it to me.

'But what if it's not, I mean I drank and smoked for the first bit, didn't I? I can't even remember the last time I took anything. I mean, I can't remember if I took drugs when I was pregnant or not. I might have . . . I might have . . . killed it!' Bursting into tears she rubs her knuckles roughly in her eyes and her body shakes with sobs. So grief stricken is she that I figure this has to be more than just a mood swing. I drag my chair closer and put my arms around her. Two slices of toast bounce out of the toaster, one actually escaping and landing on the worktop.

'Come on now, Rosie-Posie, it *will* be fine. I'm *sure* it will be.' I try to think of something to say that will reassure her. 'Look at all those rock stars' kiddies, all of them perfectly healthy. I bet they were all on a bit of a bender before they found out they were pregnant.'

Rosie sobs even harder and buries her face in her arms. 'They all go on pre-conception regimes! I read it in *Hello!*' I have seen Rosie cry a lot in my time, sometimes quiet tears and sometimes sad and angry mourning and sometimes laughing because she is crying for no reason, but I have never seen her weep with such abandon. I wonder how long it will be until Selin gets here?

'OK, OK. What do we see whenever we step out of our front door?' I've hit on a plan.

'Pizza Gogo?' she sniffs.

'I mean up and down the road, what do we see? We see mothers and babies, right?' That was my plan, now I have to improvise.

'Yes? So?' Her tear-stained face emerges from the nest of her hair and arms.

'Lots of healthy bouncy babies. Well, I bet not every one of those mums planned their baby, and I bet you that for a few weeks they didn't even know they were pregnant and carried on life as normal. And what have they got to show for it? Lovely healthy gorgeous babies. Just like yours will be.' It's a tenuous link, but it might just work.

'Do you think?' she says croakily but with a half-smile.

'Yes, I'm sure and the doctor will say the same thing. I bet.'

'OK.' She sits up and pours the tea, and then reaches behind her to grab the toast from the counter. So it *was* a mood swing. One day I'll get the hang of these things.

'It's going to be strange, isn't it?' she says as she butters her toast. 'I mean, no matter how much I've thought about it, and planned for it, it's all seemed a little bit like it's happening to someone else. But today, I'll see the baby. Today it will be really real.' We look at each other for a moment, both trying to imagine how her life will alter, how in some way all our lives will alter when the first one of us has a child. It's like trying to imagine the size of the universe. Both of us seem unable to quite grasp the reality of it.

'Well, better get going soon-ish, I guess,' Rosie says, shaking herself out of her reverie. 'I've got to have a shower and then I need to find something to wear that looks, you know, responsible, and then I thought, hair up or down? What do you think?' She now looks bright as a button.

'Down, you don't want any hairpins sticking in your head when you're lying on the trolley thing, do you?' I beam at her. 'Now, I'm going to get dressed because Selin will be here soon and you know she'll shout at us if we aren't ready.'

This is obviously a hint for Rosie to get dressed as Rosie is never ready on time, but it washes over her and I leave her spreading jam on her toast and staring contemplatively at the landlord's yellow print of two blue finches in a blossom tree that hangs above the table.

I've just finished blotting my lipstick when the doorbell chimes and without bothering to speak through the intercom I buzz the main door open and leave ours on the latch. Rosie is no longer in the kitchen. A quick investigation confirms that she is now in the shower.

'Rose, we'll have to go in about twenty minutes,' I call through the door.

'OK!' comes the breezy reply.

'Hello!' The deep sound of a man's voice makes me jump in shock a moment before I recognise it as Josh's. Selin's head appears over his shoulder and grins at me. I'm not surprised

176

that he has turned up. He seems to have been around all the time recently. The last time was a few days ago when he came round with two bottles of nice wine, both priced over six pounds (I checked the stickers). Rosie was out and he got stuck with me the whole evening. Give him his credit he didn't scurry off or make excuses, in fact we had a really nice time in the end, we got a bit tipsy and made up an entry for the next Song for Europe contest called 'Hoop-a-loo, I Love You (And World Peace)'. In the end I had to kick him out otherwise I would never have got up for work the next day.

Selin looks impatiently at her watch. 'Where's mum-to-be? Let me guess, in the shower?' she says and shouts through the bathroom door. 'Get a move on, bird!'

'OK!' comes the same cheery reply. The sound of the shower drums on.

'Do you want tea?'

Selin declines but Josh wants one so I lead them into the kitchen.

'This kitchen is a work of art,' he laughs. 'You should enter it for the Turner Prize as the ultimate antithesis to Tracy Emin.' For some reason his comment offends me and I pat a shiny worktop defensively.

'What are you doing here anyway?' I ask in a slightly more challenging tone than I meant.

'Oh well, I've got my car back from the garage and no work on today so I thought I might as well drive you. I mean, if you like.'

I look him up and down. 'Well, thanks,' I say ungraciously and pass him his tea. This nice-guy act is all very nice, but he could be going a tiny bit over the top.

The four of us waiting in the antenatal clinic together has elicited some raised eyebrows, and Josh thinks the other

177

mums-to-be think he must be some kind of love stud with three women on the go.

'You wish,' I say to him, and gratifyingly he blushes.

When the midwife eventually calls Rosie's name and we all stand she looks us up and down sternly. 'It's only a standard consulting room, you know, not a football stadium.' And then she bursts into sunny infectious laughter and we all smile nervously. 'Oh, go on then, you can all come if you want to, but usually it's only dad I let in. You dad?' She points at Josh who shakes his head guiltily.

'Oh, well then, what the hell,' she says cheerily. 'Support during pregnancy is very important to mummy and baby, no matter who gives it.' We file into her room and she tells us her name is Fehmi, and she's been a midwife for thirty years both here and in Africa, and she loves every one of her babies.

'I tell you what, we just *laugh* those babies out,' she tells Rosie and I see her tight face gradually begin to relax. After a series of questions that make Josh slightly uncomfortable she sends us up to the scan suite, where the waiting-room is quieter and almost empty except for a young couple sitting silently, hands entwined. We're lucky I guess that everyone is in a good mood. The scan technician laughs when we ask her if we can all come and says we're welcome if we keep quiet and don't knock anything over.

At first it looks like a satellite picture of stormy weather. Then you see a tiny pulsing beat in the centre and you realise that it is the baby's heart beating. After that the scan technician shows you its head and you can almost see a tiny profile, or maybe you're imagining it. And best of all, when Rosie coughs it wiggles up and down like a frantic little hard-house fan.

Rosie's hand reaches out to mine and, unable to take her eyes off the monitor, she whispers, 'Look, look, there's my baby.

Hello, baby.' The look of wonder on her face is reflected on each of our faces.

The scan lady tells us everything looks fine and we take the scan prints away with us. Rosie's check-up has been fine, the scan has been fine, everything about her was wonderfully normal. As we sit in the hospital café Rosie cries again, but this time she laughs as well.

'I'm really, really pregnant,' she says. 'I'm going to be a mum!'

Chapter Thirty

The usual foreign throng of Leicester Square mills thickly around me as I wait for Michael again. Under normal circumstances, the fact that I have waited for him twice in a row would be grating by now, after fifteen minutes surrounded by blonde pony-tailed exchange students called Heidi or something. What little natural light there was has started to surrender to the square's neon finery and the evening has grown chilly. I still haven't quite got the hang of the summer-to-autumn transitional wardrobe, my boots are pinching my toes and the so-called adaptable white shirt I refused to buy a size bigger than I think I am is gaping open over my bust because they only make clothes for flat-chested women, as if we are all mass-produced Kate Mosses.

However, these aren't normal circumstances because something happened today that has jangled me, something that might be nothing to worry about or might be, something that might not be my business at all but something that I know I won't be able to prevent myself from becoming involved in.

Things had gone fine after the scan, we were all in a good mood, and Josh took Selin back to work as arranged although he *did* try to offer us a lift into town.

'Don't be mental,' I'd said. 'We'll get a cab.' His new-found gentlemanly behaviour was getting on my nerves. Rosie had wanted to call Kaled but I persuaded her it wasn't really fair to make him come all the way across town when we could get a mini-cab over the road.

'But he'd love to see the scan photos!' she'd protested before eventually seeing sense.

Rosie gets pretty tired pretty quickly these days but a big street full of shops seems to revitalise her in a way that ten hours' sleep and a nice cup of decaff just can't manage.

We went from one maternity department to the next. We discovered items called sleep bras, maternity thongs and, most alarmingly, nipple pads and breast pumps. We went from floral frock to linen shift to wide-legged stretchy pants more times than I can remember and by the third set of denim dungaree shorts I could see Rosie was desperate for designer.

'Why doesn't Donna Karan make maternity wear?' she sighed, sinking on to an MDF platform sporting a foam rubber mum-to-be in M&S.

'Well, they might well do. We haven't even been to Selfridges yet,' I said brightly.

'It's all, well, it's all so *mumsy*,' she complained, 'Madonna never looks mumsy when she's preggers.' Her shell-pink glossed lip formed a pout. 'I need a drink and a big piece of cake.'

'I sort of think mumsy is the point,' I told her, and taking her by the hand I led her out of the store and off Oxford Street, walking silently past Browns and Karen Millen, carefully averting our eyes from a rose-pink flounced frock embroidered with silk and sequins.

If I was in a more frivolous mood I'd say there was something, a siren call or an inner compass that guided us towards our true North, but at any rate something altogether heavenly brought us to a boutique called Formes, Collection for Pregnant Women, Paris.

'*Paris*,' Rosie breathed and before I could say 'Eighty pounds for a T-shirt' I was installed on a stool sipping cappuccino as two sales assistants brought Rosie an array of clothes to make her heart sing. I'm the sort of girl who feels as if I'd be letting the sales ladies down if I didn't buy something after they had been so nice to me but Rosie was doing no one but herself a favour when after forty-five minutes and four hundred and twenty pounds she left the store flushed and triumphant, the proud possessor of no less than four waxed paper bags swinging from twisted cord handles.

'Now we really need a drink,' she said, and we headed for the nearest café giggling like two schoolgirls who had just come off a roller-coaster ride. Who says you need to be high up and going fast to get an adrenalin rush?

'Yeah, we do,' I agree, thinking about a large gin and tonic.

'Not you, you and me! We.' She pats her tummy. 'Me and my little baby in here. I wonder how long it will be before I feel it move. Remind me to look that up in the book when I get back.' I nod and smile. Now that she's had the scan and seen her baby the reality of her pregnancy seems to have lit her up from the inside.

So everything was fine until we went into the café.

I saw him first. Actually, I saw the woman first. If I'm completely honest I saw her legs stretched out across the aisle between two tables in a long shapely taunt, then I saw her immaculately tailored suit and the back of her head, a work of art in retro-eighties City greed, finished off with a little velvet bow. I took her in for a couple of moments and then sitting opposite her I saw Chris.

Rosie's-ex-husband-father-of-her-child Chris. His hair had grown a little too long around the collar, his square jaw had become weighed down by the early onset of jowls, and the eyes that Rosie had swooned over seemed to have retreated just a little behind droopy eyelids. But it was unmistakably him.

By this time Rosie had taken a seat by the window and I could see her peering into one of her bags, debating whether or not to break the seal on the tissue-bound parcel inside to re-examine her purchases, and I had a mini brown tray replete with two pieces of carrot cake, a *latte* and an orange juice for Rosie.

I couldn't get her out of there without her seeing him and we couldn't stay here without her seeing him. I had to tell her he was here. Stalling, I took the long way to our table and slid into the seat opposite her.

'Rosie, don't panic but . . .' Before I could finish the sentence his unmistakable voice boomed across the café and in two seconds he was at our table.

'Rosie!'

She looked up and her face blanched, she swallowed and smiled nervously and in that moment I could see, despite everything she'd said, that she was still not 'so over him'. Her eyes slid from his face and over his shoulder to the woman he had been sitting with and then back to him.

'Chris!' she said with brittle bravado. 'How nice to see you.'

He took a chair at our table and, just as I knew he would, he flipped it to face him and straddled it, folding his arms across the backrest.

'And you, sweetheart, and you. God, I haven't seen you since . . .' He clicked his fingers as if to jog a memory.

'Since the Vickers & Walmsley do,' Rosie finished for him. His memory caught and he threw back his head and laughed.

'Now *that* was a reunion.' He winked at her and to my horror she smiled coyly in reply and fluttered her lashes.

'How's Melanie?' I asked, maybe a little cruelly. Melanie was the 'love of his life'. The woman he had met shortly after Rosie and he were married. The woman he could not live without.

'Well, you know. It didn't work out,' he mumbled and he shifted a little in his seat and grinned sheepishly.

Seeing first hand that her life had been laid to waste for the sake of another empty affair, Rosie bristled.

'Well, we'd better be going,' she said, standing and beginning to gather up her bags.

Chris seemed keen to find a way to make her stay.

'Oh God, I can see you've been going shopping crazy again! How much money have you spent this time? The usual suspects, is it?' he patronised, but as he picked up one of the bags to examine it the grin froze on his face. 'Pregnant Women? Paris? Who's pregnant?'

Rosie sank back down into her chair.

'I am!' I said gamely, but Chris never took his eyes off her.

'I am,' Rosie said quietly.

'You're pregnant? How far? Whose?' A fleeting expression of shock quickly transformed itself into a still, proprietorial air combined with a hint of jealousy which ignited Rosie's temper.

'Yes, *me*. About fourteen weeks. Who's the father? Well, let me think, I last had sex in the bogs at a work do. Oh, I think it must be you.' Her green eyes sparkled with rage and the beginnings of tears. The knuckles on her hand bleached white as she clenched the edge of the table. Chris stood up, turned his chair back the right way and sat down.

'Are you sure it's mine?' he said quietly and without the arrogance I would have expected.

'Yes, I'm sure,' Rosie spat. 'Some of us don't fall in and out of love quite as easily as others. There hasn't been anyone else since you.'

To his credit he didn't argue but only sat staring at his hands. After a few moments he asked, 'Why didn't you tell me?' His voice was gentle and calm.

'Let me see . . . maybe I didn't think the man who ran out on his wife after only a few months of marriage would make the best father in the world?'

He rubbed his hand across his forehead and pinched his brows. 'Rosie, I've wanted to talk to you about that, to explain. I've been meaning to, and now this has happened . . . We have to talk now. No time to stall any more.'

During this exchange I obviously had more to say than the average fundamentalist on Hyde Park Corner but I managed to keep my mouth shut. Just.

'Look, we need to discuss this properly. Alone.' He looked pointedly at me.

'I'm not going anywhere,' I said staunchly. Rosie looked out of the window for a moment, took a couple of deep breaths to steady her temper and tears, and then turned back to look at me.

'Jen, he's right. Look, I'll be OK.'

I eyed her meaningfully but obviously not meaningfully enough for her to read 'Don't do this, he'll hurt you' in my eyes. Or if she read it she ignored it.

'Jen, I've been putting off the inevitable. We have to make some kind of arrangement. If only for the baby's sake.'

And yours, I thought. I suppose that in reality we had been kidding ourselves that Chris would never find out. Rosie wanted to wait to tell anyone at work until after she had the scan, but as soon as she did the bushfire would ignite and it would only be a matter of time before Chris heard about the baby and began to wonder.

Chris stood suddenly and went back to his table. After a short and heated whispered conversation with long-leg woman he returned and she slammed out of the café. There's always a silver lining.

'Come on.' He held out a hand to Rosie.

'Are you sure?' I said, looking at her.

'Yes. We have to do this,' she said and as I watched them leave my heart sank.

I finished my coffee and then her juice and phoned Selin at work.

She listened in silence as I told her what had happened.

'Bollocks,' she said.

'Yeah, exactly,' I replied.

'What shall we do?' She was just closing up at work and I could hear her pull the shutters down as she spoke. I pictured her with the phone tucked under her chin, the curly cord stretched to its limit as she moved around the office.

'Wait for her to come home, I suppose. I was supposed to meet Mi . . . a friend from work tonight to see a film but I guess I could cancel.' I thought of Michael already on the train from Twickenham and my heart sank a little further.

'No, don't do that. You shouldn't drop everything for one of Rosie's escapades. Look, I'll go over to yours after work. I've got the spare key. If she comes back before you I'll be there and if she doesn't we can worry about her together when you get home. OK?'

I smiled. 'OK, mate. Cheers.'

'No probs, sweetheart, I'll see you later.'

And so here I am now, having waited a grand total of twenty minutes for Michael's distinctive head to appear in the crowd, waiting to find a way to shake off the feeling of gloom.

Finally he appears by my side and grabs my shoulders as he kisses me firmly on the mouth. His lips are cold and dry.

'I can't tell you why I'm late, you'll chuck me for sure.' His confident laughter makes me smile straight away and the background annoyance of the last twenty minutes vanishes in a flash.

'Go on, you can tell me. I've had enough emotional conflict

for one day. I can't face the hassle of binning you yet. Maybe after the film.'

He flops his arm across my shoulders and his breath tickles the back of my neck as his lips brush my ear.

'Detention,' he whispers.

Chapter Thirty-one

The film Michael has picked would not have been my first choice. I had expected some kind of sci-fi extravaganza with billion-dollar special effects and maybe Keanu Reeves thrown in for good measure. Instead I'm watching a movie about two American teenage boys trying to have sex with as many American teenage girls as they can, teenage girls with improbably pert breasts that they don't seem to have any career quandaries over exposing at the drop of a pair of string panties. There seems to be a running joke involving sperm and at some point it looks as though teenage American Boy B is going to be tricked into having sex with a goat.

This was never really going to be my scene, but the subtle torture of knowing that Johnny Depp is showing one screen over, playing a fey Italian love-lorn poet, makes it all the more difficult to enjoy.

Michael's hand is resting on my thigh, his forefinger absently running along the seam of my jeans, back and forth, back and forth. He rests his chin in his other hand and at every punchline throws his head back with a deep husky laugh that makes me smile despite myself. Throughout my entire and, it's probably fair to say, extensive dating career I have never yet managed to spend a date necking in the back of a cinema. I suppose at the back of my mind I thought that this was going to be the day, but instead we have a centre aisle seat and Michael's hand on my thigh is the nearest thing to making out that I'm likely to get. To console myself I watch his profile out of the corner of my eye, the contours and shadows of his face flickering and altering with reflected Hollywood light.

The last few weeks with and without him have certainly been unusual, preoccupying I suppose. It seems that the higher his sun has risen in the sphere of my existence, the colder and darker the year has become and the further and more distant thoughts of Owen seem to be. This has become exactly the diversion, the distraction, that I was looking for – but now what?

A miscellaneous teenage American boy skids through a slimy patch of vomit that for some reason is strategically placed outside a teenage American girl-occupied shower cubicle and careers headlong into the steam. More breast-exposing antics ensue. Michael's mouth curls into an appreciative teenage English boy's leer and then, feeling my eyes on him, he turns to face me looking a little sheepish.

'What do you think of the film?' he whispers, taking his hand from my thigh and sliding it around my shoulders.

'Yeah, funny. You?' I whisper back, awarding him points for deliberately taking his eyes off the near-naked girl. His fingers slide inside the neck of my shirt and rest at the back of my neck.

'It's all right,' he says, leaning closer and looking at my mouth. 'I'm a bit bored with it now, it's basically just one joke anyway.' He closes the last few millimetres between our lips and to my horror and delight his free hand clamps itself over my left breast. Before I relax fully into my first-ever full-on cinema snog experience I check for people sitting behind us (the seats are empty) and wonder fleetingly if this sudden interest comes from feeling frisky because of the total of naked girls to date in the film. Deciding not to debate it, I sink a little further into my seat and stifle a giggle as Michael's hand slides up the inside of my shirt and his fingers find their way inside my bra with an almost imperceptible tear of lace.

The last thing I see before I close my eyes is American Teenage Boy B being tricked into having sex with a goat.

Twenty minutes of base-two smooching makes us a little befuddled and dazed when the lights go up at the end of the film. As we wander out of the double doors and take the escalators back down to street level we are quiet, our hair ruffled, our skin flushed and in my case a tiny smile of triumph on my lips. That's one more thing I wanted to do before I was thirty checked off the list. Now I've just got 'learning to drive' and 'being a jazz-club singer' and I've got six weeks to go. It's achievable. Oh, and that career thing. Well you can't win them all.

As soon as we're out in the cold air Michael pushes me up against a wall and kisses me deeply. I can feel how turned on he is. We pull apart and gaze at each other for a moment. Maybe like me he's thinking that perhaps we should always factor a bed into our meetings from now on.

'Time for ice-cream?' he asks and I nod and follow him to the Häagen-Dazs shop, our fingers finding each other's like old friends now. The queue isn't too bad and we are seated and served before too long. He holds my hand across the table, which if I weren't having such a good time would really piss me off as I only have one hand free to chase the last pecan nut around the dish with my spoon. But I like the feel of his fingers so I let it pass.

'You know it's my birthday tomorrow, Thursday,' he says slowly. I had forgotten the exact day of his birthday, if I ever knew it in fact, but I did know that it was soon. Here it comes, he is going to ask me to the party again and I'm going to have to find a way to turn him down this time. No more stalling.

'Yes, about that . . .' I begin.

'It's just that . . .' he interrupts.

'I've been meaning to say . . .' I continue.

'I don't think it's a good idea that you come.'

'I really don't think that it's a good idea for me to come.' We finish together. We laugh. We cough and are silent.

'I *want* you to come,' he says, still clasping my hand. 'It's just my mum will be there and now that I've told her you're Holly and every other single person there knows you aren't . . . it would be a bit risky, you know. And you'd hate it anyway, there would be no disco unless some DJ has sampled it in a loop for some bloke to rap over.'

A mixture of relief and chagrin folds in my stomach, the same old story. I don't want to go to his party, but I don't want him to not want me to go. I suppose that if I am determined to pursue this 'diversion' away from Owen I'm going to have to accept it as just that. For all the hand holding and cinema–related necking we've only seen each other a few times; he doesn't owe me anything special and vice versa.

'No, it's fine. I didn't really want to come anyway, to be honest,' I say, a little more bluntly than I had been planning.

'The party's on Friday and then I've got the whole weekend free. I thought we could meet up, do something?'

'Get a hotel room maybe?' I suggest mischievously. He blushes and I feel mean. Leaning across the table I take his face in my hands and kiss him softly. 'Yeah, we'll do something this weekend, something special for your birthday, OK?' That hotel–room thing might not be such a bad idea, I'll check my bank balance when I get in.

The waiter hovers, waiting for us to leave so that he can let some other unfortunate sweet-toothed queue member into the warmth, but I don't feel ready to go yet. I order another coffee.

'I went shopping with Rosic today,' I tell Michael, who shows his level of interest by an imperceptible rising of his brows.

'We bumped into her ex.'

'Exes. Bummer.' He nods, looking at me with a laid-back air in anticipation of a subject change.

'Ex-*husband*,' I stress, forgetting that he probably has a string of ex-girlfriends installed around Twickenham ready to ambush him at every turn, according to his mother at any rate.

'*Husband?* Way heavy.' He nods again, this time furrowing his brows with sincerity. He is making the effort, bless him.

'Well, anyway, he found out that Rosie is pregnant—'

'Rosie is pregnant! Bloody hell!' His shock makes me realise that we have talked about absolutely nothing every single time we have met.

'Yes, by him. Long story. Anyway, he found out about it and they've gone off to "discuss" it. And I'm a bit worried about her so I should be getting back after this coffee really. Just in case.' I down the lukewarm cappuccino, wave my debit card at the waiter and wait for the bill.

'Yeah, no worries,' Michael says. 'I've got to get back anyway. It's a school night!' He chuckles and I smile at him, glancing around for eavesdropping social workers or ChildLine volunteers at the same time.

'But surely it's good Rosie is talking to her ex, right? You know, him being the father of her baby and all. I mean, if they sort stuff out it's good for her, isn't it?' he asks.

'Well, with any other bloke maybe. But you don't know what a total *Rupert* Chris is.'

Michael shakes his head at me and as we leave the restaurant he pushes a fiver in my hand.

'For my ice-cream,' he says. It's a small gesture but it obviously means a lot to him to pay his way. I wonder if I should have given him my half of the cinema ticket money. That's probably a month's pocket money.

'What do you mean a Rupert?' he asks as we leave.

'Long story,' I say. 'But basically he walked out on her after a few weeks of marriage with a serious case of cold feet and a new girlfriend to boot. Now he suddenly wants to be back in her life, but for how long? Men have a habit of walking out on you when you're most vulnerable,' I say, thinking about Owen. If there is one thing I'm certain of it's that Chris can't be any better than Owen and if I've managed to break away from him then Rosie has to break away from Chris too, for good. It's almost as though we made a pact and if she breaks it I'm left out there all alone on a limb wondering about my own choices, maybe the only one who really fucked up big time, when I thought I had an ally. But it's *not* like that, Rosie and Chris together would be genuinely bad news.

'I won't walk out on you when you're vulnerable,' Michael says sweetly, taking my hand. 'But if Rosie and this Chris geezer still like each other enough to conceive a baby, well then maybe they still have feelings for each other. Maybe, you know, they might work things out, don't you reckon?'

'No,' I say and we drop the subject.

We walk up through Chinatown and the smell makes me wish I'd gone for the real-dinner option over the sweet swift high of confectionery. We stroll through Soho and past the Coaches, the allure of a double brandy almost tempting me in. Hand in hand we stroll through the chilly night up Charing Cross Road to the beginning of Tottenham Court Road, until we reach the bus stop for the number 73. As usual it is heavily populated with tourists, drunks, couples and commuters thronging on the roadside, jostling each other for pole position, anxious to make it on to the long overdue bus should it finally lurch around the corner.

'You don't have to wait with me, you've got a lot further to go home than me, and it is a school night, right?'

He smiles and stands behind me, wrapping his arms around

me and resting his chin on the top of my head. 'I'll wait,' he says mildly.

As it turns out it's not too long before the bus arrives, in fact three 73s arrive in convoy, so that I have time to kiss him once more before I run on to the last bus.

'What about the weekend?' he calls after me.

'I'll ring you when I've come up with something,' I shout over my shoulder. I swing into a seat nearest the pavement side and wave to him as the bus pulls out.

I turn on my phone but there are no messages. I phone home but Selin picks up and there is no sign of Rosie.

I sit back in my seat and watch the city slip away under the gloss of street lamps and moonlight, the warmth of Michael's kiss still tingling on my lips.

Chapter Thirty-two

As I let myself into the flat I can see Selin in the living-room at the end of the hallway, sitting on our blue sofa, her long legs tucked up under her chin, surfing channels.

'Any sign?' I call down the corridor but before she can reply Rosie appears out of the kitchen, mug of coffee in hand.

'I'm here! You can call off the search party!' She lifts her mug at me. 'Do you want one?'

'No thanks, I'll be up all night the amount of coffee I've had, and I thought you were cutting down too. Are you all right?' I reach out to touch her arm but she flounces away.

'It's not for me, it's for Selin. I don't need you to tell me how to look after my baby, thank you.' Selin silently takes the mug of coffee she was clearly not expecting and sends me a look of warning. Rosie flops back into the armchair, and breathes out through her mouth so that her fringe fans away from her forehead. She looks tired, shadows have bruised the underside of her fair skin and her usually perfect make-up has clearly been disrupted more than once by tears. I should probably leave it – if this was something to do with me I'd want them to leave it – but instead I ask, 'So how was it with Chris?'

'Fine,' Rosie replies curtly. Selin shakes her head at me but I figure that months and months of mutual-misery therapy entitle me to probe a little more.

'What do you mean fine? Did you sort something out about the baby? Money or something?'

'You know what, you two really get on my tits sometimes. I *am* capable of making some choices for myself, you know. I don't need you watching my every move. I mean, *you*,' she says, pointing at me. 'You don't even feel you can go out without having a minder waiting up for me. Do you think I'm going to top myself or something?' She flings the magazine she has been reading at the telly, toppling the latest casualty of our attempts to cultivate house plants to the floor.

I am used to her mood swings but it has been a long time since I've seen her temper flare up like this. Not since the last time she was with Chris, in fact.

'We just worry, Rose, that's all,' Selin says quietly. 'We were there, remember, when he hurt you? We can't help worrying, we love you. But you don't have to talk about it if you don't want to.' She gives me another look that tells me to keep my mouth shut or else.

'Sorry, mate,' I mumble insincerely. After all, it was my bed she climbed into three nights out of four in the aftermath of the affair. I didn't go through all that sleep deprivation for her to swan off and play happy families with the evil perpetrator of her misery at the drop of a hat. Rosie sighs and flings her head back to look at the ceiling.

'He thinks we should make a go of it,' she says flatly.

Rage and disbelief begin to hurtle towards my mouth as Selin's hand grips my wrist and her dark eyes hush me. I shut my mouth under protest.

'He says that the baby is more important than our little differences and that it deserves a proper family. He says that he's had time to think while we've been apart and that he's realised he has missed me. He said he'd been plucking up courage to get in touch since the night we ... well, you know.'

'Little differences! So, that bird in the café was helping him pluck up courage, was she?' I blurt out before Selin's tightening and painful grip quiets me.

'Look, I'm not a total moron, you know, I know what a wanker he is. Has been. But he's got a point about the baby. I mean, Jen, how many times have you told me how much your dad abandoning you hurt you, how much you've missed having a father figure? Well, it was the same for me. Maybe I haven't got the right to deny my baby the chance to have two parents. And anyway, he does seem . . . different, like he's changed. You didn't talk to him today. He made a lot of sense.' Rosie hugs a cushion under her chin and stares blankly at the TV.

I sit in silent fury; after nearly twenty years without a father it has never occurred to me that no father might be a better option than a bad father. I can't change my mind just like that, can I? Time and time again I've thought about how different my life would have been in a million small but important ways if my dad had only been around during my teenage years. If only I had had him to give me a lift to Hull on my first day of university instead of struggling scared and alone on the train with two rucksacks; if I had had him to change the plug on the lamp in my bedroom instead of having to ask my new flatmate's dad to do it. But I still think having had him for a while and then feeling his loss so acutely is worse, it must be worse than if I had never known him at all. If I'd never known him I wouldn't miss him, would I? And if Rosie gives her baby a dad who's likely to duck out at any given time, things will be just as bad for that child too, won't they?

'But you don't have to be with him to have him in your baby's life, do you?' Selin says. Good point, that is exactly what I was going to say.

'Don't I? You know as well as I do that my dad and Jen's never made the effort once they were gone.' I couldn't argue with her there. I think I had six or seven embarrassed weekend trips to Brent Cross every other Saturday, but then I decided I couldn't stand it any more and my dad didn't feel the need to coax me. Soon after that the calls stopped and then the birthday cards. Once when I was about eighteen I got back in touch and tried to re-establish some kind of relationship. It ended in a stand-up fight in a Chinese restaurant. He blamed me for not bothering to get in touch with him, for letting us drift apart. 'But you're the dad,' I had said. 'You were the adult. You left me.'

The problem is that as far as I can see Chris and my dad have a lot in common. They are exactly the same kind of man. At some inevitable point Chris will be saying the same goodbye to Rosie again and this time to her baby too. Maybe it would be better for neither of them to ever have to face that pain.

'So what are you going to do?' I ask belligerently.

'Well, he wants me to think about it. He's asked me to go down to his cottage in Oxfordshire for the weekend. I'll be *alone*,' she says, silencing the protests before they begin. 'He'll still be in London. He just thought I might like the space and the fresh air, and I would. I'm going Saturday morning.' She twists in the chair to look at us, resting her face on the arm.

'No lectures, girls, OK? Not until I've sorted this out?'

'No lectures,' Selin says and I press my lips together in silent mutiny, managing to refrain from exchanging tortured glances with Selin. Maybe nothing I can say to Rosie is going to make a difference to what she decides. But I haven't given up yet.

'Cheers, oh and by the way I got you these.' She chucks two Miniature Heroes Mars sweets at us and turns back to the TV. 'I ate the rest.'

After Rosie goes to bed, overtaken by that weary kind of calm that washes up after a day of heightened emotion, Selin and I sit together on the sofa for a little while longer listening to her move around the bathroom, pour a glass of water in the kitchen and then retreat into her room. We idly watch the TV for a few minutes more until we hear her light switch click off.

'What do you think?' I say immediately, in an unnecessary stage whisper that causes Selin to raise her famous eyebrow at me with disdain.

'I think she shouldn't get too stressed out and if Chris is stressing her out we shouldn't add to it with lectures she won't listen to and opinions she won't take any notice of. She'll come to the right decision eventually. I expect. Don't forget what the midwife said about support, she needs our support.' She leans a little closer to me and I notice she is wearing a heart-shaped locket around her neck with an engraving of her initials. Another present from her doting dad, I expect.

'Nice,' I say, nodding my head at her neck, and her hand closes instantly around the locket.

'Um thanks, present,' she says quickly. 'How did he seem to you? Chris? Did he seem like he had changed at all?' I note her obvious embarrassment and think how sweet it is that she should be worried about upsetting me. She knows how much I wish I had a dad like hers. My thoughts turn back to Chris.

'Well, he's got a bit jowly. But apart from that he did seem really affected by the news. I don't know, the bloke's a serial romanticist.' I have no idea if that is a real expression but I did humanities at college and Selin did maths, so I can pretty much say what words I like and she'll go for it. She could do the same to me with the square root of anything and probably does.

'What I mean is,' I continue, 'he falls in love with one woman after another at the drop of a pair of knickers and every time she's *the* one! He's in love with being in love. Maybe he could fall for the idea of fatherhood in the same way.'

Selin leans back and examines her shell-pink nails. 'It must be different with your own kid, though, surely?'

'You'd be surprised,' I say. 'So, you and me this weekend,

kid? Friday we've got disco with Jackson and then Rosie's off to the country. What do you fancy doing?'

'Um, actually darling, I meant to say. I won't be able to make it out Friday. I've got this thing on.' Selin has this habit of pulling one side of her mouth right down when she is feeling sheepish, it makes her look like a rather charming frog.

'Thing? On? What sort of thing?' I ask. Selin never has things on unless they are things with us.

'Family party – you know the drill.' She rolls her eyes and does her frog face.

'Oh, *that* kind of thing. Fair enough. Someone getting engaged, are they?' When you live round our way there is a Turkish wedding every Saturday, it seems, and more often than not Selin is related to or acquainted with either the bride or groom. But even before the ribbon-decked cars process up and down Green Lanes and the misty-eyed bridal portraits appear in the local photo studios, there is an equally big and impressive engagement party. I have been to a couple with Selin before; they are always top entertainment.

'Yeah, something like that. You could come, but well, I suppose you don't want to let Jackson down, do you?' she asks mildly. I'm sure she thinks I fancy him.

'Well, never mind. What about the rest of the weekend?' I ask, half hoping she won't be around to find out what I'm up to.

'No can do, sweet cakes. Families, huh?'

'Oh, OK. I'll just be a Ken-no-mates on my own then,' I say, feeling two seconds of sorrow.

'Sorry, love,' she says, patting my arm, but of course before she finished uttering the words, in my mind's eye I'd got Michael in my bed all weekend long and for a whole night too.

Things couldn't have worked out better.

Chapter Thirty-three

As ever, Friday morning is easier to wake up to with the sure and certain knowledge that I and the rest of my colleagues will spend the working day getting ready for it to be 5.30 and for the weekend to begin.

Carla will make her lunchtime trip to Miss Selfridge and after coming back to her desk twenty minutes late she will tantalise the boys with glimpses of her latest clubbing-bikini-masquerading-as-a-dress acquisition. If the rest of this week has been anything to go by she'll then throw herself at Jackson for a good fifteen minutes before his good manners cave in and he scuttles off to the coffee machine, preferring even work-machine coffee to her dreadful skinny-legged preening.

Either Kevin or Brian will ask Carla out and she will turn either Brian or Kevin down, depending on whose turn it is. Carla will spend the rest of the afternoon discussing her hairdo on the phone with a mate called Kelly or Trisha and the boys will end up in the pub next door from 5.45 until closing time, nudging each other every time a likely-looking girl goes past and never once plucking up the courage to talk to her. Eventually some poor cab driver will lose that night's lottery and take them back to wherever it is they live in zone four and consider himself damn lucky if there is no vomit to clean up. They will stumble up the stairs in their respective parental homes, desperately hoping not to wake mum and dad up but looking forward to mum's greasy fry-up in the morning. If their mums are lucky neither one of them will have poohed in the bath by mistake this time like Kevin did last New Year.

Georgie will leave half an hour early if she's not working from home, which she rather tends to do on a Friday. This Friday specifically, Jackson and I will get changed in the loos (separately, of course), have a couple in the pub next door (gaze with smug pity at Kevin and Brian for a while) and then meet Rosie for a couple of Sea Breezes and Cosmopolitans before hitting a club. And then, of course, I have the rest of the weekend to spend with my nubile and athletic lover during which we can work on improving his performance time, and I don't mean speeding him up.

Ha, Carla, you practically pre-teen minx, I beat you this week.

'I've asked Carla, Kev and Bri to join us tonight. I hope you don't mind?' is the first thing that Jackson says as he sets a tall *latte* from the deli down the road on my desk. As predicted, Georgie has left me a message to tell me she is working from home and Jackson has discarded his tie, exposing an intriguing length of tanned bare neck. I'm sick as a pig.

'Mind? No! How nice, a work outing.' Bollocks bastard bollocks. I think about my glittery halter-neck languishing in my kitbag, which will surely look prim and dowdy compared to whatever scrap of shimmery something Carla will shoehorn over her non-existent behind. Jackson settles himself in my visitor chair and pops the lid off his own coffee.

'I mean, they aren't exactly my cup of tea, as you English say, but Carla asked herself and I thought at least if I asked the guys we could lose them later if it got too dire.' Or he asked them so he could lose me if I got too dire.

'Sure, no problemo.' I smile at him and sip my *latte* and make small talk until he departs. Bollocks bastard bollocks.

I phone Rosie to moan but she's out on a client lunch, and yes, it isn't quite 10.00 a.m. yet. I phone Selin to moan but rather surprisingly she has the day off to go shopping. Selin *never* has time off. I must remember to ask her about it.

With all moaning avenues firmly blocked I reluctantly open a spreadsheet for cover and spend the morning surfing the internet for cheap flights that I will never take whilst picking up calls about every two minutes. The fax hasn't called me for a while and when I got the switchboard to look into it they said it was probably a fault in my set and gave me a new one. It must have just been echoes on the line that I thought I heard on the other end, or myself breathing into my own headset.

The day passes slowly and when the tinny bell sounds on my PC to let me know I have an e-mail I pray it's not from Lizette chasing all the invoices I haven't signed off in three months, but from one of the girls or maybe even Jackson. Just something that is going to give me five minutes of relief from sodding area-sales figures.

When I check, I see it's one of those anonymous greetings you can send from some sites. I open it up and there's a link through to a website where a card waits for me to pick it up. I smile to myself, thinking of Michael, and I double click on the link. While I wait for it to open, the egg-timer turns somersaults on my screen and I tap a finger against my keyboard.

Eventually it opens on to a big red love heart pulsating and releasing other tiny little hearts floating into my screen until they seem to bounce off the edges of the monitor. A musak version of 'Heaven Must be Missing an Angel' rattles out of my rubbish speaker and as I watch a message floats out of the heart in big fat bubble lettters. 'I'm watching you,' it reads before each letter swells and then bursts. The animation begins again.

I'm puzzled. It's not exactly high romance, in fact it's a bit spooky. I glance up across the office to where Jackson is sitting and he catches my eye, winks and smiles at me. Ha-ah! So not Michael at all, Jackson in fact. Well, that certainly is an intriguing development and does rather make the prospect of this evening slightly more bearable. Of course he could just have meant it as a friendly prank without any connotations but in my experience a boy never does anything remotely out of the ordinary without any connotations.

In the taxi Carla talks about her hair, her bare-look stockinged legs seeming to take up most of the cab. I cross my denim-encased legs demurely at the ankle and admire my impulse-buy boots. Fully aware that after any period of sustained foot action lasting over ten minutes I will be a virtual cripple, I love them nevertheless. They are sophisticated, cool, sexy and hip. Carla's silver platforms, that are even now making predatory contact with Jackson's loafers, are showy and cheap. Shoes, like dogs, say a lot about their owners, and that's all I'm saying. Jackson's eyebrow-raising, aimed at me from across the cab, reminds me of the unspoken secret of the e-mail card and instigates a tiny uncurling of my smile.

As a proper adult I really shouldn't be so peeved by Carla's invasion into my night out. I really shouldn't be so jealous of her just because she is younger than me and skinny and clearly isn't wearing a bra under her dress. I should be confident in my maturity, confident that the allure of the breadth of my experience makes my blue eyes much more interesting to gaze into, and not just because of the first faint tracings of fascinating laughter lines that I have begun to notice recently. In fact, I *am* perfectly happy to be my age in the presence of such a naïve and shallow young slip of a girl, with nothing to talk about apart from herself and her leg-waxing regime. I am *not* remotely intimidated by her.

The stuck-up anorexic bimbo cow.

We're meeting Rosie in Langley's off Covent Garden, in time for the cocktails happy hour. It's one of my favourite places to go, not only because about six or seven months ago it was the place to be (I think it was anyway, I first came here during the summer) but because I love the metallic, retro feel of the place.

I have got an unformed idea that Jackson, three or four cut-price Cosmos and I might go down pretty darn well on the dance floor later on in a *Saturday Night Fever* kind of way. I wouldn't want to brag about my disco-dancing prowess but I reckon people must think I'm pretty good, they certainly always stare at me when I'm shaking my stuff to 'Yes Sir, I Can Boogie'.

Rosie is late, and so I offer to order Jackson and me our first drinks at the bar and leave Kevin and Brian to fight over who gets to buy Carla a drink. As Jackson and I break away from them I feel Carla's hungry little eyes follow us through the crowd. *Nul point*, Carla love.

The bar is crowded, about four or so people deep thronged in a dense mix of suited salesmen, Red-or-Dead-and Diesel-clad media girls and those who would have been models if only fate had made them taller, thinner and better looking, but who gamely sport the 'fuck you' pout anyhow.

The secret weapon that I have over pretty much all of these people is that even though some of them have been queuing for nearly ten minutes, I will almost certainly get served before they do. How? It's simple. I squirm my way towards the edge of the bar, disarming normally competitive men by activating weapon 'cleavage stun' and negotiating feisty girls with a well-placed rib-bound elbow. When the target site is taken I stand on the foot rail that runs along the bottom of the bar with both feet and lean as far over it as I possibly can, exposing at least three inches of cleavage. Unless I'm very unlucky and the bar is entirely worked by mean-minded women or gay men I will be served straight away. Tonight is no exception. One guy, temporarily wrenched out of my thrall, mutters, 'Bloody typical,' under his breath but I've started a tab, left my card behind the bar and made my way back to our much-coveted table before he'll even make it back to the bar's edge.

It's not fair, I know. It's exploitation and it's probably dreadfully politically incorrect, but at some point during the history of the world evolution decided to turn men into blithering idiots at the sight of a partially exposed mammary and I feel it's only my duty to make the most of it.

'Neat trick,' Jackson whispers in my ear as we negotiate our way back through the rows.

'Just lucky, I guess,' I throw back over my shoulder with a three-cornered grin, but I feel a secret rush of pleasure that he is certainly not blind to my charms.

When we reach the table Carla is alone, having despatched her minions to a long and thankless campaign at the bar. I take my straw in my mouth with my tongue and smile at her before I take a long suck. Jackson shifts his chair a little closer to mine so that we can talk and I suck a little bit harder on the straw, sinking slightly in my chair so that we are shoulder to shoulder, heads tipped towards one another.

After this drink, or maybe the next one, I'll work out exactly what my intentions are regarding Jackson. Michael is somewhere, right now, in some hired-out scout hut in Twickenham drinking cider and black with a gaggle of school-girls and somehow his constant presence in my mind and his impending visit tomorrow seem suddenly very far away. I briefly recall an eighteenth I went to all those years ago and the vivid recollection causes me to push the now faint thought of Michael and his party even further into the distance. My glass is half-empty in what seems like seconds.

As Jackson comes back from the bar with another round we both smile in delight: whoever is in charge of the music has put on 'D.I.S.C.O.'. It makes the metal table hum and I find myself tapping my foot and singing the words to myself as the mixture of vodka and brandy hits the back of my throat and my brain moments apart. The tensions of the day begin to fade and I get that sudden rush of star-crossed sensation again as the beginning of an evening full of promise and possibilities begins to unfold. Something is going to happen tonight.

It's too loud to talk normally and so Jackson leans his lips closer to mine and tells me about his apartment in New York and his dog, Trooper, who still lives on his parents' ranch in Texas. I get in another couple of drinks and as he reminisces he tips his head back a little and casts his bright blue eyes at the ceiling as if watching a distant movie. As I watch him talk I wonder if, just maybe, something's going on here and if it is, what I'll do about it. I mean, the whole e-mail thing. It must have been from Jackson, who else is there? And he is really cute, although it's not that I've just forgotten Michael, well, not exactly. A brief fling with a colleague from overseas, I can't think of anything more stupid or insane to get involved in, but then again . . . ?

And then this happens.

Imagine that you are an Elizabethan playwright. You've had this idea knocking around the back of your head for a while about a couple of Italian teenagers who fall in love, but after a nice bit of poetry and a couple of exciting fight scenes they end up tragically dead. And then one day, as you take your morning constitutional before you finally settle down to commit it to parchment, you come across a poster for *Romeo and Juliet* and you think, 'Oh well, there's no point then. Shakespeare's gone and created a masterpiece *again.*' Or, let's say, you're a composer in the eighteenth-century Austrian court and you've spent the last ten years working really hard on a piece of music that's going to finally make your name with the Emperor. Just as you think you've cracked it, some seventeen-year-old kid called Mozart goes and knocks the Emperor's socks off with a full-scale symphony and well, you might as well just go home now and hock your harpsichord.

Can't quite see where I'm coming from? OK, let's say you've sort of had your eye on this bloke, you're not sure really, but you think he likes you and you wouldn't mind seeing if there's a snog on offer later even if you decide not to take it. You've think you've just about vanquished the skinny youngster in the non-existent dress when, suitably late, your film-star-beautiful pregnant best friend makes an entrance Grace Kelly couldn't have pulled off. In about three seconds you lose his sexual attention for ever and get relegated right back down to the role of his girl mate, her less beautiful friend.

Basically it's the same principle.

Now don't get me wrong. I'm not pissed off or upset or jealous. That would be like getting annoyed because the sun rises or sulking because the tides came in *again.* Rosie in full sail, happy, glowing and untroubled, is like the brightest star in the sky; all eyes are drawn to her and judging by the way his jaw dropped, swiftly found its place again and then supported his most winning smile, Jackson is no exception. She must have secured that client she had the four-hour lunch with because she looks radiant, as if she has managed to push all her Chris-related dilemmas firmly to the back of her mind. If there is one person I know who's better at denial than I am, it's Rosie.

We've laughed about this kind of thing over the years, Selin and I. It's not that Rosie has had more boyfriends than us, or more opportunity. It's not that she has ever pinched anyone we've fancied. (Well, she did snog Josh back when I had a crush on him, which pissed me off for a week, but that was only because I had pretended I didn't have a crush on him any more when I did. I slapped her face and we had a laugh about it and then we snubbed him. I don't think he noticed, he was too busy avoiding us.)

Plenty of men have been beguiled by Selin's exotic long-legged grace and flashing dark eyes and been blind to Rosie or me. And I've had my fair share of devotion from many a man who goes for curves and curls over the china-doll look. But despite all that, while Selin and I can happily consider ourselves attractive, pretty, charming, sexy or gorgeous depending on the year, the outfit and/or the time of the month, Rosie is properly beautiful pretty much all of the time and Jackson is clearly enchanted.

Rosie leans over to kiss me and envelopes me in Allure by Chanel. I've been hoping that she's going to give me her half-full bottle but apparently it's a timeless classic and I'll have to buy my own. I take my bag off the seat I've been saving her and she slides into it.

'Hi, darling. God, what a fantastic day, I've landed the most incredible deal. Christmas bonus, here I come!' She eases off her tailored black leather jacket and smiles at Jackson, seeing him for the first time.

'Well done you,' I smile. 'Jackson, this is my flatmate Rosie. Rosie, Jackson who is on a short visit from New York.' Jackson leans across me to take Rosie's hand but luckily for good taste and decency he does not kiss it.

'Hey,' he says, not taking his eyes from her.

'Hello,' she says in her poshest Lady Di voice. Funny how he always gets that response, even Carla picked up an 'h' for him. As they regard each other for a moment longer than is strictly necessary, I look at over at Carla and for the first time ever we exchange a 'Oh well, win some lose some' glance and a wry smile.

'How are you feeling?' I ask Rosie. She is wearing a top and some trousers we bought in Formes. The top is orange and red silk and billows out over her tummy before it tapers to a 1920-style tie that fits snugly around her still-slim hips.

'Pretty good actually, might not make it to the club though.'

'That's a shame,' Jackson smoulders at her.

'Yeah, well, I'm pregnant, so you know I have to take it easy.' Absolutely nothing changes in the expression on Jackson's face but in some abstract way all of his features fall.

'Oh, you've left dad at home then?' he asks.

'Nope, the father and I are divorced.' I watch this exchange with fascination. I had fully expected Rosie not to mention the pregnancy thing at all in preparation for an evening's flirtation. Never before have I seen her bring up her divorce in the first few seconds of meeting someone. She usually waits for date three or four. Even more intriguing is that news of Rosie's divorced status cheers Jackson up just as imperceptibly but equally as clearly as his disappointment had shown in his handsome face. So it's not the baby that puts him off. Does that mean he's a genuinely nice guy or a cad? Does that mean the e-mail card was a cheap trick or a friendly gesture with no overtones? When he offers to go back to the bar to get Rosie a vodka-free Sea Breeze and another couple of Cosmos I turn to Rosie and say, 'You appalling slut.'

She laughs and tips her head back, smiling like a cat after a couple of pints of cream. 'You fancy him, don't you?' she asks sweetly.

'Well, *ye-heah*! Look at him. But not in a getting-off-with-him way.' Well, only in a pretend-TV-crush way.

'He is rather scrummy, isn't he?' Rosie licks her lips. 'Mmmm,

American Eighties Fox Man.' And henceforth, thus shall he be known in the kingdom of Rosie.

'Aren't there rules about pulling when you're preggers?' I tease her.

'I don't know, maybe there's a section on it in that scary book. Let's get it out from under the doorstop when we get home.'

Slipping into good-friend mode, I say, 'Look, he goes back to New York soon, so just watch yourself OK? Don't get hurt. You've got enough on your plate at the moment. What with crying when the Crunchy Nut Corn Flakes run out and all,' I say, glossing over the Chris situation. But she knows what I mean. We both watch Jackson return with three tall glasses, turning his fair share of heads on the way.

'Do you know what?' she says softly into my ear. 'I've got a feeling that Jackson and I will get on just fine.'

At about ten Rosie announces that she's ready to go home and Jackson offers to walk her to a cab. As I wait for him to return I look around for the others. Carla is nowhere to be seen and Kevin and Brian are now standing furtively near a group of girls who are determined to remain oblivious to them despite their stage-managed bursts of laughter, gung-ho shoves and reckless drinking. Poor Mrs Kevin and Mrs Brian; I can hardly bear to imagine the state of their bathrooms later.

Cosmo-fuelled rhythm keeps my foot tapping to some ungodly garage track with some squeaky bird repeating the same phrase over and over again. Her enunciation isn't great and I might be a tiny bit tipsy but I'm fairly certain she keeps hollering, 'Take me up the arse!' That's the trouble with the music of today, no tunes, no proper instruments and you can't hear the lyrics. I wonder if there is some kind of exorcism I can have done to rid me of the spirit of Auntie Marge for good? Or maybe it's worse than that. Maybe I am *becoming* Auntie Marge. God help me.

The responsibility of keeping our four-seater table unoccupied by strangers falls heavily on my shoulders and I try my best to look as sulky and as threatening as possible. Some young kid from the Kevin and Brian school of flirtestry winks at me from a few feet away. I glower at him.

Like a kickback from a tequila slammer, the pain of missing Michael suddenly crashes into my head. He is somewhere with his friends right now pogo dancing as if he invented it to a band called Soggy Wafer or something. Or worse still, Sarah has washed her hair for once and she's fluttering her eyelashes at him from behind a can of Top Deck. After all, he's offloaded his virgin thing, hasn't he? He probably wants to go after scalps of his own now, not spend his time on a tired old has-been like me. Even at this very moment the inexorable wheel of fate could be spinning an empty bottle of Thunderbird slowly towards him, marking him out as the next person to full-on snog Holly, the girl who is good at improvisation.

I close my eyes and feel the world shift a little underneath me. I might possibly have had one cocktail too many. The only problem with drinking spirits sitting down is that you can never be sure if it's safe to stand up again. I open one eye to look at the table. It seems to be fairly static, if a little blurred. I count the number of tall empty glasses on the table, divide them by three and wince. There should be a law against making alcohol taste like Ribena. Not only am I suddenly far too pissed to go dancing, I'm also jealously obsessing about a fling, a meaningless thing. A rebound affair, another one; God knows I've had enough practice. He's not supposed to mess with my head like this.

Missing Michael so badly now, alone and, let's face it, drunk in a busy bar is like fancying a Mars Bar when spending a weekend at a fat farm. You always want most exactly what you can't have. (Although personally I have to say I pretty much feel that way about Mars Bars wherever I am).

I concentrate on his sweetness at our last meeting, his long and ardent kisses in the cinema and his excited and happy tone on the phone when I invited him over tomorrow morning.

Christ, he's coming over tomorrow morning! Look at me, I'm ratted. If I go home *now* and take two paracetamol, drink two pints of water and remember to take my mascara off I might just scrape a pass when I see him. Any other course of action is personal suicide.

Jackson returns to the table, after a suspiciously long time finding Rosie a cab, and the faint whiff of Allure lingers about his person.

'Come on then, dancing queen, let's boogie,' he says, holding his hand out to me.

That strange little drunk-goldfish-short-term-memory thing kicks in and for a nano second I forget he's come down the stairs and is standing in front of me. I see him as if for the first time and remember again that he's been there for the last ten seconds just after I blurt out, 'Jackson! Thank God you're here, take me to a cab, I can't walk.' Which my time-lagged memory immediately follows up with, 'Hi, Jackson, do you know? I think I'll go home. Bit squiffy.' Even talking slowly so that I can double-check that I'm not accidentally saying, 'Please take me home and fuck me,' it seems that I am slurring.

'Oh, baby,' Jackson laughs and helps me to my feet. My heels give way like Bambi legs beneath me. We try again and slowly totter towards the Everest of stairs that leads to the exit. When we finally make it outside I stand for a moment under the false illusion that several deep gulps of pollution will make me feel better.

'Are you going to blow chunks, honey?' Jackson says, holding my forehead. I'm dimly, ever so slightly aware, in the last tiny bastion of my brain that remains unassaulted by Ribena's evil twin, that I shall be so seriously mortified by this moment next time I see him that I'll go pink and stutter. Please God, let me forget it and let him be kind enough to laugh about it behind my back.

'No, no,' I say, standing more or less upright. 'I'm fine, really I am.' I lift my chin and totter to the pavement's edge.

'Taxi!' I yell to a cab-empty street. 'Where are you, you bastard?'

Luckily for me, Jackson can hold his drink and it is only through his careful marshalling that any driver worth his salt would let me in the back of his cab.

It is Jackson who makes sure that I don't get into any passing Mondeo and holds out for a licensed cab. It's Jackson who bundles me on to the back seat and interprets my garbled address for the driver. Jackson hands the driver a tenner and a fiver and asks him to make sure I get through the door. The driver swears and Jackson gives him another fiver. All this I am watching as if from a distant universe, or from the other side of one of Jackson's misty-eyed recollections as he recounts this tale to Rosie next time they see each other. Must not forget to quiz Rosie about this later.

For a while, slumped low in the seat, I watch the orange blossom of the street lights slide by and then the intermittent blinking of the red door light and then, well, I'll just close my eyes for five minutes.

Chapter Thirty-four

'Jenny? Jen love? Jen?'

The evidence of my head turning inside out, my eyes stuck together by industrial tar and the transplant of the Arizona desert into my mouth tells me that I did not complete any of the three steps that I usually recommend to avoid feeling like an early-bird member of the living dead after a night out. Slowly I sit up. The bed creaks like a coffin lid.

I focus on Rosie, who is biting back a smirk and holding a cup of coffee tantalisingly just out of my reach.

'Bleah fime if id?' I try to say before I realise someone has Superglued my tongue to my mouth during the night. I reach for a glass of the night before last's water and down it. Rosie sits on my bed, unable to prevent a snort of derision escaping from her nose.

'You were in a *right* state last night.'

'Me? Was I? Weren't you in bed?' I say, gradually gaining control of my vocal chords. 'Give me that sodding coffee, will you.'

She hands it to me and flops back on my bed with a blatant disregard for my personal safety considering that I'm holding hot coffee and my hand-to-eye coordination isn't quite in conjunction yet. I retreat as far back from her as possible, huddling against the security of the headboard, and resent her fresh-faced dewy-eyed unhungover look. You tell me: just what are the just deserts for irresponsible sex resulting in unplanned pregnancy? Because if it's a gaggle of foxy men hanging on my every word, and never feeling shit due to alcohol poisoning again, then line me up for some. I'm going for it.

'I wasn't in bed. You arrived about ten minutes after I got in. It wasn't even eleven! You couldn't get your key in the door and you couldn't remember the number of our flat so you buzzed everyone until you got me and then I thought you were taking a rather long time getting up the stairs and when I looked, it was because you were crawling. Unfortunately for you, two of our neighbours had a good look too. Anyway, when you did get in you gave me permission to marry Jackson, told me Chris was a Rupert and passed out pretty much as you find yourself now. I took your jeans and top off in the interests of personal hygiene.'

I peek under the covers and see I'm still in my underwear down to my socks. I hate it when Rosie is the grown-up one. She just milks it so much.

'So have you woken me up this early to fit in all the smugness you can before you go?'

Rosie laughs, quite unnecessarily loudly, in my view.

'No, darling, because your mobile's been going every five minutes for the last half hour and you've had about ninety text messages. I was going to read them but then I thought it was probably nicer to bring you the phone and then sit over you while you read them yourself. Have you got a secret boyfriend, lady?'

'Chance'd be a fine thing,' I mumble, genuinely grumpy enough to be able to get away with bad acting. Looking at my phone I can see that, sure enough, it does show twelve text messages waiting for me. I guess that half of them are from my messaging service telling me I have a phone message.

I open the first one. It's not from Michael's usual number, but it must be from him. 'I'll see you soon,' is all it says, spelt out in full with none of that funky text abbreviation the kids are all so fluent in these days. Michael must have taken pity on my total inability to suss it. Either that or he's trying to impress me with his ability to spell. I dial my messages and Michael's voice crackles into my ear.

'Hi, it's me. It's nine thirty and I'm just on the way to the station. I think I'll be at yours around eleven, OK? Call me if the coast isn't clear. I missed you last night. Anyway, bye!' I catch myself smiling soppily and Rosie studies me intently. I decide not to pick up the rest of the messages as I'm pretty sure they are just a chain reaction caused by my diligent little phone trying to tell me someone was calling. I switch it off.

'What's the time?' I ask again, but this time with words.

'Coming up to ten. Why, have you got to be somewhere?' She thinks that just because I murdered half my brain cells last night she'll be able to catch me out.

'No, but you've got a train to catch, haven't you?'

'No, smarty-pants. Josh offered to take me. He said the last thing I needed was a stressful train journey on top of everything else. He really is a lovely bloke, you know.' She stresses the last sentence as if I haven't known Josh for just as long as she has and aren't perfectly aware of how nice he is. Good old Josh, so nice and helpful for no reason at all, oh no, just because he's nice. I'm peeved.

'Josh! Ha! He might be nice but no one is *that* nice for no reason. Haven't you worked out his ulterior motive yet? Haven't you wondered why he's suddenly always round here, doing stuff?'

Rosie nearly falls off the bed in hysterics.

'Of course I have, have *you*?' she laughs incredulously. I

think she's being a tiny bit harsh on him; his crush on her isn't a laughing matter.

I'm about to tell her off but then the doorbell chimes and I put down the coffee and dive under the duvet.

'I'll talk to you about this when I get back,' Rosie says sternly for no good reason. After a couple of moments I hear Josh's deep tones in the hallway accepting Rosie's offer of a quick coffee before they go. I've got to get up and face them. For starters, I've got to begin getting my face sorted out – I've only got an hour – and secondly, I have to make sure they leave here pretty quickly, I don't want anything to go wrong. I reach under the bed and pull out my pyjamas, use a baby wipe to take off most of my make-up and drag a brush through about as much hair as my pain barrier can bear. I shuffle into the kitchen. Josh has had his head shaved again, it makes his head seem strangely appealing. I resist the urge to touch it and sit next to him at the table.

'Good night?' he asks with that wry little smile he has.

'Mmmm. After a fashion. You? Did you go to the family do, or did you manage to escape?'

He suddenly looks about as guilty as a man can get.

'Um yeah, I went,' he says.

'Ha! You snogged someone, didn't you?' I can't resist taunting him in front of Rosie, who obviously thinks she's got him wrapped around her little finger, but at the same moment I find am horrified by his infidelity. Josh! Our Josh snogging women left, right and centre when he's supposed to have a crush on Rosie. It's very uncharacteristic.

'Me? No! I . . . well, I did go. That's all.' His dark complexion has taken on a rosy tint and I settle back in triumph. I try to pin down why I feel so pissed off at him; after all, I've already decided that he and Rosie wouldn't work out, but that doesn't mean I think he should keep his options open in the mean time.

Josh isn't meant to snog other girls. He is meant to be Josh, the bloke in my life who doesn't snog other girls. He's supposed to be neutral, damn him. Either that or my befuddled brain has lost all ability to work cognitively. I like the sound of that option, I'll go with that.

Rosie shakes her head at me from over his shoulder. She really is excelling at smug soberness this morning.

'Right, I'm off to get my bag. Are you ready, Josh? It really is nice of you to give me a lift. You really are a nice man.' She looks pointedly at me again and Josh shrugs a bit and looks self-consciously at his coffee.

'I like your pyjamas,' he says into the silence. I stir my coffee. For some hangover/hormone-related reason, I'm sulking.

'Do you still want to come to my exhibition when it opens? Not so long to go now – I'm getting a bit nervous about being ready in time. I reckon it'll be good.'

'Yeah, probably,' I mumble.

'I didn't snog anyone, you know.' He seems to feel that he needs to make his point, and something in his tone makes me believe him.

'Josh, you big lug, I don't care if you did!' My sulk evaporates as quickly as it came and I cave in to the urge to stroke his head across the table as the weight of my hangover lifts momentarily. We smile at each other stupidly for a second before Rosie appears in the doorway.

'Right, come on.' Josh sets down his cup and takes her bag from her.

'Will you be all right?' I ask her, remembering to be a good friend for five minutes.

'What, you mean in a luxury six bedroomed "cottage" with a fridge full of gourmet food and satellite telly? I reckon.'

'Well, call me if you need me. And don't make any rash decisions until you've spoken to me and Selin, OK?' If it wasn't for the fact that I absolutely have to get her out of the house before Michael gets here I'd give her another full lecture on the 101 reasons why Chris's hospitality is the only thing she should accept from him, but that's going to have to wait until she gets back.

'OK.' She rolls her eyes and we hug. As I close the door on them I realise I never got to ask her about Jackson. Talking of whom, I hope I didn't do anything too embarrassing with him last night – that would be awkward.

I look at the wall clock. 10.22. I'd better get moving.

Chapter Thirty-five

It's actually 11.22 when the doorbell finally chimes and for once I don't mind Michael being late. I have only just stepped out of the shower, my wet hair is drizzling down my back and the big towel that I have haphazardly wrapped around myself is very damp.

'Hello?' I suppose I'd better check it is Michael and not Rosie returning because she's forgotten to pack enough pairs of really big maternity knickers.

'All right? It's me.' I buzz him in, put the door on the latch, run to the hall mirror and hastily examine my face. There are shadows but they aren't too deep. I do look exceptionally pale but maybe that will add to the brunette version of pre-Raphaelite charm that he's always banging on about. I grab another towel from the radiator and give my hair a quick rub over when he politely knocks on the flat door before entering.

'Hello there,' he says in the style of Leslie Philips, looking me up and down.

'Hi, sorry about this. Woke up a bit late.' I go to him and try to kiss him whilst still holding up my towel. The texture of his clothes through the cotton feels rough.

'Listen, never apologise for being practically naked. In fact, you should be damn sorry you've got anything on at all.' With a wicked smile he grabs my wrists and forcibly raises my hands so that the towel drops to the floor.

'You bastard,' I manage to say as he looks me up and down again, devouring me with his gaze and then shoving me against the hallway wall, my arms above my head, taking both wrists in one hand and allowing the other to explore. The feeling of his cold hand and his clothes running the length of my body makes me forget everything but the feel of his fingers.

'Bedroom,' I whisper in his ear and he leads me into my room.

He pushes me on to my bed and I watch him watching me as he finds his way out of his clothes. Outside, the traffic rumbles up and down Green Lanes, some kids yell and shout at each other and someone with a radio tuned to a Turkish station parks outside. When all his clothes are in a pile on the floor he climbs on top of me and pushes my legs apart with his knee.

'Later on,' he whispers, 'I'm going to spend hours and hours practising all of the fantasies I've dreamt up on you. But right now you look too good for anything else but this.' I arch my back to meet him and sigh as he enters me. We move together quickly, my fingers creating valleys in his back and before I realise what's happening I come just before him, in a quick explosive burst of pleasure. A second later he too is still, his face buried in my wet hair.

For a moment we are silent. Out of the window I watch a tumult of white cloud slowly drift across a blue sky. I can hear the clock ticking in the hallway and the central heating click on.

Michael raises his head and looks at me. 'I feel as if I'm never going to get enough of you,' he says.

'That was something else,' I say, not really sure what to say when he's being romantic. 'I mean you really . . . you made me feel really good.'

He smiles down at me and rolls on to his side.

'But I just went for it, like no foreplay or anything.' Sometimes I wish he'd stop being so literal.

'Foreplay doesn't matter when you're already turned on. You turned me on in seconds. Although that does not mean that I don't expect you to carry out your promise on every last inch of me, OK? That concludes the lesson for today.'

His smile deepens as his hands travel lightly over my breasts 'OK. The first thing I wanted to try is this.'

Somewhere behind the clouds the sun moves across the sky and turns the morning into afternoon. Finally evening begins to tint the daylight and we lie quietly together, drifting in and out of sleep.

'How was your party?' I ask him at last.

'It was OK. Cool. Eight people threw up. Mum and Dad gave me a car. Now all I need to do is learn how to drive.'

'Cool,' I say, trying to remember if I used to count incidents of vomiting at my teen parties. Michael's face is inches from mine and I can tell by the look in his eyes that he doesn't want to discuss vomiting contests any more.

'Listen, you remember the other day on the phone. I said I think that I love you?'

I blink awake and chew my bottom lip. 'Did you? I don't remember. I was probably in a bit of a rush.' I had hoped we'd forgotten about that. He props himself up on his elbow, and his smile is so sweet and shy I just want to stop him speaking but my fingers aren't fast enough.

'I do, you know. I do love you. I realised it last night at the party, and even more when I saw you this morning. You are like no one else. I love you and want everyone to know about us. I want you to come back to my house tomorrow and I'll introduce you to my mum and dad as who you really are. My girlfriend.'

Now probably isn't the right time to reflect back on the several moments in my life when I have made the same or similar speech to various men and they have replied with the same deafening silence that I am now inflicting on Michael, or to think about how I'd try and save face by saying something like, 'You don't have to say anything. You don't have to say you love me. I just love you and wanted you to know, no strings.'

Exactly as Michael has just done.

'But I . . .' I sit up and look at him, think of how much I missed him in the bar last night, how much I wanted him from the first moment I set eyes on him this morning and how much I need him at the moment, need him to reflect the me I used to be before Owen ripped me up.

'I do love you,' I say. Not because I do, but because I don't want to hurt him the way all of those various men hurt me.

Michael buries his head in my neck and I look down at the crown of his head and his strong fingers circling the tops of my arms, and I feel every one of the eleven years between us.

Fortune interrupts the silence by sounding the doorbell and I leap out of bed perhaps a little more quickly than is polite just after such a mutual revelation. I don't especially want to see anyone right now, but I do want a break from the tension and pathos of the moment.

'Hello?' I enquire into the whistling feedback of the intercom.

'Hi? Jen? It's Ayla here.' Her voice sounds very young and distant from three floors down.

'Ayla! Hello.' I'm surprised, I haven't seen her since Mrs Selin cooked us dinner.

'Um, can I come up?'

'God, of course you can, sorry.' I buzz her in and race back into my room to pull on a pair of jeans, a bra and a top.

'Selin's little sister,' I whisper to Michael as I race out of the bedroom and pull the door shut behind me.

'Hello,' I say again as I open the door to her. She towers above me in her Nike Airmax and bends to kiss me on either cheek, brushing an ironed shiny strand of hair behind a multi-pierced ear as she stoops.

'This is a nice surprise, fancy a coffee?' I lead her into the kitchen and pick up the kettle to fill it.

'No thanks.' She wrinkles her nose. 'Got any juice or Coke?' I check in the fridge, find some of Rosie's organic apple juice and pour her a glass.

'This is a really nice place,' she says, looking around. 'It must be great to have your own place.' As she speaks she nods her head with quiet contemplative persistence. I make myself a cup of instant and settle down next to her.

Just as I wonder what the likelihood is of Michael making his presence known and beginning his new policy of outing our relationship, he strides into the kitchen. At least he had the good grace to get dressed first.

'Hello, I'm Michael, Jenny's . . . cousin.' I can't work out if his last-minute denial of our love was a general back-down or if he merely revised the status of his devotion to me when confronted with a beautiful girl much closer to his own age. The latter definitely figures if the long assessment he has bestowed on her person is anything to go by.

'This is Ayla, Selin's sister. We were just talking through girl stuff, weren't we, Ayla?' I say briskly. Ayla stands up again, her cheeks burning with the unexpected heat ignited by an unknown foxy boy in her presence.

'I'm sorry, Jenny, I'll go, I didn't realise that you had company,' she says, but I reach out and gently push her back into her seat.

'Nonsense. Michael is just passing through. Michael, go and

watch TV.' He nods and backs out of the kitchen. 'See,' I psychically transmit to him, 'I talk to you more like your mother than your mother does, and you think you love me!'

'See you around then,' he says to Ayla, treating her to one of his playground-special smiles and ignoring my telepathy. A few moments later we hear the theme tune to *Blind Date* blare out, switch briefly to *The Generation Game* and then back to the *Blind Date* tune again.

'He's pretty cute, your "cousin",' Ayla says with an impish smile; I can't work out if she's being sarcastic or not. I choose to ignore any possible undertones given that she's sixteen.

'Is he? I've known him since he was a kid, you know, so I don't really look at him that way.' I thank God for the first time that one thing Michael can't give me is stubble rash. I hastily change the subject.

'Well, how's it going with that chap, thingummy?'

'Jamie? He asked me out!' Her voice rises in a little high-pitched squeal at the end of the sentence and her solemn face breaks into a grin.

'Cool!' I say genuinely impressed.

'Yeah, but I can't go out with him.' Her face falls again. 'Tamsin says she'll break both my legs if I do.'

'Tamsin? Isn't Tamsin your mate who you went to Ibiza on a family holiday with in the summer?' I can understand the tremulous tone to her voice. Ayla has had 'friends' turn on her before.

'Yeah. But since term started everything seems to have changed.' She drops her head so that I can see the hours of work that went into the perfection of her zig-zag parting.

'But she was joking, right?' I ask hopefully. For her to be involved in another incident like this could really knock her confidence for good.

'No.' She lifts her face to look at me and her beautifully lined eyes are full of imminent tears.

'I'm in big trouble, Jen,' she whispers and the first big fat tear runs down her face.

'Oh, darling,' I say, dragging my chair next to her and flinging an arm around her shoulder. I'm thinking teenage pregnancy, drug addiction, shoplifting ring?

'It's Tamsin and the others. They h–hate me.' Her tears break into full–blown sobs now and her head drops to her forearms. I hand her a piece of kitchen roll.

'I'm sure it's not that bad, if you've just fallen out. They're probably just miffed because all the boys fancy you and you don't get spots. Ever. Do you?' I have always wondered what genes the Mehmet family carries to avoid any type of teenage acne whatsoever, not even the sort of outbreak I'm still prone to from time to time – and I've got six grey hairs.

'It's worse than that.' She looks at me again and takes a couple of deep breaths. 'When I first met them, right, they were really nice to me and like, that lot, Tamsin and Aisha and everyone, they are the coolest in the year. So I was really chuffed when they asked me to hang with them. Lots of the other girls didn't like them, but I thought they were just, you know, jealous.' I nod as she speaks, recognising a scenario from my own school life, but with more expensive trainers on.

'Anyway, after I'd known them a while they started messing around with the juniors, teasing them and that. And then they started to nick their dinner money off them and threaten to beat them up if they didn't pay. I did too. I was there. We'd go and spend it on lipstick and fags. I don't smoke though!' she adds quickly in an attempt to negate the rest of her confession.

'Ayla!' I cry, unable to repress my dismay. This is exactly the kind of behaviour that has ruined so much of her school life recently. I can't believe someone as sweet natured as her would inflict the same thing on someone else. Not little Ayla who wanted to marry Gary Barlow when she grew up and used to trail around after us suffering in turn our adoration and annoyance with her toddler devotion.

'Yeah, I know. It's the worst thing I can do, isn't? But they were my mates, you know. My only mates.'

I keep silent and let her talk.

'Well, then there's this girl in our year, Lucy, she's nice and that, but she's almost deaf, you know, got a hearing aid, she talks a bit funny. She's a bit overweight, not much, but a bit. Well, they just started laying into her every day. Calling her names, writing stuff about her in the bogs, spreading rumours, saying she was a slut. That she'd give any boy a blow-job for a quid. At first I thought it was just messing but yesterday I was with them when they caught up with her in the park. They hurt her. They made her bleed. I'm not like that. I told them I'd had enough of it. Tamsin said I'm a stuck-up cow anyway, she called me a slag. She said if I talked to anyone I would be next. I took Lucy home. She says she's not going to tell.'

'*You* have to tell someone,' I say firmly. 'You can't stand by and let that happen to someone else.'

She shakes her head. 'Yeah, but they *carry knives*, Jen, and Tamsin is a real psycho. And I don't know anyone else. No one else in that school is going to be my friend now. And Tamsin said she'd cut me if I told.'

My blood boils when I think of some jumped up little bitch, with a penknife trying to lord it over kids like Ayla. There's no excuse for kids like Tamsin – her parents are working, they live in a nice Victorian semi on Lordship Lane. They go to a time-share villa in Ibiza every year.

'Ayla, why haven't you talked to your mum and dad, or Selin?' I'm touched that she came to me, but her family is a close one.

'Because they'd bloody kill me! After everything I put them through, with the old school and the doctors and that. Can you

228

imagine how let down they'll be if they find out what I've done? And they're really busy with everything right now and I hardly see Selin at the moment, what with everything she's got going on. And Josh would just go round there and he doesn't really get it.'

I can't imagine Mr and Mrs Selin not having time to talk things through with their own kids, they have each taken time to talk things through with me in the past. But I can imagine how hurt they will be when they find out about this. I can see how difficult it must be for Ayla to tell them.

'You have to tell them, Ayla, at some point.' I can't get involved in covering this up from her family.

'I know. I know what I have to do. But I thought maybe if I could sort it out before I told them, they might not kill me so much?'

I bite back a smile and nod. 'Go to the head, face out Tamsin and the girls. If they're carrying knives they'll be expelled for sure.'

'Excluded. And I don't think that will make much difference to how they feel about me.'

'Look, Ayla, excuse me for saying this but girls your age are all mouth and no trousers. Girls *my* age are all mouth and no trousers. They won't really hurt you, not if you show them you're strong. And I bet Jamie will still be your friend, won't he, hey?' I nudge her gently in the ribs with my elbow and a tiny smile softens the tense line of her mouth.

'Yeah. Jen?'

'What, honey?'

'Will you come with me, Monday morning? To see the head?'

'Of course I will,' I say, with no idea how I'm going to explain yet more absence from work. 'And then later I'll bunk off work a bit early and come and meet you from school, OK?

Then we'll both go and tell your mum and dad about it. They can kill us together.'

'All right, thanks.' She delicately dabs the end of her nose with the kitchen roll. If I remember correctly it's hard to be sixteen. You look twenty-five but inside you're still just about twelve. I've always thought that I haven't changed inside since my eighteenth birthday but looking at her I can see I have, I've changed a thousand times, like a butterfly constantly cocooning and emerging. Maybe I don't have to be stuck in a rut after all. Maybe I'm changing right now.

I watch Ayla walk down the stairs and give her one last wave as she turns on to the next landing before I shut the door. Striding back along the hallway I push open the living-room door and look at Michael spread out over the entire sofa.

'Right, Cousin Mikey. I'm starving. Go and get us some fish and chips.'

Chapter Thirty-six

As soon as I open my eyes I am wide awake, despite the fact that it is Sunday morning and my alarm clock says it has only just gone 7.00. I wish some big-bearded astrophysicist-biochemist person would explain why this early-morning alertness only happens on weekend days next time they're making mind-blowing discoveries about the universe in a lab in the middle of the Arizona desert.

I roll over and look at Michael's back. His broad shoulders and the faint heatwave given off by his body prove tempting and I scooch in behind him and wrap my arms around his chest, tucking my knees into his. He stirs a little and one hand reaches back to squeeze my thigh before he drifts back into deep sleep. One thing about being eighteen; you never suffer from insomnia.

This weekend we have had the chance to become properly close. We have had the hours and the space to become intimate. We have talked about music (he's a lost cause), books (he doesn't read real books but is quite partial to graphic novels), football (he supports Chelsea and wishes he could play like Zola, I support Arsenal and wish Tony Adams had been my dad), and after a brief (very brief) discussion about sexual politics I had teased him about the possibility that he might be a bit homophobic.

'Homophobic?' he replied with horror. 'I'm not scared

of the fuckers!' We laughed but I'm not entirely sure he was joking.

And we even discussed our futures briefly. I asked Michael what he wants to be when he grows up. A rock star. He asked my why I told his dad I want to be a journalist.

'Because I do, one day,' I'd said.

'You don't reckon you might have left it a bit late then?' he asked cheerfully.

I changed the subject.

Late last night after I'd taken an excursion to the kitchen to down a glass of cranberry juice he asked me how many men I've slept with.

'I'm not telling you!' I replied, horrified by the question.

'Why not?' he asked, grinning but perfectly serious.

'Because. Because haven't you seen those films or read those books where the bloke persuades the girl to tell him how many men she's slept with and then he feels jealous, sexually inadequate and secretly thinks she's a slut?' In fact I didn't have to watch any films or read any books to garner that piece of experience, I'd fallen into that trap many a time myself. Even Owen, who increased his bedpost-notch tally *during* our relationship, had thrown a tantrum when I finally told him.

'It's a lot then, is it?' Again he adopted this jokey but edgy tone.

'See! See! It is *not* a lot but it is more than you, OK? It doesn't go into double figures. OK? Subject closed.' Of course it does go into double figures, but frankly it's none of his business. In fact, it's about fourteen, assuming that I haven't forgotten anyone (and let's face it, some of them deserve forgetting). Fourteen that I've had actual sex with. People I've kissed? That could run into three figures frankly, I've always been a fan of kissing. Fourteen sexual partners is not a huge number given that I started doing it twelve years ago. Fractions aren't my forte but it is a lot less than two a year. Girls are prettier than boys, sex is more available to us, so in my experience no matter which girl you are, if you've had more than one partner you are likely to have shagged more people than your current squeeze. The golden rule is *never tell him the truth*.

I'd taken his mind off the question with oral sex in the end, which seemed to make him decidedly happy, and after that we drifted off to sleep.

This morning, with every inch of my physical self screaming, 'Why aren't you asleep? You were up most of last night, you will get bags!' all I can think about is, where do we go from here.

After all the revelations and discoveries about each other and after all the sex that each time has been a little bit different, a little more emotional and eventually downright fabulous, I can't pin down how I feel about him. It's not Creeping Repulsion. I still want him, I'm still happy to be welded to the warmth of his body and don't have the compulsion to invent an early five-a-side game of soccer for him to go to in the park. (I'm not joking, it's worked in the past. You can make boys do almost anything with the promise of a game of footy, even an imaginary one. It's like a metaphysical blow-job. Probably.)

It's more a question of what I want from him. When this began I wanted a quickie with a teenager, then I wanted his admiration and reflected glory. Now that I know him properly that's changed. He's sweet and inexperienced. He's not cynical yet or cruel. He's open and still growing emotionally and probably physically. In some ways I feel like an aged vampire trying to suck back some youth. I am one of the partners he'll never forget, simply because I'm the first (and really rather good at oral sex). I don't want to fuck him up for the next one. I love Michael but this is going nowhere, when it comes right down to it. I have always known from the moment I agreed to take him from Ye Olde Parson's Nose that this would end in tears one day. The only questions are whose tears and when?

Despite everything, I'm not in love with Michael, I'm in love with the idea of him and what he does for me. I'd really love to be in love with him, to confront everyone we know with our relationship and bravely say, 'So what? This is love!' I could blame it on the fact that it's still too soon after Owen to meet the love of my life, but I know that's not true. I know you can fall in love seconds after a relationship if you want to, if you meet the *right* person. I know that all the months we give ourselves to get over someone are really just an excuse while we wait for the *right* thing and sometimes it takes a year or more and sometimes it takes two days. Michael and I is a lovely thing, a joyous thing but it isn't the *right* thing. I decide the only question has become whether I should finish something that makes me happy just because it isn't quite right, when it is very nearly so.

He stirs again and his muscles tighten and stretch before he twists to face me, circling his arm around my waist and pulling me as flush to his chest as is possible. He's no exception in the early-morning erection stakes then.

'What's the time?' His voice is husky with sleep.

'Seven-ish,' I reply, brushing his fringe out of his eyes.

'Seven! I never wake up this early. It must be the irresistible allure of a naked woman in my bed.' His hand moves from the small of my back to my bottom and we kiss.

Oh, well. Now doesn't seem like the right time to think about endings.

Chapter Thirty-seven

Michael is still my boyfriend. The rest of the morning he was so sweet and pleasant that I decided the fact that we are both happy is reason enough to continue. In fact, it took Rosie's call from the train to chuck a cold bucket full to the brim of reality in my face and to finally get Michael chaperoned out of the front door.

The moment he left I became instantly and happily exhausted. I flopped face first on to the sofa and have spent the last hour or so drifting in and out of the half-dream world of the *EastEnders* omnibus.

'Hello!' Rosie calls down the hall as she lets herself in.

'Mmm,' I mumble back, unable to muster the energy to take my face fully out of the cushion it's buried in. She bustles into the room, chucks her overnight bag in a corner and stands in front of the telly, leaning forward to scrutinise me.

'Bloody hell. Have you been shagging all weekend?' I stifle a yawn and drag myself up into a sitting position. I know that lying this one away is going to be a bit tricky given that my hair's a mass of knots, I have shadows under my eyes and my mouth is bruised and swollen with kissing.

'Yes,' I say, casually.

'Fuck me! Who, who was it? Was it Jackson?' Her voice doesn't waver but I can tell she wouldn't like it if it was.

'No, no. It was this guy, I met him ages ago at a party. We just bumped into each other and, well, one thing led to another. Very satisfying.'

Rosie elbows her way into my sofa personal space. 'Well? Are you going to see him again?'

'No, probably not.' This half-truth thing is more complicated than I feel like dealing with on no hours' sleep.

'Why not? You look like you got great value for money.'

'Oh, I just don't think I will. Anyway, how about you? Come to any earth-shattering conclusions about your horrible ex?'

'Well, he has got a really nice cottage in the country and lots of money,' she sighs wistfully.

'That's reason enough then, get back together with him.' I shake my head at her with about as much sarcastic vigour as I can muster while suffering from the jet lag of too much sex.

'But after the way he hurt me so much, common sense tells me I'd never be happy. I do still have feelings for him, but even so, I'm sure you're right, it could never work out,' she says with a total lack of conviction.

I flop a comforting hand on to her shoulder and pat her a couple of times with limp-handed apathy.

'Well done. Good girl.' I pat her again.

'Yes, but it's not just about my happiness, is it. It's about the baby too. The baby's happiness. In the olden days people got married because of babies and they stuck together through thick and thin. And arranged marriages, those people don't know each other very well, do they? But love grows. Maybe Chris has changed and maybe we might *make* it work.'

I blink at her and take a moment to repeat what she has just said to myself.

'Are you saying you are going to go back to the slimy chinless weasel?' Over my dead body.

'No, Jen, I just haven't decided yet. You can't decide things like that in one weekend, you know. I still have to think about it. And please, he's not a slimy chinless weasel *and* after all these years you should know that the more horrible you are about the men in my life the more I defend them and the more I like them. You're practically forcing me back into his arms.' We laugh and smile during this exchange but each one of us is aware of the serious undertones. Eventually I take her hand and say, as kindly as I am able, 'Rose, if you go back to Chris it will be the worst thing that you ever do and you will surely live to regret it.'

'Will you still be my friend?' she asks defensively, expecting the answer we have always given one another. And perhaps it's because I'm overtired or maybe it's because I'm angry at myself but I don't feel like mincing my words.

'I love you, Rosie, but I don't know that I could face going through all that pain with you again.' I don't really know what I mean by that, and I'm honestly rather shocked to hear myself say it out loud.

'So you're asking me to choose between you and the father of my baby?' Tears well up in her eyes.

I shake my head. 'No, no. Look, I feel pretty strongly about this. I don't have the answers, but I do know that at some point, in order to be proper friends, we all have to stop being so accepting of each other's mistakes. I'm only saying what I think because I love you.'

Rosie nods her head, but looks bewildered and hurt. 'I see, well, I understand that,' she says softly. I feel cruel, but for once I'm determined to stand by my convictions. Rosie continues, 'It's just that, well, maybe I should have done the same thing the second or third or fourth time you went back to Owen instead of giving you all my support and standing by you no matter what?' She sighs heavily and eases herself off the sofa. 'I'm off to bed,' she says, and as her door shuts the small amount of distance between us opens up just a little wider.

Chapter Thirty-eight

The clock on the wall opposite me ticks audibly. If you stare at it for long enough, your brain tricks your eyes into believing that the second hand travels backwards in time, just for one brief moment. And time should go backwards, it must. Everything that has happened over the last few hours is wrong. It's a mistake.

Somebody has to correct it.

Everything started as normal this morning, as expected. It had rained during the night but the morning was bright. When I looked out of the window I could see puddles of blue sky reflected in the wet road surfaces. The leaves on the trees that line the nice end of the road had begun to turn and small flame-coloured piles of leaves had collected in the crevices of their roots. Every single one of these tiny details I remember absolutely.

Rosie and I went through our breakfast ritual, silently handing each other mugs of coffee, pieces of toast, pots of jam, warily avoiding dicussing Chris. I spent ten minutes sitting over the steam from my drink trying to think of a way to ease the situation but by the time I'd thought of something to say Rosie was in the shower and the door bell announced Ayla's arrival. I let her up and she sat silently on the end of my bed while I brushed my hair and put on my morning make-up: foundation, mascara, lip gloss. I had decided to get into work late and blame it on the buses, something that's easy to do when you live in a tube-free zone like Hackney. Georgie hasn't been near public transport in the last fifteen years at least so I was pretty sure she wouldn't rumble me. I hadn't worked out how I was going to get off early to meet Ayla from school yet but I decided to cross that bridge when I came to it.

Ayla sat quietly on my bed and watched me. I was in a mood; my fight with Rosie had put me out of sorts. I wasn't rude to her, but I was grumpy. I might have made her feel awkward, as if she was putting me out. I didn't mean to.

Once outside, the brisk bright morning made me feel better. We discussed what we were going to say to the head.

'Now, the thing is I think you have to be totally honest. It's no good pretending you've been a total angel, is it?' I'd said sternly. I just wanted her to see how serious these things could be when they got out of hand.

'I know. I'm sorry,' she said, apologising to me for the sake of saying sorry.

As we approached the school, herds of kids began to swarm in our direction, shuffling along in noisy twos and threes, skidding past on scooters and skateboards, gradually falling into flight with the rest of the flock. Teen couples strolled hand in hand, pausing every now and then to kiss with dogged open-mouthed passionless enthusiasm. The kids swore as much as they ever did and talked with a strange slang mix of North London and New York. I felt sorry for Ayla, isolated in their midst.

As we crossed the playground to the main entrance a shrill voice hailed us across the tarmac.

'Oi! Slag! I'm watching you.' I turned around and saw Tamsin posed against a nearby railing, a thunderous scowl scarring her face, her minions standing sentinel on either side of her. I watched her until she felt self-conscious enough to tug at the hem of her skirt and turn her back on us, muttering, 'Fat bitch,' over her shoulder. Despite my suit and thirty years her words stung and I felt as intimidated as I ever have on a playground.

With my hand on Ayla's shoulder I guided her down the once-familiar corridors until we reached the head's office.

'We need to see Mrs Edgerton. It's urgent,' I told the same secretary who used to glare at me when I was hauled into the plastic chairs opposite her desk for some minor misdemeanour, usually involving too much make-up and back combing. She looked the same to me; why do people in education never get old? Maybe it was my suit and conservative make-up, but she didn't recognise me, question me or try to stall me. She took one look at Ayla's sheet-white face and went into the head's office. A moment passed and before long we were both seated in low orange-covered easy chairs, each with a cup of instant coffee neither of us wanted in our hands.

'So, Ayla, what's all this about?' Mrs Edgerton asked her.

It was almost ten when I left. Ayla had been sent back to class, pupils had to be interviewed, parents had to be called and procedures followed.

'You do understand that they have threatened her?' I said finally, taking in the stricken look on Ayla's face precipitated by the news that she had to go back to lessons. 'It could be very difficult for her out there today.'

'Her teachers will be alerted of the situation, Ms Greenway. This is Stoke Newington, not Bosnia. Nothing will befall Ayla on school property. You have my word.' I looked at her sensible, calm face and took her at her word. She agreed to contact Ayla's parents last, to give Ayla a chance to talk to them in person after school.

'But I will be calling them first thing in the morning, Ayla. Do you understand?'

'Yes, miss,' she had mumbled, looking about as wretched at the prospect of a confrontation with her family as was possible. It almost made me smile.

I had been in a hurry, I needed to get on the bus and into work before my public-transport excuse became null and void. I didn't stop to take an extra moment with her, to check that she was OK.

'See you later then, kiddo, about 3.30, yeah?' I ruffled her hair in a way that would really have annoyed her. 'Cheer up. It's never as bad as it seems.'

'Yeah, 3.30.' She paused and turned in her toes just the way she used to as a child when she'd been up to no good. 'Cheers and everything,' she said and she kissed me on both cheeks, turned her back on me and went to class. I remember thinking how tall she was and how young really, for all her plucked eyebrows and gelled-back hair, her adult airs and graces.

Georgie and Jackson were both out of the office when I finally made it in. They had gone to a seminar on e-marketing, which I think I had known about at the back of my mind, and wouldn't be back in the office for the rest of the day. There were three voice mails from Georgie on my office phone giving me jobs to do, and a further seven that just clicked off after a short pause. I guessed that she'd been phoning me all morning and stopped bothering to leave messages after a while. Georgie isn't exactly Gordon Gecko but even I got that sinking feeling of being caught out and possibly landing in trouble. I phoned her mobile, which I knew would be switched off, and left another apology for being late.

And then the worst thing that I thought could happen happened.

After Friday night I hadn't expected any more fun-and-games flirtations from Jackson but as I logged into my e-mail unread mail poured into the in-box, stacking up in intriguing little yellow envelopes. Out of twenty-two messages, eleven were anonymous messages from the same website as my message on Friday. At first I thought it might be a virus but our IT department checked them out and said they were clear, said they were just mails from a secret admirer. I opened them one by one. Each came with the same kooky animation and a clunky nursery-style tune as the first one, but each had a different slogan:

> I never stop thinking about you
> You are the one for me
> I saw you Friday
> Be my valentine all year round
> Pick up my calls
> I want to fuck you
> I'll see you soon
> Wait for me
> You are in my dreams
> We should be together

And then in the final message was the only repetition:

> *I'll see you soon.*

It clicked; these messages weren't from Jackson. There was no way they could be from Michael, he didn't have my e-mail address and even if he did, this wasn't his style.

Ostentatious declarations, insinuating ways of grabbing your attention, egomaniacal refusal to let the past go. Owen had never e-mailed me in the past, but I guess it's not that hard to get my address, and I suddenly knew with instinctive certainty that they were from Owen. He'd love this, he'd love the fact that he'd surprised me with these unexpected communications. I imagined his sudden conversion from Luddite quill user to internet café fly. It makes perfect sense really, coming from Owen who wants to insinuate his way into one's life and still keep his distance. The internet is his heaven and a new-found way of reaching me from beyond the grave of our relationship.

Instant big silent tears plopped on to my desk and I had to turn my back away from the window to my only solid wall. God, I was never going to be allowed to make that final break. With a heavy heart I picked up the text messages that had been languishing on my mobile phone since Saturday morning. Owen again, I was pretty sure. It didn't take much of a leap of imagination to connect him with the constant hang-ups at work either, although it wasn't really his style not to have anything to say. This was a new departure for Owen, using technology to court me, and typical of him to insist upon spelling every text message exactly. Once, his overtures would have made my skin tingle with anticipation, I would be thrilled, caught all over again in the romance of our doomed relationship as it turned on its upward circle. Now I just felt exhausted, and thanked God that he no longer knows where I live. All I can do is wait it out until he finally goes away.

I called the IT department again and had them set up my e-mail so that all mail from this site would be automatically deleted. If he sent me anything from another address I would have to call them again. I wanted to phone Selin but I was scared I'd blow Ayla's cover, it only seemed fair to let her do the talking herself, poor kid. I couldn't phone Rosie because we still weren't talking and I couldn't phone Michael, he had double physics. The rest of the day passed slowly, my body aching with tension and anger. Still under Owen's thumb after all this time.

When two o'clock came around I knew I should start winding up my work and find a reason to leave the office, but as soon as I started to pack my things away a call came in from Georgie. She wanted me to check for an urgent order on the fax and make sure it had gone through before the end of the day, it was a new client and a big order. She didn't say anything about my lateness but she was pretty sniffy with me and I could tell the next couple of days would be icy until I had proved again that I wasn't a total slacker. Shame I was planning to walk out of the door just as soon as I could then, but I have always believed your real life is more important than your job. The order wasn't on the fax. I called the client who said they had sent it half an hour earlier. I checked everyone's in-tray, and then everywhere I could think of until I found it in the recycle bin amidst a ream of the discarded status reports that the machine automatically churns out.

'Please check these through before you throw them away,' I shouted uncharacteristically. People raised their eyebrows and little 'ooooh's echoed from behind monitors. It was good to know they respect me so much.

It was just after 3.00 when I finally left. I would be late for Ayla. As I left the building I found myself looking long and hard up and down the street before I went to the bus-stop, just in case Owen was there. Silly really.

The bus crawled along, the lurching movement making me feel sick. The man who sat next to me had his mobile soldered to his ear and his inane drivel about the girl he claimed he had shagged Saturday night and how many ways he'd done it to her on Sunday didn't exactly improve my mood. The poor cow was probably sitting by a phone somewhere waiting for her new future husband to call.

Another rainstorm cleared the air and by the time I made it off the bus and stepped on to Newington Green I was running about fifteen minutes late and was around fifteen minutes from the school gate. Thirty minutes late. I had planned to be early, to be there when she came out. I hoped that with any luck she would have overestimated the whole thing and walked the short walk home alone, but I'd promised to meet her so the least I could do was try to catch her halfway.

Walking as fast as I could in my work shoes, my toes stung as I took each step.

As I walked past the Mehmet firm window I peered in through the slatted blinds. Both Selin and her dad were there, their heads bent over their desks, Selin leaning into the earpiece of her phone, a smile on her face. It didn't look as though Ayla had gone home, or if she had she'd gone straight upstairs to her room to avoid talking to her father, maybe to practise what she was going to say.

But then at the corner of Clissold Park and Green Lanes I saw her. Either she hadn't waited or she hadn't been given a choice; at any rate she was pinned up against the park railing with Tamsin's face millimetres from hers, Tamsin's right forefinger stabbing her point violently home, the fist of her other hand coiled around the neck of Ayla's biker jacket. So she hadn't underestimated them, things really could get that bad. I picked up my pace, but the road was busy and the traffic stopped me getting across as quickly as I wanted. To scare them off I shouted across the busy road. To get them to leave her alone, I shouted Ayla's name as loudly as I could.

'Ayla!'

The tick of the clock on the wall moves forward again and for a moment I let my eyes wander to the peach stipple-paint effect of the wall it hangs on and the tatty fruit-themed frieze that runs along behind it. My eyes are drawn back again to the second hand, and it marches haltingly forward. No amount of concentration can turn it back now.

'Ayla!' I shouted across the busy road.

All heads in the group turned towards me, relief flooded Ayla's face. She seized the moment and pushed Tamsin away from her, shoving the others clear as she ran towards me, her eyes locked on me.

She ran towards me, across Green Lanes, glancing at the changing lights on the crossing before locking her eyes on me.

A lorry driver ran a red light. Over the road a terrier tied up outside a newsagent began to bark. The way I remember it, I saw his owner come out of the shop to quiet him and cover her eyes with her hands before I saw everything that happened around me.

A world of noise and chaos crash landed into the afternoon.

The lorry skidded across the road and crashed into a parked car, its horn sounding a long and unremitting note. Cars braked to a panicky stop, doors slammed, people ran out of shops and leaned out of windows. Tamsin and her friends ran away into the park. And during the single moment that all this happened Ayla's body curved through a violent arc in the air. A moment later her head hit the kerb at my feet, the rest of her sprawled in the road.

It took me time, just a fraction of a second, to take in what had happened, to realise that she had been hit by the truck, to realise that she was bleeding at my feet.

I knelt beside her.

'Ayla? Ayla?' I repeated. Her brown eyes were still fixed on mine but they were not focused. I fumbled for the mobile in my bag, but someone in the crowd called out, 'It's all right, love, they're on their way.'

'Are you sure?' I asked.

'Yes, love, five minutes they said.'

I knew enough not to try and move her, so I covered her shoulders with my coat.

As I moved I said, 'Her parents, her parents . . .' But some one must have told them already because all at once Selin and her parents were at my side.

'Oh, my baby,' Mr Selin whispered as he sank to his knees in the gutter. Selin's mother pushed me out of the way and took her daughter's hand, whispering to her to wake up, rocking gently on her heels.

I looked up at Selin, and met her gaze. Her eyes were wide with horror and disbelief.

'She ran, she ran into the road,' I whispered, unable to find my voice. Selin nodded silently and turned her back on me, kneeling to wrap her arms around her mother, gently rocking her back and forth. I felt as though I had stepped into someone else's nightmare, an invisible ghost. From then on everything seemed like a dark dream.

The ambulances arrived. I was dimly aware of the lorry driver being bundled into one of them and it left quickly. The police arrived, closed off the road and began asking questions. I remember thinking that they would have to put the buses on divert. Further up the Lanes, car horns had begun to sound angrily, unaware of the reason for the delay to their journey.

We all stood back on the kerb while the paramedics tended to Ayla. Gently, quickly and quietly they prepared her for her journey without exchanging a look and only the occasional word.

'She's my daughter,' Ayla's mother said and the paramedic nodded and let her climb into the ambulance. Selin and her father looked at each other, at a loss for what to do, when a police officer offered to take them to the hospital.

'Do you want me to fetch Hakam?' I asked as they climbed in to the car. Selin's father looked at me as though he had seen me for the first time.

'Jenny? Why are you here?' A sudden panicked sense of guilt knotted into my stomach. I called to her across the road, she ran to meet me.

'I . . . I came to meet Ayla, we . . . I came to meet her,' I finished lamely. Mr Selin looked around him as if he had just been dropped into an alien world, I don't think he really heard me. For a moment he focused again and caught my hand.

'Don't worry about Hakam. He's at his grandmother's, he'll be fine there for now. Let's leave him for now,' Mr Selin said. He pulled me down towards him. 'Jenny, find Josh, tell Josh and bring him, please?'

I nodded, relieved to be given something to do. 'Of course, right away. I'll bring him. Leave it to me.' I paused only to watch their quiet pale faces as the cars pulled away.

The squat Josh lives in is maybe twenty minutes' walk away. I began the journey at a brisk walk but soon I found I had broken into a run and I kept running until my chest felt like bursting, my head pounded and my feet screamed each time they touched the pavement. Eventually I was forced to come to a halting stop and I bent double gasping for air, my stomach lurching in revolt. Passers-by carefully avoided looking at me. I reached into my bag and pulled out my inhaler, taking two doses in quick succession and breathing deeply.

There wasn't far to go now, I could have just walked it, it wouldn't have made much difference, but I knew that I couldn't.

I kicked off my shoes, shoved them in my bag and began to run again. Five minutes later, out of breath again, with torn tights and bleeding toes, I pressed the bell of Josh's house and didn't remove my thumb until the door had been opened. A girl I didn't recognise opened it and I pushed past her into the hallway.

'Josh,' I wheezed, looking around me for any sign of him.

'Hang on just a minute,' she said indignantly. 'Just who the hell are you?' I ignored her and burst into the living room. Danny was watching *Ready Steady Cook*.

'Where's Josh?' I asked him, gulping in air, my heart pounding, feeling sweat cool on my forehead. I couldn't see him, it hadn't occurred to me that he might not be here. 'Where's Josh, I need to see him?' I repeated anxiously.

Dan eyed me speculatively. 'He's upstairs, working. What's going on? Has something happened?'

I didn't bother to answer him and headed for the stairs.

'Josh!' I called as I closed the gap between us. He met me at his bedroom door, and at the sight of me backed in again and sat on his bed. His walls were covered with charcoal drawings and a painting in progress leant on an easel by the window.

'Christ, Jen.' He looked me up and down and pulled me into a hug. 'Fuck, darling, what's happened to you?' He took my face in his hands and said, 'Did Owen do this to you?'

I shook my head and prized myself out of his embrace. 'No, no. It's you. I came to get you.'

He stood up, confused and concerned. 'Get me?' he said, his voice filled with intuitive dread.

A moment's silence ticked by, I spread my hands out before him, unable to bear what I was about to say.

'Josh, it's Ayla, she . . . there's been an accident.' As I watched him take in my appearance again from a different perspective, as his face crumpled and rearranged itself, my chest imploded with pain for him.

'Is she OK?' he asked hoarsely, blinking hard.

'She's badly hurt, she's at the hospital, it happened about half an hour ago. I came, I came to get you. As fast as I could. To take you there.' For a brief moment he pulled me to him once again in a tight, fierce and frightened embrace, and for just a second we stood limb to limb in silence, gaining strength from each other as we took in the enormity of the afternoon's events.

'Come on.' He headed down the stairs and I followed him.

Dan and the unknown girl stood in the hallway as we headed for his old Capri.

The journey to the hospital seemed to take for ever. We drove in silence, Josh's jaw working against tears and fear. I put my shoes back on and focused on the pain. I tried not to think about Ayla looking at me instead of at the traffic as she left the safety of the pavement.

At the hospital we were ushered into the family room where Selin and her parents were already waiting. As the door opened they all stood up, Josh strode into their arms and they were caught in a family embrace.

I sat in a chair in the corner and began to watch the clock.

Chapter Thirty-nine

It's been almost three hours now. I have sat here quietly in the corner feeling that I shouldn't be here, feeling that I can't just leave, not wanting to leave. Mr and Mrs Selin talk to each other in hushed Turkish. Josh sits quietly, his head in his hands. Selin sits with her arm draped around him, staring out of a window at the view of a brick wall. We all jump a little when she stands.

'I'm getting a coffee, does anyone want a coffee?' Her family just look at her blankly.

'I'll get us all one.' Selin looks at me as if she is surprised and perplexed to find me still present. 'Jen, will you help me?' I nod and stand to follow her out of the room.

'Seli, darling,' her father speaks. 'Call Nene, tell her what's happened. Ask her to keep Hakam for a while longer. Try not to upset her too much, he doesn't need to know anything. Not yet.'

Selin holds her father's gaze for a moment, swallows hard as she contemplates an impossible task and blinks back tears. 'Yes, Dad, OK.'

I follow her out of the room.

'How are you doing?' I ask her. She can't look me in the eye, I know that if she looks at me she's afraid she'll lose it completely, and she'll never be able to get it back. I know this instinctively even though I can't remember a time when I have ever seen her really lose control.

'I'm fine. I'm fine, it's how *she's* doing. That's all that worries me. The doctors haven't really said anything since we arrived. They said it was critical, that's all, they said to be prepared for the worst. They haven't been near us since.'

Finally she finds the resolve to meet my gaze, with a questioning look. 'What happened, Jen, why were you there?' I concentrate hard on slotting two twenty-pence pieces into a vending machine and watch as beige-coloured liquid bubbles into a plastic cup, trying to map out what happened in words, trying to circumnavigate the lumpen sense of dread that has fossilised in my chest, the certainty that everything is down to me. This time I can't look Selin in the eye.

'I was meeting her after school. I was late. She was on her way home when I saw her across the street.'

'But why? I mean, why were you meeting her?' I pause, hand her the coffee, position a second cup, slot in two more coins and witness a brief replay, a dog barking, someone's scream, the screech of tyres, Ayla's dark eyes looking into mine, but not seeing. How could something that should have been a minor teen drama, a bit of trouble at school, maybe a couple of nights being grounded . . . ? how could something that I should have been able to control have turned into this? For the first time in my life I had been the designated adult. I had failed, and failed at what cost? As I hear my own words I realise how impossibly ordinary and mundane my explanation seems.

'She'd got into a bit of trouble with some girls at school. She didn't want to worry you, any of you, what with all that other trouble at her old school. She wanted to try and sort it out herself before she told you. I was just there for moral support.' Some moral support, I think.

'I was late,' I repeat lamely. I am trying to tell Selin, without telling her. It's my fault.

'Bullies? She was being bullied again? Bullies caused this?' I can see the storm of emotions she is trying to battle through focus on anger and I quickly try to calm her down.

'No, no. More complicated than that. She'd got mixed up with the wrong crowd, got herself into a bit of trouble. She was doing the right thing. The head was, *is*, going to call your parents tomorrow to talk it through with them. She'd stuck up for another girl. She's *been* very brave.' I realised that I had unconsciously been talking about her in the past tense. My clumsy change of gear stuck out like a sore thumb. I handed Selin another cup of coffee and began again, the synthetic aroma making my stomach lurch.

'But then, how did it happen? The accident?'

I tried to think of a way I could describe it without making it sound as senseless as it was.

'I was late. When I saw her, the girls she'd . . . the girls she'd told on were giving her hassle. I was going to her but I, I wanted them to know she wasn't alone.' I paused and braced myself for Selin's reaction. 'I called out her name, Selin. She saw me, and she panicked, I suppose. She ran across the road. It was a mistake, stupid really. She should have been fine because the lights were changing, but she didn't wait for the traffic to stop. The lorry driver ran a red.' With the last two cups of lukewarm liquid in my hands I turn to look at her, flinching before I even meet her eyes.

'That's what happened,' I say, ready for recrimination. But she only nods again, her face a dark-eyed mask. She's heard what I've said but she hasn't really understood. I called out Ayla's name.

'Listen, I, I don't think I can talk to Nene, not without, you know. Losing it.' Her voice is tense and strained. She's talking but really, behind her tear-glazed eyes, she is still trying to make sense of it all, slotting the puzzle pieces together.

'Give me the number and I'll call her. She knows me. I'll tell her not to worry,' I say. I'll lie, I think to myself on the way to the pay phone.

A few moments later when I go back into the visitors' room, Selin is recounting what I told her. Josh smiles absently at me as I hand him one of the coffees that I'm still carrying. As I pass one to Selin's dad he catches my hand and squeezes it a little.

I was late, I want to tell him. I was late. But the family don't look at me, they don't demand explanations or reasons. They merely turn to each other once again, communicating with silent solidarity as the second hand on the clock jerks forward. I settle back into my chair across the room and watch its endless progress.

It's odd how quickly a strange situation can become the status quo, and for a few minutes more that room becomes the whole world to us. So when the door opens and a doctor comes in we are almost surprised, it's almost as if we have forgotten why we are there.

Everyone stands.

The doctor composes herself and in that moment we know it is bad news.

'Mr and Mrs Mehmet, when Ayla came in she had sustained very serious head injuries. Further investigation uncovered extensive internal injuries that caused a massive amount of blood loss. The vehicle that hit her was going very fast. We tried everything we could to save her. I am very sorry to tell you that a few minutes ago your daughter died on the operating table. There was nothing more that we could do.'

The family look from one to another, speechless. Hands reach out and fingers link, but no one says a word.

The doctor coughs.

'If it's any consolation, should Ayla have survived the operation she would almost certainly have been brain damaged.'

'*Consolation?*' Selin rounds on her. 'Don't you think we'd rather have our sister back in any condition, instead of dead and alone up there, with people who don't even know her? Who don't even care?' Josh takes her in his arms and she begins to weep; the sounds of her mother's sobs soon join her.

The doctor tries again.

'I'm sorry, I really am. You can see her now, if you want. I'll take you.'

They file out one by one and leave me alone in the room.

'You were at the scene, weren't you?' the doctor asks me, just as she is about to close the door.

'Yes,' I say quietly.

'The police want to talk to you, can I send them in?'

'Yes,' I repeat. 'Doctor, what about the lorry driver? Was he hurt badly?' She looks away and shakes her head.

'No. Small head wound, minor concussion. He'll be sent home in the morning. He hadn't been drinking,' she adds as an afterthought and she shuts the door.

The interview with the police took longer than I could cope with and they've asked me to go down to the station tomorrow to make another statement.

As I walk out of the softer lighting of the family room into the harsh strip fluorescence of the casualty department, I blink under the bright lights. I can't see anyone I recognise. I expect they've gone home. The pain in my feet kicks back in as the numbing effects of shock begin to wear off. I look in my purse for some change for the bus but when I hobble outside I find Josh, his shoulders huddled against the chilly evening, smoking a cigarette.

'I didn't think you smoked any more?' I said with a weak smile.

'I don't. I just ponced this one off that bloke over there.'

He nods in the direction of a man with both legs in plaster, apparently stranded on a bench with no one to collect him. The man catches my eye, gives a comic shrug, and laughs at his own plight.

'Is there . . . are they still here?' I ask, unsure about things like death certificates and morgue arrangements.

'No, they've gone home. I waited to give you a lift. You'll be waiting for God knows how long for a bus round here.' He looks at the sky as if he's watching the stars that have been obliterated by the glare of the city.

'Josh, you didn't have to do that. You should be at home,' I say, more grateful than he can know that I don't have to make the trip home alone. He doesn't answer but starts walking to his car, two quick paces in front of me.

This time, with no one to see, no one to rescue, the journey home seems to take no time at all and as we pull up outside my flat I look up at the dark windows.

'Looks like Rosie is out,' I say. Another person who doesn't know. 'God, Rosie! She'll be so upset.' When I glance back at him, he is staring fixedly at the steering-wheel.

'Oh, Josh, I'm so sorry. Look, thanks for the lift.'

He nods and looks at me quickly, the silent tears in his eyes catching the glow of the street lamp. I reach out and grip his wrist for a second before opening the car door. I wait until the clatter of his car's old engine has been washed away into the tide of night-time traffic before slotting my key into the lock. Just before I go in I have one quick into-the-night look for some stars, but still they are hiding.

Chapter Forty

When I get into the flat the answerphone blinks to let me know there is a message. Warily I press the button, half expecting some message from Owen, even though I know he doesn't have my home number.

'Jen, it's Rosie. I won't be back at the flat tonight, don't worry about me, I'm fine. My mobile's on if you have anything to say to me.' Her tone is slightly imperious and huffy, but I have known Rosie long enough to know that this means she wants to clear the air as much as I do. I don't know how I'll begin to tell her about today. I remember the e-mails and text messages from Owen and my heart sinks even further. My mum always says things happen in threes. What will be next, I wonder? And how the fuck can I be so fucking shallow as to lump Ayla's death in with some stupid fucking superstition?

I dial Rosie's number and wait for the slow clicking connection to insinuate its way across space. The phone rings for a long time before she picks it up.

'Hiya,' she says briskly and for once I wish mobile phones didn't afford you the opportunity to be prepared for whoever calls you. Rosie is prepared for the wrong call, and I feel sorry for the advantage I have over her.

'Hello.' As I reply, I discover that my voice is cracked and husky.

'Oh, you're in then?' Rosie must have been waiting for me to call her to sort things out.

'Rosie, something's happened.' The tone in my voice takes the edge out of hers right away.

'What's happened?'

I tell her in as few short sentences as I can. When I finish, silence crowds the line for long seconds.

'I'm coming home now,' she says. I can't make out the tone of her voice.

'Where are you?' I expect her to be at Chris's.

'Jackson's hotel,' she says absently.

'Oh. OK.' I just want her to come home.

'I'm coming home, OK?'

'OK.'

'I'm getting a cab, I'll be twenty minutes tops, OK?'

'OK.'

She hangs up and I turn on the TV. There doesn't seem to be anything left for me to feel any more, as if the day's events have drained me of every last emotion. I'm just terribly tired and my head throbs.

When the door finally slams it wakes me up. Rosie hurries down the hallway to greet me.

'I'm here,' she says, and takes my hand.

This time, as I tell her again, we sit turned to face each other on the sofa. Rosie watches me over the rim of her mug, some of her expression masked by the swirls of steam from her camomile tea. I'm tired of telling it but I need someone to react to the way it happened to me. I need to see if Rosie sees it the same way that I do.

'So, she saw you and she just ran into the road?' Rosie asks me again. I nod.

'But, it was the lorry driver, right? Running a fucking red. The bastards do that all the time down that road. How many times have I said it? People drive like maniacs in this city.'

'But if I'd been on time, if I'd met her at school, we'd all be round Mrs Selin's right now lecturing her on the responsibilities of behaving like an adult. Instead I was late. Ayla's dead. I just don't understand it. How can something as mundane as stopping to look for a fax cause someone's death?'

Rosie shakes her head and sets her cup down. 'You can't blame yourself for this, mate. Please don't even go there.'

Although I'm relieved to hear her say the words I've wanted to hear, I'm surprised at the annoyance in her voice.

'But if I'd been there on time,' I continue, eager for more affirmation.

'If you'd been there on time, if the bus hadn't been stuck in traffic, if Ayla hadn't got mixed up with bullies, if she hadn't moved schools, if, if, if. You can't blame yourself. This was an accident, a terrible random series of events that culminated in tragedy. Blaming yourself is too easy.' Her face is hard with grief and anger, she is angry with me but not for causing Ayla's death. She thinks I'm making myself the centre of this tragedy. Maybe she's right, but maybe the alternative explanation, the arbitrary pointlessness of it all, is just too much to bear.

I lean back and tip my head up to look at the ceiling.

'You're right,' I say, suddenly afraid. 'But how fucking *awful*.' At last tears come to us both. Hugging each other for grim life, we weep together, holding hands tightly until we are too tired to cry any more.

Finally I say, 'Rosie, about yesterday. What I said . . .' She interrupts me. 'It's all right, really. I know where you stand. You've been honest. Look, it hardly seems like it matters so much right now, does it?' She extricates her hands from mine and roughly wipes her face.

'No, but . . .' I try to continue because I want to, need to, restore the equilibrium of our friendship.

'Just leave it, OK?' Rosie says irritably. 'I'm going to bed. I'm exhausted.' I look at her tired pinched face and back off. Just before she leaves the room she turns to me and says, 'Poor Seli, how will she ever live with this?'

We look at each other for a moment longer and I shake my head.

'I don't know, I just don't know,' I say as gently as I can, but she doesn't answer as she goes straight to her bedroom. She must be shattered.

For a few moments more I sit alone and watch the world for signs of change. Everything seems the same and it shouldn't. Everything seems the same but I can't help feeling that the last threads of continuity are slipping loose.

Chapter Forty-one

The arrival of October has chased away the last remnants of the summer, the fleeting blue-sky reprises and momentary reunions with warmth of September have now been completely washed away by the heavy soaked skies of autumn.

It suits us all, and since Ayla's death we have gone about our daily lives like choreographed automatons.

Rosie and I didn't go to the funeral itself. To be honest, we both felt awkward about going to the mosque and Rosie thought the trauma of the burial might be too much for her. I decided to stay behind with her and make sandwiches. I pretended to myself that it was just as good a way as any to support the family but really, in my heart, I know it was because I'm a coward. Not only afraid of unfamiliar places, but of seeing the family go through so much pain and seeing Ayla buried. I still think that if I had been on time none of this would have happened.

Loyalty to the Mehmets meant I could not run back to my mum's house in Watford as I had been tempted to do, but I took the easier option, arriving with Rosie at the house just before they left, spending the day following food-preparation instructions from a neighbour and family friend while we waited for them to return.

I have only ever been to two funerals, both grandparents who were old and, hard though it was at the time, it hadn't been a shock. Muslim funerals happen much more quickly and it was only two days after Ayla died that Rosie and I stood expectantly in the kitchen doorway as the family trailed back into the house. I had been anticipating a parade of relatives, friends and acquaintances but instead it was only the family, a friend of Selin's father and a couple of close neighbours. We had made far too much food. From my limited experience of funerals I remember afternoons beginning with hushed murmurs and cups of tea passed round, gently building into family chat and finally laughter. But this time, even whispered conversations seemed intrusive.

The family sat or stood, pale-faced and shocked. Since Ayla's death I have hardly managed to talk to Selin, but on that day I suddenly realised that I haven't really *talked* to Selin, found out what's going on with her, in months. When we've been together, if we haven't been dancing, or drinking, the conversation has inevitably come back to my or Rosie's life. Selin has sorted us out time and time again. It's almost as though the better friend she has been the more of a stranger she has become.

Seeing her for the first time since the hospital, sitting incongruously and in silence in the corner, hand in hand with Mr Selin's friend, with her chin in her hand looking at the traffic passing down the road, his gaze intent on her, was just like seeing a stranger. The recently bold, beautiful Selin seemed to have been hollowed out into an almost translucent china doll, her skin stretched taut and pale, every angle of her face etched with grief. I briefly considered trying to rescue her from the overattentive friend but despite everything I had said to myself and Rosie over the last couple of days I couldn't find a way to comfort her. I still felt as though somehow I had brought her to this state, empty and alone except for the attentions of some old man.

Hakam ran upstairs as soon as he could. Mr Selin dabbed at each eye in turn, quietly wiping away tears and sipping whisky, and Mrs Selin went to the kitchen and washed up all the plates and cutlery we had washed up earlier that day and began packing the mountains of food into freezer containers and Tupperware.

'The children can have all this for their lunch,' she said to me as she dried the same plates again. 'I mean, Hakam can.' She hid her face with the freezer door and I went back into the living-room and sat at the table where a few weeks ago we had been laughing with Ayla about Jamie Bolton. I wondered where he was right at this moment. Looking around for Rosie I saw that she had joined Selin and the stranger sitting by the window but Selin didn't move to acknowledge her. I caught her eye and she shrugged at me and shook her head. I bit my lip and went to find Josh.

The sight of him huddled against the chill on the balcony in his best shirt and one of his dad's ties hit me harder than I expected. His wide shoulders folded in upon themselves and although he was clean-shaven I could see shadows of sleepless nights under his red-rimmed eyes. I hung back for a moment in the doorway wondering whether to interrupt his reverie, wondering if I was brave enough, but before I could leave he caught sight of me and offered me a drag of his cigarette.

'I don't smoke,' I smiled weakly. 'And neither do you, remember?' He returned my smile with a tight distortion of his lips.

'Apparently I do again.' With this he took a long last drag and flicked the butt of the cigarette over the edge of the balcony into someone's back garden.

I joined him to lean on the railing and looked out over the brown and grey mosaic of the city. The gloom of the evening had already begun to settle in the sky and slowly seeped down to meet the rooftops and chimneys.

'How are you holding out?' I asked, wishing there was some alternative script for occasions like these.

He glanced at me for a second before returning his gaze to the horizon. 'She was my kid sister, you know. My baby girl. The worst thing I worried about for her was getting pregnant by some spotty kid behind the bike sheds, even though I knew that was never her style. The best things I imagined for her, college and freedom, love, a future. She was so beautiful, wasn't she? I was getting ready to fight off all her suitors. Never had a chance with Selin, she used to fight them all off before I got there. Ayla was different, more delicate somehow. More . . . breakable.'

I watched Josh's profile in the diminishing light, and felt every shadow and line of his expression so hard it almost knocked the breath out of me.

'Josh, I just don't know what to say,' I recited lamely from the script again.

He shook his head and put his arm around me, I wound my arms around his waist and we stood quietly until finally the last of the light left the sky, silent and companionable.

'Come on. We'd better go in,' he said to me, and the sudden withdrawal of his warmth made me shiver. He looked at me for one more moment before opening the doors back into the living-room.

'You've been a really good friend, Jenny, I just want you to know I appreciate it.' I watched his back as we returned to the warmth inside and I felt terrible. I haven't really been any kind of friend at all, everyone is misjudging me.

Hoping to rectify this a little bit, once inside I made my way over to Selin, who looked as though she hadn't moved once. Rosie had gone somewhere.

'Seli?' I whispered her nickname, and she slowly turned her face to me and focused.

'Jen, hello, come here.' I went to her and she hugged me for a long time, covering my face with her fragrant hair, her shoulders stiff and brittle under her shirt.

'Are you OK?' she asked me.

'Me? I'm fine, are you OK? We haven't really had a chance to talk, have we?' I looked pointedly at the man with her, a tall and slender man with short grey hair and intense dark eyes, but he only smiled at me and nodded.

'Oh, it's just, I can't really think of anything to say, but thank you, thank you so much for being here. It's meant a lot to me and Josh. And Mum and Dad. And Hakam.' She smiled weakly. I sighed and squeezed her hand.

'Selin, I just wanted to say that, well, maybe it wouldn't have changed anything but I'm sorry, so sorry that I didn't get to Ayla in time.'

Selin looked confused for a moment and then shook her head as if trying to clear it, a tight smile emerging.

'Don't be silly, this was just a pointless accident. No one's fault. Well, not yours anyway.' She squeezed my hand again but the tight restraint in her voice made me wonder whether she was entirely convinced by her own words. I felt suddenly like an intruder.

'Well, maybe we'd better go, it seems to me that you need time with your family.' I glared at the man again, but he only smiled and nodded.

Selin sighed and any traces of anger dissolved into exhaustion. 'Maybe you're right, but thanks for being here. Where's Rosie?'

'I'm here.' Rosie stood behind us with both our jackets over her arm. 'I think Jen is right about the family thing, we should be going.'

Selin nodded, hauled herself from the window-seat and walked with us down to the front door.

'Don't forget, call us whenever you need us. Whatever time,' I told her. She smiled and hugged us both again.

'OK. I'll see you. Oh, and it's Josh's exhibition coming up in a few weeks. He almost pulled out of it, it took Dad and I ages to persuade him not to. Ayla would have been so cross, she always said he should hurry up and be a proper artist instead of pissing around being a gardener, it embarrassed her.' She smiled at the memory. 'We all have to be there to support him, OK?'

'Of course,' I said. Selin shifted uncomfortably from one foot to the other for a moment and then took one of each of our hands in both of hers.

'Look, I do need to talk to you. I've got something to tell you. I was meant to tell you on Monday but . . . but . . .' She couldn't finish her sentence. We re-engaged in a hug.

'Shhh, it's OK. You can tell us when you're ready, OK? If you want us, either of us, any time, we're here.' Rosie smoothed Selin's hair back from her forehead and gently wiped away her tears with the ball of her thumb.

'Thank you. I needed to hear that, but I think I need to be with this lot for now,' she smiled, nodding back up the stairs. 'It means a lot to me to have both of you around, I'll be in touch.'

Rosie and I walked back in silence through the damp and foggy evening, not exactly on bad terms any more but not exactly easy with each other's company either. In fact, Ayla's death was a very convenient way for neither of us to feel that we had to discuss our differences very much.

For the last hour we have sat in silence in front of *When Harry Met Sally*, both cradling cups of tea, our feet outstretched before us, too exhausted even to change from our funeral clothes. Rosie's sudden movement from the sofa startles me.

'Do you want another?' she asks, holding her hand out for my mug.

'Yeah, cheers love,' I say and then, remembering my manners, 'I'll make it, you must be knackered.'

'No, no, I'll make it.' She peers into my mug. 'I swear, you shouldn't be allowed a full mug of tea, you never finish one, always leave a good two inches in the bottom.'

I laugh; she always teases me about this. 'You know I don't like it when it's gone cold,' I say just as I always do.

'You must have an asbestos throat,' she says just as she always does. I sense that the familiarity of the exchange signals a truce between us. I let myself relax a little and feel the aches and strains of the day start to corrode into my muscles.

'Oh, I meant to tell you,' Rosie calls out from the kitchen. 'My mum's over with Hubby next weekend for a few days, they'll be staying at his country residence, you know, the bungalow in Godalming. Anyway, it's the only chance I'm going to get to see her and I suppose I should, so I'll be away Friday night and Saturday day, back Saturday evening. Sunday they do his relatives. Do you think that's OK? Leaving Selin?'

I had hoped that the three of us would be able to spend some quality time together at last, but life goes on, I guess.

'Well, it's not exactly as if your mum's round the corner so you must go. Selin would understand, and anyway, I bet your mum is dying to talk babies with you.'

'You're joking, aren't you? My mum and the concept "granny" in the same scenario, that's not the kind of label she's used to, darling. By the way, who was that guy who kept hanging around Selin?' Rosie returns from the kitchen, wrinkling her nose at the memory of him. 'He looked like a right letch.'

I nod in agreement; she has only filled my mug two-thirds. 'I know, but Selin is too polite by far to tell anyone to leave her alone. And anyway, she probably didn't feel like confrontation today of all days.'

Rosie nods and flops on to the sofa.

'How do *you* think she's handling it?' I ask Rosie.

'I don't know, it's hard to tell with Selin, isn't it. She's such a rock, always has been. I mean, you can see how devastated she is, it's written all over her, but somehow if she'd gone to pieces, tears, hysteria, it would be easier to see how to help her. I mean, I always go to pieces, I'm very easy to deal with in that respect.' We smile at each other tentatively, trying not to make light of the situation but really tempted to blow the tension with a good giggle. Rosie continues.

'It's like when she split up with Max, when was that now? God, *seven* years ago. I mean, they'd been together all through uni, hadn't they? Her dad and his dad were best friends, they were both accountants and they really did seem made for each other, you know, in their own way. But then he goes and proposes and that's it. It's over. No dramatics, no endless nights of weeping round yours, no vodka binges round mine, no sleeping with other people to get back at him and then feeling shit about yourself. Don't you remember? She just told us the news one night, you and I went into classic post-relationship mode, got steamingly drunk and pulled those two blokes that looked like rejects from Take That, *and* I got Gary Barlow – bloody hell – and she went home before midnight sober as a judge and alone. In fact, the next day she came round to yours and cooked *us* breakfast.'

I nodded as I remembered what could be classed as Selin's only serious emotional upheaval until this week. 'Yeah, but I mean maybe she never loved him or something, and she just felt a bit relieved that it was over. She's not, you know "showy" is she, with her emotions? But this, I mean we know she adored Ayla, they all do. This is different.' I'm searching for easy access to an experience I can only feel peripherally.

'Of course it is. But the thing with Selin is it's really hard to know what she wants, what she's thinking, how she's coping.'

We sit in silence for a few moments more and then I say. 'Don't you think we should know?'

We watch the end of the film without answering the question.

Chapter Forty-two

I compare this Friday to last Friday morning and I think about how much can change in a week. I have to go back into the office today. Actually I don't have to, Georgie told me I could take the whole week off, but for once the prospect of a mundane office job seems more appealing than an unarmed exploration into the world of daytime television. Under normal circumstances I am fully equipped with a full battery of irony, sloth and indifference but for the last couple of days the vapid lull of the TV has only set my mind free to think about Ayla, Selin, Josh and Michael.

It's a tough choice between thinking things over in my living-room and thinking things over in the office but at least at the office I'll have Jackson's and Carla's endless prattle to preoccupy me. When I think that dithering over some fax in a desperate attempt to get back into Georgie's good books made me late for Ayla I feel suddenly overcome with angry fatigue. Something that insignificant should not play a part in someone's death. No one would have died if that order hadn't gone through, if it had been chucked out with the rubbish. Georgie would have acted as if someone had died, probably me, but no one actually would have. And yet if I'd treated the fax like the stupid piece of pointless money-making paper that it was someone might even have lived. Someone I cared about.

This is the side to irony I never wanted to become acquainted with, the real-life implications of the messenger missing Romeo on his way to find Juliet dead in the chapel.

I've phoned Selin a few times, but her answerphone has always picked up and I've felt awkward about phoning the family home. I don't want to intrude.

Michael. After nearly a week, I only spoke to him briefly yesterday and I'm expecting to see him tomorrow morning. I was on my way back from the police station after giving a full statement, walking down Stoke Newington High Street closely followed by an angry drunk mumbling obscenities under his breath. I had ducked into the safety of Woolworths and was spending some preoccupied minutes looking for an all-the-rage Barbie my niece desperately wants for Christmas when my phone rang. I answered it quickly, for the first time in my life keen to silence 'Disco Inferno'. It briefly occurred to me that it might be Owen, but I had said, 'Hello?' before the thought registered.

'It's me, how are you doing?' It was Michael; straight away his sweetly cheerful tone annoyed me. 'I just I thought I'd say hi. We haven't spoken since the weekend?' He finished the sentence as if it were a question. He really wanted to know why I hadn't called him.

'Not good, actually. You remember Ayla? The girl who came round to my flat? She's . . . um, she died.' The fact that I was telling him several days after it had happened suddenly threw our relationship in to stark shadow and light.

Normal boyfriends you phone straight away under those circumstances, you expect them to rush over or talk you through it and be there for you. It's a long, long time since I have had a normal boyfriend, but the dull philosophy student I told you about, he would have come over with some red wine and discussed existentialism with me, that sort of thing. For a moment I wistfully missed his stolid predictability and even his beard. I realised that I hadn't even wanted to talk to Michael as a distraction, and really he's the best kind of distraction there is.

'She died! No way, you're kidding, right?' He laughed. I knew it was nervous laughter but it was exactly the wrong thing to do. I bristled.

'No, I am *not* kidding and it is *not* funny. She is *dead*. She was run over on Monday. Right in front of me, actually.' I realised my voice had risen and become tight with tears and that people were watching me. I put down the Barbie I had been clutching and marched swiftly out of the shop. Some Twickenham static crackled in my ear.

'Fuck,' he said eventually. 'But she was only, what, seventeen?'

'Sixteen,' I said and turned from the cut-price squalor of the high street into the bohemian café society of Church Street.

'Fuck, I'm only a couple of years older than her. Fuck.'

I sighed impatiently as the enormity of mortality hit Michael for the first time, my temper stopping me dead outside an estate agent's window.

'Michael, I should go really, OK? I'm on my way to the police station to give a statement,' I lied.

'Look, should I come over tonight? Do you want to talk about it? I could skip school tomorrow and we could go somewhere, forget about it.'

I swallowed hard. I didn't want to forget about it, but I thought back on the last time I saw Michael and how nice it would be to spend some more time like that with him, in our little bubble of denial. But not with Rosie in the next room.

'No, look, it's not a good idea just now. But Rosie's mum is in the country at the weekend so she won't be around Saturday. Why don't you come over in the morning, we can spend the day together. You'd have to go before she got back though.'

I said it quickly, feeling guilty for making arrangements when I probably should be seeing if Selin wanted some company, especially when Rosie was going to be in Surrey with her mum. The invitation is out of my mouth before I realise what I'm saying. I'm not sure how seeing Michael will help me, to be honest, but at least he can't make things any worse.

'Yeah sure, I'll cheer you up in no time,' he said brightly, with an absence of tact I knew he did not intend.

'I'm not sure it'll be that easy, Michael,' I said harshly despite myself. 'Someone I have known for most of her life is dead; a very good friend – two very good friends – have lost a sister. I need to deal with it. This is grown-up stuff. I'll see you Saturday, now go and play football or something.' I hung up and stormed the last twenty minutes home full of rage. I knew I had taken my anger out on him when he didn't deserve it but I felt a nasty pleasure that for once the recipient hadn't been me, and a seedy kind of triumph that despite my cruelty I would still see him Saturday morning, keen as a puppy.

Since then I've had my phone turned off. To avoid any more messages from Owen as much as anything else. It occurs to me that I should maybe sit down and think about the whole Owen thing, try and work out where he's coming from, what he's likely to do next, but I can't and anyway I refuse to. For me to be dwelling on the mysterious ways of Owen is exactly what Owen wants. I put it out of my mind. He'll get tired, some poor girl will take his fancy in a bar or a club or a library and he'll leave me alone in favour of some novelty. Despite his self-delusion, not even Owen is so overdramatic as to keep this up for long.

The office seems quiet when I get in and I realise that I'm almost half an hour early, an eventuality that I never achieve by design, usually timing my departure from home to ensure that I am at least ten minutes late into the office, maybe more if the buses don't come on time. I spend a moment trying to commune with the psyche of the rest of the city's worker drones. How many of them get a kick out of going to work and how many, like me, see it as a way to fill time until real life starts in the evenings? Hmm, filling time. Probably shouldn't be filling time when you don't how much you've left. For some reason a memory of Josh's desolate face as he hunched over the balcony railings after Ayla's funeral flashed back to me.

I stare at this week's filing and speculate on the reality of the paperless office as I look at the colour-coded and yet indecipherable array of Post-its that adorns my monitor.

Ayla used to love stationery.

I don't know why I've suddenly remembered that. When she was eleven or twelve she used to collect reams of pretty writing paper and notelets, scented erasers and matching pencil-and-sharpener sets.

In fact, somewhere around here is the three-colour Tipp-Ex set she so longed for that I'd pinched for her a couple of years ago. I never did get around to giving it to her before she grew out of that phase and into aspiring after a belly piercing.

On impulse, I root around in my desk drawer and look for the set. I find an old toothbrush, a single earring and half a pot of glitter eye shadow, the other half of which has spilt over the rest of the drawer's contents. Under the office lights' fluorescent glow it gives off an oddly festive feel. Right at the bottom I find the Tipp-Ex set and right under that something else I'd forgotten. The application form for the journalism course I'd always wanted to apply to but had never got around to.

I lift it out of the drawer and gently blow the glitter remnants away. I think of the look on Ayla's face when she used to pack her pencil case for a new term full of promise. I could fill it in, couldn't I? I could send it off, see what happens.

And anyway, it would give me another reason to ignore that filing.

After completing the form and slipping it in with the work post, I wondered if my last phone call with Michael had constituted even more of a shift in the power balance of our relationship and if that was what I had actually wanted, actually meant by being so unkind. It made me think about the countless cruel things that Owen had said to me over the years. For the first time I think I understood him in a small way, understood his impulse to hurt other people rather than himself, to be in control. Thinking about Owen made me wonder what delights might lurk in my in-box this morning, or how many silent calls I might pick up. I thought about Ayla's sixteen years of life and my thirty. And I made a decision. As soon as this time, this hiatus, is over I am changing everything. As soon as everything is back on an even keel I'm going to go back to college, or at least I'm going to do *something*. My birthday is in a few weeks. By the time the next one comes around I *will* have achieved some personal success, damn it.

Jackson is next in and he strides straight to my office and to my visitors' chair, tipping it back on two legs, a habit he has probably picked up from Rosie. I smile to myself.

'Hey,' he says in an unusually downbeat tone.

'Hey,' I reply, with the false ring of an English person speaking American.

'How are you doing?' As we talk I go through my morning routine of booting up my tortoise-speed PC and opening internal mail envelopes stuffed full of invoices and external circulars offering me security guards or cut-price office furniture. I absently-mindedly bin what I hope is the junk mail.

'Oh, not so bad. Well, terrible really,' I smile at him wanly and he returns the favour, very sweetly not turning on his full-power smile.

'Yeah, Rosie seems to be taking it pretty hard too.'

I fish an invoice out of the bin and replace it with a letter about water coolers that I had mistakenly shoved in the dark and rarely sorted world of my pending tray.

'So, what is the deal with you and Rosie?' I ask, in the vain hope he might tell me something she hasn't.

'Nothing, no deal. We're friends. I'm hopelessly in love with her, of course,' he says lightly, 'but she's got a whole lot of baby on her mind, not to mention a repentant ex-husband, and I'm going back to NY in less than a month. Friends is about all we can be.' He nods, his handsome face a picture of resignation, and somewhere beneath the tan I detect a nuance of genuine sorrow. I have got so used to Jackson that I can't believe he's going back.

'Less than a month? That's gone quickly. But you'll be back on a regular basis, won't you? And as long as you've persuaded her not to go back to Chris, you never know what might happen,' I say hopefully, watching the interminable turning of the PC egg-timer as it attempts to open my e-mail in-box.

'Well, I gave it my best shot, it's true. You never know what's going to happen.' He tips the chair back on to its four feet and rises. 'Do you want to have lunch later?' he throws over his shoulder as he leaves.

'Lunch? Yeah, lovely.'

My unbelievably slow, unbelievably noisy, unbelievably archaic PC finally finishes its whirring and my in-box opens. Thirty-six new e-mails. I check them quickly: several from Georgie, a couple from Jackson, something jokey with an attachment from Selin that she sent on Monday, just a few hours before Ayla died. And the rest the usual complement from my colleagues throughout the building. Nothing that looks as though it might be from Owen. I breathe a sigh of relief.

Maybe he is somewhere out there still, hunched over some pay-as-you-go terminal in an internet café, sending me alliteration-heavy missives like there's no tomorrow but they don't get into my mail box, so they don't really exist as far as I'm concerned. I'm just not going to think about him any more.

The relief makes me feel bold and I turn on my mobile. I wait with baited breath for it to ring to tell me I have messages but it is silent. There is one text message, however. I chew my lip as I open it, it's from Michael.

'sry sry. pls call. mxx.' I look at it for a moment. I probably should call him and make him feel OK, confirm our plans for tomorrow morning but instead I delete it. I'll think about him later. Right now I feel elated. Owen has finally found something better to do; I don't have to think about him any more.

The afternoon runs down slowly and the absence of anything much to do has left me exhausted and almost looking forward to a quiet night in.

'Bye then,' I call to Jackson as I leave dead on five.

'Yeah, bye, I'll see you Monday,' he calls back.

'Yippee yi yay,' I reply glumly as I exit the doors.

I have the bus-stop in sight when I feel a stranger's hand fall heavily on my shoulder. I whirl round in shock, crashing the arm away with the full force of my forearm. My heart is pounding and I clutch my bag to my chest, thinking 'Owen', and 'Don't be such a fool' in one brief moment of panic. I find myself glaring into Michael's eyes.

'For Christ's fucking sake, you idiot, you scared the fucking shit out of me!' I scream at him. No one around stops or bats an eyelid, lucky he isn't about to murder me.

'God, I'm sorry, I'm sorry. I called your name but you didn't seem to hear me.' Michael backs away from me, his palms raised to placate me. I look at him with disbelief and then I let him pull me into his arms and I am glad to have my face buried in his shoulder for a moment, breathing in his warm scent. Finally my blood pressure drops and I only feel incredibly tired.

'Michael, why are you here? I told you I'd see you tomorrow,' I say, watching hurt spread over his face as I finish my sentence. My bus comes around the corner and, wearily, I let it pass, tutting and sighing for his benefit.

'I had to see you face to face, to find out if you're still angry with me. If we are . . . you know. OK.' I close my eyes and take a deep breath. He really scared me. I hadn't realised that I could be so easily spooked.

'Look, can we go somewhere to get a coffee and talk?' he asks. I look up at a rain-filled sky. There is no reason why he shouldn't come home with me tonight, Rosie will have gone by the time I get back, but for some reason the thought of spending this evening with him wears me out.

'No, look, I've got plans for tonight. Go home. I'll see you tomorrow.' I listen to my patronising and detached tone with mild bewilderment. Who am I today?

'I've made a twat out of myself, haven't I?' he says sullenly. Pity and regret flood my chest with warmth as I fold my arms around his waist. The look of relief and gratitude on his face makes me wince.

'You haven't, it's just that we'd made an arrangement and I've already made plans. And this week has been tough, you know. I'm not at my best.' I stand on tiptoe and softly kiss his warm mouth.

As we part he looks at me with a puzzled smile. 'You're always on best form for me,' he says. I smile back at him but really I wish he'd stand up for himself a bit more. Another number 73 bus turns into the bus-stop and I start towards it, hoping to beat the throng for a seat.

'Look, I'm getting this one. I'll see you in the morning, OK? About ten-ish or something?'

'OK. See you. Love you.'

I smile at him once more over my shoulder, but I don't look back as I get on to the bus and I don't turn to wave goodbye as the bus departs.

Chapter Forty-three

When I get in the flat is empty and in darkness and for a few seconds I wish I had brought Michael home with me.

Rosie has left me a note telling me she'll be back Saturday evening around seven-ish and not to pinch all her biscuits. I smile as I take the packet out of the bread bin and help myself to one. Things with Rosie have been better since the funeral but not the way they used to be. Since I told her exactly what I think of Chris and how I feel about the whole thing we haven't spoken about it. This used to be the sort of thing we'd talk over endlessly between us, working out a conclusion in unison, but it's obvious that whatever she is going to decide it will be without my input, and it's when the decision has been made that we'll really find out where our friendship stands. I just don't understand why she doesn't see him as clearly as I do.

I phone Pizza Gogo and order a large vegetarian thin crust on the grounds that the vegetable content (i.e. sweet corn) makes it healthy, getting a kick out of watching the pizza man out of the living-room window as he picks up the phone and then, realising it's his laziest customer, finds my face in the window and gives a little wave.

'You come and get it, yes? Save my legs?' he jokes as he takes my order.

'No, no, your leaflet says free delivery within a five-mile

radius, it doesn't say anything about not delivering within a hundred-yard radius.'

He laughs and tells me fifteen minutes.

'I'll see you in half an hour then.' I hang up.

I call Selin next, hoping she'll be in and want half of my pizza. Her phone seems to ring for a long time before the answerphone picks up. I think she might be call screening.

'Selin? It's Jen, darling. Are you there? Pick up if you are? I'm home and I wanted to see how you are. I haven't managed to get you for the last couple of days and I'm not around tomorrow, so I wanted to check in. Are you OK? Selin?' Eventually I hang up and look at the phone for a moment. Rosie hasn't managed to talk to her either. I try Selin's mobile, but it's switched off.

The family business had been closed all week but I just can't bring myself to phone her at her parents' house. I suppose she'd call us if she wanted us. We told her she could, she said she would. On impulse I call Josh's mobile.

'Jen,' he says, answering in a couple of rings.

'Hi, where are you?' I ask routinely.

'Um, walking along Clissold Park. Mum's just fed me and I'm going home to try and get some kip. I was up all of last night and most of today. Thinking, you know. Trying to do some work.'

'Right, of course. Listen, Josh. I haven't been able to get hold of Selin. Was she at your mum's? Is she OK?' I listen to the sound of Josh's breathing for a second.

'Um, yes, she's there.' There is something he doesn't want to tell me. I'm sure Selin blames me.

'Do you think I should call her? I don't want to intrude,' I say, trying to work out what he's thinking.

'Maybe tonight isn't the best night. Look, don't worry about her, she's being looked after, she'll call you when she's ready. You know Selin.'

Feeling rejected in some oblique way I start to feel sorry for myself.

'I don't suppose you fancy staying awake for a couple more hours to help me finish off a veggie pizza?' I ask hopefully.

'After one of Mum's meals? Are you joking? She's still cooking for . . . for six.' He finishes the sentence quietly and I kick myself for being so insensitive.

'Josh, I'm sorry,' I say. 'Look, take care and call me, OK?' Another couple of beats of silence follow.

'I could bring round some wine and watch you pig out, though,' he says suddenly and my heart lifts. I hadn't realised how much I didn't want to be alone tonight, even though I'd turned down the pleasure of Michael's company.

'That would be really nice, if you're sure,' I say, trying to keep the potential pressure of gratitude out of my voice.

'I'm sure. I'll pop into the Venus 21 off-licence and I'll be there in ten, OK?'

'OK,' I say, smiling to myself.

The pizza arrives and I shove it in the oven while I wait for Josh. Catching sight of myself in the hall mirror I quickly go into the bathroom, cleanse the mascara seepage from under my eyes and brush my hair back from my face. It seems pointless before pizza but I brush my teeth anyway and squirt on a bit of Rosie's perfume.

He arrives a few minutes later with two bottles of wine, a couple of days' stubble and hollows under his eyes that throw his cheekbones into stark relief.

'Fuck, you really haven't slept, have you?' I say without thinking. He laughs.

'So direct and to the point, as always. That's my girl.'

Finally, with beakers of wine, Billie Holiday in the CD player and the pizza laid out before us, we settle on the sofa.

'This is nice,' I say. 'I don't mean, you know what I mean,

I mean it's ages since you and I have just hung out.' Which isn't strictly true, we've hung out a lot recently but everything before Ayla's death now seems like light years away.

'Yeah well, I usually have to try and catch you between bouts of Owen,' he smiles wryly.

'And I have to catch you between bouts of creative temptresses with a special line in papier mâché and henna hairdos,' I retort for good measure.

'Not any more, I've given them up. Can't trust a girl who gets turned on by soggy paper and glue. I'm thinking maybe chicken wire and plaster of Paris might be my next avenue of romantic exploration.'

I raise my eyebrows.

'Oh really? Well, I've given up Owen, so until chicken-wire girl comes along we can do this more often.'

'That'll be nice,' he smiles. 'Unless another fatally-flawed-personality boy comes along in the meantime.'

We both laugh at ourselves and take a large gulp from our glasses, holding each other's gaze as we do so. I fill the glasses up again. We have silently agreed that we are going to get bladdered. Josh is sleep deprived and I haven't eaten much today so it shouldn't take too long. This means I'll have a red-wine hangover for Michael in the morning. Oh well.

'How are you holding up?' I ask, not for the first time. 'Stupid question really.' The wine sizzles in my empty stomach.

'Stupid? No, I'm holding up dreadfully.' He takes another gulp of wine, emptying half of his glass in one go and topping it up again. I try and think about what I can do, what I can say. I can't just not talk about Ayla, but I feel as if I shouldn't simply let him sink into overtired drunken maudlin oblivion either. If I can't be there for Selin I can try and rescue Josh in my own small way.

Suddenly an old memory pops into my head.

'Do you remember when you had that girl up in your room, what was her name? You were about twenty, you must have been because we were in the lower sixth and Ayla was three. I bet you were trying to get your leg over and anyway, Ayla was just talking properly and we got her to run into your room and shout, "Josh is gonna do it! Josh is gonna do it!" at the top of her voice and your mum came storming up the stairs and dragged you out of that room by your ear. And that poor girl, what was her name? She ran out of there quicker than a bat out of hell. God, that made me laugh for weeks.'

Josh tips his head back and laughs, nodding at the memory. 'Janine Whitman. That was her name. She refused to see me again after that, so thank you very much. She might have been the one, you know,' he says with a look of mock reproach.

'Trust me, it *wasn't* Janine Whitman,' I say with conviction.

'No, I don't suppose it was.' He smiles as another memory comes back to him and I feel pleased with myself that I started this.

'What about the time she poured all of Mum's best perfume over that stray dog she brought home? Or when she was nine and she decided to become a nun. Dad nearly had an embolism!' We laugh again, both picturing her appearance one tea-time in a home-made tea-towel wimple and bed-sheet habit.

'Your poor dad, he was ready to pack up and go back to Turkey!' I smile.

'She was a lovely girl,' Josh says, the laughter and light gradually draining from his voice. I reach out and take his hand. He grips my fingers and looks away from me.

'It just seems so arbitrary, Jen. So pointless.' Threatened tears constrict his throat.

'I know,' I say, 'I know.' I shift down the sofa towards him. His arms pull me into a hug and he buries his face in my neck. Before long I feel his shoulders begin to shake and his tears dampen my shirt. Minutes pass and he gradually becomes still. As he raises his head he turns his face from me again and drops his arms to his sides. This is all so unbearably hard for him.

I position myself in the crook of his arm, my back curved into the warmth of his chest, pick up his limp arm and tuck it over my shoulder.

'Do you want to talk about something else?' I ask after a short silence.

'No, it's good to talk about her, to remember and laugh. Mum can't bear to mention her name at the moment. That house is so quiet and dark. Poor Hakam, I think he feels it worst. It always used to be Ayla he'd talk to, the rest of us must seem like pensioners to him.' I feel his other hand brush the hair back from the nape of my neck in an absent-minded gesture and I settle my head back on to his shoulder. Without warning, my niggling worries about Selin spring to the surface again.

'Josh? Is Selin angry with me?' He moves abruptly and the bristle of his stubble grazes my ear and makes me shiver.

'Angry? Whatever for?' he says, reaching for the next bottle of wine and filling our glasses.

'Well, I know it's really selfish to think this at the moment but I get the feeling she is avoiding me because I was there, wasn't I? Do you think she . . . do any of you blame me? Because I'd understand, I would. I'd just rather you didn't pretend that you don't.' I twist round so that I'm looking him in the face, trying to read his thoughts in his eyes. He must be able to read the anxiety on my face as clear as day.

'Jen, no one blames you. Mum and Dad don't, Selin doesn't and I certainly don't. You were trying to help, everyone understands that. You mustn't think anyone blames you.' I sigh and turn back to my original position. As the warmth of more wine settles in my stomach, I realise I haven't touched the pizza.

'I think I blame myself then,' I say finally and the warmth of my own tears burns my face.

'Oh, Jen,' Josh says softly, wrapping his arms around me. We sit in peace and I listen to the quiet rhythm of his breathing gradually lengthen. I relax, my tears finally stop, and my body gives in to the strains of the day, my eyes growing heavier.

Josh has drifted off to sleep, and I carefully take the half-empty glass from his hand and put it on the floor. The video tells me it's just gone ten. It doesn't seem fair to wake him, not just yet. Putting my own glass down carefully, I settle back into the crook of his arm and turn my face to the back of the sofa. I'll just doze here for a bit and then send him home.

Chapter Forty-four

A searing pain shooting down one side of my neck and biting into my shoulder wakes me again. For some reason it takes me a couple of minutes to open my eyes, and I wince and straighten my neck out, slightly alarmed by the loud crack it makes. At some point during my nap I have changed position and my head now rests just below Josh's chin. I look at the video clock. 8.32 – well, that's not too late then. Except it was ten something when I last looked, which means it's 8.32 a.m. and not p.m. We've managed to sleep on a two-seater sofa, the pair of us, for ten hours. Blimey.

For several moments I stare at the dim light that has managed to seep through the curtains, then at the cold and congealed pizza, which neither of us touched, on the floor, and then at the video clock again. I have a vague feeling of disconcerted unreality, I can't believe that it is still possible for so many hours to escape me without my permission. The sort of feeling you get when you really do sleep through your alarm clock for once, or when you really can't remember what happened the night before, or probably when you have been abducted by aliens and you lose a few hours and gain an implant, that sort of thing. We must both have been tired, very tired. Two adults on a two-seater sofa, ten hours, that's tired.

I let myself listen to and be lulled by the rise and fall of Josh's chest for a few moments more before I gingerly extricate myself from him. The side of my face stings as I sit up and I'm fairly certain that right now I have the perfect imprint of one of his shirt buttons displayed on my cheek. As I carefully slide away from him I notice that I have dribbled on his shirt. Nice.

Despite my efforts, I fail to not wake him.

'Mmm, c'm'ere,' he mumbles, maybe not quite awake yet, and with his eyes still closed he grabs my wrist and pulls me back towards him.

'Josh!' I squeal loudly, afraid that he is dreaming of someone else and that reality will disappoint him and embarrass me. He opens his eyes, blinks at me a couple of times and then a slow smile spreads through the even more stubble that he seems to have accumulated overnight.

'Hello, Jen, sorry about that. What time is it?'

'Morning. That's what time it is, can you believe that we managed to sleep the whole night on the sofa?' I want him to be as amazed as I am.

'No way! Well, I did need to catch up on some sleep. The whole night on the sofa? That's tired.' He hasn't let me down. I nod with satisfaction and walk stiffly to the kitchen; a quick stop at the hall mirror reveals my new facial button imprint and an array of sleep creases. That's it, my skin is officially old. I never used to get sleep creases. Not until this year.

A few seconds later Josh ambles in after me and we both look stupidly at the kettle as it rattles and boils.

'Shall we go to the Sunshine Café?' he asks and I nod gratefully, not trusting that I have the hand-to-eye coordination to make a cup of tea myself. I silently slip into shoes and a coat, somehow enjoying my day-old clothes, the hungover buzz between my ears and the easy known-him-for-ever joy of Josh's company.

'Josh, how do you define being old?' I ask him as we troop

down the stairs. 'I used to think I'd be able to define it by wages, mortgages, number of kids, that sort of thing. But it occurs to me this morning that I identify it with the fact that my skin no longer has elasticity. I have an old woman's skin, therefore I am old. I'm suing.'

'Suing who?' He shakes his head and smiles at me with quiet indulgence.

'Oh, I don't know. Boots, Oil of Olay, Clinique, Clarins. The celestial being who decreed that there should be no halcyon time of complexion perfection between spots and wrinkles. That sort of thing.' Josh holds the external door open for me as I wander out into the damp air.

'I think you've got lovely skin. Now see that?' he nods at one of those telephone terminal things on the street corner. 'That makes me feel old.'

I frown. It hurts.

'A telephone terminal thingy?' I am nonplussed. Maybe he used to harbour a secret wish to become a BT engineer, but now believes the opportunity has passed him by.

'No, not the terminal thingy, those fly posters advertising a new single by a new band.' I look at the poster featuring an image of a pig's head on a doll's body. It reads 'Tomorrow Never Comes/Lacklustre'.

'I don't get it,' I say. Admittedly this morning I'm not likely to get my own name, but still I want to know.

'No, neither do I. What I mean is, I don't know if "Tomorrow Never Comes" is the name of the single or the band. I don't know if "Lacklustre" is the name of the single or the band. I've never heard of them, or it, whichever. There was a time, not so long ago, that I would have heard of them before they had heard of themselves. I'd have been at their early gigs. I'd probably have known the bassist. I'd have been their biggest expert fan, until they broke the charts and I ditched them for being too mainstream. Now I know nothing. Not knowing about new music is a sign of being old to me. Not knowing which is the band and which is the title of the single on the fly poster means I'm old.'

I cover my face with my hands and wail.

'What's wrong now?' Joss asks me with mock concern.

'If that's true, I've always been old!' I cry, peeping out of the corners of my fingers to catch him smiling, taking his play punch on the shoulder like a man. I lean gratefully into his bulk and he swings a friendly arm around my neck.

A couple of fry-ups and two milky coffees later I look at the grease-filmed clock on the Sunshine Café's wall and remember that Michael is coming over. I'm overtired, emotionally drained and laden down with saturated fat but even so I think I should probably be feeling a bit more upbeat about his visit than I am. I sigh and drain the last of my coffee.

'I have to go,' I say to Josh, who for the last five minutes has been quietly attempting and failing to make a roll-up fag.

'Oh, do you? I thought you might fancy a walk in the park after this?' He finally cobbles together a thin and untidy creation, looks at it and then tucks it behind his ear. I smile to myself and think that an alcoholic weakness-fuelled walk through the park with Josh is just what I would like, safe in the knowledge that we'd make each other giggle, or be happy to be quiet together, that at no point would there be any pressure to feel one way or another or to struggle against some kind of display, no matter how mild, of something approaching Creeping Repulsion. Very many times during my life I have been accused of not picking up obvious warning signs, of sticking my head in the sand but even I, mistress of telling it like I want it to be, can tell; I'm not *really* looking forward to seeing Michael. I think the precarious reasons I invented not to finish it may just have completely evaporated.

Either way, I've got to see him this morning.

'No, I've got to go. I've got to meet someone.'

Josh looks at me for a moment and says, 'Oh. Well, OK.' He seems a bit peeved.

'Not a boyfriend or anything,' I find myself saying. 'Just a mate. Arranged ages ago.'

'OK,' Josh says, but I know he has picked me up in a lie and I can tell it bothers him in just the same abstract way that it bothers me. I feel as though I've let him down somehow. I push my chair back and stand.

'So, well . . . tell Selin I love her and to call me if she wants me. And, um, why don't you come round, you know, any time. Last night was really . . . well, it was really good to spend time with you. Despite the whole sofa incident.'

'Yes, I will, it was. The sofa incident was the first time I've slept since the accident. And thanks, Jen. It's good to have someone to talk to outside the family. You seem to be able to . . . well, what I'm saying is you're a really good mate.' I can't help the little warm burst of pride in my chest and I smile shyly.

'Oh well, no problem. So I'll see you then?' I sound like a needy girl in search of date two.

'You'll see me.' He sounds like a lothario boy already in search of the next date one.

I leave the café feeling jangled and confused. Josh. Maybe it's because I haven't seen that much of him for ages and then when I finally do it's during a time of grief, of heightened emotions, but something seems to have happened to my perception of him. Now that I'm leaving him a little out of sorts in the Sunshine Café I feel a bit down, almost as if I miss him. I analyse these feelings for a moment longer. They do not compute. It has been a really difficult time recently, we are all jumbled and mixed up. Plus I'm hungover, I'm emotional,

I'm almost thirty but still spending time with Josh is so easy. The next time I meet someone who might mean something to me I'm going to go for a bloke a bit more like Josh, I mean really, what more could a girl want? I let myself into the flat and turn on the bath taps. Someone just like Josh maybe, exactly like him. Maybe even Josh, I find myself thinking.

'Jennifer Gillian Greenway,' I say out loud to myself, 'this is *no* time to rekindle an unrequited adolescent crush during a time of extreme emotional upheaval. It would definitely be the most stupid thing you have ever done. Oh, apart from initiate an affair with a teenager.' As the bath fills I look at myself in the mirror which is clouding over with steam. My face retreats into the mist and with it any sense of self-recognition that I thought I had.

Lying in the steaming water, I think about the last time I'd just got out of the bath to greet Michael at the door, dressed only in a towel. It seems like years ago, the frenetic rush into sex had seemed like a turning point to me, like a final page ushering me into a new chapter of my life. That weekend had seemed like a release, so why does the prospect of his arrival now make me feel like a prisoner?

Yet again, I have wet hair and only a towel on when the doorbell rings.

'Déjà vu,' I mutter to myself as I pick up the intercom. 'Hello?'

'Hi, hi, it's me.' I buzz him in without speaking and hurriedly rush into my room and pull on my habitual pair of jeans and a jumper, *sans* underwear but slightly more respectable than just a towel.

'Hello!' He is panting when he comes through the door and suddenly my bedroom is filled with his large presence. I smile, unable to not be pleased to see him. He strides over and kisses me hard, his tongue taking possession of my mouth and his hands sliding up under my jumper.

'Mmm, damp skin, no bra,' he says, pushing my jumper up to expose my breasts to the cold air. As he holds the material up under my chin and looks at me I feel a detached, turned-on tingle in my gut, as if I'm watching a film of myself. I let him tug the jumper over my head and pull me on to his lap, watching him suck and kiss my breasts, listening in silence to his sighs and groans, but this time I'm not there with him, I'm far away, my own voyeur, intrigued by how removed I am from the whole process.

He doesn't seem to mind or notice my emotional absence and I let him remove my jeans, push an enquiring hand between my legs, flop me back on to my bed and hastily disrobe. I let him cover me with his body and his mouth. By the time he enters me I want sex, but I feel so far away from wanting him that I feel like a stranger in my own bed. He wants to be slow, but my own impatience finally prompts me to engage and I begin to move under him and push him to work faster and faster until I come in a quick aggressive spasm. My sudden apparent ignition of passion pushes him over the brink and he shudders, tenses and relaxes against me. A few seconds pass before he slides out of me and rests his head between my breasts.

'That was fantastic,' he says.

I look at the grey sky outside the window and for the first time ever feel the power that comes with using someone just for sex. Immature feelings for Josh aside, I am now certain of how I feel for Michael. He is a wonderful, kind, funny boy, but all I have ever wanted of him has been to cheer me up, has been to turn me round from the gloom of Owen. All I've ever wanted is his adoration and his body. I have never really wanted to give him anything in return at all. I have treated him in almost exactly the same way as Owen treated me. Ayla is gone and life is all too short for something as wrong for both of us as this is. For once in my life I have to be decisive, to really do the right thing.

'Michael,' I say, knowing what I'm going to say, but not sure how to say it.

'What?' He raises his head and smiles at me.

'Michael, we can't see each other any more.' He sits bolt upright and smiles at me, checking to see if I'm teasing.

'What . . . What do you mean?' he asks uncertainly.

I brace myself.

'Listen, you're a fantastic person, a wonderful person, but . . .' I watch his face begin to crumble but I swallow and carry on. 'Michael, it isn't you. It's the timing. A lot of things have happened to put things into perspective for me. I've been lost and lonely and I wanted you to rescue me. That isn't fair to either you or me. I'm sorry,' I say and I mean it.

His slow sweet smile fills his face.

'I don't mind. I don't mind. That's what I'm here for, for you.' I withdraw my hand from under his and rub my finger across my forehead. I knew that this moment would come all those weeks ago in the Ye Old Parson's Nose when I agreed to take him home that night. I knew that all the wrong turns I had deliberately made would bring me back here one day. To a place where I have to hurt someone for the sake of not getting hurt myself. The thought that I might have something, no matter how small, in common with Owen makes me wince.

'Michael. I just don't think we can see each other any more,' I repeat. His face drops and he blinks hard twice.

'Why not? I mean, we get on OK, don't we? Is it . . . is it the sex?' To have this conversation moments after sex must really hurt him, but I can't see that delaying it any longer will help. His face is so open and vulnerable that I have to resist the urge just to push real life away once again with all my might in favour of the comfort of pulling him into my arms.

'No! God, no. Sex with you has been fantastic, this morning was fantastic. It just makes me realise even more that I'm with you for the wrong reasons. Great sex isn't enough. Michael, I'm thirty in a couple of weeks, I need to feel that I'm going forward, even if I'm going forward alone. With you I'm standing still. Standing still in a wonderful, sunny happy place, but standing still.' I watch his face and search for the right words, some way to end this without hurting him too much. 'You and I, we just aren't right. We don't fit together properly, not in an emotional sense. Every time I see you I have to rationalise what I'm doing. It's all wrong, and I don't want that kind of relationship, Michael. I want one that is part of my whole life, not an appendage to it. If I want a relationship at all it's got to be the sort that will allow me to be myself and be free. Not the kind that's going to have me worrying about "it" every second of the day. I want one that isn't a secret from my friends or family, that doesn't have me pretending to your mum to be a girl from drama club. I think maybe I just need to be on my own for a while.' I shrug lamely and bite my lip. For the first time in my life I realise that there is no way, no place or circumstance that makes this kind of speech resonate with anything more than hollow regret.

'That's it?' he asks defensively, and he has every right to. When I say it out loud it sounds as if I can't see that what we have, what we had, is worth fighting for. And the truth is, I can't.

'Yes, that's it,' I say, already sounding cold and distant.

'It's not about how great we get on? How good we are together? How we make each other laugh? It's about how *respectable* we are?'

I can't think of a better way to explain something that I am only just beginning to understand myself. I find I don't want to have to explain it any more. The pain and complication, the inevitable consequences of my actions, weigh down too heavily on my tongue.

'I think you should go,' I say, avoiding his eye, climbing out of bed and getting dressed.

'But, wait. I can fix that!' he cries, scrambling out of bed and back into his clothes. 'I can make that better. I can make it so that I can be a whole part of your life. I can!'

I look at him and throw him his trainers.

'I don't think you can,' I say with a deliberately cold voice. 'We are just too far apart.' I walk to the front door and hold it open. Filled with justifiable anger, he hurtles towards me stopping short a few inches from me.

'You're wrong. I'll show you how much you mean to me,' he says. 'Then you'll see.' And he is gone, slamming into walls as he rushes down the stairs.

I don't go to the window to watch him walk away, I go into the living-room and look at the sofa which still holds the impression of Josh's head and neck in its cushions. I sink into his familiar dents and close my eyes, rubbing my pounding temples.

Have I treated Michael badly? Did I make that more painful than it had to be? Was I more cruel and cold than I had to be? Saying all that just after sex, that would hurt him. Would waiting any longer have hurt him more? Would an uncomfortable day of distances and silences have been better for him? I do feel bad, I feel wretched, but as is always the way if you're the person who ends it I feel relieved. At least I didn't leave him a Post-it note.

So, where do I go from here?

When Rosie comes through the door later that evening I have barely moved off the sofa all day. I spend a lot of time on the sofa these days.

'Hi,' she says. 'Seen Selin?' I hear her bustle in and out of her room, haul myself into an upright position and shake my head.

'No. I keep calling but no. I saw Josh. He said she was at their mum and dad's and not to worry but, well, I keep thinking there's something he's not telling me. How was your mum?'

Rosie comes into the living-room with a waxed Sephora paper bag.

'She seems to have become even more American. Except that she's still thin. Good genes, you see. Hubby is fine. She told me I should have an elective caesarean so I didn't have to bother with the fuss and worry about my vagina stretching. She said, and I quote, "Well, honey, you're still not married, you know. I think you should at least get a ring on that finger before you let your vagina get slack." Said it right in front of Hubby and his niece. Mortified.'

I let my jaw drop before bursting out in giggles.

'Your mum, she always was a one,' I say. 'Can you imagine my mum saying that? Can you imagine my mum saying "vagina"!' We laugh. Rosie's mum has always been the glamorous, skinny, dressing-young, roots-always-touched-up mum. When Rosie's dad left she picked herself up and got right back out there, remarried within two years and relocated to the States as soon as Rosie left home.

My mum met my dad when she was fourteen. She married him at a time when being a wife and mother was what marriage was all about, and she did that better than anyone for nearly quarter of a century before the secretary came along. When my dad left my mum was hurt and bewildered, punch drunk from a blow she didn't see coming. Suddenly forced into a world of work she didn't want or understand, just to keep a roof over our heads. She did it, she held down one job and then another until gradually she began to make friends and enjoy her working life, right up until the time she retired. But I'll never forget those first years after we had the rug pulled out from under our feet. Coming home from school to an empty house for the first time ever, to find the electricity had been cut off or the phone bill hadn't been paid. Going to bed before eight so that I didn't have to hear my mum cry. I'll never forgive him for abandoning us like that. If he had to leave us, why did he have to be so unkind?

I pull myself out of my reverie and admire the array of cosmetics Rosie has begun to set out on the floor.

'Say what you like about your mum but she gives good gifts.'

'I know!' And for a few minutes we sniff newly opened pots of face cream, test lipsticks and spray perfume just as we used to in our old bedrooms all those years ago with 'borrowed' or discarded Avon products.

'Got another antenatal next week,' Rosie says, admiring the rainbow of Tuscan Spice through to Glacier Cherry Gloss that she has created on the back of her hand.

'Yeah? Routine one? Do you want me to come?' She ignores my question.

'You know I woke up last night in Mum and Hubby's guest room in total panic, literally gasping for air. Finally I calmed down and I thought, what is it? And then I suddenly realised that I am going to be responsible for another human life, like, *really responsible*. To the extent of keeping him or her alive. I'm going to have to remember to feed them and clothe them and not drop them or leave them in the bath or on the bus. I mean, I've thought about it before now, of course I have, I thought about nothing else when I decided to keep my baby. But the closer it gets the more I realise how much my life is going to change. It's not just going to be *my* life any more.' I listen quietly to her outburst and have begun to formulate a reassuring response when she continues, 'The thing is, I don't know if I can face it alone. I don't know if I want to.'

I close my mouth and swallow. Chris.

'What does your mum say?' I ask through tight lips.

'She says that when it comes to marriage and children you have to give it every possible chance before giving up. But then she does watch a lot of Oprah Winfrey.' She smiles at me hopefully.

'Well maybe, but you're not married, are you, Rosie, and why is that?' Her face falls and she silently packs her cosmetics back into her bag.

'You just don't want to understand, do you?' she says, as she goes to her room. 'And I don't need you to come to the clinic with me, Chris is.'

I pad wearily to my bedroom, wondering how many more hits our friendship can take and how many more bridges we can build. I can't see past how wrong it would be for her to go back to Chris and she can't see why I'm right. My neck and shoulders hurt from too much time spent on the sofa over the last twenty-four hours but despite spending most of it asleep I find I'm shattered. I am grateful to go to sleep again.

Chapter Forty-five

I'm standing in a field full of tall flowers, with stems that reach over my head and heavy scent-laden flowers that act like parasols to shade me from the heat of a mid-summer, midday sun. Somewhere ahead of me I can hear a happy child, laughing and calling my name. I think I am lost.

'Jenny! Jenny!' The cries seem to get further away each time I hear them and each time I look around me I have become even smaller and smaller in a never-ending summer.

'Jenny, mate, wake up, for Christ's sake.'

I sit bolt upright and rub my eyes, blinking. The clock reads 9.30 a.m. Rosie is leaning over me.

'Rosie, I was dreaming . . .' I say, slightly befuddled, pushing my hair out of my eyes and smoothing sleep creases from my skin. 'It is Sunday isn't it?'

'Oh yeah? Well, I thought *I* was dreaming but it turns out that there really *is* a mad woman downstairs demanding that you let her in now!' Her tone is not a happy one, and I wince as I remember last night's conversation.

'A what?' I can't seem to get my act together

'This woman, a Frances Parrott. She was ringing the bell for bloody ages. I was in the bath, but anyway as you clearly weren't going to wake up I got out of the bath and answered it for you. Who is she? She is most insistent that she talks to you. And frankly, she sounds mightily pissed off.'

Frances Parrott? Fran. "Call me Fran, dear." Oh fuck. Michael's mother. I can think of only one reason why Michael's mother is here.

'I can fix that,' he had said, or something like it, when I told him that the reason we couldn't be together was because I wanted a proper relationship that I could have in public. He's gone public. He's told his mother.

'She's . . . um, tell her I'm not here?' I ask Rosie hopefully as I climb out of bed and into the same jeans and jumper I put on for Michael yesterday. The jumper looks too tight across my chest so I change it for a baggy one, fully aware that it is probably too late to make a good impression.

'Too late, she knows you're here. She demands they come up here now before she calls the police. That's the *police*, Jenny?' Rosie tells me with furious precision, just in case the situation hasn't quite sunk in yet.

I pace up and down by my bed a couple of times, trying to think of a way out of the flat without using the stairs.

'Jenny! Snap out of it! Talk to her yourself, will you? What's the problem anyway, do you owe her money or something?' If only I could write a cheque to get out of this one.

'Or something,' I say, taking a deep breath and preparing to bite the bullet. I walk to the door and pick up the inter-com phone.

'Hello?' I say banally.

'Miss Greenway, it's Michael's mother here. I demand you let us in right now.' Oh fuck, she's brought him with her. This gets better and better.

'Come up,' I say briefly. I turn and look at Rosie, who is eyeing me speculatively from the kitchen doorway.

'Rose, you are about to hear some things that you may

find . . . surprising. Please would you just remember that I meant to tell you everything, and promise me that you will wait until you've heard my side of the story.' She raises her eyebrows in a way that clearly says, 'Why should I?' and the front door shudders behind me as Mrs Parrott bangs on it with the full fury of a mother scorned.

I open the door.

'You manipulative hussy,' she says, pushing past me and marching down the hallway. Hussy? If this wasn't so serious I'd be tempted to laugh. 'What kind of a woman are you to lure an innocent boy into sex. You disgust me, you pervert, you're nothing but a . . . but a filthy disgusting paedophile.'

Now I take offence. Rosie watches in silent horror as a tear-stained Michael files past her into the living-room and stands behind his seething mother.

'Mrs Parrott, Michael is eighteen. He's old enough to vote, old enough to die for his country. And he's more than old enough and ready to have sex with whomever he chooses, believe me,' I say, instantly regretting the implication of my last words. I sink on to a chair. Mrs Parrott bubbles over with wrath.

'He only turned eighteen a few days ago, he is still a child no matter what he may think. You know that and I know that. You come into my home, abuse my hospitality, lie to my face; although how I could ever have been fooled into thinking you aren't every single one of your thirty years I *don't* know. You lead him on, you corrupt him and then finally, *finally* demand that he tells us about you or you'll finish with him! What did you expect, Miss Greenway? What did you expect? An invitation to dinner? Perhaps we should ask you along to his next parents' evening, maybe *you* will be able to explain to his teachers why his grades have slipped? Can you? I bet you've got a pretty good idea what he's been up to when he should have been studying, haven't you? You filthy . . .' Apparently she can't think of a word low enough to describe me and at last her tirade runs out of steam and she just stares at me red faced and open mouthed. I can't find the words to defend myself, I just raise my hands, palm towards her, and then let them drop into my lap. I remain speechless. What can I say?

'Mum.' Michael reaches a hand out to her but she slaps him away. I can see from the blotches on his stricken face and the shadows under his eyes what a dreadful night he has had, and my heart goes out to him. Patiently, he begins again.

'I've told you, it wasn't like that, Mum, Jenny wanted to end it. I was the one who didn't want it to end, I was the one who wanted to tell you. I wanted to show her I wasn't ashamed of us, of what we have. Had.'

She shakes her head at him with pity and turns to look at me again.

'Oh, so you'd had your fun with him, had you? Novelty worn off, had it?'

I catch Rosie's eye. She shakes her head at me, turns and retreats into her room.

'I don't know what to say to you, Mrs Parrott,' I say. 'I can see how it looks to you, but really it wasn't like that.' I'm not sure that is exactly the truth but I'm certain that it is what Michael needs to hear. 'Michael and I cared about, care about, each other. We really do. But I could see that the practicalities were never going to go away. I just wanted to end things before they got out of hand, before anyone got too hurt. I never meant to take advantage of your son, I don't think that I did. We had a relationship that wasn't going to work out, that's all.'

She shakes her head at me this time and picks up her bag.

'If you never wanted anyone to get hurt or damaged, "young" woman, you should never have let this farce begin. You were the adult here, not a teenager. Now I am warning you, it might be technically legal, but if you ever, *ever* go near my son again I will have an injunction out against you faster than you can say your own name, and believe me I'll make sure that everyone you know knows about this. Do you understand me?'

'I understand you,' I say to my hand, feeling powerless to defend myself.

'Right, Michael, come on. We're not spending one second longer in this place than we have to.'

Michael stands and looks at me for a moment.

'*Come on*, I said!' his mother bellows.

He stands his ground.

'I'll be down in a minute, mum. I want to say goodbye to Jenny.' She looks from him to me, her face a picture of despair, and she heads towards the door.

'You have one minute before I come back up here and drag you out on to the street by your hair,' she spits and then she is gone.

'I'm so sorry,' he says, standing a few feet from me, swinging his hands by his side like a ten-year-old, 'I thought maybe . . . I don't know what I thought. I didn't want us to end.' I stand up and catch his hand in mine. My chest feels tight with sorrow and regret. Not regret for the last few weeks with him, but regret that I caused this to happen.

'Michael, it's not your fault, it's mine. I should never have let this happen.' He jerks his fingers from mine and pulls his shoulders back, raising his chin a little.

'Don't say that! *Don't ever* say that! I have had the best time ever with you. My first time with you. It was everything to me. And I'm not a fucking kid, you know. I *did* know what I was getting into and I got into it because I wanted to. And my grades are down at school because I'm basically not that bright and I should have taken Art instead of physics, but oh no, Dad said I needed a science.'

His mercurial switch in tone makes me smile. He always did make me smile. Our fingers link again, sending a physical memory of his touch up and down my spine. Deep breaths.

'I'm sorry that you have had to go through this,' I say, gesturing at the morning in general. 'And for the fact that you will presumably be grounded until you're twenty-one.'

He laughs. We both laugh and step into an easy hug.

'I won't forget you,' he whispers to the top of my head. 'Not ever.'

'I should hope not, not after all the good times we've had.' I smile and tip my chin back to look into his brown eyes. 'If things had been different, you would have been the one,' I say, and maybe it's not true now but maybe it could have been once, before life snuck up and changed me all around. He nods and delves into the pocket of his combats.

'I want you to have this. I can't listen to it any more and well, I think you should have at least one thing that is fairly modern in your CD collection. Your cred's rock bottom, Jen.' He hands me his David Gray CD and I swallow the lump in my throat.

'Oh, thanks,' I say dumbly. I clutch it to my chest, like a soft toy.

'I'll see you around then?' he says, although both of us know that he won't.

'Yes, sure,' I say anyway. 'Send me a postcard from uni.' It seems that anything I am going to say will sound trite, it has just become impossible to find words that express how I'm feeling. I walk him to the door and he bends to kiss me lightly, brushing his warm lips against mine before turning down the stairs. I do not watch him go. For a quiet moment I stand and look at the CD cover, and a brief vision of his sofa bed flashes across my memory; for one crazy second I think about chasing after him and asking him to run away with me somewhere, somewhere where it's summer all year long. I hear the downstairs door slam shut. I want to go into my room, put on David Gray and lie quietly looking at the ceiling, but I've got one or two things to sort out before that can happen.

'That was thingy, wasn't it? The boy from the party and Soho Square. Ginger Teenager.' Rosie looks at me from the doorway of her bedroom at the other end of the hall, her mouth half open with disbelief and a look somewhere between hysterical laughter and self-righteous preaching hovering around her eyes. How am I going to handle this one? She crooks her finger at me and beckons me to follow her into the living-room.

'So, you're telling me you've been out with Ginger Boy? You, know, secretly?' She's looking at me as if I've dropped in from another planet as she flops on to the sofa.

'I *was* planning to tell you. I mean, we didn't exactly go out together, it just sort of happened, you know. One minute I'm being all responsible and letting him down gently and the next minute he's getting my kit off in the back of a cab, you know how it goes.'

Rosie bursts into shocked laughter. She starts to count on her fingers.

'But he's, like, *twelve* years younger than you. When he was born you were . . . wearing a ra-ra skirt and fantasising over Limahl.'

I interrupt her. 'Yeah, yeah, been there, done all that stuff. I know he's too young for me and that's why I only saw him for a bit and I'm not about to go on a Kilroy special about forbidden love to announce our engagement. But for a while there, the age gap thing didn't matter. He was so . . . refreshing and new.' I try to explain what it was about Michael but it seems that Rosie can't keep her mind out of the gutter.

'My God! You busted him! What's it like doing it with a

306

virgin? Was it crap? Did you have to go on top? Did you droop? Did he?'

I smile and shake my head. This reminds me of our old sleepover days, and I'm relieved that she seems to be letting me off so lightly.

'Honestly, Rosie, all you think about is sex, sex, sex. Actually, he was pretty good after a few practices.' Rosie clasps a cushion to her face with embarrassment. I smile. 'And let's just say what he lacked in expertise he more than made up for in stamina!' We both giggle and I settle down next to her on the sofa.

'But actually what I meant, when I said refreshing, was that he isn't jaded by life or relationships. He still sees the wonder of everything, the possibility of a future. After Owen it was nice to be with someone like that for a while. Yes, I admit it was partly an exercise in pretending I'm not a thirty-year-old with no prospects. It started out that way, but well, if things had been different I could have fallen for him maybe. If he'd shut up about *Star Wars* and heavy metal for five minutes.'

Rosie tucks the cushion back behind her back, her smile fading. 'Why didn't you tell us?' Her tone has gone from curious hilarity to slightly defensive.

'Well, you know. He's ginger,' I say, trying to go for a laugh.

She smiles but persists. 'No, but really?' I look around the room and try and think of a way to say that if anyone had known they would have spoilt it. It was never meant to be something real enough to talk about, but somehow I can't bring myself to say that, to show how messed up I still am.

'Well, why didn't you tell us about Chris wanting to get back with you?' I retort unwisely.

'I did!'

Oh yeah. She did. Plan B. 'OK, why didn't you tell us about the baby, when you'd known for ages?'

She rolls her eyes and shakes her head. 'Jen, that is so different, and you know it.'

I shift in my chair. 'Well, we don't always tell each other everything. We're not obliged to. I don't know why, OK? One or two things have been going on around here recently in case you haven't noticed. It didn't seem important.' I think about the e-mails and messages from Owen that I haven't told anyone about either. Talking about things means you have to accept that they are real.

Rosie sighs. 'It's just that we used to tell each other everything. We used to be close. Maybe too close. Maybe you just didn't want to hear the truth from people who know you better than you know yourself.'

Maybe, and maybe I don't want to start now. 'Well, you can talk, you won't listen to anything we've told you about Chris. I mean, you're still thinking about getting back with him, aren't you? After all he did to you?'

Rosie bristles visibly and turns to face me. 'You *really* don't know him, you only think you know the bit of him that hurt me, the image of him that I created in order to get over what had happened. That was just a part of him. When you get past that stuff he's . . . well, I didn't go up the aisle because I thought he was all right. I married him because I loved him, *really* loved him. And love like that doesn't just disappear after a few months. I think I still love him. He says he still loves me, he says that he ran away from it all because it all seemed too much too soon, but now he realises what he's almost lost. He says this time he's grown up enough to handle how much he cares about me. Me and the baby. When you get hurt you have to pretend it was all a mistake, and maybe getting married so quickly was, but the more I think about it the more I think that Chris and I weren't a mistake, the more I think we're exactly right.'

After everything we've been through together I can't believe that she doesn't see what I see, or remember what I remember. That she is repeating an almost exact rendition of one of Owen's speeches that she always told me was a load of crap.

'You think what? Christ, Rosie, don't you remember what he did to you? Don't you remember he packed your bags for you *before* he told you he'd met someone else? Don't you remember that he told you that you were too boring in bed and the thought of being married to you for the rest of his life made him feel suffocated? That he told you you were too clingy? Too demanding? Because I do, I remember the nights and nights and weeks and weeks of listening to all the things he said and did to you. Christ, he can't even commit to his *cat*, the poor thing moved in with his neighbours and he didn't even notice! Do you think he's going to commit to you and a baby once the novelty's worn off? You stupid little fool. You have no idea.' I shake my head.

'You sanctimonious cow,' Rosie snaps at me, her venom hitting me in the face with the full force of her sudden anger.

'All this time you've been fucking doing my head in about Chris, coming all high and mighty with me and you've been shagging some kid behind my back, behind all our backs! What the fuck did you think you were doing? He's eighteen, for Christ's sake! At least I'm trying to sort out an adult life. You're too messed up to even try. You'll be scrubbing around in pubs and clubs, getting used up by going-nowhere scum, still getting paid shit money in the same dead-end job ten years from now.'

Her portrait of the future I most fear pushes me further into a red rage.

'Well, at least I'm not thinking of throwing my life away with some bastard serial philanderer! Don't you ever learn? You want to end up like both our mums, used up and stranded, traded in for this month's latest model?'

Rosie shakes her head and her tone drops to quiet fury.

'Have you ever noticed that every single opinion you have about men comes back to your dad? Every single man you've ever been with has got something to do with him. Your whole relationship with Owen was about finding a replacement dad, someone older, someone who'll keep you in line, tell you what to do. You think it was Owen who wore down your self-esteem and broke you up. But it was your dad, the day he left you. It always has been. Owen just played around with the pieces he left behind. You judge every single relationship you see by the way your father treated you. You think you've made it without him, but that's bollocks. You've never got over him. Not ever. He's still ruining your life, and he doesn't even know or care.'

I shake my head at her, speechless with anger and hurt.

'That's not true,' I whisper.

'You don't know Chris. You only see one side of him,' she repeats, getting up to leave. I shake my head and tuck my feet up under my knees.

'I'm sorry to hurt you, Jen, but I think maybe it's time you woke up and took a good look at yourself. I'll see you later.'

The door slams and she is gone, leaving me alone with Michael, Owen and my father.

I have been looking at the Artex on my bedroom ceiling for around two hours now, but so far its swirls and peaks have not revealed any secrets which might get me out of the mess I am currently in. I feel guilty on about every count I can possibly conceive of. Guilty about how Michael is feeling, guilty about how I upset his mother, guilty that I was late for Ayla, guilty that I have been so caught up in myself over the last few weeks that I have hardly noticed whatever's going on in Selin's life, guilty that I've stressed Rosie out when she's pregnant and in need of my support. And to cap all that I feel guilty about how I have treated myself, hiding from the ghost of Owen in any corner or excuse I could find, bouncing off the walls of our relationship yet again, trying to pretend to myself that I've put it all behind me. Just look at the last few months. Who am I trying to kid? Not even I am going to be suckered by that line any more. Well, no more, he has nothing to do with my life, my decisions or my actions any more.

I don't know if Rosie is right about my dad or not, I don't know if I want to know. But I do know one thing: if he, she or anyone else thinks that I am where I am because of him, or because of anyone, I'm not having it. Everything I do, everywhere I go from now on, is because of me.

I've got to try and sort out the gaps that have pulled us all apart over the last few weeks.

Maybe it's not that hard; all I've got to do is try to explain myself to Rosie, have one last-ditch attempt at making her see what a mistake getting back with Chris would be, discuss everything with Selin, really find out how's she's doing, and come clean about my secret love life with her. That's all. I have exactly a month before I'm thirty to find out what I really want from my future, maybe even get on a journalism course, sign up for driving lessons. That will leave only one ambition totally unfulfilled and frankly I never did really think I would cut it as a jazz-club diva. Between you and me, I'm not entirely convinced that I can actually sing.

In fantasy arguments, friends, enemies and boyfriends never interrupt you. They are usually wildly impressed with your rhetoric and you are allowed to make a dramatic exit before they run after you agreeing with absolutely everything you say, begging for your forgiveness and thanking you for the enlightenment you have bestowed upon them. I'm an optimistic girl. It could happen. But just in case it doesn't, I am fully prepared to grovel. I just want my friends back.

Chapter Forty-six

Well, the best-laid plans of mice and men and quarter-life-crisis chicks don't always come off, it seems.

For the last two weeks I have hardly seen Rosie. She came back later on the day Michael's mum came round and we looked at each other for a long moment before she sat down.

'Do you remember when we used to go out Friday nights, stay in the pub all day Saturday and then go out again?' I asked her, faced suddenly with the prospect of yet another weekend in.

'Well, things change,' she said flatly.

'Rosie, please let's not let this get out of hand,' I'd said, ready to launch into the speech I had worked on most of the afternoon. 'We've been through a hard year, we've been through a lot together, so let's not fall out now over what are, after all, only men . . .'

But Rosie didn't want to hear my speech. 'Nope, let's not. OK? I'm off for a bath, see you later.' Interrupted mid-soliloquy, I watched her retreating back. It could have gone worse, I suppose.

Since then we have smiled at each other across the breakfast table; Rosie takes all her calls in her bedroom when she's in the flat and a lot of the time she isn't here. I wonder who she is with?

One day at work Georgie forced me to attend a debrief with Jackson over how the exchange had gone so far, on the pretext that I'd have valuable input but really so that I could take the minutes. After an hour and a half with only bottled water for refreshment, I collared him in the corridor and said, 'Do you see Rosie a lot?'

He looked me up and down and said, 'Some. Why?'

We continued to walk back to our offices.

'Well, Jackson, I think if you saw Rosie *that* much you'd know why,' I said, convinced now that she was seeing more and more of Chris.

'You mean you think I'd know more about the affair with the teenage kid and your views on Chris and your latest big row and the frosty atmosphere round your house?'

'Oh,' I said. 'Well, if you know why haven't you said anything?'

'Well, because I like Rosie a lot. I like you a lot. But despite this and my considerable abundance of talent and charm, neither of you will sleep with me and frankly spending any time worrying over your latest schoolgirl fall-outs seems to me to be pretty pointless. Now if I was getting laid by at least one of you, I might *pretend* to take an interest.'

My face must have been a picture of horror because he laughed and patted me on the back.

'Oh guys, hey?' he joked, rolling his eyes. 'No, stupid, do you want to know the real reason?'

I nodded.

'OK, so hear me out, OK? Rosie and I have talked a lot. She was pissed at you, sure, because you got into that whole teenage thing – which by the way I do want to hear more about some time – and because you didn't tell her anything about it until some middle-aged axe-wielding maniac mom turned up. You know, you two have always talked about everything. I think

313

she minded that more than anything. But also, considering how close you are, it seems that you just don't want to listen to how she feels about Chris. It seems that you've built up this image of him as a monster that you have to rescue her from. Granted, it's an image to which she did initially contribute, but hey, you've broken up with a few guys, right? You don't exactly paint them as Mr Nice in the aftermath, but maybe a few weeks or months or years later you might think, "Oh well, he wasn't that bad." Right?'

I thought about Mr Philosophy who left me because despite the fact that I didn't love him I wanted him to love me so much that I badgered and pestered him into a commitment he wasn't ready for. About six months after we broke up he met Miss Right. Got engaged and got cats. Jackson's right, I don't think he is such an evil heartless bastard now. In his position I'd have done the same thing. But Chris is different.

Jackson continued. 'Well, we've talked a lot about it over the last few weeks and believe me, I've tried every machiavellian trick in the book to get her to think that he's not the one and run back home with me, but the more we talk the more I think I might be wrong, much as it depresses me. The more I think about it, that whole marriage-divorce fiasco might just have been one of life's regular reality-check mess-ups, not a modern interpretation of a Jacobean revenge tragedy. In fact, I've met Chris. And I hate him, but that's because I'm in love with Rosie. Objectively? He's immature, sure, a bit too "English" for my taste, maybe needed a bit longer to shop around before seeing what a good thing he had with Rosie, but he's no wife beater. He's not evil, just misguided. He's just a guy who got it wrong big time and wants a second chance.'

We paused outside my goldfish bowl and I leant my forehead against the glass.

'You weren't there, Jackson, after it happened. You didn't

see her. If you'd seen her you'd understand,' I said wearily.

'Well, maybe, but my point is I like you a lot and I like Rosie a lot. I don't want to fall out with either of you, so if you want to talk about stuff, as long as it's not fast-track global invoicing systems, then let's talk. But I won't be doing any go-between stuff or telling you what she said and her what you said, and that's the last time I offer my opinion. OK?'

'Fair enough.' I didn't want to fall out with Jackson as well.

'Now, office-machine coffee or ritual suicide by biro?'

'Ritual suicide by biro, please.'

I did eventually see Selin. Both Rosie and I had left messages on her answerphone every other day, and one of our few conversation topics recently has been:

'Heard from Selin?'

'No, you?'

'No.'

Getting more and more concerned about her, I decided to walk past her office window one evening on my way back from work and sure enough I saw her dark head still bent over her office desk.

I rattled the door but it was locked so I knocked, and she looked at me for a moment before letting me in. She looked thinner, fragile.

'Selin, we've been so worried about you. Are you OK?'

She smiled and took my hand and hugged me.

'OK as I can be. I'm sorry, Jen, don't take it personally, I've just been spending time with the family. I've got your messages and I've been meaning to return your calls, but never seemed to find the time. After a while you dread someone asking you how you are. Not that I'm not glad to know you care or anything,' she added hastily.

'That's OK,' I said. 'I understand.' But I felt hurt nonetheless that she hadn't wanted me. Every crisis that had happened to me, I had always wanted her, but then nothing this big had ever happened to me.

'How are things at home?' I asked. Despite her declaration of dread, there really didn't seem to be very much more I could say. I sat opposite her desk and looked at a poster depicting a Cypriot coastline that hung on the wall above her shoulder.

'Well, quiet, devastated . . . you know. The shock has worn off now; we're just left with the grief and the empty space without her. Surprisingly, Mum's doing the best, cooking her way through the whole thing – but she's the rock, she's holding us all together. Dad has just gone to pieces, I think he feels that he let her down, somehow failed his little girl. Hakam tries really hard not to come out of his room. He won't talk to me but he spends a lot of time with Josh. They play on the computer and watch videos and they talk about it. Josh has been really good with him. And as for Josh, well, you've seen Josh, haven't you? He said he'd been over. I think it did him good. He'd exhausted himself, refused to sleep. He comes round to Mum's every day for dinner and then he's been working, painting, getting ready for the exhibition, it's his way of escaping, I suppose. So that's how we've been.' She smiled a tired smile and then leant back in her chair with a weary resignation. 'And you?'

'Oh God, Selin, you wouldn't believe . . .' I began but then I saw the shadows under her eyes and the tired line of her mouth and stopped myself. 'Well, the edited version is that Rosie is still umming and aahing about Chris, can you believe it? Anyway, we've sort of fallen out about it and one or two other things but I'll tell you the details another time. I can see you're tired.'

Selin smiled and looked at her watch. 'Look, I'd better get going. Family dinner, you know?'

'OK, well, I'll stop leaving you messages every five minutes now I've seen you. You call me when you want me, won't you? If you want me.' I stood and buttoned up my coat, it had started to drizzle outside.

'Of course. If I don't see you before, I'll see you at Josh's exhibition anyway, won't I?'

'Definitely. OK then.' As I opened the door I collided straight into Josh and, strangely, Mr Selin's tall, silent friend who had looked after Selin at the funeral.

'Hello, Jen,' Josh smiled at me.

'Hello,' I said to him. 'Hello,' I said to the friend, who nodded at me in return.

'We've just come to pick Seli up, working too late as usual. Come on, sis. Mum's cooked up a storm.'

'OK, I'm coming, I'm coming.' Suddenly Selin seemed to become more like her old self again and I watched with bemusement as a wide smile spread over her face when old-tall-silent-friend-man strode across the office to her and sat on the corner of her desk talking softly to her as she shut down her PC.

'Well, I'll be off then,' I said to Josh, my eyes still on Selin.

'OK,' he said. 'Fancy a drink later in the week? You and Rosie and the pub? Maybe Seli if we can drag her away from . . . home.'

'Yeah, love to if you're up to it, give us a call.' I looked at Selin and the man once again and shook my head. 'See you then.'

'See you.' Josh shuts the door practically in my face.

That was over a week ago. Josh's exhibition is next Saturday and it looks as though I won't hear from either of them until then. And it's another wet Monday and, OK, I am feeling sorry for myself.

The last few weeks could have been worse, I suppose. There haven't been any more messages from Owen, although there was one evening on the way home from work when I thought

I'd seen him. I thought I caught sight of his familiar shock of blond hair and his angular jaw standing out in the commuter crowd and I braced myself for confrontation, but when I looked again all I could see was an army of grey raincoats and umbrellas. Realising that I must have imagined it I worried all the way home, wondering whether my brain had conjured up his image because I was anxious about just that kind of confrontation or because deep down part of me missed him.

And then, one night, after sitting though the maximum number of bearable hours of Carla's latest bedroom tales in the pub along with Kevin, Brian and a very bored Jackson, I'd come back on the bus late and alone and sort of tipsy, but moreover tired and depressed, and for a moment I thought he'd turned up again.

For once the usually busy short stretch of Green Lanes that leads to my road was quiet and abandoned and I could see as I followed the bend of the road that even the Pizza Gogo lights had been turned off. For a moment I thought I heard Owen's familiar brisk walk behind me, characterised by the steel toe reinforcement he insisted on having on his second-hand shoes, but when I turned to look the road was empty. I stood for a moment and looked around me at the empty shadows, peering through the steamy windows of the coffee houses for a familiar face, and suddenly I felt afraid to be alone outside in the night. I was only fifty or so yards from my door but I ran that last stretch and didn't stop until I had slammed the door behind me.

I stood for a moment at the bottom of the stairs getting my breath back, and then I laughed. Spending too much time alone or in the company of my mostly moronic colleagues was clearly making me slightly crazy. Even if Owen had once been inclined to follow me – and I'm pretty sure he'll have found some other distractions by now – he's got no idea where I live.

Now I'm sitting on the telephone chair listening to the rain stream down the ancient double glazing and looking at the phone. I miss Michael, or at least I miss the idea of him, or maybe just being able to think about the idea of him. I hadn't really expected our last goodbye to be our last goodbye. I'm certain that if I had been in Michael's position I would have written letters, phoned and probably begged at least a few more times before finally giving in, but it seems that Michael has more presence of mind and dignity than I gave him credit for.

This morning I dithered around considering deleting his number from my phone but something like sentiment stopped me from doing it — that and the memory of our first kiss under the trees in Soho Square. It sounds corny but if he had been a bit older then maybe he would have been the one, or maybe in ten years' time life and love would have turned him into someone else, someone who couldn't love someone like me.

I stare at the phone. I'm not expecting anyone to call me, I can't think of anyone I want to call (although I should call my mum) but even so I'm tempted to pick up the receiver and check the dialling tone just in case.

Just as I reach my hand out the doorbell chimes and I jump out of my skin. I run to the front door and pick up the intercom phone.

'Hello?' I say in breathless tones.

'Hello, Jen, it's me. Do you and Rosie fancy that pint?' It's Josh. I resist the temptation to kiss the handset. A visitor!

'Rosie isn't here but I'd really love to,' I say, completely failing to not sound grateful.

'OK, I'll wait for you down here then. See you in a sec.'

'Josh! I'm a girl. Monday night or not, I have to brush my hair and put on make-up. It's raining, you'll be soaked by the time I get down there. Come up.' I buzz him in, leave the door on the latch then skip into my bedroom in search of my hairbrush.

When he arrives in the door frame I have my head between my knees as I brush out the tangles of my unruly hair.

'There won't be anybody there, you know, except two drunk old men, an Australian barmaid and me.' I fling my head back and smooth the untangled waves away from my face.

'You never know,' I say slowly. 'And anyway, I'm not doing it for men, I'm doing it for myself.' I lift my chin.

'Yeah, course you are.' He smiles and perches on the edge of my bed.

'To be honest, Josh, it's so nice to get out of the house to a place that isn't work that I'm pretty tempted to get fully glad-ragged up.' I hastily brush on some mascara and lippy. 'How about you? How are you doing, or are you fed up with people asking you that question?' I think of Selin who has not been in touch since I saw her.

'Not fed up exactly, just sort of depressed by the inevitability of being unable to say, "I'm OK." Gradually things settle into a pattern, I'm not saying it's getting easier for us, it isn't, but it's getting bearable and in some ways – I'm not sure how I can put this – somehow I feel like Ayla is inspiring me. The last couple of weeks I've completely rebuilt my part of the exhibition, I've added three new paintings, the fastest work I've ever done and maybe the best. They're not paintings of her but they are paintings for her, paintings of her spirit, if that doesn't sound too hokey.'

I zip up my boots and pull on my jacket. 'Not at all, I can't wait to see them.'

'Well, you'll have to until next weekend, and anyway, one of them isn't even dry yet.'

As we walk out into the night air I'm pleased to see that the rain has subsided into a drizzle and that it's light enough for me not to have to go back upstairs and get an umbrella.

'And Selin? Couldn't persuade her out?' I ask tentatively.

'Selin, no. She'd really rather just be at home right now, you know.'

The light and the warmth of the Rose and Crown beckon and as we walk into the large airy pub I look around. There are two old men and an Australian barmaid. But it's only early, not quite eight, there may well be more of Stoke Newington's young hip set — not quite as thin as Ladbroke Grove's, nor as happening as Brixton's, but generally attractively affable in a bohemian kind of way — about to arrive.

'What are you having?' Josh asks me and I go for a whisky mac, my favourite bad-weather drink.

'I'd better grab a table — beat the rush,' I say and slide into a comfy corner and remove my coat. I catch sight of my reflection in the mirror. The damp air has curled my hair up in exactly the way I least like and my mascara has run a little. I lick my thumb and pull it under my eyes but I can see little improvement when I check again.

Josh settles opposite me with a pint of Guinness and places my drink in front of me.

We look at each other.

'How's Dan?' I say on impulse.

Josh rolls his eyes. 'You're not thinking about going there again, are you?' he asks with exasperation.

'No-oh! I'm just asking. I'm fond of Dan now that I've got over the horror of having . . . thinged with him. Yuck Yuck Yuck!' I gag theatrically. Josh makes a squeamish face and sinks some of his pint.

'He's OK, working himself up into a tizz about Saturday. Basically, his whole piece revolves around him making plaster casts of bits of his body and reassembling them in a creative way, and no, I don't know what he means either. But there is one body part he hasn't quite got around to yet, keeps putting it off, can't think why, can you?'

I almost choke on a mouthful of ginger wine and whisky and splutter. 'No! Poor Dan. Perhaps he should ask you to do it.'

We both laugh and I ask myself if I really have just brought Josh's private parts into the conversation. In any event, Josh has gone slightly pink and sinks another good portion of his pint, shifts uneasily in his chair and changes the subject by saying, 'So, after the day you moved house we all thought Owen would hassle you big time, but nothing? Maybe he's finally out of your life.'

I finish my drink and let it melt my chest before I answer.

'Well, not quite. There were one or two e-mails, phone messages for a bit. But they've stooped now.' I finish brightly.

Josh leans forward with concern. 'What do you mean, e-mails, messages? When? Why didn't you say?'

'Oh, it was just before the accident. I would have said but it wasn't really a big deal, just a typical Owen gesture. I had his e-mails blocked and he hasn't texted me since. Probably just a last-ditch attempt to attention-seek, although I did think . . .' I remember the two times when I thought I might have heard or seen him but decide I don't want to sound too paranoid. 'No, nothing really.' I shrug and get up to go to the bar. 'Same again?'

Josh nods, a frown of concern creasing his forehead.

'You're sure,' he says as I return, 'that that's all it is? You don't think he's gone all barking like he did with that girl I knew?'

'No, no. Really. I mean, I know him if anyone does, don't I?' I say, not feeling quite as sure as I sound and wondering how I can change the subject.

'Still, maybe you should mention it to the police?' Josh asks.

'Mention what? A couple of cheesy e-mails and some stupid texts? I've deleted them all now, anyway.' But looking at him I can see he is not going to let this go. 'Look, I promise if anything else happens I'll talk to the police. They'll say I'm paranoid with an overactive imagination, but I will go, OK?'

'OK then.' He nods with satisfaction and both of us take a deep drink.

By the time the landlord rings time, a fuzzy warmth has seeped through my chest and into the ends of my fingers and toes. The warmth of the whisky and the pleasure of Josh's company have cheered me up but still my good mood can't quite suppress the undertone of chaos that my current situation seems to teeter on the brink of.

'Come on,' Josh says. 'I'll walk you home.' Outside, the rain has cleared and the night has become chilly, so I tuck my arm into his and lean on him as we stroll down Albion Road.

'Rosie's got a theory about me,' I say, apropos of nothing. 'A theory about why I can't accept her prospective reunion with Chris and why I basically stuff up all my relationships.'

Josh looks down at me. 'This should be good, maybe it'll help me stop stuffing up all of mine too. What is it then?'

'She reckons that every man I get involved with is basically my father. Oh, and every man she meets, and Selin I guess. She reckons I'm incapable of trusting anyone and that I project my own insecurities on to the men I get involved with thus inviting them to treat me like shit. Which, frankly, I think is a bit rich.' In fact, Rosie didn't say exactly that but my own twisted theory has developed out of that conversation and several hours of night-time ceiling gazing. Josh tips his head to one side and bites his lip.

'Your father? That's a very specific theory and one I'm going to have a hard time applying to myself, although I might try it next time I'm involved in a break-up. "It's not my fault, it's Jenny Greenway's father – he treated her like shit and now I just can't be trusted by any woman!" Well, what do you think?'

I smile despite myself, the rain begins again.

'I think it's crap, probably. Don't you?' We turn into our road and Josh is silent until we reach the front door of the block. 'Well, don't you?' I ask impatiently.

'Well, I don't think you or your dad are responsible for the crap that Owen put you through. I think Owen is. But maybe if in some way your past does influence your choices, well, maybe she has a point . . . *in a way.*'

'Bollocks,' I say fiercely and fling the door open. 'Come up for coffee,' I demand and march up the stairs in front of him. He acquiesces without argument.

'I've got to say, if you're supposed to be such a pushover I've yet to see any evidence for it,' he says to my back.

'Well, you're different, aren't you? I say. 'You're not trying to sleep with me.'

As we get into the flat I wipe the rainwater from my face and go into the kitchen, opening cupboard doors, forgetting what it is I'm looking for.

'Are you OK?' Josh asks softly. 'You seem pretty angry.'

'I'm not angry about Dad! I'm angry with Rosie for using that as an excuse to make it OK for her to get back with Chris. I'm not angry about Dad, I don't care any more about all that. I put it behind me years ago – everything, everything . . . what . . . what . . . he . . . did.' I finally get the words out along with a gut wrenching sob. Why did I drink whisky? It *always* make me cry, I know that.

'Bastard, bastard, bastard,' I hear myself saying as I sink on to the kitchen chair. 'It's the whisky, ignore me, I'll be all right in a moment!'

'Jen, come on now,' Josh says softly, taking my hand and leading me into the living-room. He lets me crumple on to the sofa and sits next to me. 'Don't cry, darling, not over him. Not any more.'

'I'm not! It's the whisky,' I protest as another wave of tears hits me. 'I don't mean to, it's just that, it's just that it does still hurt. The fact that he doesn't want me any more, or my mum or my brother, even his grandchildren, not any of us. He just replaced us and that was it, like we never existed. Your dad is supposed to be the one man who won't do that to you, isn't he? Like your dad. Like Mr Selin. And maybe, maybe if my own dad doesn't want me, well then, why would anyone?' I listen to the whisky tell my secrets for me and I listen to my own tears rattle inside me. 'Oh God, ignore me, I'm flipping drunk and weepy again!' My voice hits another crescendo and I can't seem to calm myself down.

'Oh God, Jen. Come here.' He pulls me across his lap and I collapse into his arms, unable to hold it back any longer. I bury my head in his chest and the smell of him, the smell of oil paint, Guinness and cigarette smoke. As I cry he rocks me gently, brushing my hair away from my forehead and letting it fall, brushing it back and letting it fall. After a while the tension and pain subside and I find myself cradled between his legs, my arms around his neck, his hands around my waist. I sniff and wipe my eyes, conscious of the black panda smudges that must now surround them.

'Jen, you mustn't see yourself in that way.'

'I don't!' I say feebly. 'I'm just being stupid.'

'No, you're not, you mustn't let this hold you back. Your dad was a prick, a total prick for letting go of his relationship with you. A prick and a coward. You're not to blame, it's got nothing to do with you. You're a wonderful woman, a beautiful wonderful funny woman and you've done that without him. Remember, I knew you when you were a podgy teenager and believe me, you've made an improvement. Most men would give their eye-teeth to be with you. Any man. Not just the sociopath types you seem to think you're fit for. You should give yourself a break, aim a bit higher next time. You know, someone evolved.' Finally he succeeds in making me smile. I rub my eyes with the heel of my hand.

'God, I'm so sorry. The last thing you need is to be nannying me right now,' I say, lifting my face to his.

He grins. 'Actually, it's a bit of a relief to get to look after you for a while. My macho image was seriously going down the bog.'

'Macho image! What macho image, you're a flipping girlie artist!' We laugh more with relief than anything else.

But after the laughter something strange happens. As we watch each other's faces, quietly searching for something else to say, I become acutely aware of his hand on my waist and the feel of his torso against mine. I can't think of a more inappropriate feeling to be having about a more inappropriate person at a more inappropriate time. I begin to move away but his arms tighten around me. Before I know what I'm doing, I raise my chin so that my mouth hovers millimetres from his.

'Josh?' I manage to say before his lips close on mine and God help me I find myself returning his kiss, pressing him back into the sofa cushions with a fire burst of longing that has come from nowhere. With a surge of emotional release I find myself pressing deeper into his kiss, my back arching as his cool hands slide up under my top, his fingers kneading the small of my back. I can't think, I can only feel, and as his embrace tightens still further I hear a low moan escape from the base of his throat and my own heart thundering in my chest.

It lasts for only a few seconds, hardly more than a minute certainly, but I am lost like Dorothy drugged in a field of poppies, caring about nothing but the present moment. Then it seems that, in the present moment, a snapshot third-person view of ourselves hits us simultaneously and we stiffen and spring part, reality catching up as suddenly as that moment of uninhibited passion engulfed us. I leap off the sofa as if I've been burnt, smoothing my clothes and hair as I do so and turning away from him to gaze out of the window that looks over Green Lanes. I can't think.

'Christ, fuck,' he says angrily to himself. 'What a bloody idiot.' He is standing, too, having leapt from the sofa a fraction of a second behind me. Only when I'm a good few feet away from him do I realise that I moved out of his embrace that quickly because I so wanted to stay. But he moved just as quickly. What must he think of me, he must think I'm a stupid heartless slut.

'Jenny, I *never* meant for that to happen,' he says categorically, grabbing his jacket from the back of a chair.

'God, of course not. Just a moment of madness what with . . . everything and all. The whisky, the dad stuff. Ayla.'

'I mean, you must think . . . I mean, I'm not like your dad or Owen. I don't just want to . . . I mean, what I mean is, that I'm not the sort of bloke to take advantage of you when you're down. And right now, with both of us so confused about stuff . . .'

I don't really know what he is trying to say and I grab at words like straws in the wind. 'Yes, I mean comfort sex isn't really a good idea at the best of times, is it?' His face fills with clouds and I mentally kick myself. We accidentally kiss and I bring up sex! Sex. It was never going to get to sex. It felt as though it could have gone to *sex*, but not SEX.

'It *was* a mistake, but—' he begins but I cut him off before he has to say anything that might embarrass him more.

'I know, I know. Let's just forget it ever happened,' I say, as if reciting a tired mantra, sounding angry and cynical when I feel neither.

His chin sets, his eyes drop to avoid mine and he heads for the door.

'Yeah, well, that would probably be best, given the

circumstances. I've got to go anyhow,' he says through tight lips, and turns down the hallway to the door, unable to get out of here quick enough. I so don't want us to fall out, not us, not now.

'Josh!' I call out after him and he stops at the door, his back to me. I run to him. 'Josh. Look, the last few weeks have been really hard. Something happened between us and it was . . .' I don't what to say. Sexy? Exciting? Thrilling? Confusing? Self-preservation stops me from saying any of these things. I can't tell what was on his end of his kiss, if there was anything there at all except grief, pity, impulse and Guinness. I don't want to make things worse.

His face flushes deep red.

'It was wrong,' he nods, finishing for me. Then he opens the door and is gone.

'That's not exactly what I was trying to say,' I think out loud as I lean back against the door.

In the past I often tried to analyse first-kiss chemistry, and I know what I felt for the brief moments that we were kissing. It was all wrong and out of the blue but I felt, well, I felt passion. Real, deep, *emotional* passion. But I know only too well that feeling that way can be one-sided. I've been on both sides myself. I've agreed politely with someone who raved about how sexy we were together when I haven't felt a thing. Owen told me off on more than one occasion for becoming too emotional in bed. In the end I learnt to lock emotions away, the really big scary ones, I mean.

When Josh and I kissed I felt that knife edge of hungry passion that I had forgotten I could feel.

But for Josh? Josh who is my best mate's big brother. Josh who is a disaster with women and has stupid stripy trousers and a rainbow scarf? It can't be Josh who makes me feel that way. It can't be Josh for two reasons.

Firstly, he's Josh, who I have sensibly forbidden myself to get a crush on.

Secondly, he was obviously so mortified by the whole thing, so embarrassed and horrified that I could be so needy, that I probably disgust him now. And if he's sweet enough not to be disgusted by me then he obviously didn't get the same kick out of that kiss, judging by the way he fled out of that front door.

I just have to face up to the fact that I've been a fool and put it behind me. The next time I see him I will be polite but distant, I will not embarrass him, gradually we will get back to normal, just as we did after the sex-with-Dan episode. But to put him in a position like this, when he really needs me to be a friend and not a potential embarrassment, well, that's priceless of me, isn't it? That tops off pretty nicely my latest catalogue of adventures that involve hurting people I care about and alienating my friends. Good old me.

Flashes of Ayla's face as she saw me from across the road go off behind my closed eyes.

Chapter Forty-seven

The rest of the week has passed in a blur, between the routine of work and the largely empty evenings in the flat. I opened my eyes this Saturday morning almost with regret. Tonight is the night of Josh's exhibtion, and either I go on my own and try to sort things out, or I don't go and sit cocooned in this flat for another day waiting for things to happen to me. I've got to go. I've got to find some way to make all this better.

I stretch out my fingers and toes under the sheets and listen for the traffic outside. As has happened so often over the last week, I find myself remembering the firm grip of Josh's fingers on my back, with a short sharp intense burst of pleasure, and then for a few seconds more I let myself remember his kiss, the feel of his hot breath, that little sound he made. He had sounded then, had felt, as if he'd wanted that kiss just as much as I had. But then he'd rushed away so quickly, was so mortified, that it must have been a momentary physical impulse, an impulse he was quickly ashamed of.

The tingle of pleasure of the memory quickly evaporates into a cold horror. Oh God, is no one safe from my questionable kissing choices?

Of course, I've replayed the scene with different endings.

'Well, Josh, we kissed. It was fantastic. So what do you want to do about it?'

'The thing is Josh, I never really realised how *tall* you are until just now and how much I want to lick your neck. Oh, you feel the same? Super.'

'Josh, let's be adult about this. We kissed. It was pretty hot. But we don't have to get embarrassed, we can simply put it behind us. We could just have sex, though to make sure the whole chemistry thing wasn't a fluke.'

And once I let myself think, 'The thing is, Josh, in those few moments you made me feel complete.'

Believe me, I have thought about nothing else over the last week – what else has there been to think about between invoicing clients, picking up calls and rolling my eyes at Jackson over Carla's head? Selin has continued to be out of the picture and perhaps she wouldn't be the best person to talk the incident over with, even if she wasn't incommunicado, given that I've messed with her recently bereaved and vulnerable brother. Rosie's three visits to the flat have been brief and all but conversation-free and I bet she'd just love to hear about another one of my romantic disasters to stack up as proof of my questionable eligibility to have an opinion about her love life. And she'd be right, damn her. In some ways I've thought about nothing else because it has distracted me from everything else there is to think about. But boy, what a distraction.

So I've thought about that kiss a lot. I've relit it, reshot it, I've analysed it from a different angle. I've retraced the conversation leading up to it, the moment just before it and those few delicious moments during it. The awkward tense moments after it. I've thought a lot about the Josh I thought I knew and the Josh I think I would like to know. I've thought about his brown eyes watching me with concern in the pub when I talked about Owen, the way he really seems to worry about me. During team meetings I've found myself thinking about the way his long slender fingers always have traces of paint on them. Things I've always known but didn't really notice until those fingers traced their pattern on my skin. I've remembered the rise and fall of his chest the night we slept side by side, the way the rhythm of his heart lulled me into my first dreamless sleep in ages. The creases of his smile that fill with stubble when he laughs, his long legs and slim hips, the way his V-neck jumper reveals just a promise of the hollows at the base of his neck. I've often thought about the day he stood between me and Owen to protect me, about his loyalty and his kindness. The gentle way he's dealt with his family's grief and the bravery with which he has confronted his own, and then I think to myself, well, now you've gone and done it.

For the fist time in your life you've fallen for Mr Nice. And he is categorically and totally the one you absolutely can't have.

Well done, Jenny Greenway.

Why not? Well, during all the thinking I've been doing over the last few days a few things have become crystal clear. I am a mess, as you may have noticed. Even *if* Josh fancied me, which he might well not, I'm not the sort of person he'd want a relationship with. He doesn't even know about Michael yet, he's bound to find out and when he does, well, that would really kill off any chance I had with him. Mad Girl Seduces Teenager for Plaything. Very appealing. He doesn't want to be with someone whose life is in such a state of suspended animation, and I don't want him to be either.

Which is some kind of revelation. I find that because I have cared about him for so long in one way, I just can't and I *won't* risk flinging myself at him again and losing all that. I won't risk hurting either of us in that way and I can honestly say that this refusal to fling myself into fate's deepest crevasse just for the sake of it is really a first.

The thing is this, I've had crushes on people before, like the friend I was in love with all those years ago who wasn't in love with me, and I've got over it eventually, so that's the worst-case scenario, you know the drill. Every time I see Josh for the next few months my tummy will do little flips, every conversation will have a double meaning, every pop song will relate back to him, even 'Steps', and then one day it will just go away, probably in the wake of a new unrequited crush. Bearable for a worst-case scenario.

On the other hand, there is the best-case scenario.

For once in my life I sort myself out. I have the guts to pack in my job and try to be something I've always wanted to be. Have a go at finding a place in the world of journalism. I take control, I get over Owen once and for all and maybe I'll get over my dad. I'll start to make my life have the sort of promise that Ayla had thought was just beginning for her. But instead of waiting for it to fall in my lap I'll make it happen.

And I'll start at the exhibition tonight by bringing Rosie and Selin and me back to the closeness we seem to have lost. Somehow I'll find a way to put my differences with Rosie behind us and knit back our old support group.

First, I'll find Josh and we'll talk about what happened, in an adult way, in a grown-up way. I won't embarrass him with how I feel but I'll make it OK for him and then our friendship can pick up where it left off.

And then maybe, just maybe, in a few months when I've sorted myself out, when I've rediscovered a sense of pride, Josh will think about that kiss and see the new me and he'll think again and maybe something might happen.

And here is the really important thing; if it doesn't happen it will be OK because I will be OK with myself.

Ayla was young enough to believe that life hadn't begun yet, she was young enough to expect her future just to arrive when she was ready for it. But it was taken from her before she had a chance to find out that life is all down to oneself. I know, *I know* I only have one chance to make it happen and I'm not letting it slip away.

Before anything can happen with anyone else, it has got to happen with me. Starting from now.

Chapter Forty-eight

I love getting ready to go out. I have always loved it since the days when I used to go on first dates; I used to love getting ready for a first date, full of anticipation and nerves. Tonight is no first-date scenario but I am just as nervous and need to feel just as confident so I start to get ready a full two hours before I need to leave the flat. I haven't got ready for a night out in any longer than fifteen minutes since I was twenty-five. It's therapeutic.

I spend thirty minutes in a bath brim-full of hot water and bubbles, shaving my legs and applying every lotion I can find. Then I use both shampoo *and* conditioner and some of Rosie's shine serum on my hair, combing it through before leaving it for the central heating to dry out naturally. I look at the clock. An hour and fifteen minutes before I have to leave, too soon really to put on any make-up or choose what to wear. In the steamy heat of the bathroom I open the cabinet door and scour the shelves, looking over the years of impulse products I have bought and only used once, looking for something else to do to myself. I could apply a face mask but it's too risky, knowing my luck I'd just erupt in spots fifteen minutes after washing it off. I don't think I need to add more spray-on conditioners to my hair or give it a deep-heat vitamin treatment, it would just end up going limp and greasy looking. I have already given my face a blast of pure Retinal A (or something) in the hope that it will kill all the free radicals, which conjures up a mental image of a load of tiny little anarchist freedom fighters battling for the right to be wrinkly on my skin. I have plucked my eyebrows, I have selected my make-up. I have unwrapped yesterday's lunchtime purchase of a shiny highlighter stick thing that is supposed to make me glow (and not look damp and sweaty). There is only one thing left to do. I decide to wax my bikini line.

Twenty very painful minutes later and I'm looking through my wardrobe for an outfit that will take my mind off the searing pain I am currently experiencing in the groin region. Whose bright idea was that?

Now, I've been to these kinds of thing before and I am fully aware that I don't have the regulation sixties print dress, Nana Mouskouri black-frame glasses or suspiciously short fringe to compete with the other artist women. I do have a Whistles floral-print silk dress that I haven't worn for a long time and which is strictly speaking a summer dress, but which I could team up with a flouncy black cardigan and a pair of burgundy kitten-heeled pumps. It's a good cleavage dress.

Wardrobe assembled, I now put on my make-up. I use the shiny stick thing. Then I take off all of my make-up and begin again *sans* shiny stick thing, which, surprise, surprise, makes me look sweaty and hot. I even put on eyeliner and two coats of mascara, like it says on the tube. I take my eye make-up off again and reapply it, this time with one coat of mascara, as it made me look as though I had clumpy falsies stuck on. Finally I am ready to get dressed.

Ensemble complete, I look at myself in the mirror. I can't say for sure if I look any better or any worse than I do when the whole thing takes me less than half an hour but I feel ready to meet the evening. Ready, if a little bit sore due south.

I have never liked Hoxton, something about it makes me nervous.

It might be the tall, narrow streets of warehouse conversions that seem unnaturally silent most of time, or the fact that it is home to some kind of school for clowns which could easily be the premise of a Stephen King novel. Or it might be the arty types who spill out of the quiet street-corner pubs and clubs with periodic bursts of smug camaraderie and fake flowers in their hair. Or it could just be that any time I have got into a conversation with Josh's art friends they glaze over faster than a puddle in arctic conditions as soon as I tell them what I do. It's not even that they just can't think of anything worth doing other than making art. It's that they'd never think of doing anything as mundane as my job. As if my job defines who I am. Well, they may have had a point up until now, but not any more!

This particular street where Josh and his friends have rented their exhibition and studio space is a quiet, cobbled back alley and I would think I've got the address totally wrong except that I can hear a faint pulse of garage coming from one of the tall dark buildings and I follow it like a beacon. I have arrived an hour after the opening was due to start, hopeful that everyone else would be here already, but afraid too that they will all have ganged up on me by now. The bass gradually increases in volume and evolves into a full-on hardcore track. I check the open doorway for any sign of a number but there is none, so I just head on in, hoping that I'm not attending the wrong party.

It seems that the exhibition is up four flights of metal stairs, and in order to make it to the top I have to push my way through hordes of already drunk artists swaying or leaning, drooping or lounging against railings and walls like a fashion spread for *Dazed and Confused* or *Wallpaper*. I don't find anyone I know on the stairs but as soon as I enter the main space, Dan grabs my arms and plants a wet vodka-flavoured kiss on my lips. I resentfully rub them dry, picturing the remnants of my lip gloss.

'All right, darling?' he says, looking down my top. 'You've scrubbed up nice tonight.' It seems that he has adopted his fake cockney persona for the night. I have noticed that it's not uncommon amongst artists to decide to lose their pleasant home-counties village middle-class accent when confronted with others of their species who might have more working-class cred than they. If only they all sat down together and worked it out in advance they'd probably find out that everyone else here is probably the offspring of a viscount or something. I mean, how many children of coal miners or chip-shop owners do you know who can afford not to have a real life, with real bills, and spend all day faffing around with acrylics? That's not entirely fair, Josh isn't like that, he works hard to support his art so there must be others. It's just that they're probably not here.

'Dan, hi. How's it going? Is the *Time Out* bloke here?' I ask.

Dan nods and points out a man in a shiny brown suit and a spiky haircut. 'He hasn't got to my bit yet, that bloody tart Tamara has had him cornered for the last half an hour, bitch.'

I nod mildly and scan the room, looking for familiar faces.

'What about the girls? Are they here?' I ask him with some trepidation.

'Yeah, they're around here somewhere. Josh has had a panic attack and he's up in the studio. Panicking. Poor bastard. Fucking shocking about Ayla.' He contemplates his complimentary bottle of Smirnoff Mule for a few seconds more and then grins at me. 'Fancy getting off somewhere later?' he asks with the wholly professional double meaning of a practised lothario.

I smile and shake my head. 'No, cheers Danny, listen, where's this studio?' He takes my offhand rejection with the aplomb of someone who wasn't really that bothered to begin with and points to the ceiling.

'Next floor up, there's a ladder and then you go across the

roof and there's a sky light and . . .' It seems you to have to be some kind of climbing expert to get around this place, which I'm not, especially not in these shoes.

'Is there a conventional way of getting there?'

Dan looks nonplussed, thinks for a moment and then says, 'Oh yeah, well, you can go downstairs again, it's next door. Josh'll buzz you in.' He burps in my face and then goes off to scout the room for a more likely pulling prospect. I consider both options and my heels and begin my descent of the stairs past the artists once again. There do seem to be an awful lot of them. Josh had better actually be in this flipping studio otherwise the minute I get back Dan's going off those stairs.

The doorway of the next-door building is in darkness and I can't see any lights on inside. I press for a long moment the only buzzer I can see. There is no response. Of course, if Josh is depressed or 'panicky' as Dan put it, or upset, he might not even bother answering the door. Or he might be next door at the party up the four flights of stairs around some corner I hadn't managed to get to before Dan sent me on a wild goose chase. I press the buzzer once again, letting my finger play out a monotone version of 'Can you Feel It?' The ancient intercom system crackles into life and Josh's voice erupts into the street. 'Yes?' He does not sound happy.

'Josh, it's me, it's Jenny. I . . . well, can I come and see you?'

'Oh Jen, sorry I snapped at you. I thought you were some drunk from the party. Come up.' I wiggle the stiff door until it opens and find myself in a mirror image of the next door's stairwell except that it is in total blackness.

'Is there a light?' I call into a depth of shadows.

'No, we haven't got it fixed yet; we tend not to use this entrance. Start up the stairs and I'll come down and meet you.'

I edge my way up each stair, feeling my way along the wall with my fingertips, listening to Josh's steady and confident steps as he descends the iron staircase. My eyes gradually adjust to the dark and I see his silhouette loom above me, backlit by the glow of a room a couple of floors above.

'Here.' He holds out his hand and I take it, gripping his fingers more tightly than can be considered cool, and follow him up the stairs, enjoying the warm contact with his skin. The ascent is silent save for the sound of our steps on the staircase and our breathing. In the darkness the sensation of the touch of Josh's fingertips seems even more acute. Once we are in the light of the studio face to face, the easy silence of our stairway odyssey evaporates into awkward silence.

'So, how have you been?' I ask with false brightness, blinking under the strip lights. He seems unable to look at me.

'I've been . . .' He pauses, and starts again. 'Well, it's tough, you know. Sometimes I forget, just for a second, and then I catch myself thinking, wondering, what's wrong? Why aren't I happy? And then it all comes crashing back. She's gone. Then I feel guilty for forgetting for even a moment. And I've been meaning to call you to apologise for kissing you, but I haven't had the guts,' he adds quickly with a guilty shrug.

The very fact that he mentions kissing me makes my chest tighten.

'You've got nothing to apologise for, and well, the way you're coping after Ayla, it's astounding, it really is. Don't feel guilty, feel proud.' I gently take a step closer to him, I want to give him a hug but I don't feel that I can. 'Is that why you aren't next door?' As much as I want to clear up the kiss issue I want to make sure he's OK first.

'I can't face it. Everything I've done up to now seems like kids' stuff, a sham. Nothing about it is real, it's just stuff I wanked about with in my bedroom. It's crap. Mum and Dad and the others are down there, standing around trying to understand it, and I can't face that. I can't face them pretending they're proud of something that I'm not.' He thrusts his hands in his pockets and shakes his head.

As I watch him my throat tightens and my chest constricts. It's almost unbearable to see him in so much pain. I struggle to find some way to help him. 'I can understand how you must feel, but you've worked really hard on this exhibition. Ayla would have wanted you to be proud of it, especially because you painted it for her. She wouldn't have wanted her . . . her death to change the way you feel about your work, except maybe to show you how important it is that you make the most of your talent.' My voice, bouncing off whitewashed brick walls, sounds full of empty platitudes. Eventually I say, 'You have to go back for your family if nothing else. Whatever you may think, you have to let them be there for you.'

Finally he tears his gaze away from his trainers and looks at me. 'I know, you're right. Thanks for coming by the way; I didn't think you'd want to, after . . .' His eyes return footward once again.

'Josh, we need to talk about what happened,' I say, risking a last-minute loss of nerve.

'Yeah, I know it was inexcusable, I'm so sorry.' He rubs his hand roughly over the stubble of his shaven head.

'No, let me speak. I've been practising this all day. OK, we kissed. And, well, it was a *wonderful* kiss.' I kick myself for this burst of unrehearsed candour, I hadn't meant to say that. Josh's eyes suddenly lock on to mine. I regroup myself under their gaze with a huge effort of determination. 'But it was the wrong time and the wrong place and I was crying and you felt sorry for me and maybe you needed to be close to someone too, but in any case we just sort of collided and Josh, I care about you *so* much. I really can't bear for our friendship to suffer because

341

you're embarrassed about what happened, because it was lovely and you don't have to be embarrassed. That's what I wanted to say. We kissed, I don't regret it, I'm not angry or upset by it but I just want you to know it's OK and we can just put it behind us and get back to normal. There, I've said it.' His black eyes search my face as if he believes he can find all the words I haven't been able to say written somewhere on my face.

'I thought you'd guessed,' he says, shaking his head in wonder. 'But even now you don't have a clue, do you?'

I back away slightly afraid of losing my balance by standing so close to his magnetic pull.

'What do you mean?' I say in a whisper, more terrified of what he might not say than of what I hope he might.

'Jenny, I'm not embarrassed about kissing you. I mean, I am. I'm embarrassed about putting you in that position, but that's all.' He takes a deep breath. 'Don't you see? Couldn't you *feel* how much I wanted you? How much I've wanted to kiss you for months, for a very long time.'

I stand still and let the words sink in. Disbelief tightens my throat and I struggle to swallow.

He gives a wry laugh and looks at the ceiling. 'I know exactly when it happened, last year at some party we were all at, just standing around chatting, the usual, and then you walked into the room, just the Jenny you've always been, but suddenly looking at you took my breath away, I wanted to touch you so much. I couldn't believe it, one of the few women I really connect with and suddenly the only woman I wanted most in the world. And you were with that twat Owen.' He shakes his head as if dragging himself back to the present and returns his gaze to me. 'I shouldn't have said this. I meant to make things easy for you, but well, nothing ventured nothing gained. Hanging around being your best mate for the last year hasn't got me very far, has it?'

I smile in wonder, that was going to be my plan.

'The long and the short of it is that I really want you, Jenny. I want us to be together.'

I look around and quickly find a seat. My head reels and my heart thunders in my ears. He wants me! He. Wants. Me. I shake my head and look at him in wonder. This can't be happening.

'Are you OK?' he asks me anxiously.

My high-pitched laugh bounces off the high ceilings. I nod. 'You must think I'm so stupid. I thought you fancied Rosie!'

He crosses quickly to stand beside me, and the inches that separate us seem to fizz with our physical proximity. I so want all this to happen now, but more than that I so want to get this right.

'Josh, I can't believe everything you've just said to me and, well, I think – no, I'm certain – that right now I want you too. Maybe I've felt it for a long time and I didn't realise it but everything that has happened this week has finally made me see it.' I steel myself. 'But listen, Josh, it wasn't the right time for that kiss. Now is not the right time to begin this.' It takes every effort of my being to speak each word. Josh shakes his head and hunkers down until our faces are level.

'Is there going to be a right time to kiss me, Jenny?' he asks, his voice low and soft. I want to say yes, any time starting from now, but I know that rushing into this would be the worst thing that either of us could do. No more telling people what they want to hear, what I want to hear. This is the new me.

'I don't know, Josh, I don't know right now. You mean so much to me. I . . . I really enjoyed that kiss, believe me. But things have been crazy for the last few weeks. First Owen again, and then, well, you're going to find out. I got mixed up with someone. It's over now but it was complicated. He was quite a lot younger than me. I kept it a secret because . . . well, I don't know why really. But anyway, what I'm trying to say is, is that I rushed into a "relationship" for all the wrong reasons and people got hurt. I wouldn't want to do that with you. I . . .'

I can't think of a way to tell him how I feel right now, alone with him here. Every part of me is aware of his body: the smell of him, the curves of his neck, his long lean torso under that T-shirt. Every scared and lonely part of me wants to take a step into easy affection, but this is the new me and what if I make the wrong choice again? I won't do that to Josh.

He leans a little closer to me. 'Let me get this straight. You're saying you feel the same way, well, then why not let us enjoy it?' he asks softly, his finger tracing a line down my forearm, making me shiver with longing.

'Josh, you know me. You know me better than probably any other man in my life. You know that I have to make some steps forward on my own. I have to get used to being happy to be myself, proud of myself. And I know that you're hurting and that you can't see what life will be like past losing Ayla. Neither can I. I know exactly how good it would be to let this happen right now. I mean, Christ, I came up here without a clue about how you felt, and everything you've just said is everything I have fantasised about non-stop since the moment we kissed. But for the first time in my life I'm sure about what is right, and this is not the right time for either of us to get into this. If we do this now, we could wreck everything and you mean too much, far too much to me to want to risk that happening. I'm not asking you to wait around for me while I sort myself out, Josh, I'm just saying we need to understand ourselves before we can risk getting involved. I need to try and see myself the way I really am. Not the way Owen, my dad or whoever else has made me see myself.'

A gentle smile softens his lips. I let him pick up the tips of my fingers, causing goose bumps to rise across my arms.

'Jenny, you don't have to ask me to wait for you. I'll wait

anyway. I've waited through about three break-ups with Owen and two or three rebounds for you to notice me. I've waited through this last one. I knew there was *someone*. There is always someone with you, you're afraid to be alone. I can already see the you you want to be. I can see the funny, sweet, loyal you. I can see the girl who makes me laugh so much it makes me cry. I can see one of the few people who can reach out to me when I feel so hurt that I just want to curl up and die. One of the few people who care enough about me to even want to try. I can see someone so sexy it blows my socks off, someone who deserves to be loved. I can see *you*, Jenny. I can see you when you can't even see yourself. So I'll wait. Because what you're saying makes sense and if when you've sorted yourself out you can see me the way I see you, then it will have been worth the wait. Just for the chance of being with you.'

Unable to speak, I look into his eyes as he bends his head to mine and gently kisses me. With a huge effort of will my fingers stay passively in my lap and I let the moment pass, sweet and whole. As we part, each of us lets out a deep sigh of frustration and watches the other.

'Just don't take too long, OK?' Josh says softly.

I nod and smile, pressing the palm of my hand against his face before standing abruptly. 'Come on, we'd better get back to that party before we lose it again.' I feel unspeakably happy and totally terrified all at once, I need the throng of the party to distance me from the intensity of what has just happened, to let me savour the moment at a distance from it.

'OK, come on. I'll take you on the short cut.' Ten minutes and two scary ladder climbs later I'm back in the heart of the party and he has disappeared into the crowd, true to his word, letting me have my space. My space scares the shit out of me.

'Jenny, darling!' Mrs Selin's call directs me into the crowd and after a few minutes of edging, elbowing and cleavage-stun deployment I find myself standing in Josh's area of the exhibition. Josh, however, seems to be avoiding the place like the plague and is in close conversation with the girl who was at his house the other day. It's pretty clear she fancies him.

Everyone is here and when I say everyone I mean even some who I didn't expect. Rosie is here, having managed to pull together a stunning outfit without ever once returning to the flat, and stands gazing at one of Josh's paintings, refusing to look in my direction. Jackson nods at me over her head, winks and rolls his eyes. I smile back at him and shrug sheepishly. Mrs Selin, even now, has her arm around my waist and is guiding me towards her smiling emotional husband.

'Jenny.' He greets me with a firm hug, plants a paternal kiss on my forehead and releases me towards Selin. Selin is not alone. The tall man from the funeral, the over-attentive uncle or whoever he is, is at her side, his hand resting on her shoulder. I can see the strain of the last week in her eyes, and she stands mutely in the crowd looking frightened and alone with this great shadow of a man hanging over her. This time I go in for a rescue.

'Excuse me?' I beam up at him and taking Selin's elbow I lead her away. She follows compliantly. The tall man rubs his hand over his mouth as he watches her depart.

'Who *is* that guy? Are you OK?'

She shakes her head. 'No, no, I'm not OK. Not really. I'm trying to be OK. We all made Josh go ahead with this, but I feel numb. I . . . Oh God, Jen, is every day for the rest of my life going to be like this? Shouldn't I want it to be? Shouldn't I always want to feel the pain of not having her? I just don't think I'm strong enough to bear it.' She keeps her voice calm and low as she stares at me intently and I'm taken aback by her sudden unloading of feeling, restrained as it is. It's typical of Selin that she refuses to make a fuss in public, even as she mourns her sister. I look across the group and see that the man is still watching us and is preparing to make his way over.

'Come on,' I say lamely, 'let's get drunk.'

Unsurprisingly, Danny is at the bar, now fully bladdered and totally pissed off. 'The fucker never even gave it a second glance, the fucking fucker. I knew it, I knew I should have been a fucking poet.' He sticks two fingers up at the departing *Time Out* Man's back. He seems to be going over to Josh's work.

'Cheer up, Dan, no one liked Van Gogh's work until he was dead, did they?'

He snorts at me. 'I don't want to be famous when I'm dead! I want to be famous now, get minted, get all the chicks and have a restaurant! Bloody formaldehyde, bloody dead cow, and bloody unmade bed. I've been doing the flipping unmade bed thing for bloody donkey's.' He pouts but is distracted from his tirade by a passing debutante type in a cut-off top.

As we make our escape I hand Selin a bottle of Moscow Mule and I am relieved to see her smile as we return to our group. Just before we rejoin them I stop her and say, 'Selin, I don't know, but I think that one day you'll be able to remember Ayla without the pain. And I don't think it means that you will love her any the less. Honestly.'

She squeezes my hand and takes a second to compose herself before walking back over to the tall man who has been joined by Josh and her parents, a family group. Who *is* that man?

At least it's obvious that Rosie hasn't yet told her about our fight. I catch Rosie's eye involuntarily but it seems her curiosity has got the better of her chagrin and she nods at the tall man and raises her eyebrows with a question. I shake my head to show her that I know nothing more about him and our brief truce is over as she sniffs, shoots me a daggers look and turns back to Jackson. I don't really think it's that we're cross with each other. I think it's that we're cross with ourselves. No, actually, I am pretty cross with her.

Seeing no one to latch on to, I turn to Josh's paintings. Unlike many of his colleagues he's not into installation art, he likes to paint in the old-fashioned way. He loves the smell and feel of paint. He loves the wonder of colour. I love his paintings, although I'm never sure if it is for the right reasons. I love them because they are bold and beautiful and I'm not really sure being beautiful is a good enough reason. I am always badgering him to give me one, but he has always held back. Perhaps he's waiting for me to see his paintings the way he does. These paintings, the three painted in the aftermath of Ayla's death, are spectacular and wonderful, I wish I had the right language and knowledge to describe how I feel about them.

'What do you think?' My thoughts are interrupted by *Time Out* Man, who nods at Josh's painting. Christ, I don't know what to say, what if I let Josh down and say something rubbish?

'I, um . . . well, I'm not an expert or anything, but I react to them in . . . in an emotional way, they make me feel . . . They make me feel.' I look at him, trying to gauge his reaction to my inept comment. 'To be frank, most of the other stuff in here looks like a Blue Peter project to me.'

He laughs and looks around. 'Well, I wouldn't quite say that. But there is quite a lot of chaff to sort through before you find the wheat. It's like looking for a pop star, so many of the hopefuls should have stuck to being a runner-up at the local pub karaoke night.'

I like him, he makes me laugh. 'So, you're the *Time Out* Man, aren't you?' I ask.

He looks a bit pleased with himself and nods. 'Sort of *Time Out* Man, more freelance really. I do the odd review here and there and I run a gallery down the road. Always looking for new talent. Are you his girlfriend, then?' He nods at the painting again.

'Me? No, no, I'm no one's girlfriend.' He is a bit short, but he has nice hazel eyes and yes, I am flirting. Just a bit, for old times' sake.

'So you aren't an artist, I take it?' He turns on a flirty smile.

'Oh, and how can you take it?' I reply archly, flirt feigning offence.

'Well, the Blue Peter comment gave it away.' He laughs and looks down my top. I flick my hair off my shoulders, no point in obscuring his view.

'Fair enough. No, I'm not. I work in computer hardware sales, but I've decided to make a career change. I'm going to enrol in a journalism course, a good recognised one, full time if I have to. Give getting the career I want a go.' He is the first person I have said it out loud to. I am instantly afraid of failing and suddenly see the merits of one mundane spreadsheet after another, and a million, 'Hello, UK sales, how may I help you?' a day.

Time Out Man looks back at my face, and I'm fairly sure that not all the admiration displayed there is purely for my person.

'Good for you, you should ring the *Time Out* office, they might give you a couple of weeks' work experience, it never hurts to network. I'll mention your name if you like,' he finishes with a flourish. He must think he's just cinched a snog for sure.

'Really? Really, would you?' Calm down, try not to sound too grateful.

'Yeah, sure I will, but I can't guarantee anything, OK? What is it, by the way?'

'What is what?' Is he asking me about the painting again? My cup size?

'Your name!' His laugh borders on the patronising.

'Jenny, Jenny Greenway,' I say quickly and I watch him write it on the back of a business card.

'Jenny, and what's your number, Jenny?' I tell him, knowing that the likelihood of any desk editor ever seeing it is slim to nil.

'Can *I* call you some time?' The inevitable line.

I sigh and look at the back of Josh's head, the sweep of his shoulders under his T-shirt. You never know, maybe this bloke is a nice bloke under his libido.

'What's your name?' I ask him, with a polite smile.

'Mike,' he replies. Christ, not another one. There really should be more male names to go around. Has the person in charge of thinking up names never thought that in the twenty-first century the small Anglo-Saxon name pool often causes confusion and heartache to the average sociable girl?

'Mike, will you still mention my name if I turn you down? It's not that you're not cool. It's just that I broke up with someone recently. After his mother told me I couldn't see him any more. And I'm sure you don't want to get involved with a needy commitment-crazy girl on the rebound, do you?'

He takes a hurried step back, already searching though his repertoire of 'I have to be going now' excuses. When in a sticky corner push the commitment-phobe button, works almost every time.

'Well, I appreciate your honesty. Of course I'll mention your name, Jenny. And, well, I have to be going now, lots more art to look at. Good luck.' And he's gone, clearly unwilling to waste any more of his time on a dead prospect. I hold out little hope for the name mentioning, and frankly, as I have never experienced the benefits of professional nepotism, I'm not entirely sure what I would do about it anyway. But I guess I should ring them up and find out about work experience. Work experience at nearly thirty, well, whose fault is that?

Selin has managed to pry herself away from the grip of her aged admirer and is chatting to Rosie. Jackson must have gone to the bar. Well, here goes the bridge-building exercise phase two.

'Can you believe it?' Rosie says with unrepressed incredulity to Selin who stares at her open mouthed.

'Hi!' I say as brightly as I can. Selin smiles at me, and I feel annoyed that whatever Rosie has told her has diverted her sufficiently to forget herself.

'Hello there, I thought you'd pulled?' she says sunnily.

'Oh no, I've given up men for a bit.' I look Rosie in the eye. 'I've decided to have a shot at growing up properly this time.' Rosie purses her lips and drums a false nail against her glass of water, but won't look me in the eye.

'Anyway, can Selin believe what?' I ask, bracing myself for the worst.

'Jackson has asked Rosie to go back to the States with him! To live with him!' Selin exclaims.

It's my turn to be open mouthed. After my corridor conversation with him the other day I was sure he'd given up any hope of winning her over. She must really have caught his heart for him to go for this last-ditch attempt, it's the kind of thing I'd usually try. Would have, in the past.

'Bloody hell, he's keen,' I understate, but I'm delighted that something has happened that might take her mind off Chris.

'Of course I can't go, I've only known him five minutes and we haven't even, well, we haven't even had sex,' Rosie says, primly.

'Ohhhh,' Selin and I say together. We did wonder.

'And anyway, I can't go, so there. We'll keep in touch though, you know, and maybe after the baby is born and big enough, we'll have a holiday. But I haven't told him one way or the other yet so, shhh.' She presses her index finger to her shell-pink glossed lips. Rosie is the only person I know whose lip gloss doesn't go tacky and dry, ever.

Selin nods conspiratorially, but I think I hear uncertainty in Rosie's voice. This is not like Rosie. If Rosie wants something, she'll just go for it, long-term future or no. She must be having a second go at growing up too. Anyway, I decide to implement my plan to bond us all back together properly.

'Look Selin, why don't you come back to our place for a nightcap? Hot chocolate and toast, a pyjama party? What do you say? Rosie, were you planning to go back to Jackson's? It's just that we haven't all been together for a while, have we? I thought it would be a good chance for a proper talk.'

'I agree, there are things we need to discuss,' Rosie says meaningfully. I hope she means her apology to me and her grateful acceptance of my opinion and advice, which will make my grudging acceptance of her life choices unnecessary. 'I was planning to come home, anyway. What do you say, Seli?'

Selin glances over her shoulder at her family and nods. 'Yeah, sure. I've got something to tell you, too.'

Tonight we must let Selin talk. We must not turn this into the Rosie-and-Jenny show yet again.

'Shall we make a move then?' I say.

Rosie takes out her mobile. 'I'll call Kaled, and then say goodbye to Jackson,' she says.

As we make the round of goodbyes Josh gives me a hug and kisses me primly on the cheek. The memory of the few minutes we spent together next door hovers hungrily between us and we exchange a quick glance of mutual remembrance. I won't take too long, I think.

Rosie appears suddenly at my side and gives us a knowing

look. 'Come on, Kaled's outside,' she says, turning to look at Josh's face one more time before we depart.

I can still feel the impression of his lips as we step into the cold night air.

Chapter Forty-nine

Back at the flat Rosie makes the toast, while I get some milk in a pan and heap two more than the recommended number of teaspoons of chocolate powder into our orange mugs.

Selin is in the other room looking for something on the TV, I guess. Eventually I say to Rosie, 'I'm so sorry about everything, especially that you had to get caught up in the end of Michael and me. That was really crap. Some mad woman comes over to your house, screams and yells and then I have a go at you about Chris. I'm sorry about what I said, I mean, I'm sorry about the way I said it. But you're right, I don't see the Chris you do and I love you, I don't want you to get hurt. It might be stupid or impulsive but I think running off with Jackson would be more sensible than getting back with Chris. That's all I'm saying.' I lift my hands palm up and back away from her.

'Let's just put the Chris debate on hold for a second, OK? I'm sorry for what I said about your dad. It wasn't fair and it's not true.' She doesn't look me in the eye as we both know that neither of those two things is strictly true. But I'm glad she's said them anyway. In return, I offer a partial explanation for Michael.

'Believe it or not, I genuinely hit it off with Michael. I really did. I cared about him. Actually, I'm really going to miss him, and the whole thing hurts quite a lot. More than I expected.'

I hadn't realised it until I said it, I had been so prepared for the end right from the start, but I hadn't been prepared for how I would feel afterwards. Not the gut-ripping trauma of an ending with Owen but real sadness and loss, a chapter closed. I suppose he was a sort of swansong.

Rosie rewraps the bread and considers the simmering milk. 'I don't really understand what you and the ginger kid were up to, and I don't really want to know. It wasn't so much him, or his age, it was more you getting on your moral high ground over Chris when all the time you were behaving in just as, if not a more, irresponsible way. Not that considering a life with my baby's father *is* irresponsible, actually. Anyway, it was *that* that really pissed me off. Plus, as you know, pretty much everything makes me cry at the moment. Especially love-lorn teenagers and furious red-headed mums. I understood how she felt, you know, she was protecting her baby.'

I sling a conciliatory arm around her shoulder. 'I know, I'm sorry it all went off here, mate. Really I am. And I'm sorry I went off on one about Chris, it was only because I love you, and I don't want you to be hurt,' I repeat my disclaimer.

Rosie pours the milk onto the chocolate and I stir.

'Well, sometimes you just have to understand, don't you?' she says as she piles up a tray with chocolate and toast and we go into the other room. 'Talking of which, let's make this an evening for Selin to talk, OK? Enough of our problems for five minutes?'

We agree, and I catch sight of myself in the amazing makes-you-look-thin hallway mirror and think, 'Maybe getting outside of my own stuffed-up head for five minutes will do me some good.' Typical. Even when I'm trying not to think about me, I think about me, me, me.

Selin is sitting on the floor crosslegged. The TV is not on.

She looks nervous. I hand her a chocolate and a plate of toast but she touches neither.

'I've got something I have to tell you,' she says.

Rosie and I look at each other and join her on the floor. I wait for Selin's first-ever extensive emotional unburdening. 'It's OK, mate,' I reassure her. 'We're listening.'

She pauses, delves about in her bag for a moment and then brings out two Mars Bars. She pushes them across the floor to us. Mars Bars. From Selin. The first ones ever. The significance of this moment cannot be underestimated. Rosie and I look at each other. We don't pick them up but only look at them, symbols of Selin's new-found frailty.

'I meant to tell you before, but well, you know.' She pauses and takes a deep breath. 'I'm engaged. To Adem. The guy at the funeral. The one you were asking me about. He was there tonight. We're engaged. We're going to be married. It happened a few weeks ago, I was about to tell you when Ayla was killed. He's been at my side through the whole thing, he's made it bearable. There, I've said it.' She smiles at us nervously.

Rosie and I look at each other again and then at the Mars Bars, and then at Selin. This was not what I was expecting, and oddly I feel let down.

'That old bloke?' I say bluntly.

'He's not that old. Forty-six.' Sixteen years her senior. An age gap bigger than mine was with Michael. I try and think back over the last few weeks, but we've hardly seen each other. When did she meet this man, how did she meet him?

'It's old enough, Selin. Who is this man? You can't just tell us you're getting married. Is it an arranged marriage? Does his wife know?' I ask stupidly, some old anger stirring.

'No! I mean, no, it's not arranged. He's not married any more. I met him when I was out with Dad, on our pool nights. Dad has known him for years on and off. We got to know each other.' She smiles to herself. 'He's a nice man. He's kind and loving. He's been fantastic since Ayla's accident. He's your landlord, by the way.'

'*He's* our landlord?' All the things that should have clicked into place so much earlier if only I hadn't been so self-obsessed and if Selin hadn't been so sodding secretive. Yes, I *know* that's rich coming from me.

Rosie picks up her Mars Bar and studies it, shaking her head in bewilderment. 'You don't do anything for fifteen years and then you do this. I don't think I'm grasping it, you're getting married to someone you hardly know who could actually be your dad. That's the sort of thing I expected from Jen, to be honest. Look, it's not just some knee-jerk reaction to what's happened, is it?' she asks.

Selin looks horrified. 'What, you mean as a reaction to my grief? How can you say that? I've known about this for weeks, I just couldn't find the right time to tell you.'

'But Selin, what about passion, excitement, discovering the world together? All that stuff?' I ask her. Surely she must see that she could be signing her young life away.

'Oh yeah, all that stuff you did with Owen between him sleeping around and throwing you out, you mean?' Selin loses her patience and snaps at me. 'Or Rosie, all that honeymoon stuff you did with Chris the three minutes you were married before he dumped you for the love of his life mark one hundred and twenty six? Actually, there is passion and romance with Adem. It's just not the sort of addictive crap you two are so fond of getting wrapped up in, safe and sure in the knowledge that good old dependable Selin will be around to pick up the pieces, because let's face it, I never have anything else to do, do I? I *love* Adem, I am going to marry him. That's that. My family are happy for me, even if you can't be. And you wonder

357

why I didn't tell you? First of all, you haven't been around to talk to properly in weeks, and if you are it's either one or the other of you that needs to talk, because both of you have got yourselves into yet another mess. You never ask me, do you? You never wonder how *I* might be feeling, not even now. And secondly, I knew exactly what you would be like, you hypocrites. You say that I've been doing nothing for fifteen years. Actually, the pair of you have been too wrapped up in yourselves to notice *anything* I do, but I have had a life apart from being your counselling service and Adem is part of my life. A far more rewarding part than either of you.' Her eyes flash with anger. She springs up off the floor and perches on the edge of the armchair.

Rosie and I look at each other in stunned silence. Neither of us had a clue that Selin felt this way. We just assumed, or I did at least, that everything was cool in the world of Selin. Everything until Ayla, that is. I never imagined that there might be other stuff going on. I feel terrible.

'But he's so old,' I say, reflectively. I just can't get my head round this.

Rosie, on the other hand, has let her shock boil over into anger and she lets her bombshell drop. 'Listen, Selin. Chris and I might have been through a rocky patch, but we've worked it through now.' Rosie reaches into her own bag and throws two more Mars Bars on to the pile, like gambling chips. 'We're going to give it another go. I'm moving back in with him.'

'What?' I shout, all my good intentions of tolerance evaporating into thin air. 'You're going to give it another go? You're fucking mad, the pair of you. You and Selin. You're insane.'

Rosie whirls on me, pointing her finger in my face. 'I don't know why you're so high and mighty when you've been shagging someone eleven years *younger* than you behind our backs for God knows how long! And all that crap about giving men up. I saw you tonight with Josh, you've got him wrapped around your little finger now too, haven't you? Stringing him along until you get bored with him now, are you?'

A dense silence falls over the room. Nice one, Rosie.

Selin looks at me. 'Is this true?'

'Well, yes, sort of. I was going to tell you, tonight.' I had my Mars Bars hidden underneath a magazine. It seems pointless revealing them now.

'The Michael thing, I was going to tell you about that . . .'

'You mean the kid from the party, the ginger kid from the park?'

'Yes, I . . .'

'You hypocrite. How come it's OK for you but wrong for me?' she interrupts me.

'Because, it was just a fling with Michael. You're planning to ruin your life for ever with some pensioner!' I retort with a defensive reflex that inflames Selin even further. This is not going the way I planned it.

'How can you possibly know that? Since when have you been an expert in *not* ruining your life?' She stands now and roars at me. 'And Josh? You decide to mess around with Josh *now* of all times? You don't care about him in the slightest, do you? You selfish arrogant bitch.'

My face stings as though I have been slapped. 'Josh and I have sorted things out. *We're* fine about it. So there is no need to go leaping to his defence,' I argue, aware of how lame I'm sounding. Aware that I should be trying to smooth things over and make things better, but finding that every chance I get I'm throwing it away.

Selin walks to the door. 'Oh, he's let you walk all over him again, has he? Well, I'll tell you this. I won't let you get your claws into him, do you understand? So you can forget that little fantasy, you'll never touch him again.' She knocks over a cup of hot chocolate in her path. 'And as for you, Rosie, I've had enough of you and your stupid ideas too. Go back to Chris. Good luck to you. But I don't want to know when it goes wrong, OK? I don't want either of you on my doorstep any more. My counselling sessions are now closed. Permanently. And thanks for your understanding, by the way. I knew all those years of me being there for you would finally pay off. Yeah, right.'

She slams the front door so hard the pictures shudder and the next-door neighbour thumps on the wall, probably finally pushed to the brink by the recent week's rash of door slamming.

'Well, thanks for dropping me in it, Rosie,' I say bitterly, cross at her and cross that I didn't handle this better.

'You did it to yourself, sweetie,' she says archly, reaching over to mop up the chocolate with some tissues. Her prim self-satisfaction drives me mad.

'And you're about to do it to your baby. To think I even thought you might make a good mother. What a joke.' It's out there before I can do anything about it.

Rosie turns to me with a face like thunder, and throws the damp tissues at me. 'No, Jen. I'm not the joke. *You* are. You run around after Owen for three years, when everyone but you can tell he doesn't give a fuck about you, you sleep with everyone you can lay your hands on except the one decent man that's interested in you, and then you fuck a kid. That's a joke. Ha fucking ha.' And she's gone into her room.

I pick up the chocolate-sodden tissues and bin them, then pocket a Mars Bar.

We have never fought like this before. We have never been so cruel or so honest. I feel as though everything has gone, that the so-called fortress of our friendship has shattered like sugar glass. I can't see any way back to how it used to be, but then if we are all so happy to lie to each other, if we're all so blind to each other's hopes and hurts, maybe there is nothing to go back to?

I climb into bed, turn off the light and eat chocolate in the dark, mulling over everything they said. None of it was that far off the mark, but there was a time when a fight like this would have been impossible between us.

What has gone wrong?

Chapter Fifty

It's Thursday and I have seen neither Rosie nor Selin since last Saturday. I guess Rosie has been staying with Chris, and Selin is just staying out of my way. Rosie did come back to the flat while I was at work and left me a note, a Post-it stuck to the front door. I'm sure she appreciated the irony.

'Will be back at the weekend to pick up the rest of my things. Will pay rent until end of month, please sort out return of deposit. R.'

It hadn't even occurred to me that Rosie moving out would mean I'd have to find somewhere else to live. I've been so used to having my own place for so long, and now it looks as though I'll have to go back to an affordable house share with strangers, who are probably psychotic, or have rotas for washing up or who write their names on the milk. Oh God, a few weeks off thirty and I'm turning into a student again. Right, calm, calm deep breaths. I can handle this.

All week I have considered ringing them and trying to make peace. My finger has hovered over both their numbers on more than one occasion and I have always chickened out, childishly deciding that it is *always* me who makes the first move. Always. For once in my life I'm going to stick up for myself. And besides, they were just as right about me as I was mean about them. It's much harder to be defensive under those circumstances.

The only thing I have been able to do is begin to sort out my life, by which I mean making an attempt to steer its direction rather than letting it drift along in limbo.

The new prospectus for the journalism course has arrived, inviting me to an open evening and requesting a personal statement about why I'm committed to journalism. The course takes three months and it can only be done full time, so I'd have to give up work.

The prospect of giving up work seems like a dream on the one hand, but on the other, the prospect of making ends meet on minimum-wage bar jobs does not. Josh is the only adult I know who doesn't have a proper job, but then he doesn't have nice shoes, forty-seven lipsticks and three maxed-out credit cards either. I have more debt than a small country. Following my dream might be the one tiny push I need to get me off the repayment treadmill and into the as-yet-uncharted land of the credit blacklist. I'll be scouring the papers for those any-purpose loan advertisements where they lend you money even if you live in a car. And it's not yours. Still, if I did join the course I wouldn't be able to start until next April. That *would* give me a few months to save. Save money, there's a novel concept.

Anyway, I have the reply slip agreeing to attend sitting in front of me. I have the biro in my hand. I'll fill it in later.

Jackson went back to New York today, a bit earlier than planned in the wake of Rosie's rejection, I guess. We had a last lunch before he was picked up to go to the airport. He was on good form, but I think he was hiding how down he really felt.

'Jackson, I'm sorry, mate, but as much as I'd love it, you can see why she decided not to go back with you. You hardly know each other.'

He nodded and stirred his coffee. 'I know, but you know what? I think we could have made it. Jesus, Jenny, you don't expect to go falling in love with a pregnant English girl at the drop of a hat. I mean, we didn't even have sex! God forbid that that woman who wrote *The Rules* was right about that one. You know, I should have stuck to plan A.'

I laugh. 'Oh, and what was plan A?'

'Well, to seduce you and have a fun sex-filled affair until it was time to go home, of course.' He rolled his eyes and laughed but I don't think he was entirely joking.

'You were going to seduce me?' I laughed. 'Well, that's a bit arrogant. I don't even fancy you,' I lied. 'And anyway, I was seeing someone at the time. So I was not available,' I added primly.

'Yeah, *the Teenager*. Baby, I could have improved on his act, let me tell you.' We both laughed this time, but I blushed, my cheeks burning bright with the last flames of my office crush.

'Well, *if only* Rosie hadn't come along and interrupted your nefarious and shallow plans for me. Darn it, if I'd only known I could have fallen out with her for another reason too!' I laughed but as I glanced out of the window at the afternoon drizzle I sighed hard.

'You know, she's full of bravado but I get the feeling she's scared as shit that this is all going to go wrong,' Jackson told me gravely.

I shrugged my shoulders.

'She misses you guys very badly,' he said to the back of my head.

I turned to look at him. 'Well, she knows where I am,' I said. 'Or at least where I am until I have to move out because she's landed me with a flat I can't afford.'

Jackson shook his head, checked his watch and stood to put on his coat. 'I have to run. Look, you've all had a bit of a strange time lately. A bad time. Now is the time when you need each other more than ever. One of you has got to make the first move,' he said, obviously enjoying his moment as paternal influence.

I affected petulance with full teenage force. 'But why me? Why do I always have to make the first move?'

Jackson leant over, ruffled my hair and kissed me on the lips. 'Because I've got to lecture someone and you're the only one of you dimwits here. And because it's written all over your face how much you miss them too.'

I shrugged again and stood up to hug him goodbye. 'I'll miss you,' I said, and I meant it.

'I'll miss you too, but I'll be back in six months and maybe by that time I'll have gotten over Rosie, you'll have gotten over . . . whoever it is this week and we can have that affair I talked about.'

I laughed again and pushed him away. 'Jackson, I *never* said that I wanted to sleep with you!'

He gave me one last lingering look. 'Honey, you never had to *say* anything.'

By now he's probably back in NYC. I do miss him. He was just about the only person I'm talking to at the moment.

The other thing I've done is to enrol for driving lessons. My first one is tomorrow night. I deliberately planned it for a Friday night so that I would have something to preoccupy me during the day and so that I won't have to say, 'Oh nothing,' when people ask me what I'm up to that evening.

And in between planning my career, taking to the highways and not making up with my friends I think about Josh. Josh, Josh, Josh. Our brief encounter on the sofa and our brief encounter at the party. In fact, I'm having such a problem maintaining my resolve over Josh that I even find myself, like right now for instance, staring at the phone and repeating over and over again in the back of my mind, 'Phone me, Josh, phone me, Josh.'

So fully absorbed am I in my new role as love-crazed spinster that the ring of the phone makes me jump and nearly spill my tea on my still-blank application form.

'Hello?'

'Hi, Jen, it's Josh. You all right?' The sound of his voice sets a flutter going in my stomach. Josh whose voice I always recognise and who nevertheless always feels obliged to remind me who he is every time we talk on the phone anyway, Josh who makes my cheeks turn pink. He sounds in an upbeat mood.

'Um well, you mean apart from the recent Armageddon to hit my social life? I'm fine. How are you?' I've changed my mind about being sensible, I can't stop thinking about you and I miss you and do you want to come over right now and have sex? I mouth silently into the mouthpiece.

'Oh, you lot will sort it out. You always do,' Josh says, oblivious to my silent plea. 'And look, I'm sorry I didn't tell you about Adem. Selin really wanted to tell you herself. He is a really sound bloke, you know,' he adds loyally.

'Yeah, well. We'll see.' I bet his ex-wife and kids don't think so.

'Anyway, the reason I'm phoning you – ' I feel a brief flurry of excitement and anticipation that Josh might ask me out and break the expected tedium of the up-and-coming weekend, and I know that my willpower will dissolve under no pressure at all in about 000.01 seconds. ' – is that I wanted to know if you've read *Time Out* today?'

'*Time Out*? No. I don't need *Time Out* any more, I don't have any friends,' I say, wondering if he's spotted some cool club we can go to, or some new restaurant in town.

'The review of the exhibition?' I had totally forgotten it came out today. I can tell that even Josh is becoming impatient with my introspection.

'Oh God, Josh, sorry. What did it say?' I hold my breath.

'Yeah, it was good, really good. It said the collective had some good ideas and it was worth a look, but best of all he mentions me by name. Listen: "Painter Josh Mehmet may be traditional in his use of oils and canvas but all that is ordinary ends there. He has an eye for form and colour that is startling and engaging, and an emotive and passionate style that connects with his audience".'

'Bloody hell! Josh, that's great. Emotive and passionate. Imagine!' I imagine him being emotive and passionate with me and take a deep breath.

'Yeah, and today I sold a painting. The one that was up for one hundred and fifty quid!' Here we go, he's going to invite me out to share his new good fortune.

'Josh, that's fab, are you going to celebrate?' I prompt him.

'No, not at the moment. I'm still not quite in the mood for celebrating and anyway, I haven't got time. The *Time Out* bloke is interested in me exhibiting some work at his gallery. We're having a meeting tomorrow, I have to go and paint before the terror of it all petrifies me into artist's block!' He laughs and I try to mask my disappointment. It turns out that the man actually *does* think about something else apart from me. This secret-admirer business isn't all it's cracked up to be. But my empty weekend aside I really am pleased for him, he deserves it.

'Josh, that's great. Thanks for letting me know.'

'No problem. It sounds stupid, but I somehow get the feeling that Ayla is behind this. That she is helping me on. Does that sound stupid?' His detached voice suddenly sounds very young and vulnerable.

'No, not stupid. Not stupid at all.' We listen to the sounds of each other's breathing for a moment.

'About the other night, everything I said . . .'

I wait for him to continue with bated breath. 'Yes?' I'm terrified.

'Well, I meant all of it and, and well, the more I think about what you said the more I think you're right, that we need to wait a bit. And the fact that you've insisted on it makes me realise you care about this too. It makes me feel good. Optimistic about the future, for the first time in ages.'

My heart melts and I'm glad I managed to keep my trap shut for once. 'And me, me too,' I say simply.

'I'll see you soon, yeah? Call me,' he says. I say goodbye and hang up the phone.

The doorbell chimes. I'm not expecting anyone, Rosie said she wasn't planning to come back until the weekend. Maybe she's come to her senses and is back with her tail between her legs.

'Hello?' I ask the intercom system.

'Jenny? Hello. It's Adem, I thought we should talk about the flat.'

My heart sinks into my toes.

'I understand you will be moving out soon?'

Rosie must have contacted him already. Good old Rosie.

'Yes, come up,' I say blankly. I leave the door on the latch, return to the living-room and slump into the sofa.

'Hello? May I come in?' he calls down the hallway. His stupid politeness rankles.

'Yes! I'm in the living-room,' I snap. 'You know where it is, presumably.'

He appears in the doorway, and takes the chair by the phone. 'Actually, I haven't really been here since I bought the place. It's looking pretty good though.' He smiles at me and I have to admit his laughter lines are quite pleasant. At least he hasn't gone totally to seed like some men his age, he's still slim and he's got most of his hair. Well, let's get down to business.

'So, I have to move out. End of the month. Can we have our deposit back, please? Two cheques would be best.' I don't think we really needed a personal visit to sort this out and I just want him out of the flat as quickly as possible so that I can go back to moping alone.

Adem shifts in his chair and leans forward, clasping his hands together as if he is about to pray. 'Actually, Jenny, I wanted to talk to you about Selin.'

I sigh, audibly. 'Really?' I say with as much icy disinterest as I can muster.

'You must think she is crazy, wanting to marry an old man like me.'

I nod. 'Well, yes.'

'I expect you wonder why on earth we got together . . . ?'

'Oh no, not really, I've seen it a million times before. Man hits middle age, man dumps wife and kids and goes off with first bit of young stuff he can find who's blind enough or stupid enough to shag him. Man forgets he ever had a family.' My dear old dad, still breaking my pretty heart in two after all these years.

'Jenny, I was married, yes.'

I rest my case.

'I met my first wife, Andrea, when I was twenty-two.'

'I'm not really sure I want to hear this,' I say.

'Please. Let me speak. I met Andrea when I was twenty-two. She was eighteen. I hadn't lived in London long, she was a barmaid in the local pub. I'd never seen anything like her. She was so full of life. A very pretty blonde girl. Vivacious, you know. Every night for two months I went to the pub and ordered a cola – I hadn't found work yet, so I sat at the bar and made it last for as long as I could, just to talk to her.'

This is possibly the cheesiest story I have ever heard. 'I'm sure the memories will comfort her on the day you marry your second wife.'

He looks at his hands, takes a deep breath and carries on.

'Finally I found some building work, and I thought, well, now at least I can take her out somewhere decent, so I went down to the pub that night, but I couldn't work up the courage. I thought I'd have a drink, just one and then I'd do it, but it never seemed like the right time. When she called time I was pretty drunk and I thought, that's it. I've blown it, she must think I'm a fool. Just as I was getting ready to leave she marched round the other side of the bar and said to me, "Are you going to take me out, or what?" I was speechless, so I just nodded. "Good," she said. "Friday's my night off, meet me here at seven, we can go for a meal." And she put her arms around my neck and kissed me on the mouth. Three months later we were married.' He is smiling to himself as he recounts the tale, the hypocrite.

'So, what you're trying to say is that you got married too young, neither of you really knew each other and after twenty-odd years you've finally realised it's never going to work?'

He winces at my words, I've finally managed to hit home. These are the things I never get to say to my father. He swallows and looks me in the eye.

'Three years later she was dead. We had been planning to try for a baby. Back in those days there wasn't so much screening or health checks for women. She had cervical cancer. She didn't know until it was too late. By the time it was diagnosed there was nothing that could be done. She was dead in three months.'

I let the clanking sound of the radiator cooling off fill the silence. So he's had a tragic first love. That doesn't make it right.

'I'm sorry about that,' I say. I am sorry for poor Andrea.

'Well, in time it hurt less and I have met other women, but never one who could make my heart sing like Andrea, not until I met Selin. She's so different from Andrea, so brave and independent, so shy and gentle. But she has given me back my heart. I love her, Jenny. I love her with all the passion a human can muster. She thinks I'm mad for coming here to tell you all this. She thinks I'm was mad for telling it all to Rosie too. She thinks it is no one's business but ours. But I can see how hurt she is. I know she is too stubborn to try and explain it to you, so I persuaded her to let me try. I hope you will be able to be happy for us one day. God knows, the last few weeks have been sad enough, but we have helped each other through and we do make each other happy, truly truly happy.'

I nod silently. It's hard to let one's opinion evaporate in a moment, even after a story like that, but I do believe he means what he says. I also believe that Selin is right, really it is none of my business. It just reminds me, at face value anyway, of all those years ago when I said goodbye to my dad, as my dad.

'Don't forget I love you, sweetheart,' he had said. I never did forget. But he did. Right, snap out of it.

'Adem, I'm sorry for being so rude. Maybe if Selin hadn't insisted on keeping this a secret from us we wouldn't have got so cross and we wouldn't have jumped to the wrong conclusions. It will take some time to get used to but, well, if Selin is happy, I am happy for her.' I continue tentatively, 'What did Rosie say?'

'She cried a lot, Selin said she would. And then she said more or less the same as you. The pair of them spent two hours on the phone, talking things over.' I suppress a spurt of jealousy. Why Rosie first? Where's my two-hour phone call? But seeing as getting Rosie and me in one place at the same time these days is nigh on impossible I let it go.

'I'll try and make it up to her, I promise. I'll call her tonight.'

He nods and smiles. 'Good, there is one other thing. The flat.'

My heart sinks again and I look around the flat I have come to love.

'I don't want the hassle of finding new tenants at this time of year.'

I am about to say that he won't have any trouble finding new tenants at any time of year in London but instinct keeps my mouth shut.

'So what I propose is that I cut the rent in half until the New Year. At the end of that time maybe you will have found a new flatmate, or maybe something else will have turned up and we can review the situation. In return, you being here will make sure the pipes don't freeze up and cause me flooding.'

So, buy my friendship with an act of unparalleled kindness, is it? Nice one. However, I'm not about to fly in the face of the one piece of good fortune to come my way for a long while.

'Adem, that's really kind of you. Thanks. Thanks so much.'

'No need to thank me. Well, I must be on my way.'

This time I stand and follow him to the front door.

'There is just one other thing,' he says with his hand on the latch.

'Oh yes?' He's not going to spoil it all by demanding sex in return for rent, is he?

'There's someone else who wants to see you.'

He opens the door and Selin is sitting on the stairs, a bottle of wine clutched in her lap.

'Selin!' I say with a smile.

She stands and takes a step towards me. 'Jen, I'm sorry, mate. I said some horrid stuff.'

'And me! Me much worse!' We engulf each other in a hug and then stand back and smile stupidly.

'Fancy splitting this?' she asks, holding out the wine.

'Yeah, I'd love to. Come on in, you two, I'll get some glasses.' I head back into the flat.

'No, not for me. This is for you two. Enjoy your night,' Adem says. He kisses Selin and waves over his shoulder as he heads down the stairs.

Back in the flat, Selin and I look at each other and burst into tears. It has been a tense few days.

A few minutes later we are sitting on the sofa, glasses of wine in hand, and Selin is reading through the college prospectus.

'This is great, you should go for it. I'm so proud of you, actually being proactive for once.'

I smile sheepishly, noting the 'for once'. 'Well, I will go for it. But I'll need to do more than just turn up. I have to show an "active interest". I'd better get some work experience somewhere. I really wish I hadn't left this until I was geriatric.'

Selin pats me on the head. 'Better than leaving it until you're dead.' Her own words hurt her and she takes a deep gulp of wine.

'How is everyone, your family and everyone?' I had always imagined that grief like this would be so overwhelming that the whole world would stop, that it wouldn't leave any time for thinking or feeling just exactly as you did before. But it does, and when you remember, you feel guilty for carrying on like normal.

'The same,' she says, obviously at a loss to find new ways to describe her pain. I nod and hold her hand.

'I know,' I say.

She takes another sip of wine and raises herself up in her seat.

'I've got to say, Jen, I'd just about given up on you taking any initiative with your life. I thought you'd be stuck in that God-awful job for ever, just waiting until they promoted you to head of paper-clips or something. I actually thought you liked it.'

'Yes, well, so did I for a while. It's taken me a very long time to get motivated but well, here I am. Ready to give it a go. Knowing my luck I'll probably have to go back to Georgie and beg for a job after six months and I'll end up working for Carla, but well *at least I will have tried*,' I say with mock sincerity, and at least I *will* have tried.

'So, you go to the open evening. You network. You phone around the local newspapers and use some holiday time to get work experience. OK?' Selin recaps for me, just in case I'm not capable of sorting this out myself.

'Yes, sir,' I say, performing a mock salute. 'And I've got a driving lesson tomorrow,' I add proudly.

'Bloody hell, you really are going hell for leather, aren't you. Have you got yourself lined up with a gig at Ronnie Scott's too?'

I look at her sideways. 'Whatever do you mean by that?' I ask suspiciously.

'All the things you want to do before you're thirty. Decent career, learn to drive, nightclub diva.'

'I've never told you about the singing? Have I?' I say cautiously. Oh God, maybe she overheard me in the shower one time.

'Yes, remember? That night when we were at your old place? We'd found a bottle of Jack Daniels that Owen had left behind after one of his binges, and we played truth or dare. Anyway, you told us about your dream to sing just once, in front of a proper audience, and then you did your version of "I Will Survive". I've got to tell you, Gloria Gaynor didn't have too much to worry about that night! Mind you, neat whisky probably doesn't enhance one's vocal chords too much, unless one is Janice Joplin or Bonnie Tyler. And then you cried for ages. Whisky makes you cry, doesn't it?'

I laugh, but I really wish I hadn't chosen to share that particular secret with my two dearest friends. I know it's a pipe dream, but it's one that had kept me amused for many years, and other people knowing just makes it seem all the more silly.

'God, I hate people who remember what's been said after a drunken game of truth or dare. I never remember, it's so unfair. You could have told me you had a secret thing for wearing soiled Y-fronts and I wouldn't know it. Anyway, I obviously made it up just for something to say.'

Selin shakes her head. 'Of course you did.'

I share the last drops of wine between our glasses and reach for my purse to see if I have enough cash to get another bottle.

'But say that you hadn't, and that you really were going up on stage to sing, what would it be? The ultimate song you'd really love to sing? "I Will Survive"?'

I laugh but get drawn in despite myself. 'No, it wouldn't be disco, disco is the best music in the world to dance to. But not as much fun to sing as say . . . some classic soul track, some Aretha Franklin. "Respect". "Respect", by Aretha Franklin. That's a kick-ass song. That's what I'd sing,' I daydream.

'Cool,' Selin says. 'I'd do "Total Eclispe of the Heart" by Bonnie Tyler.'

I shake my head at her in despair and before I can stop it Bonnie's tune insinuates itself into my head, preparing for a tortuous night of replay on a loop. With an easy peace between us, I have to finally ask her.

'Selin,' I say tentatively. 'You would tell me, wouldn't you, you would say if you . . . What I mean is, if you blame me for Ayla's death, you'd say, wouldn't you? Because I've been blaming myself since it happened. I'd understand, but I just need to know.'

Selin looks at me in horror.

'Blame you? God, Jenny, no, no.' She blinks and shakes her head. '*Maybe* just after it happened and you were there and I didn't really understand why, maybe then I got you and the accident all mixed up just for a moment, and I was angry at you, at everyone. But I've never blamed you. The more I thought about it – and I've done very little else recently – the more I'm glad that you were there. I'm glad the last face she saw was someone who she knew and trusted. She wouldn't have felt so alone,' she says softly, taking my hand.

Neither of us speaks. The weightless feeling of relief that floods through me takes the dull protective edge off my own grief and I see the world without Ayla more keenly than ever. We sit in silence for a long time, listening to the distance traffic's boom. After maybe ten minutes have passed I have one more important thing to say to make things right.

'Selin?'

'Yes, love?'

'I just want to say I'm sorry, you were right. I've been a terrible friend. It's all been one way for so long. That's not the sort of friend I want to be. I want to be the kind of friend that you have always been to me, and from now I will be. I'm sorry. If I ever act like that again just poke me in the eye and tell me to stop it, OK?'

Selin smiles indulgently at me. 'OK, Jen,' she says.

'Selin?' I say again, same tone.

'*Yes*, Jen,' she repeats.

'Well, will you really kill me if at some point in the future, when everything settles down a bit, Josh and I give it a go? Because the thing is, as it turns out, I really like him a lot.' I say the last bit in a rush. 'Don't tell him I said that.'

'Well, let me see. Do you like him because he is a wonderful talented generous person or because he is the first grown-up man to be nice to you since Owen?'

'The first option,' I say sincerely. 'Really, and because for no apparent reason I stopped thinking of him as your brother and started seeing him as a living breathing sex bomb.'

Selin giggles and puts her hands over her ears. 'Jenny! He is still my brother! Yuck,' she screams.

'Soz,' I say, and laugh. Filled with a startling rush of joy. 'So you won't kill me?'

Selin looks me right in the eye. 'No, I won't kill you if you two get together. If you ever, *ever* do anything to hurt him, or muck him around, then I'll kill you. And the same goes for him too.'

'How can we fail,' I say with a cheery grin. We pause for a moment and look at our wineglasses.

'Selin?' I say again.

'Mmmmm?' She sounds as if she's tolerating a three-year-old.

'What am I going to do about Rosie? I mean, now you and I have made up. And you and her have made up. I should try and make up with her, right?' I finally check my purse and find only small change. I get up to put the kettle on, probably best for my overworked liver.

'Well, yes. Yes, you should. And I think you should do that playground rhyme as well while you're at it, you know, the "make up, make up, never ever break up" one. Somehow it seems appropriate,' she says dryly.

'OK, OK, so maturity hasn't been much of a factor recently, but it's not actually my fault. It's the pressure of being my age at the dawn of a new millennium, and that's the truth, there's a book out about it. Too many choices, that's my trouble.' Selin raises her famous eyebrow at me sceptically. 'I don't know if I can make up with her, though. I mean Chris. *Chris*?' I say, as if my protests over the last few weeks haven't made my views clear enough. I rise to go to the kitchen.

'I know. I know, but well, Rosie and I had a good talk about it earlier on today,' she calls after me as I pad down the hall. 'She's aware of what's she's doing and well, they seem to have sort of bonded again recently and anyway she wants to give it a go and not spend her life wondering if it might have worked out. If I've realised anything recently it's that life is too short for crap like this. I think we have to swallow our reservations and just hope it works out for her. And anyway, I think Chris might actually have changed.' She follows me into the kitchen.

'And what if he hasn't? What if it doesn't work out? Will you reopen the doors of your therapy centre for her?'

'Of course I would, we'd all do the same for each other. It's not my fault I'm the only one who's not fucked up.'

I flick her shoulder with a tea towel and smile. 'So you're really happy with Adem then. You really, really are?'

'What you mean is, is he any good at sex, right?' she asks me with a sideways look.

'Right,' I say. Obvious really.

'It's fucking fantastic. It's fucking *Company* magazine 101 ways to achieve orgasm in one fucking go. I'm telling you, Jen, I may not have been around as much as you, but I know quality when I come across it. So to speak.'

We break down in a fit of schoolgirl giggles. Selin starts opening the cupboards.

'Oh God, I'm starving. Got any junk food?' she asks me. I open a drawer to display six untouched Mars Bars.

'Here you go. Take your pick.'

Chapter Fifty-one

Despite the prospect of an empty weekend watching the after-noon film on BBC2, putting on my going-out make-up for a trip to Sainsbury's, and finally trying to finish that book I've been reading for the last year or so, which according to everybody else is the best book ever written about anything ever, I feel that today, Friday, has been a pretty positive day.

First of all, being friends with Selin again has made me feel much better. Of course, it doesn't mean she'll be around this weekend, Adem is taking up most of her time, but it means that at least some of the old order is back as it should be. Secondly, I closed my office door this morning and composed a speculative letter requesting work experience, copies of which I sent to *Time Out*, the *Hackney Gazette* and all the other localish newspapers I could think of, hoping they won't laugh too much when they see my age. Then I wrote my personal statement to send to the college, mentioned all the places I've had work experience at (creative licence) and posted my reply slip.

The rest of the afternoon at work was made slightly easier by the fact that Carla has fallen in love and so her usual Friday trip to Ann Summers or wherever it is she gets her outfits has been curtailed. Instead she went to the supermarket and came back with a selection of gourmet pre-prepared food. Tonight is their first date 'in' and she told me she was feeling quite nervous as she piled a packet of rocket salad, fresh pasta, ready-made carbonara sauce, a bottle of Pinot Grigio and a tiramisu that looked as though it would benefit from going back in the freezer any time soon, on to my desk for my appraisal.

'I've never cooked for a bloke before, see,' she told me. 'Do you think it's all right?'

'Mmmm, looks delicious.' I smiled at her.

'I just don't want anything to go wrong, not tonight!' Her voice almost trembled.

Bless her, I thought, she's obviously quite fragile underneath it all. 'Tonight going to be "the night", is it then, Carla?' I asked her with the confidential tone of a slightly older sister.

'"*The* night"? Oh, you mean are we going to shag? Oh no, I already shagged him. This is just the first night it will be in a bed. At least, I hope we're going to bloody shag, it cost me nearly fifteen quid, this lot.'

Like I said, fragile.

On the way home I had a good think about Rosie and Chris, trying to sort out my feelings. Everyone else says I'm wrong about this. Even Selin, who is never wrong, has eventually come around to the idea. Everyone says we should give Chris a chance, even Jackson, Jackson who tried to whisk Rosie away to another continent. Even Jackson who cared so much for her and stepped down in the end; he wouldn't have done that if he didn't think it was for the best. And even Michael, bless him, didn't seem to think he sounded like the personification of evil I have him pinned down as.

If I really force myself to think about it – and you know how much I hate that I think my main objections are still valid; Chris really messed her up. But really, deep down, I think I'm jealous. I think that I didn't want Rosie to have a second chance with Chris. I didn't want her to have the opportunity to make right the dreadful wrongs of their relationship when I couldn't. Even

Rosie who I love so much, I didn't want her to have the chance to heal all the same wounds in her that I thought I could never heal in myself – the damage done by Owen and, yes, by my father too. I wanted us both to carry our scars for ever. It's still hard to adjust to the idea, for sure, but now that I realise I can make myself whole without either of them I can begin to see Rosie's side. I think I might have been wrong about Chris, and first thing tomorrow I'm going to swallow my pride and call and tell her so. I just need one more night to make sure I've got everything straight in my head, to make sure we get it all sorted without yet another bust-up.

And to top off a productive day I have just got back from my first ever driving lesson. I think it went pretty well: I didn't crash. The instructor, Jim, recommended that I sign up for twenty lessons rather than ten but given that I didn't know where to put the ignition key when I got in, it could have been a lot worse. I reassured him that I was a fast learner once I got the hang of things.

'Let's bloody hope so,' he had joked, 'I haven't got much hair left as it is.' What a card.

And so now, here it is: my Friday night in, alone.

I've got that feeling again that it might not be quite as boring as I anticipate, but that has probably got more to do with the sugar rush I experience after eating a king-size Aero bar and drinking a can of full-fat Coke instead of having a sensible cup of tea. I have got a bottle of wine but somehow drinking alone on a Friday night seems much more needy and desperate than drinking on your own any other night of the week, so I have left it chilling in the fridge. As the evening progresses I'll decide how needy and desperate I feel.

I have a bath early, and lie on the sofa painting my nails as Friday night TV passes me by. I catch five seconds of some boring top-ten music programme dedicated to thrash metal and

I think of Michael. A tiny little bit of me wants to chase my latest star-crossed feeling and try his mobile, just to test whether or not it would be possible to get him to spin his mother a line and have him on the 9.20 from Twickenham and heading right into my arms. For a moment I imagine him coming through the front door again and I let myself drift into a little trip down memory lane, but to be honest the only reason I want to call him is to find out if I still have power over him, not because I miss him at all, not really.

This is no good. I'll think I'll open the wine.

The theme tune to another rerun of *Friends* greets me as I return from the kitchen with my wine. As the first glass slips down I spend fifteen minutes trying to work out which one of them is trying to shag which other one who may or may not fancy the first one. I can't tell, but the second glass of wine makes it seem less important and I find myself giggling out loud.

Around ten o'clock I think about Josh. Call me, he said. He meant for me to call him. He is so intent on keeping our agreement and staying out of my way until I've 'found myself' that he has lumbered me with the heavy burden of making the first move. Well, it's the twenty-first century, I'm fairly sure he won't blow me out, so I reckon I can manage it. When the time comes, which is not going to be in five minutes, I will have the willpower.

Instead I try to work out why how I feel about him changed so radically.

It's an odd thing being a girl, now bear with me here. Because attraction to one person or the other can be sparked off by the oddest little things. Just look at Dan, for example. Ha, ha. No, but seriously. I've known Josh for most of my life and I've always liked him, he makes me laugh, he's a good listener, he can dance pretty well for an artist, but I have never, apart from that brief time as a teen, really fancied him, and even then I think it was in the safe-distance-crush kind of way. The sort of unformed fantasies you have about boys that involve nothing more scary than imagining the kind of kiss where your noses don't bump. But two things have happened to change how I see him. The time that we kissed, it was definitely a kiss that I could go to bed with, no doubt about that, and secondly, it's his neck.

His neck and shoulders to be precise. It's his warm olive-coloured skin and the little hollows at the base of his neck that lead into the mysterious and powerful breadth of his shoulders. Ever since his opening party last week I have been thinking about running my tongue along those little hollows. It always does start with a single body part for me – hands with Michael, but it has been forearms, eyes, ears and now neck. Oh, that neck.

Feeling reckless, I reach into my bag and pick up my mobile phone, turn it on, and scan through the numbers until I come to Josh's. I could just press Call and get him over here right now. In half an hour or so I could be discovering the delights of that torso for myself. But something tells me that sex with a frustrated and drunk girl isn't what Josh wants out of me, and it's not what I want him to want either, so I toss my phone back in my bag and content myself with a little more fantasy.

Now that I've established that I *lust* after Josh and that I really like him, I should probably question the ethics of going out with someone who has always been a friend, but suddenly I feel quite sleepy and after all, tomorrow is another day. Well, you can't expect me to dump years of happy denial all at once, can you?

The lovely thing about having an early bath is that all I have to do now is brush my teeth and I can fall into bed. I turn the heating on because I'm too tired to put on my pyjamas and climb naked into bed, stretching out against the clean sheets and turning off my bedside lamp.

As I lie on my back and wait for the familiar shadows to emerge out of the darkness I smile to myself. My evening hasn't turned out to be as exciting as my intuition had told me, except for the fact that I have decided that one day, quite soon, if he hasn't changed his mind in one of those horrible twists of irony, I'm going to find out more about Josh naked. And that is an exciting thought to go to sleep on.

I can't breathe. I'm trapped. I'm trapped under a rock or a tree, it's dark and I can't breathe, I twist and struggle but I can't move. I force myself awake.

I can't breathe.

I blink in the darkness. There is a hand covering my nose and my mouth. There is the weight of another person on the bed. On me.

I blink again. I swallow.

I *am* awake.

'Hello, Jenny, I said I'd be seeing you soon,' Owen whispers in my ear.

Chapter Fifty-two

My first instinct is to struggle, but he has pinned me to the bed, the duvet the only thing keeping me from him. I'm not afraid yet, I'm still half asleep, I'm probably still half drunk. I have no idea what time it is, I have no idea how he got here, all I know is that he *is* here right now. I don't feel afraid yet, I feel angry. What's he playing at this time? I try to shake my head clear of his hand, but his fingers dig into my cheeks. I don't *feel* the pain but I stop moving. I don't feel the pain, but I know he is hurting me.

'I'm going to take my hand away now, don't scream. If you scream that will make me very angry and you know what that means.'

I nod dumbly. His breath stinks of alcohol and his fingers of stale smoke.

As he slowly releases his hand from my mouth I gulp in some fresh air. He reaches over me and turns on the bedside lamp.

I look around the room, and listen to the familiar rumble of the constant traffic along Green Lanes.

He is here. I am not dreaming. He *is* in my house.

Now I am afraid.

'You always did prefer it with the light on, didn't you?' He has straddled me but now he sits back, smiling down at me with the same indulgent smile he used as he poured me wine, or presented me with a meal or a gift. I don't know if I am supposed to speak or not. I free an arm from under the cover and pull the duvet up as far as it will go.

'So modest, that never used to be one of your more obvious traits,' he smirks.

I wince, remembering. What does he want? Has he come here for sex, has he come here to hurt me? I take a deep breath, I remember his tempers, I remember his moods. Try to be rational, try to be smart. Talk quietly in a neutral tone. I won't provoke him.

'It's just a surprise, that's all. I didn't expect you to turn up like this?' I attempt a smile.

'Well, let me see, you won't talk to me face to face, you won't speak to me on the phone, you won't reply to my e-mails. I had no choice, Jenny. I needed to see you and you left me no choice.'

I want to ask him how he knew where to find me but I daren't, I'm too afraid of making him angry, of reminding him that I didn't want him to know.

'I'm, I'm sorry. I never meant to shut you out. I was . . . trying to get over you. You know how hard I find it.' If I pander to his ego, maybe that will calm him down.

Suddenly he lunges down until his face is millimetres from mine; the stench of his breath forces me to resist the impulse to gag. His hands grip both of my wrists. I can't be sure, but his irises are almost entirely obliterated by the black of his pupils, he's probably taken some coke too.

'I didn't *want* you to get over me, you stupid little slut,' he whispers. 'I still love you, don't you understand that?' I feel his knee dig its way between my legs, pushing them apart under the covers.

I am not going to let him do this to me. Not without a fight. Think, be calm. You know him.

'Owen, I didn't realise. The last time we finished it seemed so final. I really thought you didn't want me any more.' I try to stay calm, to stay still, I don't want to move. I think furiously: where is my phone? In the other room. Is there anything here? Anything heavy, the wine bottle? Not within reach. Don't make him angry. He doesn't seem to have a knife or anything. But he's big, he's bigger than me. He's strong.

'That's why I'm here,' he says, bending his lips to my neck. 'To show you how much I still want you.' His hand releases one of my arms from its grip and begins to make its journey under the duvet, a sickening reminder of our sex routine.

I will not let him do this to me.

'Owen, wait!' I say with more command than I could have expected to muster.

He withdraws his hand and looks at me. 'Come on, you know how you love it when I fuck you,' he says mildly.

'Look, you say you love me, you *know* how I feel about you. But this is all too fast, we can't just jump back into bed. We need to talk. Let me get dressed. I'll make us some tea. Let's talk things though.'

He studies me through swollen and red lids. I hurry on.

'I can see just by the very fact that you're here how much you care, but it's still a bit of a shock. We need to talk things through, like we always do. I bet you've got things you want to say to me, haven't you?'

Even this Owen, the drunk and drugged Owen, must surely be the same Owen deep down, the Owen who loves the sound of his own voice. With one movement he springs off the bed and takes a seat in the corner.

'Women, they always want to be wooed. Fine,' he says. 'Get dressed. We'll talk. I'll undress you later.' I can see that he is not about to provide me with any privacy. I can see that in his drug-addled eyes rape wouldn't be a problem for him. My instinct is to shy away from him, curl and hide, but instead I steady myself and dress as quickly as I can without looking as though I'm afraid, letting him watch me, keeping him calm. I keep waiting for the dream to end, to blink myself awake to the sounds of my alarm clock. Keep waiting for those few confused moments just as I wake when I work out that it's all a dream.

He follows me into the kitchen and I fill the kettle. I could throw boiling water in his face but it wouldn't knock him out, it would just make him angry. He would come back at me. I open the cutlery drawer for a teaspoon, I could go for him with a knife, but he's stronger than me, he could turn it on me instead. All I can think about is keeping him calm, staying safe. I look at the clock on the microwave: 3.28 a.m. It seems like a long time until dawn. From somewhere the statistic that women are more likely to be raped or murdered by men they know insinuates itself into my mind and I nearly lose it. Tears sting my eyes as I turn my back to him. My knees buckle and wobble, the wine I had earlier on rises in my throat and before I can stop myself I find that I'm retching into the kitchen sink.

Owen is instantly at my side, smoothing the hair away from my forehead. I force my stomach to be still and stand back from him, wiping my mouth with the back of my hand.

He hands me a glass of water.

'Must be the excitement,' he says and something in his eyes at that moment tells me that he knows exactly what he is doing. And that he is loving every minute. I gulp down the water and return to making tea. Stay calm.

'Let's go into the living-room,' I say. If I can get to my mobile . . . What then? What if I can get to my mobile? One step at a time.

I take a seat on the sofa, hugging my tea between my knees, my bag at my feet. I try and think back to earlier on. Is my phone switched on? Yes. Who did I call last?

Owen takes centre stage opposite me and begins to pace the floor.

'The thing is, Jenny, it's the arrogance of it all that hurts me. The way you think you can simply drop me — as if *you* have the choice. You don't have the choice, you belong to me, *I* make the choices.'

I nod at him and think back. I was going to ring Josh, that's right. I had called up his name and then I hadn't had the guts to go through with it and I chucked my phone back in my bag. If the battery hasn't run down, right now the display on my phone will say 'Josh, call?' I can't talk to him, of course, but maybe he'll be able to hear, maybe he'll know, maybe he'll understand what's going on and he'll get help. *If* he's there, *if* his phone is switched on, *if* it wakes him up and *if* it doesn't go to messages. It's all I can think of right now. I make a show of finishing my tea and I bend to put the cup on the floor. As quickly as I can I reach into the open bag, find my phone on top of the clutter and press the Call button, sitting upright again slowly, carefully, not distracting Owen.

Maybe Josh can help. *If* he can make out what's going on.

'You're the only one, Jenny, the only who has ever really touched me, who has ever really given me what I need. So I can't just let you go, can I?' As Owen talks on, warming to his theme I strain to catch the faint call tone, terrified he'll hear it too. It seems to ring for ever before it is cut short. I *think* I can just make out the tinny sound of a voice on the other end. Either he's picked up or it's a recorded message. Now what? If he's there I can't let him hang up.

'Owen,' I say, as loudly as I can get away with, 'I understand how you feel but you can't just break into my flat and expect everything to be all right. Expect us to have sex, just like that.' It's not what Owen wants to hear but it is exactly what I want

Josh to hear. If he can hear me. There is no sound coming from my bag now.

'Look, you silly little cunt, I had to get your attention somehow, for Christ's sake. I tried everything else. If you're pissed off about this you've only got yourself to blame. God knows, I tried to talk to you. You made a mistake when you thought you could ignore *me*. I don't like to be ignored, Jenny. I don't like it at all. And you know how it upsets me to lose my temper. Well, maybe the time for talking is past, maybe I should just show you how much I care.'

'OK, OK, wait. I understand. Let's talk then. Let talk.' He sits next to me on the sofa now, taking my wrist in his hands, and he talks. Hearing his words but trying not to listen as he makes his plans for me sickeningly clear I sit perfectly still oddly calm against the rising waves of physical fear that have begun to break over my body. I'm waiting for what I know will be my only choice. Over his shoulder I watch the minutes tick by on the video clock, each minute seeming like an hour. I nod, I agree, I pacify him, six minutes. I sit still as he strokes my hair and I agree with him that I do love him, and that I could never love anyone else. Eleven minutes. I hold my breath and swallow hard as he grips my chin in his fingers and turns my face to his, forcing my mouth open with his tongue. Fourteen minutes.

I blink hard to fight back tears as he whispers, 'I can't wait for this any more.'

Seventeen minutes. No help is coming. I am not letting this happen to me. This is my last chance.

I take a deep breath and with all the force and anger I can muster I punch him in the throat and make a dash for it. He catches me at the living-room door. I fall, twisting on to my right shoulder with a wrenching thud; from somewhere else I can feel pain. He looks at me with disgust and straddles me. I open my mouth to scream, but before I can it is filled with

390

blood. He has hit me. He's going to hurt me and I can't find the strength to fight any more. I close my eyes and pray, 'Just let it be over quickly and please don't let me die.' He's won.

The loudest sound I have ever heard rips through the flat, the door is flung off its hinges and suddenly the room is filled with shouting men.

'Back away, get on the floor. Get ON THE FLOOR.' Before my eyes Owen is wrestled to the ground by two policemen. They are followed in by at least half a dozen others. I draw my knees up under my chin and watch them. A woman police officer crouches down next to me, helps me to my feet and takes me into the bedroom.

'It's all right now, love, it's all right. Has he . . . ?' I shake my head, unable to speak, and watch as Owen is taken out of the flat.

'You fucking bitch, you fucking bitch, I'll kill you, I swear, I'll kill you,' are his last words to me. I look at the woman sitting next to me and open my mouth but I can't speak.

'You're all right now, aren't you? You did well. Your friend called us straight away, we listened to the conversation on the phone. We got here as quickly as we could. Just in time, and you're OK.' She seems to be reassuring herself more than me. I can't feel my toes or my fingers, I can't speak.

'It's all right, love, there's an ambulance on its way. We'll take you in to get checked over. Oh look, here's your friend. You're OK now, OK?'

I nod, hoping to shut her up, and suddenly Josh is kneeling in front of me. I flinch as he takes my shoulders but then I throw my arms around his neck and let him hold me.

'Were we in time?' he whispers. 'Jen, you have to tell me, did he hurt you?'

I shake my head and relief floods his face.

Chapter Fifty-three

Having been a terrible, uncommunicative daughter for some months, I've now been at my mum's house for the last few days, sitting on her brown velvet sofa, watching winter insinuate its way into her garden.

My brother and mum came and picked me up from the hospital. There was nothing broken, only bruising and a lost tooth, near the back. I keep running my tongue around its empty groove, making my mouth sore. Mum's taking me to the dentist tomorrow, just as she used to when I was a kid. I don't want to go, just as I never used to when I was a kid.

Owen's on remand. The police are pressing charges. It seems surreal, to say the least.

The first morning (or was it afternoon?) that I woke up after it happened, I woke up to Josh's face. We watched each other, solemn and still for a moment, and then he said, 'I'll get your mum.' He leant down and kissed the back of my hand before he went. I haven't seen him since, he's called several times, but I just don't feel as though I've got anything to say.

The hospital had given me something, drugs to make me feel calmer, or to take away the dull throb of pain in my jaw and my shoulder. I felt peaceful and detached, totally fine. My mum cried whenever she looked at my face. It wasn't pretty, I guess. Swollen and bruised.

'I can't believe it but they say they need your bed, darling,' she said angrily, shedding tears on to the sheets.

'They probably do, Mum. I'm OK really, aren't I? Just a few cuts and bruises,' I said mildly, hoping to cheer her up.

She sobbed again and hugged me so tightly that I winced. 'You're so brave. When I think about what might have happened it makes my blood run cold. Well, the doctor's on his way to discharge you so come on, let's get you dressed.' I looked at the jumper and jeans I had pulled on so quickly the night before. It still seemed like a dream, even then.

Then there were the police, statements, checking, double-checking. They wanted to work out exactly what happened when. At that point, for the first time, a deep freezing fear lurched in my chest. I shook my head, no.

'Jenny, we only want to make sure we have as much evidence as possible. This could really help put him away.'

I shook my head, rigid with horror. 'No. You found him *in* my flat, *after* forcing entrance, beating me up and on the point of raping me. If that isn't enough, what is? No. Not now anyway.'

I knew all that would have to come out eventually. I knew without anyone having to tell me that for weeks Owen must have been following my every move. All the time I had my head in the clouds over Michael or Josh he was close behind me, planning his attack.

Arrangements were made for me, phone calls and leave from work as long as I liked. Adem promised to re-secure the flat, once the police had finished with it. I was taken back to my mum's house.

She brings me in a plate of the nursery food she has been feeding me since I got here. Baked beans on toast and a glass of milk.

'Here you go, love. You've got to eat. I've got you some of

393

those little cakes you like for after.' She pats me on the arm and sits across from me.

'Fancy watching *Neighbours*?'

I don't fancy watching *Neighbours*, I fancy turning my face to the wall and closing my eyes, but I know she does. Since her retirement Mum's TV and dog routine have become pretty much set in stone.

'Yeah, why not.' I let the taste of childhood sink into me with a comforting warmth and watch the wind beat the rain against the trees outside. Mum's dog, Horatio, presses his nose up against the glass of the door. He looks at me and Mum in turn through a shaggy fringe, picking his paws up and down in a little dance, giving sharp high-pitched barks which hardly seem fitting for a dog of his age and size.

'Oh you,' Mum says to him as she gets up to open the door. 'No sooner are you out there than you want to come in with your muddy paws all over my floor. It's no wonder this carpet has gone to rack and ruin.' Her whole face is filled with an indulgent smile as she ticks him off. His big floppy paws leave small pools of muddy water across the carpet on his trip to the kitchen in search of food.

'That's your lunch, that is,' Mum says to me. 'He knows he doesn't like baked beans really, but it's the smell. Drives him crazy, but I bet you, if I went out there now and put some in his dish, he wouldn't touch them, the mad old dog, and I'd end up throwing them away.' I smile at her. I'm sure she fusses more over that dog than she ever did over us when we were kids. She looks at the kitchen door.

'Oh well, there were a few left over. Maybe I'll just pop out there and see if he's changed the habit of a lifetime. Could have changed his taste in his old age.'

A sudden gust of wind hurls rain at the window pane like a handful of stones, and I shiver. This is it, limbo. I can't imagine going back to work. I can't imagine going back to the flat, new lock or no. I can't imagine leaving the house and going to the dentist, I definitely can't imagine seeing the counsellor who has been arranged for me. All I can think about right now is this sofa, the trees outside the window and the dark dense clouds above them.

I had three years to avoid that moment, that look on Owen's face when he hit me. I can't be sure if I remember it accurately or if it has become a nightmare vision that has stuck in my memory, but all the same, when I close my eyes, when I see his face, I see that at that moment he wanted me dead. Three years when, almost daily, I had the opportunity, all the clues to see why Owen was all wrong. I had countless chances to get out and be safe. To let him let me go before he got this way. Before whatever anger and hate he had harboured against the world for so long finally crashed into overdrive. I had *three years* and only have myself to blame. I just didn't see it coming. I didn't let myself see it coming.

I jump out of my skin as Horatio erupts in a barking fit worthy of any Rottweiler and I hear him hurl himself at the front door. I put my plate on the coffee table and hug a cushion to my chest. More police? Owen? The thought, no matter how irrational, starts my heart thundering in my chest.

'We're not expecting anyone, are we?' Mum says curiously. 'It had better not be that bloke from the catalogue again. I've told him. I'm not interested in his special offer on shoe storage. Horatio, if it is I give you full permission to bite him.'

She hauls Horatio back between her legs and opens the door a crack. The dog's bottom waggles where his tail would have been if he wasn't an old English sheepdog.

'Hello, darling! What a nice surprise!' I hear Mum say and then her voice drops to a more confidential tone. Overcome with the excitement of a visitor, Horatio runs back into the living-room and looks for a gift, sees my toast on the table and grabs it, leaving a sticky trail of baked beans as he bounds off to bestow his treasure on the new arrival.

'Oh cheers, mate,' I hear Rosie say to him in the hallway and she appears before me, gingerly holding a bit of soggy toast between her thumb and forefinger.

'Do you want this back?' she asks me.

I nod at the dog dancing at her heels. 'I think I know someone who wants it more.'

Horatio snaps it out of her fingers and takes it under the table to kill it before eating it.

'I'm making you tea,' my mum calls out from the kitchen. 'And there are biscuits. Or cake. Biscuits or cake, girls?'

'Either thanks, Mum.'

Rosie sits next to me and for a second or two we watch the TV *Neighbours* getting aerated in swimwear.

Everyone has called me since I've been here. Josh, Selin, Rosie and even Jackson. But I just haven't been able to talk to them. I haven't been able to find anything to say. And now Rosie is here, in person. She looks well, the shadows and strain around her eyes seem to have diminished and the small curve of her belly has begun to grow into a rounded bump.

'Do you mind me being here?' she asks tentatively.

'No, of course not.' I am genuinely relieved to see her. 'I mean, thanks for coming. We didn't exactly part on the best of terms.' Everything we said to each other seems so trivial now. It doesn't even seem worth talking about. A look between us silently agrees to let it go without discussion.

'Selin said we should wait until you felt like talking about it, or felt like coming home. You know how sensitive she is. But well, I go for the bull-in-the-china-shop approach to friendship. I said, "I have to talk to Jen, face to face. I have to let her know I

love her. That I'm still her friend, no matter what." So I came.'
She shrugs and grins.

I sink back deep into the sofa. 'How are you? How's it going
with Chris?'

Rosie smiles and nods. 'He's outside in the car,' she says. 'I'm
fine, good actually. I'm starting to feel really well with the baby.
And Chris . . . well, things are very good at the moment. I'm
keeping an eye out. Taking one day at a time. I'm prepared
for the worst but optimistic for the best. I think he might have
grown up, you know. Finally.' I nod and hope with all my heart
that she gets what she wants.

'But I didn't come here to talk about me. I came to talk
about you.' I brace myself for the quiet sympathetic questions,
questions I don't have any answers for. Over the last few days I
have gained a fraction of insight into what Selin and her family
have had to endure.

'I mean, fucking Owen, what a cunt, hey? What a fucking
nutter!' She looks at me with such incredulous comic horror
that I start to giggle.

'I mean, we always knew he was a total dickhead, but fucking
wanker or what? Never saw that coming.' Rosie claps her hand
over her foul mouth as my mum enters with a tray of tea and
puts it on the coffee table. She looks at us laughing and smiles
at Rosie.

'I knew you'd cheer her up, you've always had a knack for it.
There are the biscuits. Don't give that dog any, he's had far too
much today already. Well, maybe save him the end of a couple.'
And she's gone again. Horatio appears from under the table and
positions himself between Rosie and me, his brown eyes fixed
on each of us in turn. I think about what Rosie has just said
and the light-hearted moment slips away.

'*Didn't* you see it coming, Rose? I mean, really? I keep
thinking I had an awful long time to see it coming, but even

when I did, even when I *knew* it I never let myself see it. I tricked myself into believing that it would just go away. I feel as though it's my fault.' I scrape my dirty hair back from my forehead and tie it into a knot to keep it off my face.

'Don't you dare say that! You must never say that. It's not your fault. None of us knows what's going to happen around the corner, none of us. We just hope and pray it's not going to be something horrific. Dreadful things happen to ordinary people all of the time. Out of the blue.' She bites a chocolate biscuit in two and then throws half to Horatio who makes it disappear in an instant.

'What a fucking few weeks, hey?' She bites another biscuit in half, making Horatio's day. 'I mean, first of all I'm knocked up with my ex's baby, who is no longer my ex, then you have a secret affair with a teenager. Selin plans a secret wedding, well, not that it's a secret any more. In fact, after helping her write out the invitations the other day I can safely say that the marquee will be visible from the moon. And I tell you what, if she manages to get us into those fuchsia bridesmaids' dresses she's got her eye on, we will be too.' She pauses and looks into her mug of tea. 'And there's Ayla. And there's you.'

I shudder as if someone has walked over my grave.

'Can you believe,' she continues, 'that it was only a couple of months ago that we were all sat in Soho Square just like always, moaning about how nothing ever happens? So much has changed. None of us saw any of it coming. But you made it out, mate, that's the main thing. You didn't let him win. You should be proud.'

I sigh heavily. I want to tell her the truth. 'The thing is, Rosie, just at the point that the police came through that door, no, just before it, I had stopped fighting. I didn't care what he did to me at that point. I would have let him do what he wanted. I just wanted to stay alive. I just fucking gave up.' Something from somewhere – shame, horror, fear – overwhelms me. Rosie wraps her arms around me and I sob into her hair. Horatio pushes his head into my lap and leans against my legs in solidarity. I let myself cry.

Eventually I find I am quiet. Rosie looks at me. Her own mascara has run onto her cheeks.

'You know everything makes me cry,' she says quietly. 'You are seeing a counsellor, aren't you?'

'I'm supposed to. I don't know if I want to.'

She looks at me with annoyance and reaches for another biscuit. All of them and the dog have disappeared.

'Jenny Greenway, if you cut off your nose to spite your face, don't come running to me when you wake up in fifty years' time and find out that you can't smell the roses, or something.' I laugh at her practice maternal tone. 'Seriously though, give it a try, OK? If it's awful we'll think of something else to help you. Yoga maybe, or ballroom dancing. OK?'

'OK,' I say reluctantly, spurred on by the prospect of being bullied into activities even worse than therapy.

'Promise?'

'Promise, Mum-to-be.'

She nods with satisfaction and pats her bump.

'When are you coming back?' She asks the question I have so far managed to avoid.

'Um, well, I'm not sure. I think Mum needs to look after me for a bit and—'

'Yeah, yeah sure, for a bit but it's your birthday in . . .' she does a quick calculation, rolling her eyes to the ceiling, '. . . Sixteen days. And you're going to be thirty.'

'I know that, thanks, Rose.' Thirty.

'Well, that's over two weeks away. Your mum can look after you, you can start the counselling, and then you can come back to London and we can all go out and have a big party for your birthday. Cool. You're the first to go over the hill, so to speak, so we have to mark it in style. And you owe it to the rest of us to let us see what it looks like. This thirty business.'

I frown and punch her in the arm.

'Hitting a pregnant woman,' she says 'Nice. Oh, before I forget, here's your post.' She passes me a couple of bills and two long cream envelopes, which when opened reveal that I'm welcome to work experience at both *Time Out* and the *Hackney Gazette*. I just need to call and arrange dates. It's funny how the future turns up just when you least want to see it.

'I'll see,' I say, tucking the letters behind a cushion.

Exasperated now, Rosie leaps to her feet and stands over me. 'Were those letters what I think they were? They were, weren't they? You are going to call them, aren't you?' I press my lips together and look out of the window. 'You don't see it, do you? Now look, you didn't let Owen win without a fight that night, you were the one who got through to Josh, you were the one who kept Owen talking, you were the one who kept things calm right until the last minute. So what if help turned up seconds after you could see no way out. You made it happen so that it did turn up. You beat him that night, Jenny, but if you don't get back your old life, or create yourself a new life, if you don't take chances like those ones you've just stuffed down the side of the sofa, he *will* have beaten you. For good. And anyway, we all need a good night out, God-damn-it!'

I sigh, fish the letters back out from behind the cushion and read them again. I'm tired, my legs drag with tension and sleepless nights, my chest is heavy with hurt and my jaw aches. But she's right. Before this happened I had turned a corner, I was making progress in the world, for the first time in my adult life I could see the way ahead. I don't want to give Owen the satisfaction of pulling me back and keeping me down. I'm alive, I'm untouched. I don't expect it to be as easy as just making up

400

my mind to get over it but I'm going to try and make it, I am not going to give up now.

'OK, OK. I'll be back by then,' I say to Rosie with determination.

'OK, then. Good.' She nods and sits down again and hugs me.

'You know what I've been thinking, about everything that's happened?'

I hesitate to ask, but I don't feel I can politely change the subject.

'It's like everything that's happened has been like that thing, you know.'

I shake my head, mystified. 'What thing?' I ask her. I see her pregnancy short-term-memory problem hasn't improved any.

'Like, that *thing* that we were going to have when we went away to the country that time to find ourselves. Like the dead barmaid from *EastEnders*. What was her name? Tiffany.'

It all becomes clear. 'You mean an *epiphany*!' I say, laughing out loud. Only Rosie.

'That's it, epiphany. Exactly. I'm not a religious person, but well, I do think that things happen for a reason. Lots of people let their life slip by without realising how precious and rare it is. I don't think any of us will make that mistake again. Do you?'

That certainly is one thing I can agree with wholeheartedly.

'No, I don't think we will. You're completely barking, but you're right. We owe it to Ayla, to that baby in there and to ourselves to do our best.'

'Yeah, right on, sister.'

I link my arm through hers and rest my head on her shoulder.

'There's just one thing that worries me about going out for my birthday,' I say to her, quietly.

'What's that, honey-bun?' she asks me sweetly.

'I've got sod all to wear.'

401

Chapter Fifty-four

Well, it could seem a little over the top for a Tuesday night in Stoke Newington but here I am in the Vortex Jazz Café dressed in an ankle-length deep red velvet strapless sheath dress topped off with a pair of long black velvet gloves trimmed with feathers. It *could* seem a little over the top but Selin and Rosie were so determined to dress us all up to the nines that it didn't seem fair not to join in, especially as both of them are decked out in sequins and glitter in my honour, with silk flowers in their hair, and let's face it, I've never needed that much persuasion to go glam. Even the boys – Josh, Dan, Adem and Chris – have made an effort. Some ancient seventies DJ over black jeans and a pink ruffled dress shirt in Josh's case, but he still looks pretty cool. Pretty cute too.

I've watched Chris and Rosie together all day. He handles her like cut glass. Sometimes they just look at each other and smile, as if to say, 'Everything is going to be fine.' I think they are both scared, but even I have to admit there is love there. I let the ghost of my own history slip away and looking at them with fresh eyes I see hope in their future.

I'm thirty. I've been thirty all day. So far, it doesn't seem to be too bad. There was no spontaneous growth of white hair out of the top of my head; no instant eruption of crow's-feet around my eyes and my breasts didn't take an irresistible tumble to meet my toes. The relief that flooded through me when I looked in the mirror this morning made me realise I had been waiting for the big day just as the whole world had worried about Millennium Eve. As it turns out, the world hasn't ended and it was in danger of becoming a bit of an anticlimax as far as landmark events go, or at least it *would* have been if my friends hadn't arranged this evening for me.

Apparently the venue was Josh's idea. He's got a friend in tonight's act, a rhythm–and–blues soul band complete with a horn section and the most fantastically talented voiced female singer called Coco. His friend, Jake the Lung as he seems to be known, who plays trumpet, told him about a local gig and it turns out it was on my birthday. What a happy coincidence.

'I thought it'd make a nice change from the usual clubbing palaver and this way Rosie can get a seat and even Adem might enjoy it. More his sort of era really,' Josh told me when they announced what they were planning. We'd giggled until Selin's icy stare silenced us, but really one of the things I like best about Adem is that he knows more about the music I love than I do.

The place is packed for a weeknight, and the atmosphere is great. The music is top class, the singer is wonderful and the feeling of Josh's eyes on the back of my neck sends tingles of anticipation up and down my spine. Good times.

Selin slides into a seat next to me. 'Having a good time, darling?' she asks, pouring more champagne into my glass.

'Yeah, really good thanks, this is just what I needed: a good old razzle–dazzle night out dressed up like a film star. Everyone else in here must think we're barking. Hey, go easy there with that champagne. I don't want to get too ratted too soon.'

Selin smiles to herself. 'Just a bit of Dutch courage, that's all,' she says as she tops up her own glass. 'If you don't need it I sure as hell do.' She knocks back a glass in one.

'Dutch courage, for me? I don't need it. I feel fine now really, right back on track.' Sweet of her to think that I might be feeling nervous about tonight.

She wrinkles up her nose as the champagne bubbles fizz, and suppresses a giggle. 'I know, so listen, you've got an interview for your course next week?'

I nod. 'Yeah, and my work experience sorted out. And I had my second driving lesson yesterday and the instructor looked much less frightened this time.'

She circles her arms around my neck and looks into my eyes. 'I'm so proud of you, you know that don't you?'

Seeing a bonding moment from across the table Rosie comes to join in. 'And me, I'm proud of you too,' she says, keen not to be left out.

'Well thanks, I'm proud of both of you.' And I can't stop it, I find myself saying, 'I love you guys. I really do.' We all laugh ironically, but we all secretly mean it.

'After tonight, let's make sure we never keep *anything* from each other ever again, OK? It's just not worth the hassle. OK?' Selin says.

'Sure, starting from now, I agree. I don't know why I ever did,' I say.

Rosie and Selin look at each other. 'After *tonight* then, no more secrets.'

We break our hug and I sink back into my chair, nodding my head in time to a funky rendition of 'Nowhere to Run To'. I find my glass being filled once more by Josh as he leans his mouth close to my ear and I smile.

'Are you having a good time?' he asks softly.

I turn in my chair to face him and take his hand. 'The best, this is exactly what I need. Thank you for organising this, Josh.'

His smile makes my heart jump and before I can think

about what I'm doing I take his face in my hands and kiss him. The brass section soars into a frenzied middle eight and the air vibrates with feel-good music; my body feels suddenly supercharged with unparallelled joy and lust. We break apart, heady with the sensation of each other, the heat and the music. I lick my lips, enjoying the taste of him. I look around to gauge the reaction of the girls but they are both absent, group trip to the ladies', I expect.

'I'm so glad you did that now,' he says, with a wry grin.

'Well, it seemed like the right time, after all this time. It seems perfect.' I smile into his eyes with blissful certainty.

He's suddenly looking a bit shifty, what's going on? Has he changed his mind? He takes my hand and kisses my fingertips. He hasn't changed his mind?

'It is perfect and if I survive this evening I can't wait to get you home and make it even more perfect. But what I mean is, I'm so glad you kissed me now because in about two minutes or so you're more likely going to want to kill me.'

I shake my head and laugh at him. 'What *are* you talking about?'

He nods at the stage and as I turn, the familiar intro to 'Respect' fills the room with a burst of frenetic musical energy.

'*Oh*, you got me a request!' I say over my shoulder to him. 'That's really sweet.'

'Ladies and gentlemen,' Coco says into the microphone, as she steps off the stage and in amongst the tables, and the introduction loops back and forth in a rhythmic riff, 'we often have birthday requests, but this one's a little bit special.' I smile at Josh as she weaves her way towards us. I have never seen him ·look so nervous. What *is* he so stressed about?

'Because tonight I'm not going to be the one to sing the request to you, oh no.' The crowd responds with a drunken cheer as Coco arrives at my side. The spotlight illuminates our table.

Chris, Dan and Adem are lost in a helpless fit of giggles.

'Re, re, re, re, re, re respect!' The backing singers kick in, sounding a bit ropey, to be honest. Where *are* Rosie and Selin?

'Oh, just a little bit, Oh, just a little bit. Re, re, re, re, re, re, re, re respect!' I look at the stage.

That's where Rosie and Selin are. On stage singing backing vocals. I'm certain I haven't taken any hallucinogenic drugs.

'Josh, what's going on? Have I ended up in an episode of *Ally McBeal*?' I ask him warily. He backs his chair away from me an inch. Coco waves a fantastically manicured hand at me.

'Because tonight, ladies and gentlemen, the birthday girl is going to sing to you herself!' My jaw drops and I stare at Coco in horror. She smiles in return.

'I give you Jenny and the Jennettes!' The crowd erupts with laughter and applause. My jaw drops to my cleavage and I grip my champagne glass like a drowning woman at a life-jacket. Coco hands me her microphone before I can think to refuse it.

'Go on, honey, get up there,' she says with an encouraging smile and a Sheffield accent. I look back at the stage. Rose and Selin have made up a little dance to go with their singing. Selin waves at me and winks, crooking her little finger to beckon me on stage.

'I am actually going to kill you,' I say to Josh, jumping when I realise I'm talking into the microphone. The crowd cheers with delight. Josh's grin is bigger than the Cheshire Cat's, and his very obvious pleasure makes it hard to be really angry with him. That and the sudden paralysing fear that has gripped my chest.

'I just wanted you to have the chance to do *all* of the things you said you were going to do by the time you're thirty. I wanted you to be able to start tomorrow knowing how far you've come, to be ready to start a fresh page. With me. So here we are. Go on, your mates are up there waiting for you. You know you can do it. *I* know you can do it.'

I hold the microphone away from my mouth and lean in to him.

'I *am* going to kill you, but this is the sweetest, most incredible thing that anyone has ever done for me, so I have to warn you, probably right after I've embarrassed myself and killed you, I'm very likely to totally fall for you and you'll never get rid of me.'

His brown eyes hold mine for a second.

'Warning heeded and ignored. I fell for you a long time ago. Now go!'

I down any dregs of champagne I find and stand up to encouraging applause.

'Thank God,' Rosie's voice comes over the speakers. 'I thought I was going to go into labour stood here.'

The audience laughs and claps again. I say into the microphone, 'You won't be laughing after you've heard this. Sorry, Aretha.'

I give the girls the finger as I get on stage, but I'm laughing all the same. I can't believe I'm about to do this. Jake the Lung catches my eye, asking if I'm ready.

Well, it's now or never. I'm ready, I nod at him. I take a deep breath and think about the future.

'R.E.S.P.E.C.T. Find out what it means to me.'